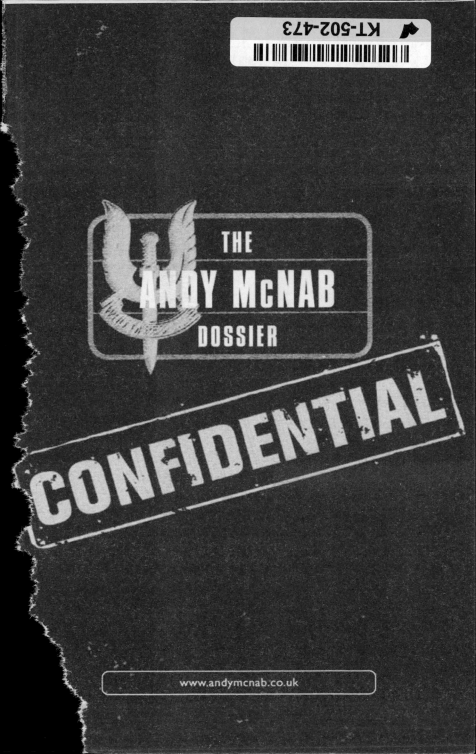

THE
ANDY McNAB
DOSSIER

CONFIDENTIAL

www.andymcnab.co.uk

ANDY McNAB

➲ In 1984 he was 'badged' as a member of 22 SAS Regiment.

➲ Over the course of the next nine years he was at the centre of covert operations on five continents.

➲ During the first Gulf War he commanded Bravo Two Zero, a patrol that, in the words of his commanding officer, 'will remain in regimental history for ever'.

➲ Awarded both the Distinguished Conduct Medal (DCM) and Military Medal (MM) during his military career.

➲ McNab was the British Army's most highly decorated serving soldier when he finally left the SAS in February 1993.

➲ He is a patron of the *Help for Heroes* campaign.

➲ He is now the author of fourteen bestselling thrillers, as well as two Quick Read novels, *The Grey Man* and *Last Night Another Soldier*. He has also edited *Spoken from the Front*, an oral history of the conflict in Afghanistan.

BRAVO TWO ZERO

In January 1991, eight members of the SAS regiment, under the command of Sergeant Andy McNab, embarked upon a top secret mission in Iraq to infiltrate them deep behind enemy lines. Their call sign: 'Bravo Two Zero'.

IMMEDIATE ACTION

The no-holds-barred account of an extraordinary life, from the day McNab as a baby was found in a carrier bag on the steps of Guy's Hospital to the day he went to fight in the Gulf War. As a delinquent youth he kicked against society. As a young soldier he waged war against the IRA in the streets and fields of South Armagh.

SEVEN TROOP

Andy McNab's gripping story of the time he served in the company of a remarkable band of brothers. The things they saw and did during that time would take them all to breaking point – and some beyond – in the years that followed. He who dares doesn't always win . . .

Nick Stone titles

Nick Stone, ex-SAS trooper, now gun-for-hire working on deniable ops for the British government, is the perfect man for the dirtiest of jobs, doing whatever it takes by whatever means necessary…

REMOTE CONTROL
⊕ Dateline: Washington DC, USA

Stone is drawn into the bloody killing of an ex-SAS officer and his family and soon finds himself on the run with the one survivor who can identify the killer – a seven-year-old girl.

'Proceeds with a testosterone surge' *Daily Telegraph*

CRISIS FOUR
⊕ Dateline: North Carolina, USA

In the backwoods of the American South, Stone has to keep alive the beautiful young woman who holds the key to unlock a chilling conspiracy that will threaten world peace.

'When it comes to thrills, he's Forsyth class' *Mail on Sunday*

FIREWALL
⊕ Dateline: Finland

The kidnapping of a Russian Mafia warlord takes Stone into the heart of the global espionage world and into conflict with some of the mos dangerous killers around.

'Other thriller writers do their research, but McNab has actually been t *Sunday Times*

LAST LIGHT
⊕ Dateline: Panama

Stone finds himself at the centre of a lethal conspiracy involving ruthless Colombian mercenaries, the US government and Chinese big business. It's an uncomfortable place to be . . .

'A heart thumping read' *Mail on Sunday*

LIBERATION DAY
⊕ Dateline: Cannes, France

Behind its glamorous exterior, the city's seething underworld is the battleground for a very dirty drugs war and Stone must reach deep within himself to fight it on their terms.

'McNab's great asset is that the heart of his fiction is non-fiction' *Sunday Times*

DARK WINTER
⊕ Dateline: Malaysia

A straightforward action on behalf of the War on Terror turns into a race to escape his past for Stone if he is to save himself and those closest to him.

'Addictive . . . Packed with wild action and revealing tradecraft' *Daily Telegraph*

DEEP BLACK
⊕ Dateline: Bosnia

All too late Stone realizes that he is being used as bait to lure into the open a man whom the darker forces of the West will stop at nothing to destroy.

'One of the UK's top thriller writers' *Daily Express*

AGGRESSOR
✠ Dateline: Georgia, former Soviet Union

A longstanding debt of friendship to an SAS comrade takes Stone on a journey where he will have to risk everything to repay what he owes, even his life ...

'A terrific novelist' *Mail on Sunday*

RECOIL
✠ Dateline: The Congo, Africa

What starts out as a personal quest for a missing woman quickly becomes a headlong rush from his own past for Stone.

'Stunning ... A first class action thriller' *Sun*

CROSSFIRE
✠ Dateline: Kabul

Nick Stone enters the modern day wild west that is Afghanistan in search of a kidnapped reporter.

'Authentic to the core ... McNab at his electrifying best' *Daily Express*

BRUTE FORCE
✠ Dateline: Tripoli

An undercover operation is about to have deadly long term consequences ...

'Violent and gripping, this is classic McNab' *News of the World*

EXIT WOUND
✛ Dateline: Dubai

Nick Stone embarks on a quest to track down the killer of two ex-SAS comrades.

'Could hardly be more topical . . . all the elements of a McNab novel are here'
Mail on Sunday

ZERO HOUR
✛ Dateline: Amsterdam

A code that will jam every item of military hardware from Kabul to Washington. A terrorist group who nearly have it in their hands. And a soldier who wants to go down fighting . . .

'Like his creator, the ex-SAS soldier turned uber-agent is unstoppable'
Daily Mirror

DEAD CENTRE
✛ Dateline: Somalia

A Russian oligarch's young son is the Somalian pirates' latest kidnap victim. His desperate father contacts the only man with the know-how, the means and the guts to get his boy back. At any cost . . .

'Sometimes only the rollercoaster ride of an action-packed thriller hits the spot. No one delivers them as professionally or as plentifully as SAS soldier turned author McNab' *Guardian*

Andy McNab and Kym Jordan's new series of novels traces the inter-
woven stories of one platoon's experience of warfare in the twenty-first
century. Packed with the searing danger and high-octane excitement of
modern combat, it also explores the impact of its aftershocks upon the soldiers themselves, and upon those who love them. It will take you straight
into the heat of battle and the hearts of those who are burned by it.

WAR TORN

Two tours of Iraq under his belt, Sergeant Dave Henley has seen
something of how modern battles are fought. But nothing can prepare
him for the posting to Forward Operating Base Senzhiri, Helmand
Province, Afghanistan. This is a warzone like even he's never seen before.

'Andy McNab's books get better and better. *War Torn* brilliantly portrays
the lives of a platoon embarking on a tour of duty in Helmand province'
Daily Express

ANDY McNAB
DEAD CENTRE

CORGI BOOKS

TRANSWORLD PUBLISHERS
61–63 Uxbridge Road, London W5 5SA
A Random House Group Company
www.transworldbooks.co.uk

DEAD CENTRE
A CORGI BOOK: 9780552161404
9780552166539

First published in Great Britain
in 2011 by Bantam Press
an imprint of Transworld Publishers
Corgi edition published 2012

Addresses for Random House Group Ltd companies outside the UK
can be found at: www.randomhouse.co.uk
The Random House Group Ltd Reg. No. 954009

The Random House Group Limited supports The Forest Stewardship Council®
(FSC®), the leading international forest-certification organisation. Our books
carrying the FSC label are printed on FSC®-certified paper. FSC is the only forest-
certification scheme supported by the leading environmental organisations,
including Greenpeace. Our paper-procurement policy can be found at
www.randomhouse.co.uk/environment

Typeset in 11/14pt Palatino by Falcon Oast Graphic Art Ltd.
Printed and bound by CPI Group (UK) Ltd, Croydon, CR0 4YY.

11

DEAD CENTRE

PART ONE

1

Camp Hope
Aceh Province, Sumatra

Sunday, 2 January 2005
15.39 hrs

Shit . . .

This was not going to end well.

The two of them were at it again, and this time one of them was going to get hurt.

Mong towered over BB, his forehead pressed hard against the top of the other man's skull to prevent him pulling back and trying a Glasgow kiss. Mong's sweat dripped onto BB's face, then down into the sand. He was breathing heavily, through clenched teeth. I could hear him even from where I was sitting.

I knew Mong. What he started, he finished.

I jumped up and skirted around a pile of pulverized, multicoloured hardwood that had once been a fishing boat. It was a week since the tsunami, and Aceh was still a disaster zone. There was debris everywhere. The coastal region looked like Hiroshima after Enola Gay. The tide brought in more wreckage and bodies with every wave.

'Mong – enough, mate! We've got work to do!'

He wasn't listening. He snorted like a bull.

'Bin it, mate. Back away. We've got no hospitals, fuck-all medical kit . . .'

But Mong was in his own little world. These boys were like two wind-up robots, grinding against each other until their clockwork motors ran out.

BB was going to get it big-time, and he knew it. But he stood his ground.

'Lads, kick the shit out of each other when we get home.'

It still wasn't happening.

Mong flicked his forehead back and then down and cracked BB right on the top of his normally perfectly sculpted hairdo. BB slumped, but before his knees hit the sand Mong swung a punch that connected with his right temple like a pile driver.

BB couldn't do much except take the pain. He flung his arms round Mong's waist, trying to drag him down as well while he regained his senses. Mong stayed right where he was, but his cargoes went south, exposing the tattooed outline of two hands, one on each cheek, which looked like someone else had already grabbed his arse.

Mong fought to free himself, but BB clung on, closed his arms round Mong's knees and threw his weight forward. Mong toppled into the sand. They both scrabbled to land a punch.

I peeled a spar off the fishing boat.

Mong wasn't shouting any more. He was saving his breath for the fight. He pulled himself up onto his knees and threw another two punches that BB managed to duck. Either would have laid him out.

He missed with the third, but the next got BB on the side of the neck and took him down. Mong dropped onto BB's chest, legs astride, and pumped his fists into the boy's body.

BB tried to curl up to protect his film-star looks.

I was nearly on top of them. 'Mong! You gotta stop, mate! Not today!'

White faces gathered by the line of NGO tents about fifty metres behind us – some of the aid workers who'd poured in from all over the world to help. Thousands of locals had fled into the hills for safety and were streaming back every day. They'd heard there was a relief camp, but few came near the ocean. They were terrified of another killer wave.

'Mong, you listening?' I stood over them. 'Bin it – now.'

It was too late. BB was fighting back. It was all his fault; it always was. He'd been having a go at Mong all day. But I had to admire the arsehole. Not many would last this long against the man mountain.

'Mong, last chance, mate. I'm going to have to hurt you if you don't back off.'

BB was about to get seriously fucked up. He deserved what was coming, but this wasn't the day.

I swung the spar down on Mong's back and kept it in place as he collapsed across BB, so he knew I was still there. BB heaved him aside, got the hint and rolled away. He crawled a metre or so, his face a mask of blood-coloured sand.

'Fuck off, BB, and get cleaned up.'

I pushed hard between Mong's shoulder-blades as he tried to get up. 'Mate, stay down or I gotta hurt you again. He's a fucking arsehole, but this isn't the time or the place. Sort all that shit out after the job, OK?'

BB got to his feet and shuffled back to our tent. The throng of aid workers parted like the Red Sea to let him through.

I sat on an oil drum bedded into the sand, still pressing on Mong's back. The beach was littered with all sorts of shit. The straits were the world's favourite dumping ground for hazardous waste, and why not? The only people who'd ever know were a bunch of Indonesian fishermen. The dumpers just hadn't reckoned on a tsunami propelling their dirty laundry into full view of a hundred tent loads of international observers.

'And pull your cargoes up, for fuck's sake. Those jazz hands are giving me the hump.'

2

They'd been in different squadrons, but I'd known Mong and BB since Regiment days. Now the three of us were out, and making a few bob on the circuit whenever and wherever we could.

'BB' was short for 'Body Beautiful, Mind Full of Shit'. He hadn't come into the Regiment the normal way, from one of the three services or the Oz or Kiwi military. He'd joined the TA off the street after watching too much SAS shit on telly. The problem was, he didn't get the culture. He didn't even speak squaddie. He was a mobile-phone salesman who played soldiers every other weekend about fifteen miles from where he lived. He was living the dream a bit too much instead of getting on with the job. He hadn't realized you had to serve your apprenticeship before going into the trade.

BB hated his nickname. He wanted all his mates to call him Justin. The trouble was he didn't have any mates.

He was OK, I supposed, and a pretty good operator.

He just didn't get it, whatever 'it' was. He was a smooth-talking Geordie fucker who fancied himself. He did all the weight training, took all the supplements. His T-shirts were two sizes too small. He plastered his face with moisturizer, and spent every spare minute building a tan for when he was back in the UK, cruising round town in his red Mazda 5.

Worst of all, he fancied Mong's wife, and didn't mind letting him know. BB had few scruples when it came to horizontal tabbing. He was plenty stupid enough to try it on with her. He'd tried it in the past, before Mong was on the scene, but Tracy soon cottoned on that he wouldn't be giving her what she needed.

Of course, BB wasn't the only one who fancied her. We all did. She was a good-looking girl. She had the kind of smile that belonged on an infant-school teacher. Everything about her was close to perfect – the way her dark hair brushed her shoulders, the way she dressed. We called her Racy Tracy, but it wasn't really true.

For everyone apart from BB she was off-limits. She was somebody else's wife. And that somebody was a mate.

This new fight had been brewing since the moment we'd met up a week ago in the UK. BB hadn't seen Mong for a couple of years, but got stuck straight in with the same old banter: 'Any time she needs a real man, just give her my number.' And he hadn't stopped there.

I gave Mong a prod. 'You all right, mate?'

'Yeah.' He lifted his head, held a finger to each

nostril and blew out a stream of sand and snot. He nodded at the waves pounding in ten metres away. 'I suppose I'd better get cleaned up.'

His accent was West Country, borderline pointy-head. It didn't fit with how he looked. Mong was a big unit; he could have been a poster boy for the World Wrestling Federation. He was tall and thickset, with crinkly dark blond hair. He never went to the gym or lifted weights, but still shat muscle. It was how he was made.

He really did have a huge arse. Each cheek was plenty big enough for those hands. From behind, with his kit off, he looked like a crime scene. After a few beers at a party, he'd drop his trousers and work his muscles so it looked like they were shuffling cards. His biggest pick-up line was 'Stick or twist?' There was still a bit of the Royal Marine in him, no matter how hard he tried to hide it. Any excuse, any piss-up, those lads couldn't wait to get their kit off.

With BB it was a totally different story. To keep his bulk he had to hit the weights non-stop and take supplements by the fistful. His day sack was filled with protein powder.

3

Mong began to ease himself up. There wasn't a mark on him.

'He's full of shit, Mong. You know that, don't you?'

He grabbed a fistful of sand and let it run through his fingers. 'He still gets to me. After all these fucking years.'

'What did he say this time?'

Mong looked away. He blinked hard, like he had sand in his eyes. 'He came out with the wedding-photo thing. The cunt. He said I'd better keep checking.'

When BB targeted a married woman, it wasn't about shagging her, or even liking her. It was about conquering her, and having one up on her husband. When he was pissed once he told me that every time he was in the new conquest's home he always asked to see the wedding photograph. As soon as he was alone, he'd ease it out of the frame, grab a pen and write 'J was here' halfway down the front of the bride's dress. If he was in a bit of a rush, he'd just scrawl it on the back, like a dog cocking his leg to mark his territory. If it was all going tits up, he'd say to her, 'Go and look at your wedding pic.'

That hadn't happened to Tracy. She was a Hereford girl who'd hung around with Regiment guys from the time she was seventeen. She and her sister had been trying to snag one for years. Why not? They got a house out of it, and a well-paid husband who was away for most of the year. For girls like Tracy, it was life as per normal, but with cash and security. She wasn't mercenary, just realistic. And it meant that once she'd got Mong, she wouldn't rock the boat. Apart from anything else, she really did love him.

'Fuck him. You know Tracy wouldn't touch him with a ten-foot pole. How long have you two been together?'

'Six years.'

'So look on the bright side, you twat. You could have ended up with Jan. Fucking nightmare. You'd be changing the wedding photo every month – it'd look like an autograph book.'

He wiped sand out of his eyes and started to laugh.

Jan was the nightmare version of her sister. Tracy's only failing was naïvety. While Jan's head was full of shit, Tracy's had room for nothing but fairies and happy endings. Before she met Mong she'd thought that meant she had to get her kit off every time she thought she'd found true love. It took her a while to realize she was just getting fucked and left to fend for herself.

Jan was a bit more cold and calculating. She knew she'd get turned over at frequent intervals until she stumbled across somebody stupid enough to take her on. Tracy had always been faithful to Mong. She didn't belong in the Hereford meat market. But Jan had thought she could handle it; she thought she could keep moving from one man to the next unscathed.

I looked over at the NGO tents, a sea of smart blue and orange canvas hooked up to brand new generators.

BB had disappeared into ours, and the white Land Cruiser crowd had gone back to doing whatever they did. Not that they'd been much help. The NGO thing had always seemed to me to be about looking good rather than doing good. BB had missed his vocation.

4

Mong clambered to his feet and wandered to the water's edge. I dropped my pacifier and joined him. 'You're a lucky bastard. You know that?'

He hesitated for a moment, then gave me a quick nod. He didn't take his eyes off the scum that swirled across the sand in front of us.

'I remember half of B Squadron telling you to steer clear of Tracy – but only because they wanted to have a crack at her themselves. They didn't see what you saw in her. She's in love, mate. And that's with you, not with any other fucker. Just you.' I pointed a finger at him like it was a bollocking.

'You've got each other, that's all that matters. Fuck BB, fuck 'em all. Just think how many of us've messed that up – BB included. They're jealous of you two. We all are.'

He nodded again.

'Why don't you just pack up and fuck off out of Hereford? Why stay?' In the film version of Mong and Tracy's life that played in my mind, they would have packed up and gone to live where nobody knew them as soon as he'd left the Regiment. Like Shrek, but without the swamp.

Mong put up with a load of shit from BB, but a whole lot more of it was dealt behind his back. He was too big and fearsome for anyone else to say it to his face.

He shrugged. 'Tracy wants to be near her mum and sister. She's a family girl.'

I felt the corners of my mouth twitch into a smile. 'No wonder they all think you're soft in the head.'

He wasn't. They were forgetting what he did for a living. And they mistook kindness for weakness. The stupid fucker was still sending cash to a woman he bumped into when he was in the Marines. He was at the checkout in Tesco one Saturday with three of his mates, each hefting a box of Stella, ready to watch the rugby. She was ahead of them, moaning that she couldn't afford to buy nappies – one of the oldest cons in the book, but Mong was suckered. He paid for all the beer, paid for the Pampers too, and hadn't stopped since. The baby had to be about twelve years old by now, and he was still sending her money.

Mong always had been a sucker when it came to kids. He was godfather to enough of them to make a football team. He and Tracy still hadn't had kids of their own, and I was pretty sure that hurt. But it wasn't something he spoke about, so I'd never asked.

Mong waded through the plastic bags and bottles and into the sea. 'Nick?' he shouted, over the roar of the surf.

'I'm not washing your back.'

'If anything happens to me – if I get dropped – you'll look after her, won't you?'

He made a bit of a meal of splashing his face in the water to avoid eye-to-eye. I knew it was difficult for him to be this emotional. Fucking hell, he wasn't the only one.

'Nothing's going to happen, is it? Unless you spend too much time in your paddling pool with that lot . . .' About twenty metres in front of Mong another three bloated bodies bobbed among the shit coming in on the waves. I nodded in their direction. 'Otherwise the only thing that could go wrong on this job is that cunt ODing on protein powder.'

He didn't laugh. He wasn't in that kind of mood. 'Everything's good at home. I mean really. But the good stuff never lasts that long for me. You know what I mean?'

He got swiped by a tumbling body as he came out of the surf. He stepped aside with the deftness of a wing forward dodging a tackle. His clothes clung to him like a second skin. 'Keep her safe, yeah?'

'I already told you, mate, of course I will. But it's not as if I'm going to have to.'

He gave his eyes another wipe as we walked back towards the tents.

I glanced across at him and was rewarded with a sheepish grin. 'Fucking sand.'

5

Our tent was a four-man job we could stand up in, a minging old grey canvas thing that stuck out like a sore thumb among the Gucci Gore-Tex affairs with blow-up frames the NGOs lived in.

BB sat on an aluminium Lacon box that contained fresh supplies of food and bottled water. It had looked lonely outside somebody else's bivvy doing jack-shit that morning so we'd decided to give it a home. We needed something to sit on and keep our kit off the ground.

BB didn't look up as we came through the flaps. He was stuffing some padding up his nose. Mong headed straight past him to his corner and peeled off his wet kit. The hubbub of French, German, American and Spanish voices in the background even subdued the chug of the generators. The NGO crews were holding a biggest-bollocks contest to see who was doing the most caring.

I brushed the crap from my cargoes, kicked off my boots and fell onto my camp cot. I'd leave the two cage-fighters to sort themselves out. We were due to set off in about three hours. We'd get the job done and then fuck off back home.

I watched the hi-tech campsite at work through our tent flaps. *Star Trek* had finally met *Carry on Camping*. Relief warriors wearing one badge or another rushed about and spoke urgently into radios, ordering somebody somewhere to do something.

I listened to the groan of aircraft overhead. Food and water were being flown in, only some of which would get where it was needed. There were already complaints that 30 per cent of the food and shelter equipment coming into the airport had been confiscated by the military as import duty. Yesterday we'd seen soldiers selling 20-kilo bags of rice – with UN stamped all over them – to the begging locals. Then the gangs demanded their cut before it could travel down the road. Even the pirates who worked the straits between Sumatra, Thailand and Malaysia were looking for their slice now there was fuck-all left to rape and pillage at sea.

Camp Hope – I had no idea who'd given it the name but they had a sense of humour – was to the south of Banda Aceh, the provincial capital and the largest city of Aceh Province. It was right at the north-western tip of Indonesia. Until 26 December last year, the only people with any interest in the place – apart from its 250,000 population – were oil companies and the Aceh separatist fighters.

Then the Indian Ocean earthquake struck about 150 miles off the coast and this part of the world was literally turned upside down. Banda Aceh was the closest major city to the earthquake's epicentre. So far, they reckoned on about 160,000 deaths in the area, and they were braced for more in the weeks to come, once the rubble started to be cleared and the sea brought more bodies back to land. Cholera would soon be spreading like wildfire, along with the contamination caused by the yellow and green shit leaking from the drums that came in on every tide.

To make things worse, the area had been at war since the mid-1970s. Gerakan Aceh Merdeka, the Free Aceh Movement, was trying to force Indonesia to accept an independent Islamic state. Aceh had a higher proportion of Muslims than other areas of the country, and had been allowed to introduce Sharia law in 2001, but GAM wanted a lot more than just religious control. They wanted the revenue from the province's rich oil and gas deposits, most of which went straight to the central coffers – no doubt with a few *rupiahs* skimmed off the top.

Major disaster or not, the Indonesian military didn't like us coming in. They didn't like foreigners at the best of times, but this last week, in the wake of the tsunami, they'd had no option. Now they were re-exerting their authority. They were starting to restrict our movements, scared our supplies would go to GAM. They wanted to keep the fuckers starving, and didn't give a shit if everyone else was too.

6

An argument erupted outside between an American and a German who sounded like Arnold Schwarzenegger with a wedgie. It was over what group was going to get the military permit to travel to some remote village with aid.

Over the years, I'd seen NGOs running around in places like Africa and I never really liked what I saw. It seemed to me that they were businesses, at the end of the day, and these two sounded like they were busy competing for a slice of the disaster pie. The locals didn't just need food and shelter. They needed protection from this fucking lot.

The MONGOs – My Own NGO – could be even worse. They were the guys who thought they could get things sorted more cheaply and effectively than the real aid workers. Most of them arrived under their own steam. Tourist visa in hand – if there was anyone around to issue one – they rented a vehicle, bunged on an ID sticker and, bingo, they were in business.

I'd Googled 'tsunami' and 'donation' just before we

left and got over sixty thousand referrals to MONGO websites, all brand new. Some of them, of course, were scams for cash.

Individual aid work was trendy in the UK, Scandinavia and Australia. And in the US, the tax authorities were granting exemption to an average of eighty-three new charities a day. More than 150,000 had been registered so far – and these were just the lads who'd bothered to go through the system. The only reason I knew all this was because Mong, BB and I had gone that route.

Aid 4 Tsunami. That was us. We carried accreditation to prove it; we'd printed it ourselves. It wasn't the most original name for a charity, but it would do. There were far worse out here. And it was as well funded as any other MONGO.

7

Our stretch of tent city was heaving with Western MONGO medics who'd dropped everything to come and help – which mostly meant setting off alone in hired wagons with a first-aid kit on the passenger seat. Some of the local lads had been examined three or four times each, and didn't have a clue what the doctors told them, what drugs they'd been given, when and why they should take them.

The docs ran around in full George Clooney mode, getting it all on video so their sponsors at home would send more money. A lot of them did a great job, of course, but others made incorrect diagnoses because they were moving at speed and didn't know about the particular challenges of the landscape. BB had a better grasp of the local parasites and diseases, and he was only a patrol medic.

The God Squad MONGOs were the worst. I'd once come across a gang of Christian hippies with guitars in Africa. They were there to round up patients for what they called their 'mercy ship'. It turned out to be an old cruise liner that had been converted into a floating hospital to bring 'hope and healing' to the poor heathens.

All well and good, but because the thing was only there for a week, they could only do operations that didn't need much aftercare. The place was crawling with people dying of gunshot wounds and machete amputations, and all the mercy ship could deal with were cataracts and hare lips, followed by films about Jesus.

There were already about four groups of happy-clappies in the camp and a hospital ship on its way. The Scientologists were also on the loose. No guitars, but plenty of mind-over-matter techniques and no sense of irony about the volcano logo on their bright yellow T-shirts.

These twenty-first-century missionaries didn't seem to realize that their message was going to fall on deaf ears. One press of the Google button would have told them that Islam had taken root here from the Middle East before it grew anywhere else. More than a thousand years ago Banda Aceh was known as the Port of Mecca.

Our problem was that these jokers moved around the city pretty much at will. Some of them even went out deliberately to get shot at by the army so they could blog home about how heroic they were. They could do what they wanted as far as I was concerned. But eyes and ears in the city were the last things we needed while we did what we were here to do.

Arnie and the American were still going at it hammer and tongs.

'What is it with these lads? They'd go to war over a brew.'

Our very own Mongo was following their argument with as much bemusement as I was. He jabbed a finger at the lump in the sleeping-bag. 'Why don't you ask Body Beautiful? They're all a few bricks short of a load. All loners. The only thing that brings them together is this sort of shit.'

BB sat bolt upright. 'How many times, for fuck's sake? I'm just as good as you cunts. What have I done that's different? I'll tell you. I didn't fuck about on a drill square for ten years, that's all. I passed Selection, all my training's the same. The only things you can do that I can't are polish your boots and square a blanket. Big fucking deal.'

'You're right.' Mong didn't bother getting up. 'And to be fair, I wouldn't have a clue how to sell someone a mobile phone.'

'Bin the fucking sarcasm. What does all that fucking trade training you're so proud of add up to? Nothing. You think life stands still on Civvy Street, but listen up. All the time you two were getting wet, cold and hungry playing squaddie, I was learning how the real world works. I'm in this because I want to be. You're in it because you can't do anything else.' He chuckled to himself. 'All those nights you were wet and cold, I was tucked up warm and shagging. So fuck the both of you. When we get back I'm going to find a job and run it myself.'

He turned away and pulled his sleeping-bag over his head.

I resisted the temptation to go over and wring his

perfectly toned neck. 'Be my guest. But until then I'm the boss and you will do what I say. You got it?'

BB's mumbled reply was drowned by Mong's snort of laughter and comment: 'Fucking great! I feel well and truly bedded in now. We're behaving just like real MONGOs.'

We had three hours left until last light. Then we were going to move into the city to deliver our own special brand of humanitarian aid. We were going to use the confusion of the disaster to recover or destroy a bunch of confidential documents from an office in the city centre. If they fell into the wrong hands, the energy company we were working for would be well and truly fucked. The last thing our employers wanted was the government and the military discovering that they were cutting deals with the separatists over future oil and gas concessions.

8

Banda Aceh had been Ground Zero on 26 December. Only 250K from the earthquake's epicentre, a twenty-metre-high wall of water had hit it within minutes. A third of the city, twenty-five kilometres square, was totally destroyed. All that remained of it was a tangled mass of rubble, furniture, cars, fridges and bodies – thirty thousand of them. Many were children, who hadn't been strong enough to resist the force of the wave. There were almost no dead animals. They'd seemed to know what was coming, and fled for high ground before the tsunami arrived.

The camp was about six K from the Krueng Aceh River, which split the city in half. It was sited so close to the sea because the roads hadn't been that well cleared further inland. Our target building was in Kuta Raja, one of the nine districts on the city's west side.

The NGOs had warned us not to make the trip.

Looters were picking through the debris, carrying off household goods, towing away cars, loading up stereos and TVs on motorbikes. If they thought we were about to report them, things could turn into a gangfuck.

To make things worse, the political conflict had also resurfaced. There'd been a firefight a couple of days ago between the army and the separatists. The separatists had hijacked relief workers and kidnapped doctors to look after their own people.

As we drove through a maze of crushed breezeblock and wriggly tin buildings and their scattered contents, we didn't see any other 4×4s. Anyone in Aceh who owned or had managed to steal one had driven it straight to the airport the day after the wave hit. The NGOs and MONGOs streaming in from the four corners of the globe snapped them up for top dollar, especially if they boasted air-con.

There was no air-con in the last of the Toyota 4×4s that had been lined up on the airport forecourt. We left the windows open instead, but with the temperature in the high twenties and 80 per cent humidity I wasn't sure it was worth it. Our skin was covered with sweat, and the breeze filled the car with the smell of sewage and decomposing flesh.

The power cables were down. Globes of light flickered among the devastation as far as the eye could see. Survivors huddled around cooking fires under plastic sheeting, boiling up whatever scraps the army had sold them. They had to use the wood from their own buildings to keep the fires burning.

We zigzagged through a random collection of sofas

strewn across the road. The tsunami had wiped whole fishing villages off the map. Large steel vessels and flimsy wooden skiffs alike had been picked up by the wave and flung down again far inland. Two twin-engine Cessnas were flattened against a wall, nose cones pointing skywards. Big Xs had been spray-painted on cars and buildings to show there were bodies inside. There hadn't been time to move them.

The army was on the prowl to try and stop the looting, but probably only so they could do some of their own. It didn't matter where in the world you were at a time like this: if you'd never had a bean now was your time. My elder brother had been on *News at Ten* during the 1995 Brixton riots, caught on camera climbing out of a shop window with a TV under his arm. In the background a policeman was doing exactly the same.

9

There was a curfew in place, but people were moving in the darkness.

BB was at the wheel. I was on his right. Mong was tucked away in the back. We all had our nice MONGO cargoes and khaki shirts on, with brassards on our right arm emblazoned with our very own logo – a Union flag on a big white circle, with Aid 4 Tsunami proudly displayed beneath it. We wanted to look the part.

BB pointed out of his window.

Mong craned his neck between the front seats to get a better view.

'Shit!'

Ahead of us, across a sea of bright blue tin roofs, a fishing boat rested on a mound of corrugated iron and breezeblocks. It was a traditionally built narrow wooden vessel with a modern cockpit and an engine sticking out of the back.

Mong's arms windmilled like a madman's. 'Stop, BB! *Stop!* Look up there!'

BB spotted it before I did. 'He's dead. Must be.'

A skinny brown leg, bent at the knee, dangled out of a smashed window at the side of the cockpit.

Mong lunged from his seat. His hand shot forward and grabbed the wheel. 'We don't know that. No cross . . .'

'For fuck's sake, look at it . . .'

Mong gripped the wheel harder. 'Nick, it won't take a minute. Let me check. It's a kid, mate.'

'BB, pull in. If he's alive, we'll sort him out and pick him up on the way back. All those lads back at the camp can fight over who'll take the credit for saving him – and maybe get themselves on the news.'

10

We climbed out of the wagon. I found myself standing in a morass of mud and ripped yellow plastic sachets. *This bag contains one day's complete food requirement for one person* was printed across them in English, French and Spanish. And next to the Stars and Stripes and a graphic of a bloke with a moustache tucking into an opened pack: *Food gift from the people of the United States of America.*

I hadn't seen HDRs (Humanitarian Daily Rations) since my time in Bosnia. Each pack weighed about a kilo and contained a day's calories. They only cost the American taxpayer three or four dollars each, but the joke going the rounds was that, with door-to-door delivery, this was one of the world's most expensive takeaways. They were designed to survive being air-dropped, thrown out of an aircraft as individual packages – much safer than parachuting large pallets of rations onto survivors' heads, and better for preventing hoarding.

The HDRs dropped in Afghanistan were yellow, like they'd been in Bosnia, before it was realized that the packages were the same colour and roughly the same size as American cluster bombs, which were being scattered like confetti. They changed them to orange-pink.

Inside would be a couple of meals like lentil stew and pasta with beans and rice. There were also fruit pastries that reminded me of Pop Tarts, and short-bread, peanut butter, jam, fruit bars – even boxes of matches decorated with the American flag, a nice moist towelette and a plastic spoon. For some reason, every HDR also included a packet of crushed red chilli.

The US Navy must have airdropped this lot. They were somewhere offshore, and their helicopters had overflown the camp now and again. Some of the packets weren't so empty. Not even the Indonesian Army could flog pork and beans on the black market.

Mong clambered across the wreckage. Wriggly tin buckled and groaned under his weight. BB leant on the bonnet as he watched him, checking his watch like we were missing a crucial meeting.

Wrinkled pictures were pinned to wood on what was left of a wall on the other side of the road. Dolls, toys and picture frames were laid out on the ground. The locals had been putting together whatever personal effects they found for others to see. For some, it would be all they had to remind them of a dead family member.

Two rounds kicked off deeper in the city and there was a faint wail of sirens. BB looked at his watch again.

'It's all right, mate, we've got another five hours until first light. It's only going to take him ten minutes.'

11

I could tell things weren't good as soon as Mong reached the cockpit. *'For fuck's sake . . .'* He stuck his head out of the smashed window. The leg dangled beneath him. 'I'm going to need a hand here.'

BB pushed himself off the bonnet. 'The kid's alive?'

Mong ignored him and disappeared inside. I climbed the crumbling concrete blocks and hauled myself onto the boat. The deck was clear. The waves had taken everything away.

Mong was easing the leg gently out of the window frame. It didn't belong to a child but a young woman. And crunched into the opposite corner of the cockpit was a man. A wedding ring glinted on a hand that was twisted up around his shoulder. His head had been crushed on the metal shelving just above him. There was no blood. The sea had washed him clean. The wound looked like a Hallowe'en makeup kit without the ketchup.

It was the same for the young woman, and the

newly born boy who lay between her legs, umbilical cord attached and placenta still inside her.

BB followed me onto the deck, face screwed up in disgust. No way was he going to enter the cockpit. 'This is fucking gross . . .'

Mong didn't look up as he pushed aside the tangle of kit covering mother and child.

BB put his hand to his mouth.

The husband's head twisted a little and fell forward as Mong tugged out a sodden blanket and laid it on the deck as best he could. 'While you were fucking about at the Carphone Warehouse we were surrounded by shit like this. Women desperate to give their babies a chance before they died themselves . . .'

'I don't give a fuck. Let's get out of here. We're going to catch something.'

I knew Mong was talking about the Balkans. Muslim women in the villages who knew they were going to get raped and killed went into premature labour as the Serbs advanced.

He gathered up the tiny body, pruned from its prolonged soaking, and cupped it in his hands. He finally raised his head. 'If you'd spent a bit more time actually soldiering instead of just playing at it, you'd understand what's been going on here.'

'Yeah? Well, fuck you.' BB spun on his heel and disappeared over the side. The corrugated iron buckled and creaked as he made his way down to the wagon.

More shots kicked off in the distance.

Mong laid the baby on the mother's breast and started to tuck a corner of the blanket around him like a shroud.

I lifted her legs so we could get the blanket underneath her. 'Mate, we won't be taking them with us.'

Mong raised the mother's head and placed the
blanket around it.

'We'll leave them here, mate. Tell the army or whoever when we get back. They can come and mark them
up.'

He was vibrating with anger. 'She shouldn't have
been left like that. Leg hanging out. It's not right. That
fucker would just have left her . . .'

'Mong, mate, you need to calm down. BB's on the
team, and we've still got a job to do.'

I went over to the husband. The meat on his legs
was squidgy. It wouldn't be long before his body
started to decompose.

Mong got out of the way so I could drag the poor
bastard next to his wife and his child. Somehow it
seemed important to have them touching. He tucked
the woman's hair into the blanket so she and the child
were totally shrouded.

We both stood there silently for a minute or two.

He looked across at me. 'Feels good, doesn't it,
doing something halfway decent for once, instead of
arsehole jobs like this?'

I put a hand on his shoulder. 'Mate, the arsehole
job's still waiting.'

12

Beyond the flood line, every football field was crammed with refugees – thousands of them – in makeshift camps. The city had suffered the magnitude nine 'quake and was now trying to cope with the magnitude six aftershocks.

There was no electricity, and therefore no light. More fires were dotted about in the darkness. Haunted eyes peered out at us from the shadows, unsure of who lurked behind our headlights. At this time of night it wouldn't be aid workers, which left looters or the army, both bad news.

We eventually hit the main bridge crossing from west to east. The mood in the wagon wasn't good. BB was expecting to go down with cholera, measles or some other fatal disease at any minute because we'd had physical contact with the family.

He had a point. It was monsoon season and rained for a couple of hours every day. The mosquitoes were out in force, raising the risk of dengue fever and worse. Thousands of corpses, hanging in trees or washed up on beaches, were rotting in the tropical heat. With open wounds and no food or clean water, the survivors wouldn't survive for long.

'Shit!' BB slammed on the brakes.

Our headlights had picked out a pair of Saracen APCs, six-wheeled monsters that had probably been bought off the Brits. BB kept us tight in to the right as they rumbled across the bridge towards us.

Mong and I exchanged a glance. As young infantry-men we'd both done too many tours of Northern Ireland stuck in the back of those fuckers.

'Three times I was blown up in one of those, Mong. Three IEDs in two years. You?'

BB's knuckles went white as he clenched the wheel. 'Fucking hell.' He swung his head round. 'Shut up, both of you. I don't want to hear your old war stories. I've had enough of that shit.'

'Calm down, mate. It wasn't a dig.'

Mong looked as though he was about to join in but I shook my head. We had to cut away from this shit. I was glad BB was going to bin it after this. With luck I'd never have to share a vehicle with him again.

The Saracens were closing. They bristled with 40mm grenade launchers and .50 cal machine-guns, Tannoy systems and searchlights. Lads in olive green stuck out of the mortar hatches, armed with M16s. In this part of the world they would have been Singapore-made, under licence from Colt. The searchlights burst into life and played across us.

We waved and smiled in the blinding light. I pointed at my armband. 'British! Aid workers!'

I knew that wouldn't necessarily guarantee us

membership of the Good Lads Club. The West had criticized the Indonesian government heavily for how they'd been prosecuting their war, while at the same time selling them the weapons to fight it with. Now the tsunami had made their lives twice as hard. They had looters to deal with as well as a resistance movement, and a massive influx of foreigners looking over their shoulders. Rumour had it they wanted the airlines to stop bringing us in. They certainly weren't on the streets to provide aid. Their aim was to kill as many separatists as they could while confusion reigned. The last thing they wanted was Western witnesses.

The searchlights stayed on us but the wagons passed by. I couldn't see the faces behind them. But I saw the M16s swing away.

13

We carried on to the other side of the bridge and headed into the darkness of the Kuta Raja district. We wanted the fruit market, straight along the road, first junction left, less than half a kilometre away. In an office block next to it somebody had been negotiating oil and gas concessions with GAM.

We didn't know who our employer was. It didn't work like that, and it wasn't as if I wanted to. That sort of knowledge doesn't give you power, it gets you dead. Crazy Dave was the broker; we never got to meet the organ-grinder. But whoever it was, they weren't taking any chances. The separatist movement wasn't all about power to the people: it was about taking control of the fossil fuels.

In the aftermath of the tsunami, there was a strong chance the deal could be exposed. Our client would be screwed; maybe our government too. Big business and politics tended to be one and the same in this part of the world.

The job was sold to us as a straight destruction of

documents – and proof that we'd done so. We'd make a video, save the SD card, and take it back. We were getting £50,000 each.

The market was deserted. It probably had been since the drama. On the recce, we'd seen nothing much more than a series of steel-framed stalls covered by bright blue tarpaulins.

The wagon stopped in the thoroughfare between two lines of stalls. We sat and listened.

A shot rang out in the distance. Then the bark of a Tannoy and some rapid, pissed-off chatter. The lads with M16s were probably telling someone with a TV in their hands to stay right where they were.

We tuned in and checked for any drama before we got to work. Mong lifted his wrist. His watch said it was nearly one thirty.

14

Making entry into the office block was going to be easy enough. We'd seen the boarded-up windows. The hard bit would be finding the documents if they weren't where they should be.

I powered up my window. 'All right, lads. Time to go.'

We grabbed our day sacks. They contained everything we'd need on-target, including holdalls to carry the docs if we had to destroy them elsewhere.

BB shoved the key under the nearside rear wheel. All movement from now on would be in slow-time and without light so we could watch and listen. The sophisticated infrastructure of electricity and comms was all down for now, which suited us just fine.

The whole area was pitch black, the atmosphere almost apocalyptic. Fires still flickered in the darkness. I expected a massive pterodactyl to fly in any minute and grab a few civvies for dinner.

There was more Tannoy action on the other side of the river, accompanied by a burst of gunfire. Two rounds were tracer. We watched as they ricocheted off something and spiralled into the sky. Then the propellant burnt out and the light disappeared.

We moved carefully through the market. Crates were stacked precariously. Rotten fruit, two weeks old, littered the ground. The two-storey office block was just ahead on the riverbank, a big square chunk of concrete and blue-tinted glass. The glass had taken a beating in the earthquake, but the structure had stood up well.

Still in slow-time, we climbed a rusty, sagging chain-link fence and landed on the solid new tarmac that surrounded the building. There was no landscape gardening here: this was a place of work. There were car-park signs and allocated spaces but no cars. The offices were rented to about twenty different companies. The one we wanted housed the Kareng Development Corp on the first floor. Room 2-17.

We walked around the building. It wasn't a tactical move. We just needed to get in and out as fast as we could, and there was a chance a new opening might have been created by the aftershocks that had followed the recce.

Large sheets of plywood had been nailed to the window frames on the ground floor to replace broken glass. Some had been loosened by looters. I gripped a sheet on the corner facing the river and pulled it out far enough to create a gap. There was no reason to waffle. We knew what we were doing.

Mong ducked his head inside and had a quick look and listen. He climbed in and BB followed. The two of them then pushed out the sheeting for me.

15

We stood on thick carpet, listening for any noise above that of our own breathing, and tuned in to the new environment. I gave it a full minute before I dug my Maglite head-torch out of my day sack. The other two followed my lead. Our beams swept across an open-plan office, maybe twenty metres long. Dozens of desks stood in neat rows. Bare wires stuck out of conduits where PCs should have been. Some computers were still in position but had been smashed. Drawers had been pulled out and papers strewn all over the place. It looked like there'd been a revolution. But the looters were looking for stuff to sell, I hoped, not read.

I headed towards the door and Mong and BB followed. It looked half open. When we got there we found out why. It had been kicked in.

We slipped into the corridor and followed the carpet as far as the wooden stairway. I started to sweat as I climbed. A sign on the landing told us 2-17 was to the left.

This floor, too, had been systematically raided. Splintered doors hung from their hinges. More redundant wires sprouted from desktops. The small, two-desk office of Kareng Development Corp was in shit state.

Our torchlight bounced around in the darkness. Paper, folders and files were scattered everywhere. I pulled off my day sack. 'Fuck it. Too much to sort. Let's torch the lot.'

BB took stag on the door. He'd keep an eye out along the corridor.

Mong set to, piling the furniture into good burning stacks. The paperwork was my responsibility. As team leader, I had to make sure it was destroyed. And we'd only get the rest of our money if we had the proof.

I didn't bother looking for material specific to the deal with the separatists. It would be quicker and easier to incinerate the lot. Fuck the building: it was either insured or would be rebuilt by foreign aid. No one was in here, and the blaze couldn't spread to other buildings or fuck anybody up. It was an island in a sea of tarmac.

As Mong threw together a pyramid of desks and chairs, I set up the handheld IR-capable videocam on a chair by the door and set it to record.

16

There are three elements in the combustion triangle if you want to make sure your arson is productive. The fuel was the furniture and paperwork. The oxygen movement wasn't perfect – the windows here were sealed units so the air-con could do its stuff – but with the internal doors open it should be fine. The fire needed to spark up as quickly as possible; we'd help it do so by stacking the chairs and desks at the optimum angle. The optimum angle was thirty degrees – which is why the perfect place to start a house fire is under the stairs.

Mong was building his second pyramid when BB slapped the wall. It was our signal to freeze.

I killed my torchlight and held my breath, mouth open to cut down internal body noise. I listened. Not a sound.

I breathed out, breathed in, kept my mouth open, and strained to pick up even the slightest vibration. Still nothing. I waited another thirty seconds. If some-one had spotted us, surely they would have done something by now.

Mong was behind me. I turned and moved my mouth to his ear. 'Hear anything?'

He shook his head.

Then we both did. Movement inside the building, down near the plywood sheeting. Then a shout.

Military? Maybe they had more than loudspeakers and searchlights on those APCs. Maybe they had night viewing aids and had been watching us all along.

Another shout.

It didn't sound military. It sounded agitated. A night-watchman? What was the point? There was nothing left to watch over. Homeless? That made sense. But I'd seen no bedding or cardboard on the floor, no sign at all of inhabitants.

I could hear the shuffle of feet. Murmurs. Getting louder. Coming up the stairs.

I went and joined BB. He pulled his head back inside. 'No lights. Can't be military. They wouldn't come in blind.'

Shouts echoed in the stairwell. I made out at least three or four different voices. Egging each other on. Vigilantes, maybe, who thought we were looters. Or just local lads who wanted to know who the fuck we were.

Mong moved alongside us.

The voices were getting closer.

I gripped their arms. 'We carry on – then fight our way out of here if we have to. They might just get bored and fuck off. We have to destroy the papers. We'll worry about that lot afterwards. OK?'

I ran back and grabbed an armful of files and thrust

them under the nearest desk pyramid. Mong did the same.

The shouts were getting louder and feistier. The newcomers hadn't got bored. They were getting more confident because we weren't doing anything. Something landed further down the corridor with a metallic clatter.

BB came back into the room. 'Five or six of them, I reckon.'

Mong stopped what he was doing. 'Fuck 'em, Nick. Me and BB'll go and clear them out. They'll do a runner. You crack on here.'

'No. This first. We go out there mob-handed as soon as this lot sparks up.'

They started chanting now, like football hooligans. The noise came from the top of the stairs.

I carried on hurling fistfuls of paper into the stacks. Sweat poured down my face. 'Let's get this done. Worry about that lot later.'

I looked up and caught Mong in my Maglite beam. He screwed his eyes shut and gave me a smile. 'No, mate. Let us two go down there and grip a couple big-time. The rest will run – they always do, don't they? You finish this off, and we'll clear the exit. What happens if we get pinned down when all this shit kicks off?'

My light moved onto BB. He wasn't happy, but Mong was chomping at the bit. 'Nick – we need to secure the way out.'

Mong was set in his ways. The halo he'd had on at the fishing boat had slipped; it was just the horns showing now.

I grabbed another pile of paper. 'You're right, mate. Go!'

BB had to shout to be heard over the chaos outside. 'Nick, what the fuck are you playing at?'

Mong tightened the straps of his day sack. He wasn't going to wait for me to answer.

He turned and prodded BB out of the door. They disappeared to my left as Mong roared at the gang outside. The noise was deafening.

17

I pulled the two-litre bottle of unleaded from my day sack and poured it over the two mounds, then lit the first match and threw it.

There was a loud whoosh and flames rushed up the woodwork. The sudden heat seared my face. I listened to the commotion outside. Chairs were being thrown; wood was connecting with bone.

I chucked a second match and turned towards the door. Both pyramids were well ablaze. I shoved the camera into the day sack and threw it on my back. I ran out to join the violence at the top of the stairs. Torchlight jerked and juddered as Mong and BB got aboard whoever was trying to stop us getting out of there.

There were other angry shouts, but from behind me this time. A chair slammed across my back and took me down. I struggled to my feet and ran towards the mêlée of jeans, T-shirts and sweat-soaked tattoos. The acrid stench of burning foam scoured my nostrils. I heard a series of loud cracks as the flames took hold of the veneer on the furniture.

A lad behind me screamed and shouted. Something hit me on the head. I didn't give a fuck. These lads weren't going to stop the fire. And soon they were going to have to leg it.

I headed for the torchlight ahead of me. The three of us needed to fuck off before the smoke overwhelmed us. I took more hits.

'Mong! BB!'

Mong turned and roared at me: 'Get a fucking move on!'

His shout became a scream and his headlight dropped. Smoke billowed down the corridor, hugging the ceiling. Shadows bounced along the walls as the flames grew. The locals hollered at each other. These lads were fucking off.

The headlight on the floor at the top of the stairs was dim. Then I realized it was rammed into the carpet. Mong wasn't moving. I gave him a kick in the ribs and yelled at him to get up.

18

He was lying on his side, head twisted. Blood poured from the inside of his thigh. The carpet tiles were soaked. It wasn't good. It was too quick. He was bleeding too fast.

'Mong!' I grabbed his shoulder and pulled him over. Blood spurted up at me like water from a burst pipe. His femoral artery had been severed. Maybe he'd been knifed. The femoral artery is connected to the aorta. Blood was pumping out of him at mains pressure.

I pushed down on the puncture site with one hand and tried to rip his cargoes with the other. Blood coursed up my wrists. I had to get my thumb and fore-finger into the wound and try to squeeze the artery closed.

'BB!'

My fingers slithered around the hole in his thigh. It was like trying to locate a small rubber tube buried in grease.

'BB!'

Mong's head lolled and his torch beam bounced

along his leg. He saw what was happening. 'Shit! I feel it. I'm going, Nick.'

'Shut up, dickhead.'

But we both knew he had less than three minutes.

'BB!'

I knew he couldn't do any more than I could but he was a patrol medic. I rolled Mong on to his back and his head flopped. No resistance from his neck muscles.

Flames shot out of the door of 2-17 and licked along the suspended ceiling. Tiles ignited. There were no sprinklers because there was no electricity. Our shadows danced as the flames advanced towards us. Thick black smoke filled the top half of the corridor. It would soon sink down to our level. Mong knew that. 'Fuck off, Nick. Go.'

'Shut the fuck up.' I stood up and pressed the heel of my boot into his groin, just above the wound. I pushed down with both hands on my knee. He groaned with pain. We both knew it was too late. We needed surgical clamps to stop it.

My torchlight fell on his face. His pupils didn't react to the light.

'Nick, remember what you promised.'

'Shut up. You're going to fucking look after her yourself.' I pushed harder. 'BB!'

Blazing tiles fell from the ceiling. The heat got more intense as the flames licked closer. I was starting to choke on the smoke. I had to bend down further. But I wasn't going to release the pressure until he was dead. I knew it was useless. He knew it was useless. But that didn't matter. I'd fucked up. I shouldn't have let him go and take on the looters.

This was all I could do for him now.

He fought to get the words out. 'Remember . . . Tracy . . .'

'Of course I'll look after her, you stupid fucker . . .'

He went quickly. No reaction to the pain. He just closed his eyes and that was it. Life had leaked out of him.

19

I lifted my boot and touched my hand to the wound.
There was no blood pumping out any more. It had all
gone. The smoke was just a metre off the floor. Staying
on my knees, I shoved my hands under Mong's
armpits and dragged him towards the staircase. I
could feel the air rush up from the smashed windows
below. The flames were sucking it in.

Mong was too big to pick up and put on my
shoulders. His legs bumped behind me as I dragged
him down the stairs.

'BB!'

I swept my torch beam across the floor to make sure
he wasn't lying there too.

I reached the downstairs office and lugged Mong
towards the exit. I had to stop under the window,
fighting for breath. Air rushed through the gap we'd
come in through. I slid down the wall and leant back
against it, with Mong's head in my lap. 'Sorry, mate.' I
couldn't think of anything else to say.

Smoke curled down the stairs. I got to my feet and

pushed the plywood further away from the frame. I had to use my head to keep it open as I eased his torso through. A gust of wind rushed past us to feed the flames.

Mong dropped to the ground and folded like a rag doll. I wasn't going to leave him there. I'd get him to the fence and then go back for BB.

Hands beneath his armpits and linked across his chest, I started to drag him away from the building.

The windows above us shattered. Flames leapt out. Mong's heels bounced over the tarmac.

Headlights on the main road ahead, moving left to right. They hesitated, then turned onto the tarmac.

The 4×4 slewed to a halt, side-on.

'Get him in!'

'Where the fuck have you been?'

'He told me to get the wagon! Get the fuck in here! The army's coming from the other side of the river.'

PART TWO

1

Hereford

Monday, 17 January

It was only a short drive from the crematorium to Mong and Tracy's place in King's Acre, to the west of the city. Cupcakes and little quarter-sandwiches were waiting for the few of us who were invited back. I took Tracy in a black Audi 6 I'd hired for the day.

The service had been standing-room only. Even Crazy Dave was there, pushing himself to the front in his space-age wheelchair. Most of the faces I recognized had sun-tans and ill-fitting suits. The ones I didn't were in Royal Marine blazers and ties, crisp white shirts and neatly pressed slacks. The Corps had also sent representatives in full service dress. Boots and medals gleamed. The only one not there to pay his respects was BB. Crazy Dave tried to cover for him by saying he'd sent him away on a job, but I knew better. There you go.

But so what? He was leaving the UK soon. The job that Crazy Dave hadn't got him was anti-piracy in the Indian Ocean, working out of Mogadishu. Sitting on a ship all day looking for Long John Silver was perfect for him. No one to work with, so no one to annoy.

All the speakers – mates, relations, people from the Corps – said fantastic things about Mong. But all I could think was what a waste it was. Then the priest or vicar or whoever got a few prayers going. I didn't listen. What a fuck-up. I was team leader, and that made his death my responsibility. I shouldn't have listened to him. I should have stuck to my guns and kept him with me.

I'd looked around me. I'd never been one for funerals, but at least I turned up. It was another part of squaddie culture that BB just didn't grasp.

The massive turnout and expressions of condolence didn't bring much comfort to Tracy. In fact they freaked her out. She wanted to be alone with her grief. Sharing it made things worse. Now she sat beside me, eyeliner streaming down her face – she looked like a poor man's vampire. All I could hear was the vehicle heater and stifled intakes of breath as she tried hard not to cry again.

I didn't want to say anything. I stared straight ahead, drove nice and gently, and left her with her thoughts.

2

The aid workers back at the camp had swallowed our story. It's always good to base a lie on the truth. We had seen a body hanging out of a stranded fishing boat and gone to check inside it. On the way back down, Mong had missed his footing, fallen awkwardly and sliced his femoral artery on a rusty reinforcing rod.

I made sure they understood this wasn't a story for their media mates. I didn't want it leaking out before I could tell his widow in person. The next thing I did was get word to Crazy Dave, who swung straight into action. He didn't just have British ex-Special Forces on his books: he had ex-Delta and Seals as well. One of the Delta guys made some calls. Favours were pulled in. A US Navy helicopter landed at the camp a few hours later and airlifted the three of us to a carrier out in the bay. They, in turn, trans-shipped us the next day onto a supply vessel that was heading to Singapore to take on stores.

In the day and a bit that it took us to steam the five hundred miles south, Crazy Dave sorted everything.

An ambulance was waiting at the dockside in Singapore harbour. It drove us straight to the British embassy, where a local pathologist was on hand to confirm the cause of death and issue a certificate. The only thing that raised an eyebrow with him was the state of Mong's body. He hadn't just been thrown into a body bag, covered with blood and dirt. He'd been given a nice wash and brush-up, and was dressed in a clean set of clothes. In fact, if you didn't know about the fucking great hole in his thigh, you'd have thought he was just having a quiet nap before taking his wife out to dinner. It was the least I could do after the care he'd taken with the dead couple and their baby.

We were on a flight out of Changi International first thing next morning. BB and I were in Club Class, Mong in cargo. During the journey, I mulled over what needed to be done next.

Crazy Dave was waiting for us at Heathrow with a funeral director and a hearse. I made a deal with him as soon as we landed. He'd give Tracy my second payment as well as Mong's. He'd tell her it was the agreed fee for the job. I'd made the old fucker a promise, and this was the start of me keeping it.

3

Tracy put her hand on my shoulder. 'What am I going to do, Nick? He was all I had.'

I kept my eyes on the road. I didn't want to crash this thing and make her life even worse. 'It'll be tough at first, Tracy, but life does go on . . .'

Her hand fell off my shoulder and back onto her lap. She nodded slowly. But then the hand came back up to her face and she started sobbing again.

I patted her shoulder, trying to drive and look at her at the same time. 'Have you thought about moving away from here? You know, try somewhere new. Somewhere there won't be constant reminders.'

She reached into a small black bag for more tissues. 'I've always wanted to go to India. On the beach. Maybe a small restaurant. Just be happy.' She blew her nose. 'But I can't. Mum's still ill, and then there's Jan . . .'

I put my hand back on the steering wheel. Jan was a problem.

She was going to be all over Tracy now she had a

few bob. But things weren't as rosy as Jan thought. Mong had died while helping the victims of the tsunami. He'd taken out a life-insurance policy to cover the mortgage, but couldn't have read the bit in the small print about not putting himself in harm's way. They weren't expecting to pay up. I'd asked BB if he'd bung in his share to make up for it, but I wasn't holding my breath.

Tracy dried her eyes as we approached the four-bedroom mock-Tudor that she now owned, or would shortly.

'I don't even have any children to be with, Nick. We tried so hard, but we couldn't.'

She looked at me. A dreadful thought crossed her mind. I could see it in her face. 'I won't lose you, Nick, will I? Just because Mong's gone it doesn't mean I have to lose you as well, does it?'

I parked up in the drive and pushed the selector to P. 'I'm not going anywhere. I'll always make sure you're OK, no matter what happens.'

PART THREE

1

Moscow

Thursday, 17 March 2011
Gunslingers Gun Club

The extractor fan was working overtime in the low-level, low-lit twenty-five-metre range. There were six hi-tech firing cubicles, each with electric wires that spun out the target between five and twenty-five metres. The fans were there to extract the lead dust that spat from the muzzles as the rounds left the weapons. Over a period of time, that stuff can line your lungs. The fans extracted the smoke and smell of cordite and cigarettes as well. People smoked everywhere in Moscow. I didn't know if there was a public policy against it, but even if there was, who was going to take the risk of telling you not to?

I pulled my Glock from its padded nylon zip-up. I hadn't been a fan of these weapons when they first came out. For a start, they incorporated three different safety systems, not one of which I could feel and work with my thumb. But now, like two-thirds of USA law enforcement and many other police and military agencies around the planet, I put my hands up. I'd got it wrong. It was an excellent weapon.

I'd misjudged Moscow, too. It had taken me a while to realize it was just an extreme version of New York. You knew where you stood with the Muscovites. People didn't open doors for each other. When you wanted something you said, 'Give me.' And as long as you had the roubles, you got. It was very clear-cut.

Muscovites had a live-for-today attitude that was infectious. Nothing you did in Moscow had consequences. It was a bit like the Wild West. The government was a dictatorship. The police were mostly corrupt. The crime rate was one of the highest on the planet. Most Russians were either unfriendly or downright hostile, especially if they were manning the doors of nightclubs. Moscow bouncers administered Face Control (Feis Kontrol). It didn't matter if you were male or female, if you were a minger they wouldn't admit you – unless you were rich. I'd even seen them split couples or groups. They were OK with my ugly face at Gunslingers, but only because I paid my membership on time.

The main reason I liked Moscow was that Anna lived there. It was nine months now since I'd taken the lease on the penthouse overlooking the Moskva River. To the right was the Borodinsky Bridge. Behind that, the Russian Federation's government buildings. It was a great place just to sit and gaze out at the city, especially at night, when the streets were full of pissed-off mingers who'd been face controlled chuntering to themselves on the way home.

Anna had been right. Moscow looked great in summer. I must have walked in every one of the city's ninety-six parks. Gorky Park had been the first. It was the only one I'd heard of. Then I discovered there was more green stuff here than in New York, and New York had more of it than London. It almost made me glad I'd left.

As the days got longer and warmer, Anna and I had headed for Serebryany Bor, an island just a trolleybus ride away. It could be walked at any time of day, but it was especially great in the evening when the late-setting sun bathed the *dachas*, the woods and the river.

I checked out the spring buds and flowers, kids on bikes with stabilizers, all the normal shit that now made sense to me. These were people who were getting on with their lives. I was getting on with mine too. It was all right. It wasn't as if I jumped up every morning and ran outside to kiss the flowers and hug the trees, but I'd been taking the time to stand and stare. For a while, anyway. Then I'd started to get itchy feet.

The more I got to know Anna, the more I realized how alike we were. We gave each other loads of space and got on with our own lives, knowing that made us both happy.

She was certainly giving me enough space at the moment. She'd just arrived in Libya, after a four-week stint covering the uprisings in Tunisia and Egypt for RT news. Since January, the only time I'd seen her was on the screen.

2

According to her reports, beamed out every day on Russia Today, Gaddafi wasn't giving up without a fight. He had just begun bombing rebel-held Benghazi. And, of course, the Brits were still having the piss taken out of them by the Russian and the German media for the fucked-up evacuation of British nationals. The Russians – and everyone else for that matter – had sent in their ships and planes and got their people out, well before the British FCO had decided to have a think about it over a nice cup of tea one morning.

I liked it when she went away. Reporting, for her, was a matter of doing the right thing. I knew it made her happy. Maybe it was the only way that a relationship would work for me, by having gaps and then coming back together. We'd probably get on each other's tits if we lived a conventional lifestyle.

I was looking forward to her coming home. Not only because I'd get to see her, but also because it'd mean she was out of harm's way. Far too many reporters were getting dropped. Russia, together with many other countries, showed the horror of war much more than we tended to in the UK and US.

Instead of a doll being placed on the rubble of a bombed-out building and some bland report voiced over, Russians got to see the mangled body of the child.

Al-Jazeera and RT reporters stood in the line of fire rather than watching from the rooftop of a distant hotel. Russians got to see dogs eating the dead. They got to see it as it was. Which was why Anna and her team were in more danger.

I didn't mind being on my own. I felt comfortable with my own company, just as Anna did. I'd been alone most of my life. I'd had lots of mates and always been around people, but I'd felt like an outsider. That was OK: I knew that was the way it was for me. I just got on with what I was doing.

I spent a lot of time in the basement gym of our condominium. For me, the gym had always been famine or feast. I did nothing for months on end because I was busy, working or injured, but when I had the time, I was in there every day.

My brain was getting a bit of a workout, too. I was reading the books I'd promised myself I was going to get through last year when I'd thought I was dying from a falsely diagnosed tumour. I did Tolstoy's *War and Peace* first, seeing as I was in Russia and Anna had suggested I started on the local lads' classics. She tested me on them, just to make sure I had done exactly what I'd promised myself. She didn't warn me the first fucking thing was over twelve hundred pages long. It had taken me longer to read than it took Napoleon to reach Moscow.

I'd just finished Fadeyev's *The Young Guard*, about the Russians' fight against the Nazis in the Second World War. Stalin had loved that guy. Now I was into Dostoevsky's *Crime and Punishment*. A poverty-stricken young man, who views himself as intellectually superior, comes up with the idea of murdering a rich money-lender he hates. I'd read as far as the crime, so I supposed the punishment bit was coming up. I couldn't wait to bore Anna to death about it when she got back.

I'd given the art galleries a pounding as well, and she'd taken me to *Swan Lake* at the Bolshoi ballet, and *Così Fan Tutte* at the opera house. I'd always thought it was a kind of ice cream.

I didn't feel I'd entered a world that I'd been missing. When I'd thought I was dying, I'd felt like I had some kind of hole that needed filling. Now it was just great to know something new. But it wasn't going to take over my life. That was why I still needed to keep my eye in on the range.

3

It's easy to shoot well, in theory. If the weapon is correctly aimed, the trigger is squeezed and the shot released without moving it, then the round will hit the target. However, the perfect or 'lucky' shot that is going to save your life is the result of years of practice. It's like building muscle at the gym: use it or lose it.

I started loading the seventeen-round magazine. A couple of punters to my left pressed their return buttons and man-shaped targets of Russian hoods with knives slid towards them. Lots of Russian piss-taking came from their cubicles as they checked each other's hits.

Gaston Glock was a genius. He'd had no experience with firearms when he entered a design competition for a new pistol for the Austrian Army in the 1980s, but he'd come up with the idea and built a prototype within a couple of months. He might have known jack about weapons, but he knew a lot about synthetic polymers, and that was one of the things that made this gun so different. The Glock's plastic frame made it much lighter and easier to handle, but it was also what made it so hard for people – myself included – to accept initially. But in the last thirty years it had proved reliable and durable, and old Gaston had done all right for himself.

I liked it here at Gunslingers. There was always a great mixture of police and Mafia, as well as gun nuts and European tourists doing the 'Russian military experience'. They paid the equivalent of five euros a round to fire weapons, and up to 16,000 euros to fly in a MiG 23. Some of these guys, mostly the Germans, blew off about thirty grand in euros over a long weekend.

It wasn't as if I talked to any of them or had mates there. Apart from anything else, I'd only learnt a phrase or two of Russian in the time I'd been in the country. There wasn't much point. Moscow was one of the big tourist destinations these days and most people knew enough English for me not to have to learn Russian. If they didn't understand me I'd do the British thing of pointing and shouting. It seemed to do the trick. I'd nod at the regulars, but only if they nodded at me first. Police and Mafia tend not to be the most sociable of people, and that was the way I liked it. I also liked coming in early, before the first tourists Rambo'd in and the place got packed.

Standing in my cubicle, I put the target out at about ten metres. I loaded a mag, pulled back on the top slide, and let go so it rammed a 9mm round into the chamber.

In the movies, when actors load semi- or automatic

weapons they always pull back the top slide and keep hold of it as it goes forward. It looks good, but it's bollocks. You've got to let the top slide go. The spring then forces the next round out of the magazine and into the chamber. Hamper this action and you're going to have stoppages. Law-enforcement agencies all over the world have trouble training recruits because of how they've seen the likes of Russell Crowe fuck it up on screen. When a Hollywood hard guy takes cover against a wall, the camera shows him with his weapon up, barrel near his face and pointing at the sky. It's yet more bollocks. The weapon's got to be pointing out towards the threat. The reason directors show it the way they do is so you can see the sexy weapon very close up, so it's next to the actor's head and you can register his emotion before they cut to the next scene.

I still used the Weaver stance when I shot. Your body became a firing platform by adopting the stance of a fighter. My legs were shoulder-width apart, left leg forward so my body turned forty-five degrees to the target. Now I was balanced forward and back, left and right.

The eyes are the aiming mechanism and the brain is the decision maker of when to fire, but everything else is used to create stability for the weapon. The web of my right hand was pushed hard and high into the grip. The higher the grip, the better the bore axis, the better the control of the weapon as the muzzle jumped when I fired. That was important. If I had to draw down outside this club it wouldn't be just one round at a time and at a paper target. Semi-automatic pistols are designed for a high grip. When the top slide comes back to reload after a round is fired, it needs to move against the abutment of a firmly held weapon frame. If not, the top slide may not go all the way back and may not be able to reload. Then I'd be fucked.

My bottom three fingers were like a vice. My thumb was wrapped round the other side of the pistol grip. Only my trigger finger was free. It was the only thing that was allowed to move. Fuck the gentle tremor that I knew would be there as I aimed. This was a lump of metal that had to be controlled if it was to do its job. If I gripped the weapon and aimed correctly, the tremor would be where I wanted to hit.

I brought the weapon up towards the target, my support hand wrapped around the dominant hand. My shoulder was forward so my nose was closer to the target than my toes. My right arm pushed the weapon towards the target as my left exerted rearward pressure so the platform was rigid.

I lifted the weapon to the centre mass of the raging Russian. Both eyes fixed on the target; dead centre of mass. The weapon's metal foresight came into my vision and became my primary focus. The target and the rear sight were now just blurs. I made sure the split at the back of the rear sight was level with the fore-sight. Then everything blurred as I focused on the foresight with both eyes.

As I squeezed, I felt the trigger safety with the first crease in my finger, the small lever that released the trigger action.

The foresight rested on the centre of mass and I finished my squeeze. The trigger went back. The round kicked off.

I didn't check to see where my round had hit. I'd find out soon enough when I retrieved the target. I just carried on firing, bringing the weapon down, then slowly up again into the same point of aim.

The only negative about coming down to Gunslingers was that it gave me itchy feet. Not to get out of Moscow, or away from Anna – far from it. But there was only so much reading, art and opera you could take in one burst. If I wanted to get out there again, it wasn't because I needed the money. There was still plenty of that left. If Anna had taught me one thing, it was that money isn't everything. It certainly wasn't her motivation. It was easy for me to say that money wasn't mine now that I had plenty of it, but I was starting to understand why Anna did what she did. Besides, going away for a bit of work the next time Anna was on a trip would make me want to come back to her and Moscow even more.

I squeezed off round after round, no double taps, just slow-time singles, making sure my skills and my eye were still in. I was in no rush. I'd bang out a couple of mags, clean my weapon, and take a walk home to get stuck into a bit of *Punishment*.

4

09.45 hrs

The coffee shop was further down the corridor, in an area that looked as if it had once been a Cold War nuclear bunker. The new owners had given it a complete makeover. It was warm and welcoming, and did a good trade in coffee and a roaring one in vodka and Baltika beer. Nobody saw a problem with customers having a few looseners before they picked up a weapon.

There wasn't one Moscow bar or coffee shop that was what it seemed. Once you were in, they didn't want you to leave. Almost every bar doubled as a restaurant, a bowling alley, snooker hall, casino, bookshop or, in this case, a gun club. Moscow is so huge and cabs are so expensive that bar owners want their customers to have everything they could possibly want from dawn till dusk – and on from dusk till dawn.

I'd only been to Gunslingers a couple of times in the

evening, and only because Anna said I should see Moscow when the cash was really being flashed. All of a sudden there were dancing girls, acrobats and laser light shows. Buying a table, which I didn't, but which gave you guaranteed entrance, a place to sit and a bar-tab, cost five thousand dollars. That was cheap; in some places it could be more than twenty thousand.

There were about five others in the bar that morning. Leather jackets weren't back in vogue as it wasn't yet spring. For now it was anything that was thick and padded.

At night, it was wall-to-wall Prada. The clubbers I'd seen were a mix of the beautiful, the rich, the well-connected, and those who wanted to be – mostly models, hookers, and girls with cocaine sparkling in their eyes as they scoped the room for 'sponsors'. And there were always plenty of wealthy men offering.

I was watching one of the six huge plasma screens hung around the walls. Two of them were linked to the ranges, so you could watch people trying to shoot under the influence. The first two tourists to come into view were German, judging by the flags sewn onto their parkas. They had that comfortable look about them, with premature beer bellies and thick moustaches.

The screen I was watching was linked to the English news channel on Russia Today. The girls always made sure it was on for me at ten a.m. so I could watch Anna's first report of the day. I never had a clue what she said because the sound was kept down, but that didn't matter. I could see that she was alive, and that she didn't have loads of holes in her. You could tell that she loved what she was doing, even in the middle of a war zone.

I was a bit early today. The screen was filled with images of Japanese military helicopters dropping water on the Fukushima Daiichi nuclear plant as they tried to avert a full meltdown. The number of confirmed dead and missing after the tsunami now stood at nearly thirteen thousand. Some 450,000 people had been staying in temporary shelters amid sub-zero night-time temperatures.

The German comedy show next door was much better viewing. The two lads were about to enjoy some AK action down one of the longer ranges. It wasn't heated, and their breath condensed around them in clouds. So did the cordite fumes kicking from their muzzles.

The AKs jerked into their shoulders and pushed them backwards. Mong was behind one of them as he fired, pushing the guy forward to try and keep the barrel pointing down the range. Rounds cracked and ricocheted off the concrete. These lads were giving it twenty-round bursts, when they'd have been told to limit them to five. At five euros a round, I doubted Mong cared that much.

He wasn't really Mong, of course. He just looked like him. Or maybe he didn't, and it was the endless news footage that made me think back to our time in Aceh. Whatever it was, every time I saw him, I wondered if he had tattoos on his arse.

5

Mong was getting a bit more pissed off. These two were tearing the arse out of it. They started to Rambo it up, firing from the hip, which made the AKs swing to the right with each burst. It was a total gang-fuck. The real Mong would have banged their heads together.

It always made me sad to think of him. Or maybe I just felt guilty. I'd kept my word after the job. I'd looked after Tracy. Jan had sucked cash out of her like a vacuum cleaner, and Tracy had paid for her mother to have private medical treatment for her cancer and home care afterwards, so I gave her money when I could.

If I was in Hereford I always went to check that things were all right. They weren't, of course. She was devastated: she'd gone into a deep depression and it was taking her a long time to climb out. The cash I gave helped her pay the bills, but it wasn't really what she needed. I never stopped telling her to get out of Hereford, to make a new start, but she didn't want to leave her mum and Jan to fend for themselves.

I got the Glock out and started cleaning the barrel

with a small brush. I smiled as I thought about all the times I used to take the piss out of Mong for being soft in the head and sending money to his supermarket woman.

When I'd got out of Russia with a few million dollars of a corrupt company's money in 2009 and bought the London flat, Tracy was the first person I wrote to. I told her I'd settle the mortgage so at least she had security. If she wanted to sell the house, she could do what the fuck she wanted with the proceeds.

She wrote back. She was really happy to have an address for me at last, and told me thanks, but no thanks. Her mum had died six months earlier and she'd finally taken my advice and got a job as a nanny in the South of France. She'd met a man. A Ukrainian guy called Frank. It didn't strike me as the commonest name for a Ukrainian, but that was beside the point. Tracy was in love. She'd sold the house and moved to be with him.

There was no return address, just thanks for all I had done. She told me life was wonderful, and how much she wished she'd taken my advice earlier.

I felt happy for her, but the last paragraph choked me up. She thanked me for all I'd done for Mong. I'd been a true friend to him, she said. I'd always watched his back. And she would always be my friend, too. Mong would have wanted it that way.

I was cleaning the barrel a bit too vigorously. I felt the same way I had the first time I'd read the letter. That she wouldn't have had to go through all this shit if Mong was still alive. And he would have been, if I'd stood firm about him not going to help BB.

6

Two Brits I'd seen there a couple of times before came into the coffee shop and ordered espressos. They reminded me of the comedians Mitchell and Webb. Their accents were almost posh, the sort estate agents might develop after a few years' running around in designer Minis selling overpriced properties to Sloanes or the Notting Hill mob.

Their hair was well cut but over-gelled, and they were clean-shaven. They wore Armani jeans and shirts, with rugby-ball cufflinks. You saw a lot of guys like them around town, with money to burn and plenty of drop-dead beautiful Svetlanas and Nadias happy to help them – for a suitable fee. These were sex-pats. They'd be down here later tonight, no doubt, watching the women who danced in cages, and buying shots from the ones wearing bikinis and vodka bottles slung in hip-holsters.

The ex-pat women didn't get left out. There were plenty of Russian men looking to provide the same service. This was an equal-opportunities town.

Companies that sent staff to dangerous places showered them with incentives. Forget bankers' bonuses. On top of their monster salaries, these guys got free rent, foreign service premiums, and cost-of-living allowances. No wonder money lost its meaning for them. After a thousand-dollar dinner at the Café Pushkin, they went to clubs like Gunslingers and ordered vodka tonics at thirty dollars a time. Then they'd select their sofas and wait for the girls to come say hi. Behind each was a private room. The menu on the table – in Russian, Japanese and English – helped you budget for what happened in there: *Intercourse 30 minutes: $500.*

Then they all turned up at their banks and law firms the next morning after about half an hour's sleep. By lunchtime they'd be having the first one of the day in the company bar or snorting a line of coke on their desk to steady their nerves.

Anna had a word for their disease: anomie. 'It means a breakdown of social norms or values, Nicholas. Distance from home puts personal values out of mind.'

It was just the kind of thing her favourite Russian authors banged on about. My new best mate Fyodor Dostoevsky certainly went for it in *Crime and Punishment*. The main character was trying to justify murder by saying it was not people he was killing but a principle.

Good luck to them. Why not? It didn't bother me. I just got on with my own life and let those jokers get on with theirs.

Mitchell, the well-fed one with the side parting, turned to me. 'You're a Brit, aren't you?'

I looked up from reassembling the weapon. 'Yep.'

'We are too.'

He pointed at the Glock. 'We like them. That your own?'

I nodded.

'I've seen you shoot a couple of times. We're thinking of joining, buying some Glocks, having some fun.'

Webb, taller, with dirty-blond hair, was concentrating on the TV. RT ran the intro to the ten o'clock news.

'Yeah, that'd be good.'

'What do you do with the gun? Do you have it locked up at home, or is it better to leave them here? Is it a drama carrying a pistol across town?'

The RT announcer was a very bland-looking guy with thinning hair and rimless glasses. The headlines kicked off with Libya. Anna would be on soon. Gaddafi had launched his first bombing raids on Benghazi. The West had called for a no-fly zone and Russia was sitting back and laughing at it all.

'I just leave mine here, mate. I don't need it at home. And I don't want it burning a hole in my pocket.'

I glanced at the screen above his head. Anna was gobbing off into her mike, with crowds of chanting Libyans around her.

Mitchell got the hint and went back to his showbiz partner, who was now watching Mong get even more pissed off with the Germans. They were larging it in front of an increasingly long queue of tourists waiting their turn.

7

Anna looked as good as ever. The water in Benghazi must have been back on. The last email I'd got from her, the day before yesterday, told me the water had been cut off and she hadn't washed her hair for a week. Her two-minute piece was done. I'd watch the full-length version when it came on later. The three o'clock news was more in-depth.

I zipped my Glock back into its case and handed it in to the armoury. I didn't bother saying goodbye to my new showbiz mates. I got my coat and headed outside into −8°C.

The Russian media took the piss out of the UK continuously for grinding to a halt at the first hint of a snowflake. Moscow hadn't seen a winter like this one for well over forty years, but it was still functioning. The mayor had gripped the situation. He'd raised an army of six thousand street cleaners.

The city was covered with gloomy grey and black slush but nowhere was impassable. Ladas and Mercedes spun a bit and people slid, but it was business as normal. There was very little grumbling about it. Some people just forgot about their cars until spring. They took the Metro, the same as I did.

The only problem was ice falling from rooftops. Two kids had been seriously injured yesterday. In St Petersburg, the roofs of a hospital and a hypermarket had collapsed under the weight of snow. They'd probably been built in the 1980s when Putin was mayor and subbing jobs out to the Mafia.

Unless there was an icicle with my name on it, I was weatherproof. I wore a North Face parka with a huge hood well and truly done up. I looked out at the world through a little circle of fur a few inches in front of my face. The hood was so big it didn't move when I turned my head. I looked like Kenny out of *South Park*. On my feet I had a pair of Dubarrys, the Gore-Tex and leather boots that were all the rage in this city. They looked like posh wellies. Anna had bought me a pair as a present for my first winter here.

According to the mayor, this was going to be the last time the city ever suffered from snow. The grey stuff reflected badly on its image, and he was going to do something about it. This boy had more money at his disposal than many a nation's GDP. He probably spent more in a day than Boris did in a year.

He'd decided to ban snow from the city. He was going to invest in the same cloud-sealing programme the city rolled out on all the major holidays to ensure the citizens of Moscow didn't get rained on. When had it ever rained on a May Day parade? Never. The city paid for jets to get up there and spray silver iodine into any clouds heading Moscow's way so they'd dump their rain upwind well before it could spoil things in Red Square. I wouldn't be needing the Dubarrys next May Day.

Alongside the biggest collection of billionaires on earth there was a massive migrant population, as well as millions of the poor, the old, the dying and the drugged. These people were all fucked big-time. I passed a collection of Soviet concrete blocks where they scraped a living.

Portable paraffin heaters provided their only warmth, but gave off so much moisture that their windows were still frozen solid on the inside – unless the residents had sold the glass and shoved up plywood in its place. In Putin's Russia, everyone was an entrepreneur.

8

One of the promises I'd made myself during my dying days was to take the time to 'stand and stare', as Anna called it – to look at trees and plants, walk through gardens, shit like that. So every time I came out of Gunslingers, I turned left through Victory Park, along 'Years of War', its central avenue. Then I got the trolleybus home.

Victory Park was a new creation. It was only finished after years of fuck-ups in the mid-1990s. Poklonnaya Gora, the hill it sat on, was where Napoleon had waited to be given the keys to the city when his troops surrounded it in 1812. He'd waited in vain.

The park was finished just in time for the fiftieth anniversary of what we called the Second World War and the Russians called the Great Patriotic War. They had little interest in what had happened elsewhere. Fair one – more Russians were killed between '41 and '45 than all the other Allies put together. And eight out of ten Germans killed were dropped by the

Soviets. In Western history books, those little details always seem to get lost in the footnotes.

The 'Years of War' had five terraces, one for each year of the conflict, and 1,418 fountains, one for every day. They weren't working at the moment because everything was frozen. But there were chapels, mosques, statues, rockets, all sorts of shit – and then, right at the centre, one big fuck-off statue of Nike, the goddess of victory. I kept meaning to ask Anna the Russian for 'Just do it'.

She was going to take me there on Victory Day, 9 May. Veterans, survivors, kids, everybody turned out. I was looking forward to seeing the old and bold. They'd be wearing more medals than Gaddafi. And it wouldn't be raining.

I was nearly at the main gate, head down, nose running, hands in pockets, making sure I didn't slip on the ice, when the front panel and an alloy wheel with the Range Rover logo appeared in what little peripheral vision my hood allowed.

'Hey, fella, want a lift?' It was the gunslinger without the side parting.

My head turned but my hood stayed where it was. I pulled the fur aside. Webb was at the driver's window of a white wagon stained grey by today's slush.

'Where are you going? We'll take you. It's fucking freezing out there.'

'Nah, it's all right – I need the exercise.'

I turned through a set of fancy iron gates. The Range Rover's engine revved behind me, but instead of driving away it turned into the park. The wagon swept past and pulled up about three metres ahead of me.

Even the number plate spelt drama. The back door swung open. Mitchell, in a big black Puffa, beckoned me inside. But he wasn't smiling. 'Come on, my friend. It's a lot warmer in here.'

The driver's window was still powered down, and I could see that Webb wasn't smiling either.

I was about to turn back towards the main when Mitchell stepped out, weapon up. He'd obviously decided not to follow my advice. 'In – the – fucking – vehicle – now.'

9

I swung back towards him, hands now out of my pockets and up by my chest. Head down, I focused on the weapon. I could smell the exhaust fumes billowing from the cold engine. I got to within a couple of paces of the open door. I could smell the rich leather interior as I leant closer, and feel the warmth of the heater.

I punched out with my left hand and grabbed the top of Mitchell's Glock. I pushed down, gripping it so I was outside his arc of fire, and jabbed at his face with my right. Short, sharp jabs, three or four in quick succession. Not caring where they hit, just that they did.

As his head jerked back, I took my chance. I found the trigger of the weapon and pushed down and round until the barrel pointed towards him.

The Glock jumped in my hand as a shot kicked out and the guy went down. I let go, turned and legged it as fast as I could, back through the gates. I screamed across the road, slipping on ice the other side and going down hard. I got up, legs flailing, and turned immediately right, out of their line of sight and fire. I kept running, not looking back – not that I could have with my hood up – and took another right.

I found myself in a service road. Steam spewed from heating vents set into the back wall of an industrial unit and engulfed a line of huge industrial wheelie-bins. I dodged between two of them, three-quarters of the way down, and fought to recover my breath.

Webb would have had to wait until Mitchell was back in the wagon before coming after me. Even if he didn't give a shit about him, he couldn't just leave the boy bleeding into the Victory Avenue snow. The police would soon be asking why.

I leant against the wall, heart pounding. Now that I was still, the cold began to eat its way into my feet. But at least they were dry; that was all that mattered right now.

I kept looking left and right to cover both exits of the service road. It wasn't long before Webb drove past the end I'd come in from. There wasn't much exhaust vapour now his engine had warmed up.

I had to assume they knew where I lived. And that meant the only thing I could do was face them up. I had to find out who the fuck they were and why they wanted me.

It looked as if Dostoevsky would have to wait. There was no way I could risk heading back to the flat or the range – or to any other known location – until I'd sorted this shit out.

And if the Range Rover's number plate was anything to go by, there was plenty of shit to sort.

10

In Moscow, real people's cars have white plates with black letters. The Range Rover had red ones with white numbers. Diplomatic plates. That could have meant jack-shit. You could buy them on the black market: they let you travel in the government-designated fast lanes and beat the Moscow jams.

Lads with red plates were never stopped. About a month ago, the police had a clamp-down on their illegal use. They pulled over a genuine red-plated wagon: the diplomat's BGs jumped out and over-powered them, spread the officers on the ground, weapons confiscated. How were they to know the police were genuine?

But even if they were black-market gear, I still had to worry. These things cost at least twenty-five thousand dollars – more if you threw in the blue flashing lights. Which meant that whoever was after me had money as well as Glocks – and that wasn't good news.

Fuck it. Running away would only make me die

short of breath. And then I'd never know what this was all about.

I started to retrace my steps. They'd be back along that street sooner or later. They'd hit all known locations: Gunslingers, maybe the flat. Then they'd cruise around for a while longer. But not indefinitely. Mitchell was going to need medical attention, unless Webb was going to let him bleed to death. So I needed them to find me before they made that drop.

I got back on the main, hood still up, but enough of my face sticking out to be able to spot the nearest mini-mart. These places were even more prolific than Starbucks. They sold everything the man who had nothing could possibly want: cigarettes, alcohol, sulphuric acid to keep your crumbling piping clear, paraffin to keep you warm and your windows frozen.

I dodged and wove my way through the traffic and went into Apricot Garden. There wasn't a piece of fruit in sight; they all had names like that. Milky Way, Cowboy's Stable, you name it.

The Russian version of *X Factor* blared from a TV mounted above the counter. An old woman who looked as though she'd been sitting by the checkout since before the Cold War puffed a cigarette and watched Simon Cowellski put the local hopefuls through their paces.

I scanned the aisles, then grabbed a hammer and some overpriced paraffin in the kind of plastic five-litre container we'd use for ready-mixed screen-wash.

I arrived at the counter as Simon gave his verdict and the singer burst into tears. A dozen or so brands of cigarette were on display, from Lucky Strike and

Marlboro to Leningrad and CCCP in bold, no-nonsense Soviet-style packaging for those who still missed the old ways. I was interested in the lighters alongside them.

I grunted and pointed. She hoovered up my roubles without taking her eyes off the screen.

I headed back to the bins, put down my newly purchased gear and unclipped the wheel retainers on the last one in the line. I unscrewed the top of the paraffin container and pressed my thumb into the seal until it broke, then left it on the ground.

I retraced my steps to the corner and looked around uncertainly, as if I was waiting for a pickup. I checked once more behind me. They'd be able to get their wagon down the service road, no problem.

11

I didn't have long to wait. The Range Rover was moving a lot faster now. Webb was still at the wheel. He spotted me and his mouth moved in double-time behind the windscreen.

He hit the brakes just past the service road and the wheels spun in the slush. Mitchell was forced up and forward from where he was lying in the back seat and I saw him give a silent scream of pain as I turned and legged it down the service road, giving my best impression of a headless chicken. I shoved the lighter between my teeth.

The Range Rover reversed at speed. I heard the engine roar as it powered into the narrow space. I reached the wheelie-bins, slid behind the last one, back against the wall, and shoved against it with both arms and then my right foot. The bin toppled into the path of the oncoming wagon.

There was a flash of grime-covered white as Webb stood on the brakes, but he was too late. Metal screeched on metal and the bin clattered off down the road.

The air-bags kicked off in the Range Rover's cabin.

I grabbed the hammer in my right hand and the paraffin container in my left.

Webb tried to exit but his door smashed against the wall. There wasn't room for him to get out. I swung the hammer at the bottom left-hand corner of the rear passenger window before they had time to draw down. The safety glass starred, then shattered.

Shouts of anger and pain came from inside. I shoved the paraffin container against the frame and pushed down on it with my right forearm. There was a fine spray for a couple of seconds, then the rest of the seal gave way and fluid gushed into the interior. The fumes burnt my nostrils and can't have been much fun for theirs.

I dropped the container and shoved my left fist through the hole, lighter at the ready, thumb on the roller.

'Show me your hands!'

They got the message loud and clear. Webb put his straight on the steering wheel. He wasn't pleased. 'You've fucked up, Stone. Just stand down.'

'Who the fuck are you? What do you want with me?'

I didn't get an answer. Maybe I wasn't sounding crazy enough.

I cranked it up. 'What the fuck do you want? Tell me or I'll fucking torch this. *Tell me – tell me now!*'

I glanced down. The paraffin had mixed nicely with Mitchell's blood on the tan leather. His leg was a mess.

I heard a squeal of brakes and the scream of an engine coming towards us from the other end of the service road. Another Range Rover, two up. Black with a blue flashing light on the driver's side of the roof. That was all I had time to register before I turned and started running in the opposite direction.

I heard no shouts, no commands to stop, no gunfire. I kept on running.

Then my head exploded. I went down like liquid. My legs moved like I was still running, but I knew I was going nowhere. Hands grabbed me and dragged my face across the hammer that had dropped me.

12

It wasn't long before I was in the back of the un-damaged Range Rover, hands secured to my ankles with plasticuffs. I rested my forehead on the leather upholstery of the seat in front of me to try to release the pressure on my wrists.

My skull had recovered from the initial pain where the hammer had connected, but I knew I was going to have a big fuck-off headache for the rest of the day. I just hoped it wasn't a fracture and I'd get the chance to sort out the cut. I couldn't feel any wetness, but I knew there had to be one. Maybe my parka had soaked up the blood before it reached my neck.

Both wagons backed out of the service road. The driver of mine was a big old Nigerian lad in a blue Puffa. Blue and red beads tied off each braid of his cornrows and he had a shaving rash under his chin. The guy beside him looked like Genghis Khan. He must have come straight from the steppes. He kept turning in his seat to make sure his passenger wasn't trying to escape – as if I was going to get far even if I did.

The blue light started to flash. I could see it bouncing off shop windows as we drove down the main. We were heading out of the city.

I was flapping. None of these guys cared about what I saw or heard, and that wasn't a good thing. It could mean they knew I was never going to get the chance to tell anybody.

I checked the dash clock: 11:17. I tried to get a view of the speedo but it was blocked by the driver's Puffa. The sat-nav was glowing, but it was all in Russian. All I got from it was our direction of travel.

Genghis had his phone out. He grunted acknowledgements to whoever was on the other end and closed it down. These vehicles were brand new. The white one must have lost its sumptuous showroom smell, but the warmth and luxury of this one almost lulled me into feeling safe.

I gave everybody time to settle down before I tried to get some sort of relationship going. I didn't even know if these lads spoke English.

'The small guy – he OK? No hard feelings, eh? I—'

With a rustle of nylon jacket, Genghis turned and put his forefinger to his lips. He shushed me like a child. I nodded, returned my forehead to the seatback and began a close examination of the carpet.

There wasn't any point in trying to talk with these guys. They were only the monkeys. And if the organ-grinder wanted me dead, I would have been dead by now. They'd have done it in the alleyway while I was half concussed. But why had they let me see their faces? And why weren't they pissed off that I'd shot their mate?

I raised my head and caught another glimpse of the sat-nav. We were still heading west, but keeping off the M1, the main motorway. Suburbia was just beginning to take shape on the Moscow margins. The media were full of it – all the usual moaning about forests having huge holes ripped out of them to make way for gated communities with names like Navaho and Chelsea.

The road was now lined with trees and the potholes were getting more treacherous.

13

An hour and twenty-seven minutes later we turned off towards a village. I'd spent every second of that time trying not to get bounced around in the foot-well, so the small of my back was now as painful as my neck.

Genghis sparked up his cell again.

This wasn't Navaho or Chelsea. The buildings were timber-framed and exuded an air of history. Enormous *dacha*s, three storeys high with huge, overhanging roofs, stood behind big walls. These were the weekend retreats of wealthy Muscovites, built in the time of the Tsar. Tyre tracks led in and out of the driveways. There was no foot traffic at all. The rich didn't need to walk and their snow was pure white.

We turned through a massive set of slowly opening wooden gates. I saw cedar tiles cladding a steeply pitched roof. Condensation billowed from modern heating ducts on the side of the old building. It looked like something out of a spy story. The whole village did.

The Range Rover crunched across the snow,

flanking the *dacha*. Huge trees circled a snow-lined playground, gardens and a swimming-pool. I could just make out the little handles round the edge to help you out of the water. We swooped round to the back of the house and stopped behind another Range Rover with red plates. Genghis jumped out and produced an eight-inch blade from a sheath at his hip. My door opened. The blade flashed in the sunlight and the plasticuffs put up only token resistance. As I straightened, he pointed the tip of his knife towards the wooden veranda.

The cold slapped me in the face as I headed up the three steps. Crows squawked in a field the other side of the trees. I touched the swelling on the back of my head. The skin had broken, but the heat of the Range Rover had dried the wound.

Three doors led off the veranda: a bug screen for the summer, followed by a triple-glazed monster with an aluminium frame and finally the hand-carved wooden original.

I stepped into a big shiny modern kitchen, all white marble and stainless steel. It couldn't have provided a more dramatic contrast to the exterior. I stood on a polished stone floor with the sweet smell of Russian cleaning fluids, that really intense mixture of rose perfume and bleach, assaulting my nostrils. And it was even hotter in there than it had been in the Range Rover.

A small man in his late forties sat facing me at a white marble table. His hair was brushed back. There was a hint of grey at the temples. He was immersed in a Russian broadsheet, the front page full of the

Fukushima meltdown. 'Coffee?' Without looking up, he pointed to a cappuccino machine the size of a nuclear reactor. 'Help yourself and sit down over here with me.'

He was wearing black suit trousers, shiny black leather shoes, a grey shirt and V-neck jumper. A white magnetic board hung on the wall behind him, covered with photos and all the normal family shit. A scaled-down red Ferrari with an electric engine was parked beneath it, next to a Tupperware crate containing every shape and size of game ball. The cappuccino machine stood beside a white marble sink large enough to dismember a body in.

'Relax, Nick. No one else is going to interrupt us, and you're in no danger. I just want to talk with you.' His English was precise, but his accent was surprisingly guttural. He sounded like Hollywood's idea of a Cold War Soviet agent.

'Please.' He nodded again towards the dozen or so matching blue mugs that were lined up on the spotless work surface. 'Get yourself whatever you fancy. Then come and sit down.'

I wasn't going to turn down a brew. It could be my last for a while. I piled in the sugar in case I needed an energy boost some time soon. I lifted the shiny glass jug from its hotplate and poured myself a generous shot of its contents.

'Do you know where you are, Nick?'

I reached for the condensed milk. 'Not a clue.'

'Peredelkino. A very nice place, steeped in history. It's known as the writers' village. Many famous Russians have lived here, Russians who have changed

117

the world with their words and their wisdom. Do you admire our great Russian writers, Nick?'

I stirred the milk into my coffee. It was so thick with sugar I could stand the spoon up in it. 'I read when I can.'

'Tarkovsky? Pasternak? Fadeyev?'

I raised an eyebrow. I knew he was taking the piss. 'The guy who said Stalin was the greatest humanitarian the world has ever known? Good writer, but I wouldn't trust his character references, would you?'

I didn't give a fuck what he thought, but I was quite pleased that he was suddenly sitting up and paying attention.

'We all need friends in high places, Nick.' He waved his hand at a huge picture window. 'Every one of these great writers had a *dacha* here, you know. They're buried here too. Peredelkino is featured in a le Carré novel – *The Russia House*.'

I finished stirring. 'Is that so?'

'There's a lot of history in these *dachas*. If only they had ears.' A thought struck him. 'Well, maybe some of them did have ears during the Soviet era, yes?'

The triple-glazed windows slightly warped the view, but I knew that if I had to leg it, I'd head for the door I'd come through and straight towards the swings and the slide. Then into the tree line, even though I didn't know what was on the other side of it. I'd go and see what the crows were up to.

The small man flicked through the pages of his newspaper with one hand, as he motioned with the other for me to sit opposite him.

'What are you reading now, Nick?'

118

'Dostoevsky.' I gave him my best poker face. '*Crime and Punishment*. But I've got a feeling I won't be finishing it any time soon.'

'When you do, you will find knowledge and enlightenment. I came to books late, but . . .' He closed the paper and raised his hands. '. . . as we all know, Nick, knowledge – of whatever kind – is power.'

I sat there with the brew. He was playing with me, enjoying the moment, even though he wasn't showing it. Not a hint of a smile crossed his face. He was like Arnie in Terminator mode.

'Thanks for the tip. But isn't it time you introduced yourself? And told me what you want?'

He waved my questions away. 'How's Anna? Is she enjoying North Africa? I watch her every day. It's a little warmer there, I suspect.'

If he was trying to impress me, he'd succeeded.

I put my mug down on the white marble. 'She in trouble?' I kept my voice even. It was pointless getting sparked up. I'd know the answer soon enough.

'This is not about Anna, Nick. No, this is about another of your women.'

My head pounded. I was starting to get pissed off. If he was going to hurt me or offer me something – I didn't really care which – I just wanted him to get on with it.

He dragged his seat backwards, turned and pulled one of the photos from the steel board. A well-manicured hand spun it towards me. Then he settled back, putting a bit of distance between himself and the table.

A woman and a young boy cuddled one another on the garden swings.

She'd changed the colour of her hair; it had blonde highlights now, and was a lot longer, well past her shoulders.

'She's still beautiful.'

He nodded. 'Of course. And you knew her husband. Knew him well. What was his name?'

'Montgomery. We called him Mong.'

He nodded, satisfied.

'So you're Frank.'

'Francis. But until we get to know each other better, you may call me Mr Timis.'

'Not very Ukrainian.'

'It puts you Westerners at ease.'

'What's happened to Tracy? Is she OK? Or is it the boy?'

'Stefan.'

'Your son?'

'Yes, he's my son. Look closer – you will see.'

I did. The boy's eyes were fixed on the camera as if he was interrogating it. The only difference between father and son was the grin on the boy's face. Frank probably hoped that in a few years' time the whole smiling thing would just run its course, and Stefan would turn into his father's son.

His eyes suddenly burnt, and I knew playtime was over. 'I have a problem. I need your help. Someone has stolen them from me. And I want you to get them back.'

14

'Have you heard from them? Has anyone contacted you?'

He leant forward, keeping my gaze. He was still remarkably cool, even for a machine. Which was probably why he managed to be whatever he was. 'No. If they had, I wouldn't need you.'

I gestured at the wound on the back of my head. 'Is this what passes for a golden handshake round here? I could have been killed. And so could that lad who bled all over your car seat.'

Frank's face was stone. 'I had to know if you are . . . capable. I only know what you used to do, not if you can still do it. What is it you Brits say – to see if you can still cut some mustard?'

He said it without a trace of a smile. The emotion gene had bypassed Mr T.

'What about the lad I shot? Are his mustard-cutting days over?'

'He'll have a fine life. He'll get drunk and tell stories of how he fought off five assassins. With the money

I'm going to pay him, the women will hang on every word. You've done him a very big favour.' He waved his hand dismissively. 'Don't worry about him. Worry instead about my son and his mother. You have certain responsibilities towards her. Or did she lie to me? This is not just personal for me, Nick – it is for you, too, would you not say?'

I took a swig of the brew and gave him a nod. 'What do you know?'

'Only that they were taken four days ago, along with their bodyguard. The pirates seized the yacht about a hundred kilometres west of the Seychelles. I'll pay them whatever they want, Nick. Just find them, and broker the deal.'

It was only a couple of days since four Americans had been killed on their yacht during a bungled rescue operation, after being hijacked off the Horn of Africa. In South East Asia this would have been pretty routine. Crew and passengers were killed and thrown overboard; the ships and their contents were seized. But this was a bit of a turn-up for the Somalis. As far as they were concerned, the people were the prize.

I didn't know if Frank knew about the US deaths, but either way I'd have to start to manage his expectations. Right now they seemed pretty high, considering he knew fuck-all about what had happened.

'You sure nobody's contacted you, even indirectly?'
'Nobody.'

'Then how do you know the yacht's been taken?'

'The crew was dumped. The yacht was taken with the three of them still aboard. The crew arrived back in

Moscow this morning. You will go and see them when we've finished here.'

'The BG, the bodyguard – is he good?'

'He's British, like you. He will be doing what he can. I know it. But I will have no further need of him once all this is over. Stefan and his mother – I want them back. I don't care what it costs.'

I looked at the picture again. 'This isn't as clear-cut as you might think. If you pay what the pirates ask, you may put them in more danger. If you don't bargain, they'll think you're loaded. They'll take your money and then they'll sell them on to another clan and the whole process will start all over again. Or rival clans could go to war over them. Either way, you'll never get them back.'

'Money talks, Nick. If—'

'There is a protocol. As long as you stick to it, there's a chance of getting them back. You understand that?'

'Of course. That is why you are here.'

'You've got to start thinking of them as dead. Plan their funerals in your head. Anything else is a bonus. Do you understand that too?'

He nodded.

'All right. To confirm, no one has contacted you? No one has been given a message to pass on? No contact number was left with the crew?'

He shook his head.

Maybe Frank hadn't heard anything yet because they were dead. Or maybe the BG was switched on enough not to give him as the point of contact.

'So why me? Why aren't you doing this through your insurance company? They have people who do this sort of thing twenty-four/seven. Or why not get the word out some other way? Knowledge, as you say, is power. And the red plates out there tell me you've got both. Why have you come to me?'

He shrugged. 'I have my reasons. I will pay you extremely well. But we can talk about all that later. Tracy respects you, Nick. I think perhaps she loves you. You have been a good friend to her, not just to her husband. You will not let her down now, will you?'

Eyes riveted to mine, he pointed his finger. 'You will be doing what you do best. And doing it for somebody you care about. What could be better for a man's soul? Read some of the books that have been written in this village, Nick. Then you will understand what I am talking about.'

I took another mouthful of my brew. The coffee wasn't hot any longer, but it still tasted good. 'I'll have to try and find a contact. Once I've done that, I'll get back to you. It's pointless talking about anything else until we know they're alive.'

He nodded again, slowly.

'Don't raise your hopes.'

He pulled a business card from his shirt pocket. The only thing on it was a mobile number. 'Call me whenever you want. Do not give this out to anyone else. Please remember the number and then destroy the card.' His eyes burnt again. 'I'm a very private man.'

The card went into the pocket of my jeans.

'I need you to buy me a flat, somewhere on the outskirts of London. No more than a hundred and fifty K. In my full name. You know that, of course.'

He raised an eyebrow. 'Why?'

I was sure money wasn't the reason he wanted to know. 'You'll find out why if they are still alive. But the only way to get them out safely will be to do exactly what I say.'

An engine rumbled alongside the *dacha*. The smashed-up Range Rover came into view and Webb climbed out.

Frank leant over the table, eyes boring into me. 'I want my son and his mother back here. Whatever it costs.'

I took a last mouthful of the brew and swallowed. Finally, I nodded.

If he was pleased at my decision he didn't show it. He sat back. 'The crew is waiting for you.'

I gestured towards the sink. 'Just give me a couple of minutes to clean my head.'

15

I kept my hood up as we stepped into the luxurious lobby of the Ararat Park Hyatt. This was an extraordinarily lavish hotel. The management would have surveillance measures to match.

I didn't look around much as we headed for the elevators. But the little I saw of the polished steel and marble atrium told me that Frank Timis looked after his people. The cheapest room would be about six hundred dollars a night, and not just because of the architecture. Neglinnaya Street was in the heart of the city, within spitting distance of Red Square, the Kremlin, St Basil's Cathedral and the Bolshoi Theatre. Property here would cost millions of roubles a square metre. We were on oligarch turf.

The one thing my hood didn't shield me from was the smell. It was roses and bleach again. Either that scent really was everywhere or it was buried inside my head.

The drive back to the city had been as talkative as the one in. We took the same route. Genghis drove this time. The Nigerian rode shotgun. He was constantly on the phone. He talked in Russian.

This suited me. I hadn't come to any decision on Frank yet. I didn't know enough about him to make a judgement, and I didn't know enough about the situation. All I knew was that it involved Tracy, so here I was.

In the exposed, space-age lift, the Nigerian pressed the button for the fourth floor. We raced upwards while the world below chatted over coffee in plush sofas. The mobile never left his ear. It had to be a woman he was talking to. His tone was far too smooth for it to be anybody else.

He didn't bother knocking when we got to Room 419. The door was ajar. He signed off his lady friend with a silver-tongued comment or two and walked straight in. More five-star-plus luxury. The walls were cream. The thick-pile carpet was the colour of bleached sand. The furniture was solid walnut. Electric curtains. A wider than widescreen Bang & Olufsen TV. A mini-bar that was even bigger than Mr T's cappuccino machine.

There were two sofas. Two men sat on each. A fifth, the youngest, was on the unmade king-sized bed. They all wore brand new shell-suits. Their faces were red and blotchy from exposure to the sun. And they all had cigarettes on the go. There was so much smoke you couldn't even see the No Smoking signs.

They eyed me apprehensively, like I was a cop who suspected them all of murder and the grilling was about to begin. Maybe it was the environment. Not many crew normally got to stay in a twelve-hundred-dollar suite in the Ararat Park Hyatt.

The Nigerian didn't even bother to greet them. He just redialled and helped himself to one of the armchairs that sat each side of a small coffee-table next to the triple-glazed window.

The oldest of the crew got to his feet. 'I am Rudy.' He stretched out his hand. He was in his early fifties, with tight grey hair and a beard. 'I am the captain.'

He was about to start a round of introductions.

'No time for that, mate. Let's crack on.'

I threw my parka onto the armchair opposite Mr Lover Man, then drew back the curtain. I was looking out of the front of the hotel. The rooftops of Moscow were covered with snow. It was like a still from *Doctor Zhivago*. The onion-shaped domes of the Kremlin were so close we could have watched Putin pumping iron.

Mr Lover Man wasn't impressed. He was too busy looking inwards, locking eyes with the crew. He might have been whispering sweet nothings into his phone, but he wanted them to know he'd be hanging on their every word.

Below me, the Range Rover was parked at the front of a line of half a dozen vehicles immediately outside the hotel entrance. Genghis did his bit for the Moscow smog by keeping the engine running. An Audi estate about four wagons down was doing the same. A couple of half-moons had been carved out of the dirt on the windscreen. It was two up. I admired the view for longer than I needed to.

Mr Lover Man closed down his mobile. Was he staying or going?

The vibe I was picking up from the crew was that it would be better if he left. You could have cut the tension between them with a knife. The atmosphere couldn't have been more at odds with the comfortable world of suede-upholstered headboards and Egyptian cotton sheets.

Mr Lover Man wasn't moving one inch.

'Does anybody else speak English?'

'I do.'

I turned back into the room.

16

He was just a kid, really, low twenties at the most. His nose was already peeling. He looked even more nervous than Rudy, maybe because he was right at the bottom of the food chain and the only other crew member I'd be able to talk to. There was definitely something wrong with this lot.

He added, 'A little.' He had the kind of American accent that foreigners pick up from *Friends*.

'You know I'm here to help, don't you? I'm trying to get the three of them back, nothing more.'

I got a sort of nod from the boy. He sat back on the bed, but he was about as relaxed as a high-tensile wire.

Rudy looked as though he'd be a serious candidate for the job of Cap'n Birdseye in a few years' time. Right now, though, the smile beneath his closely cropped beard was so rigid I thought his face might crack.

'So what happened, Rudy?'

'We were attacked by Somalis. It was so far from the African coast, I never thought—' He was still on his feet. His eyes darted involuntarily in the direction of Mr Lover Man.

'It's OK, mate, you don't have to stand for me. Go on.'

He sat down on the bed.

'The *Maria Feodorovna*—'

'The yacht?'

'Yes.'

'What sort is it? A motor yacht? Sailing?'

'Motor yacht. Forty metres. We were cruising, and then from nowhere two skiffs were coming towards us from the port side.'

The rest of the crew sucked at their cigarettes and kept their eyes down. Either the carpet was really interesting or they didn't want me to read their expressions.

'They were travelling very fast – twin seventy-fives on the back. I knew they were pirates even before they attacked. Skiffs so far from the coast. They had to be.

'We started to make speed and tried to change direction, make it harder for them to board. I shouted for Jez and—'

'The bodyguard?'

Rudy's eyes shot across to Mr Lover Man once more. No one else moved, but I knew they were even more uncomfortable at the mention of the BG's name.

'Yes, yes. He came up on deck, and he looked, but then he went down below with Stefan and Madame.'

'Where did he take them? Was there some kind of panic room? Was he armed – did the yacht have any weapons?'

He shook his head. 'They went into the main cabin.

He told me to make more speed. I was trying, but we could not outrun them. They fired a rocket across our bows. Then they aimed the rocket launcher straight at the bridge. I had no choice. I had to come off the power. The other skiff was closing behind. They had grappling hooks.'

I raised a hand. 'But did you have weapons? Did the BG take them on?'

The boy jumped in: 'If we had, I would have killed them all.'

Rudy glared at him to stand down. 'They climbed on the back, maybe five, six, I don't really know. All with rifles and big knives. I tried to make a mayday call but they must have jammed the radio.'

He sounded close to tears. 'They got everyone on the bridge. We were on our knees. There was a lot of shouting. They were kicking us, pointing their rifles into the back of our heads. They were high, chewing that drug they like. I could hear Stefan crying behind me. Madame trying so hard to comfort him.'

The crew nodded when they heard the boy's name. Their expressions seemed to soften.

'He was scared . . . so scared.'

A lad with thick dark-brown hair mumbled to the skipper and pointed at me, cigarette in hand.

'He wants to know that you will get Stefan back home safe.'

'I'm going to try. But you need to tell me everything you know. *Everything*.' I nodded at the questioner. 'Tell him, of course. I'll get all three of them back.'

Rudy translated. I caught 'Stefan' a couple of times. I shifted position so I could keep Mr Lover Man in sight. He hadn't spoken a word of English so far, but he clearly understood every word.

'You all have watches. Are they new? Didn't they take money, valuables?'

The boy answered: 'No, they didn't let us take anything with us, but also didn't take anything from us. They didn't care about us. It was Madame and Stefan they wanted.'

He was quivering with anxiety. He reached suddenly into a red nylon holdall, then had second thoughts and pushed it further under the bed with his heel.

Mr Lover Man said something in Russian. He wanted to know what the fuck was going on. Rudy seemed to be begging him to keep things nice and calm. He turned to me, hands clasped together like he was about to pray. 'I'm sorry. He has had a terrible time . . .'

'What happened next, Rudy?'

He took a deep breath as the boy sat back down. 'We were all on the bridge, on the floor. They stood over us, shouting and chewing. And then they made me steer a new course west.

'Maybe half an hour later, we saw their mother-ship, an old fishing trawler with another two skiffs tied up alongside it. They were hundreds of kilometres from home.' There was a note of profound sadness in his voice. 'They took us off the *Maria Feodorovna*. They placed us in the tender and just left us. *They took my ship.*' He finally broke down. '*They took Stefan and his mother . . .*'

The young one sparked up. 'And Jez . . .'

The captain shot the boy a warning glance.

'But, Papa . . .'

I looked at him. 'What about the bodyguard? Did he do something? Did he say something?'

His father answered for him: 'He stayed with Stefan and Madame. Trying to protect them. Please. I've spoken to my crew. They know nothing more than I have told you. I wish we knew more, but it was so quick. They came, they took. And then they left us. We never saw the three of them again. I do not even know if they had a plan.'

Of course they had a plan. This was business. There were even established pay differentials for the pirate crew members. The first guy to board a ship got paid more than anyone else. He usually picked up a couple of thousand dollars extra once the ransom money came in. Relative risk and reward, just like any other line of work.

'I need to know anything at all that anyone can remember, no matter how insignificant. It may help me find them.' I fixed on the captain. 'Can you tell them that?'

Mr Lover Man had had enough. He packed away his mobile and got out of his seat. 'We are done here.'

His English was just as it should have been. Deep and growly.

'That is all they know. That is all you need to know to make a plan and rescue them. Come.'

As he headed out of the room, the crew looked up at me with a mixture of embarrassment, fear and relief.

I glanced at the door handle and the electronic lock. It looked like the Russian equivalent of a VingCard

Classic, the magnetic card reader used in most European and American hotels. If so, the locksets would be high security, with a full one-inch steel deadbolt and three-quarter-inch anti-pick latch for added strength. The electronics worked off standard AA batteries. Their flash memory allowed the lock to be accessed and reprogrammed directly at the hotel-room door.

I followed my escort to the lift. 'Are you giving me a ride back to my flat? The Metro's a fucking nightmare around here.'

Mr Lover Man had been with Mr T too long. He didn't give it a nanosecond's thought. 'No.'

We headed down. At the main door, I zipped my parka up to my chin and adjusted the hood to hide my face from the cold. Then Mr Lover Man and I stepped outside. He took a pace or two towards the Range Rover, then spun on his heel.

'Go now and bring back Stefan.'

The Audi was still two-up. The engine stopped as soon as I turned towards the Metro. A guy in a dark overcoat and beanie stepped out of the car and his mate, in sheepskin, followed suit. Mr T had obviously tuned into Comedy Central. These boys were the spitting image of Ant and Dec. Dec hit the key fob to lock up.

I crossed the road, heading the couple of hundred metres towards the sign with the large red M. I didn't bother to check if Frank's new celebrity couple were still with me. I took it as given. He clearly liked to keep a tight rein on all his people.

17

Lubyanka was one of the first stations to be built in Moscow's underground system in the mid-1930s. Because of the city's unstable subsoil, it also turned out to be one of the world's deepest. It took passengers more than five minutes to get from the concourse to the platforms. That was just what I wanted today. I wanted to lose my new best mates, but I didn't want them to know I'd done it on purpose.

I reached the bottom of the stairs. This subway wouldn't have got Crazy Dave's seal of approval. There were no lifts anywhere. Most stations didn't even have ramps. So even if he got down here, there'd be no guarantee Crazy Dave would ever resurface.

Another thing that was going to work in my favour was the fact that you could stay down here all day. You could interchange at will, and I might have to.

Ant and Dec wouldn't find that strange. Visitors to Moscow who don't speak or read Russian can find the Metro very intimidating. It's a hub-and-spoke system, with the majority of lines running from downtown Moscow to the peripheral districts.

The Koltsevaya Line (No. 5) forms a twenty-kilometre ring that connects the spokes. There are twelve lines, each identified by a number, a name and a colour, and 182 stations. The locals often identified the lines just by colour, except for the very similar shades of green assigned to 2, 10, 11, and L1 – and at Kievskaya, where the light blue and dark blue lines converged and were almost impossible to tell apart.

It got worse. The colours on the platform signs weren't always the same as the colours on the maps, and one station could be called two or three different names depending on the line on which one was travelling.

Out-of-towners and foreigners like me had to change platforms and retrace their steps every ten minutes. I quite liked fucking about down here for a couple of hours when I'd had enough of Dostoevsky and Gunslingers. It was a great place to see the wildlife. It also reminded me of the few fun times I used to have as a kid, bunking on the Underground all day, not having a clue where me and my mates would surface. Anywhere north of the river was the Outback, as far as we were concerned.

The entry gates looked like a series of turnstiles, but without the turnstiles. They were a row of card readers, with little gates between them. Some stations had futuristic glass panels that swung open once your card had been given the green light. Most, however, had nothing – until you tried to step through without scanning your card. At that point the mechanical gates would slam shut and do their best to crush you.

I brushed my card across the sensor and went through without losing any limbs.

The Moscow Metro was designed to double up as an underground shelter in case of attack. The masses might have to spend long spells down there, but were sure not to miss out on the joys of the Communist system. There were sculptures, reliefs and mosaics aplenty to glorify the achievements of the squaddie and the tractor-driver.

Above all, it looked good, it worked, and it was cheap. A single trip – which translated as 'race' – cost 60p. My sixty-race card made it even cheaper.

All the tourist guides recommended at least one trip. But not many sightseers took in Lubyanka this year, even though it was on the doorstep of Red Square and the Kremlin. All the murals and en-gravings had gone from the ceilings and walls, leaving shiny cream tiles. It had been targeted by a Chechen suicide bomber a year ago. Forty people were killed.

Less than an hour later, another device had gone off at Park Kultury, also on the red line, raising the death toll by a further fourteen. A couple of hundred were injured.

Both stations were quickly back in business. Muscovites still had to get to work, and above ground the city was gridlocked between eight and eleven in the morning and five and eight in the evening, and no picnic the rest of the time. Down here, you never had to wait more than about a minute for a train – even if, at peak hours, it was like being caught in a stampede.

The escalator finally unloaded me onto the platform. Two dogs stretched out alongside a couple of young guys gripping beer bottles like they were gold bars. Passengers just stepped over them and went on their way. They also swept past a policeman curled up in the corner. He wasn't drunk. He was covered in dirt, leather jacket shredded, his face bloodied and beaten. This lad had been kicked to shit, but nobody batted an eyelid.

I plotted a route through the rat's nest that would eventually take me back up to Lubyanka. I wanted a better look in Room 419, without Mr Lover Man hovering over me. I'd start with what was under that bed. Another little chat with Rudy and his boy, if that was possible, would be a bonus.

This was the second busiest underground system on the planet after Tokyo's. Eight million people used it every day, and they always seemed to be sharing my carriage. There'd be no hopping on and off just before the doors closed to avoid being followed, like you see in the movies. It would be more like wading through treacle.

Losing Ant and Dec wasn't going to be easy.

18

The crowd swayed uncomfortably close to the edge of the platform as we waited for the north-west train. People shouted. Drunks sang. Dogs barked. Nobody cared. At least it was warm down there.

I didn't scan the place for Ant and Dec. I didn't want them to know I was aware. And all that mattered was that they weren't still behind me when I exited. If they were, I'd disappear back into the rat's nest. At the worst stations it was easier to take the first available exit than fight your way through the maze to get a couple of blocks closer to your destination. If the worst came to the worst I'd just make a run for it.

Our train arrived. The crowd surged. I didn't wait for anyone to get off. The doors on the Moscow Metro didn't take prisoners. They were like guillotines. If you were caught when they snapped shut, your next stop was A&E.

I shuffled and pushed my way aboard, and grabbed a handrail. The doors slammed shut, imprisoning me in a world of tobacco and beer fumes. The woman to my left was overloaded with market-stall perfume. At least it took the edge off the stench of vomit from the two drunks who'd annexed the three or four seats alongside me. Another sat by their feet, trying to navigate the neck of a vodka bottle through his full-face motorbike helmet. Nobody paid them the slightest attention. It was the Metro Derby. For 60p a race, who cared?

Head lolling with the rhythm of the carriage, I let my gaze wander casually along it at about shoulder level, trying to catch Ant and Dec's coats, not their eyes. They were probably doing exactly the same, unless I'd already given them the slip.

The train lurched. A female voice announced the next station. I was going in the right direction. It was a male voice when you were going towards the centre, a female when heading away from it.

Three stops took me to the intersection with Moscow's answer to the Circle Line. The masses fought their way on and off at the first, Chistye Prudy, giving me the chance to see a bit more of the carriage.

Nothing.

I finally spotted Ant trying hard to look as though he hadn't spotted me as we pulled into Krasnye Vorota. The train jolted, there was a surge of bodies, and I lost him again. People moaned at a bunch of teenagers with rucksacks. Women gripped their shopping bags firmly at their sides rather than risk having them trampled at their feet. Personal space was in very short supply.

The train set off again. Komsomolskaya was the interchange. There'd be a mass exodus and a mass embarkation. I'd go the six stops to Park Kultury, where the second bomb had gone off, and then take the Central Line back to Lubyanka.

The motorbike helmet shuddered. The neck of the vodka bottle disappeared once more through the open visor, then went back down between its owner's legs. This time it tipped over and made him look like he'd pissed himself.

I knelt down and righted the bottle. Nobody watched. If they had, it would have been obvious to them that any good comrade should take the trouble to ease this boy's helmet off his head before he choked on his own vomit. Maybe I'd get a medal when Anna took me to the Victory Parade.

As the train slowed at Komsomolskaya I shrugged off my North Face and bundled it under my arm, then straightened up and joined the throng at the door. The lining of the helmet stank of stale sweat and beer and cigarettes. I hoped I didn't have to keep it on much further than the end of the platform.

19

15.00 hrs

I dumped the helmet and heaved my parka back on as soon as I emerged once more into the wind and snow. It was already starting to get dark. Sunset was at six at this time of the year. The lights of GUM did their best to make up for it, glinting off the wet cobblestones of Red Square.

Before *perestroika* hit its stride, all cities in the USSR had a branch of the state-owned department store. It was the only place where diplomats could buy their Marmite and Blue Nun, and the privileged Soviet few could shop for their premium vodka while the rest of the country lined up for hours for a loaf of bread and a dodgy-looking onion.

The Moscow flagship looked like Harrods on steroids, and had a history to match. Stalin converted it into office space. Then, when his wife had had enough of him killing everybody and topped herself, he turned it into her mausoleum. In the early 1950s his successors reopened it as a store, most of which consisted of empty shelves. Now it was a shopping mall like anywhere else on the planet, except for the fantastic architecture and the eye-watering prices. The two hundred stores inside boasted all the Western luxury brands and labels. After ten years of record-breaking economic growth, high-end Muscovites had money to burn. The man in the street could only press his nose against the glass.

I headed towards the sports deck. They sold everything from trainers to canoes, but I wasn't after a pair of Versace trainers or a twenty-thousand-dollar home multi-gym. I needed a telescopic fishing rod – the one you see in gadget mags that folds down into something that fits in the palm of your hand.

20

Had Mossad, the Israeli secret service, not assassinated Mahmoud al-Mabhouh, one of the co-founders of the military wing of Hamas, in his Dubai hotel room in January 2010, I might have been trying to make entry in a totally different way.

The electronic lock of Room 419 could be accessed and reprogrammed directly at the door, but getting hold of the right box of tricks would have taken a lot more time than I had to spare. But – thanks to my mate Julian's involvement at MI5 in tracking down the source of the British passports Mossad's hit squad had used as cover – I knew a shortcut.

Burglars use fishing rods all the time to lift the keys you leave on the hall table. They then make entry with the house keys, or stay outside and steal whichever vehicle blinks in response to the key fob. Mossad had had an even better idea.

Mahmoud al-Mabhouh was wanted for the kidnap and murder of two Israeli soldiers in 1989, and purchasing arms from Iran for use in Gaza. He wasn't on Mossad's happy holiday list. They followed him from Syria to the Al Bustan Rotunda hotel near Dubai airport.

Al-Mabhouh was no fool. He'd requested a room with no balcony and sealed windows, so the only way in was through the door. He showered and changed, put documents into the room safe, and left the hotel between four thirty and five p.m. When he got back to his room at eight twenty-four that night to relax in front of a couple of episodes of *Mr Bean*, Mossad were inside, waiting for him. Half an hour later, he failed to answer a call from his wife. His body was found by a cleaner the next morning. And all it would have taken to stop his assassins in their tracks was a bath towel.

A read-out indicated that an attempt was made to reprogramme al-Mabhouh's electronic door lock, but that wasn't how the boys from Tel Aviv had got in. They'd used a method Julian had demonstrated to me in my own living room. Fuck knows why he'd brought a telescopic fishing rod with him. Maybe he thought if he could show me what fun they were all having, I'd cross back over to the dark side.

21

I headed for the house phones in the lobby, keeping eyes on the entrance for Ant and Dec. I had lost them for sure, but once they'd lost me they'd have had to make a decision. Stake out the flat, if they knew it, or go back to my last known location. Or split up and check both. Fuck it, I just had to get on with what I was here for, and as quickly as I could before one of them turned up.

I got six rings from 419 before an automated voice said what I guessed must be the Russian for 'Please leave a message'. I hung up.

I checked out the hotel restaurants, but it was far too early to sit and eat. I didn't see any of the crew having a session in the gym or the pool. But a drink or two to celebrate the fact they were alive? That was a definite maybe.

They weren't in the lobby bar. I took the lift to the roof. The view of the Kremlin was straight out of a winter-wonderland brochure.

I heard the crew before I saw them. They were well

wrapped up under gas heaters, and by this stage their breath was probably 90 per cent proof. They were having a great time and I didn't blame them.

I turned back into the lift. As it descended I started to assemble the Mossad magic wand. The fishing rod telescoped down to about seven inches, but extended to five feet when fully open. It was made of bendable alloy. I'd binned the reel that had come with it, and the low breaking-strength line. I needed to land a shark, not a kipper.

The eyelets the line fed through also folded down. I opened the one at the tip, tied the end of the shark line to it and kept the other eyes closed.

I got out of the lift and checked the corridor for movement and sound. I wasn't going to wait around. Defeating the door would take about ten seconds. The more I hovered about, the longer I was exposed. There was nothing in front of me, nothing behind. The shark-line reel on my left index finger spun as I started to extend the rod. I only needed about three feet. I put it over my knee and bent it into the shape of a bow saw.

I knelt on the plush carpet outside 419 and eased the tip, with the shark line attached, through the gap under the door. Hotel fire regulations are more or less uniform internationally. There has to be enough space – a maximum of ten millimetres at the threshold – to allow the door to swing without it touching the carpet.

I squeezed the rod through, pushing down the carpet on both sides. Once it was about three feet in, I twisted the handle and worked it up against the bottom of the door. The rod would now be going up vertically the other side. I nudged it to the right, towards the handle. The alloy clunked as it made contact with the metal.

I took a second to visualize what was happening inside the room. The shark line would be hanging between the handle and the door. The rod itself would be on the far side of the handle. I pulled down gently and heard another clunk of rod against handle a few inches from my head. The handle was trapped between the apex of the rod and the line.

I held the rod handle firmly in my left hand, rested my head against the door and pulled hard on the line. It pushed down on the handle and the door sprang open.

I slipped quickly inside, closed the door and activated the deadlock. I collapsed the deformed rod as best I could and shoved it inside my jeans.

All the Hamas lad had needed to do before he went out was roll up a towel and place it between the handle and the door. Mossad would have been fucked. Rudy and his boys also had a lot to learn.

The room still stank of cigarette smoke, and the mini-bar had been raided. Empty miniatures and beer bottles and chocolate wrappers were scattered on the table by the window. At least the bed had been made. Beyond it, the Kremlin *son et lumière* was in full swing.

I lifted out the holdall and unzipped it to discover not very much at all. There was a passport for the boy; a new one, of course. A carton of 200 Camel. Some socks, still in their cardboard packaging, and a few pairs of Speedo-type briefs. And a memory stick.

I headed for the B&O and hit the space-age remote.

It took me a minute to work out how to persuade it to do what I wanted. I finally inserted the USB end plug into a port in the side of the TV. There was only one icon on the stick. I clicked on it and got a picture but no sound.

I was glad there wasn't.

Tracy's face filled the TV screen.

Her skin was red and flushed; her face screwed up.

A pair of male hands came into shot from behind her and around her naked shoulders, pulling her away from the lens. I was dreading what I was about to see.

As the hands turned her and pushed her towards the bed, I could see that BB was still inside her from behind.

I watched for about five minutes, then sat there in shock. I thought about the pain in Tracy's eyes. I thought about BB being an arsehole. And I thought about my promise to Mong.

I threw the stick back into the bag, zipped it up and replaced it under the bed. I wasn't about to take it with me. Frank was obviously a generous employer, but I already knew you didn't want to fuck him over.

I closed the door carefully behind me and headed for the lift.

22

Back at the apartment, I had a shower and changed. I stank like I used to when I had to hang around pubs as a kid, waiting for my mum and stepdad to stop drinking and take me home. The smoke from Player's No. 6 or whatever knocked-off cigarettes they'd bought from the market that week used to soak into my clothes, hair and skin even when I sat under the table. In the morning, the stench made me feel like throwing up.

I felt like throwing up now.

I grabbed my passport and threw a few things into a day sack. It felt good to be back in that routine, getting on with a job – even though it wasn't a job until I knew they were alive.

I looked up Frank Timis online. Nothing. I even tried Wikipedia and Wikileaks. I couldn't find a thing.

I sat on the sofa and looked out over the river and the downtown lights. Steam billowed out of every building. I speed-dialled Anna. I usually called her every other day after the three p.m. broadcast. She always wanted to know what footage they'd used, and if there was anything she'd done wrong.

There seldom was. She was an old hand at reporting foreign conflicts. A lot of journos turned up in war zones without a clue. A picture of one unwittingly wearing Gaddafi green, for instance, could be valuable propaganda. It could also get you killed.

The only thing I'd commented on so far this trip was the state of her hair. Apart from that, she looked perfect. I couldn't wait to see her again. It was turning ugly out there. She'd been in Tunisia and Egypt earlier in the year, then moved to Libya. With the whole Middle East jumping up and down, she'd probably want to cover the fuck-up that was unfolding in Bahrain. Protesters had been shot and Saudi troops had moved into the country to back the government. Big drama ahead for all. Especially me, as she'd want to be in the thick of it.

The phone buzzed and crackled in my ear as it tried to get cell contact. Eventually it opened up. She sounded concerned. 'Nicholas – is everything all right?'

There were screams and chants in the background as the rebels gave Gaddafi's name a hard time.

'Shouldn't I be asking you that?'

She laughed. 'I got held up, that's all.'

She must have found a quieter spot because the noise went down a couple of decibels.

'Anna, I need a favour. Can you find out about a guy called Francis Timis? I think he's Ukrainian. He says he changed his name to Francis so it sounds more Western. He's loaded, but I can't find anything about him on the Net. There's a Romanian mining guy, but that's definitely not him.'

'Maybe he's rich enough to buy anonymity. Spell it for me?'

I heard gunfire and some scuffling as she took cover.

'How old is he?'

'Mid-forties, maybe. No older than fifty. Anything you can get.'

There was more rustling. She had to shout to make herself heard. 'Why do you want to know?'

'I'll tell you another time. You sound a bit busy. Have you got your date yet?'

She was due to be replaced by a colleague. At first she'd been looking forward to some leave. But this past week she'd started to sound less keen. It didn't make me worried, exactly, but I was concerned.

'I'm going to have to go.'

'I'll call you tomorrow, usual time.'

'Nicholas?'

'Anna?'

'Look after yourself.'

I started to laugh as the phone went dead.

My next call was to a London number. This time the line was a lot clearer.

23

I left the flat and crossed the street to the Metro. One change would get me to Paveletskaya, and from there the Aeroexpress to Domodedovo took just under an hour. That was the quick bit. Security at the airport had been a nightmare since the suicide bombing in January. The queues could snake around for miles inside the building. Passengers were missing their flights. It was going to mean I couldn't just try and grab a seat on the next Heathrow plane. I'd have to factor in at least a couple of hours of downtime before I could get airside.

As I neared the entrance, something registered in my peripheral vision. I didn't turn my head. I carried on until I was nearly inside, then stopped, checked my watch and looked around like I was weighing up my options.

About fifty metres down the road was a vehicle. I couldn't see the driver, but it was either Ant and Dec's Audi from outside the hotel or one that looked exactly like it, right down to the half-moons carved out of the grime on the windscreen and the two shapes filling the front seats inside.

PART FOUR

1

Eastcheap, London

Friday, 18 March
07.20 hrs

Coffee shops are like London buses. You don't see one for ages, then three come along at once. I sat with my frothy cappuccino and stack of Danishes as more and more people lined up like lemmings for their pre-work caffeine fix. Nearly all of them had headphones or mobiles stuck to their ears.

This branch of Starbucks was on the north side of London Bridge, by Monument tube. Jules had decided he didn't want me to come to the office. His syndicate dealt with kidnap and ransom. K&R was a private, secretive world. His bosses wouldn't want him bringing somebody in to tread across their turf – especially when Jules knew that that somebody wouldn't be wearing a suit.

I sipped at the froth. I'd gone to my flat in

Docklands straight from Heathrow and got my head down for a couple of hours. I'd had a lukewarm shower when I got up because I'd forgotten to spark up the immersion heater when I came in. I gave it a twenty-minute burst and jumped in.

The place was covered with dust. Dust sheets were for the movies, or so I thought. I hadn't sold the 911 or the flat, or even rented it out when I went to Moscow. I didn't need to. Prices had taken a hit in the recession, but they'd pick up again. As Mark Twain kept yelling from the Moscow billboards: 'Buy land: I hear they aren't making it any more!'

Besides, I didn't know what I was doing with Anna, and neither, I guessed, did Anna know what she was doing with me. We were sort of experimenting with the idea of living together.

The newspapers were still dominated this morning by the Japanese tsunami and Gaddafi's war.

Japan had raised its nuclear-contamination alert level as core damage to Reactors 2 and 3 was worse than expected after the 'quake. Panic had spread overseas. Shops in parts of the US had been stripped of iodine pills.

Libya's government was declaring an immediate ceasefire after a UN Security Council resolution backed 'all necessary measures' short of occupation to protect civilians in the country. But no one seriously thought Gaddafi would stop bombing his own people just because he said he would.

Elsewhere in the Middle East, yet another country was going tits up. At least thirty-three anti-government protesters had been shot dead in Yemen and another 145 wounded when government forces opened fire on a group of them. The Arab freedom wave kept on rolling, but at a cost.

It was hard to cut away from it and keep my head full of Somalis and piracy. Until I'd joined the Regiment and had to deal with that shit head-on, I'd thought pirates belonged to a far-off world where the Jolly Roger flew on a Caribbean masthead while all the lads swigged rum and gave it the old yo-ho-ho on the quarterdeck. But these fuckers didn't sport eye patches and headscarves. There wasn't a Captain Sparrow in sight. They ran round in flip-flops, shorts and tank-tops. They carried grappling hooks, RPGs and AK47s. And now they killed people.

2

Somalia is a failed state. Its landmass, which makes up the Horn of Africa, is stuck between Ethiopia and Kenya to the west, and the Indian Ocean to the east. Its northern coastline is on the Gulf of Aden, the other side of which lies Yemen, whose government had just taken to killing protesters. Talk about keeping bad company.

The piracy committed offshore is a direct result of the anarchy that rages on land. The same thing happens in other weakly governed states, like Indonesia and Nigeria, but it's particularly bad in Somalia. The country has been caught up in civil war since the 1990s. Come to think of it, it can't really be called a country any more.

In the early 1980s, Somali pirates were mostly unemployed youths who hung round the docks looking for work. The warlords, the clan leaders, bunged them in a couple of boats and sent them out to mug whatever they found coming from the Red Sea into the Gulf of Aden. As one of the choke-points for world shipping, it offered easy pickings.

Piracy grew into an industry. As Rudy had discovered, gangs now roved across thousands of square miles, as far east as the Seychelles, south to Tanzania, and north to the Arabian Sea and Oman. The turf was divided up. The waters of the Gulf of Aden might as well be the streets of Mogadishu.

A typical cell of a dozen or so men goes out into the open sea in two or three skiffs, small, cockroach-infested wood or fibreglass fishing boats, for three or four weeks at a time, taking only a couple of outboards. All other available space is filled with grappling irons, ladders, knives, assault rifles, RPGs and *khat* leaves, the local narcotic.

There's nothing to cook with. They catch fish, which they eat raw. The plan is always to find and take over a larger vessel, then live on it and use it as a mothership. Which was what must have happened with the skiffs that captured the *Maria Feodorovna*. They'd have binned the fishing boat and would now be using the yacht as a control base, having taken the hostages back to shore because they were European and would be worth a few bob.

Why hadn't they taken the crew as well? They were white, but maybe they were seen as fellow workers of the sea. Somali pirates had some rules. They didn't attack all shipping. They left the Indian vessels that brought expensive goodies and food from the east, mainly because the clan warlords liked to buy the stuff with the proceeds of their crimes. If the supply dried up, the warlords wouldn't be best pleased.

But the fact was, these pirates attacked anything of value that floated: oil tankers, freighters, cruise ships, private yachts, they'd have a go at anything. I found it quite funny that a dozen Somali fishermen could fuck global shipping magnates about, holding them, their crews and world trade hostage. I'd have laughed into my brew if it hadn't been for Tracy and the boy.

Back on dry land, Somalia was still in shit state. The Americans had tried to intervene in 1993 when the warlords were hijacking food aid. They'd got hammered. Nobody had tried since. The clans were now at war with each other, and Islamic militants had gatecrashed the party for a slice of the action. There was no functioning government, or even a judicial system, just chaos and disorder. Small wonder a job as a pirate seemed such a fantastic opportunity to the average Somali. I'd have been having a go at it if I was up Shit Creek.

The economic impact of piracy was actually quite small as things stood, compared with the volume of international trade. Less than one per cent of the vessels in the Gulf of Aden had been approached by pirates, let alone attacked, and most of those were only shipping garden gnomes from China. But the statistics didn't tell the full horror of what awaited victims like Tracy and Stefan.

And in the bigger picture, the nightmare scenario for Britain was that if one of the two liquid-gas ships we needed to dock here every day got lifted, we'd lose a major part of the energy supply that kept our power stations humming. If baby incubators couldn't function and the lights went out, the government might find that uprisings weren't confined to the Middle East.

Even the front-line pirates got fucked over. They received less than 30 per cent of the take. The bulk of the proceeds had to be handed over to the clan warlords, and those who had to be paid for the hostages' food and board. There were also investors. Some were Somalis. Buying shares in piracy was better than going to sea. Easier money and conditions. But some were from international criminal syndicates based in the Gulf States, with links into Europe and London.

In fact, the whole thing was a fuck-up, with everyone taking a cut some way or another. There were a lot of noses in the piracy trough.

3

I'd just started on my third Danish when Julian arrived, immaculate as ever. Today he was in a black Crombie coat over a white shirt and tie. I pointed down at the extra mug to tell him that he didn't have to go and line up, and the Danishes that were left were his. Not that he was going to eat any. They were far too unhealthy.

Jules had done really well for himself since resigning from MI5 last year. He'd gone through his moral car-wash, resigned, and come out the other side without turning his back on the good guys. He was now in the K&R business, negotiating ransoms for insurance syndicates, and trying to make sure that no one got kidnapped in the first place.

I stood up and received a soft palm and a warm smile.

'Nick . . .' He still sounded guarded. 'How are you?'

'Not bad, mate. Not bad.'

He took off his coat to reveal a black suit and double-cuffed shirt with simple silver stud cufflinks.

He sorted his Crombie out over the back of his chair, making sure it wasn't dangling in the crumbs on the floor.

'What's been happening, Nick?'

The frothing machines hissed behind us as people ordered their double skinny this, that and the other.

'Same old, same old. But I might be doing a K&R job. I need you to see if they've been pinged or not.'

'How many?'

'Only three.'

I explained the who, what and where.

'So the attack was five days ago?'

'I don't even know if they're still alive.'

He fished into a big pocket that looked like it had been specially sewn into his coat, pulled out an iPad and sparked it up.

'How are things in the K&R world?'

His fingers played about on the screen. 'Business is good. I've stopped working for a percentage of the premium saved. I can normally get them out in about three months, so it's better just to take a set three grand a day.'

'In that case, you can pay for these.' I offered him the plate of Danishes but he shook his head. I dunked one in my coffee.

'Still busy in South America, Central America, Mexico. Africa is still good, and of course Somalia's top trumps.' He finished tapping away. 'Not a thing, Nick. They don't show up anywhere.' He looked up. 'Do you know who's holding them? If they're with a clan? Has anyone been approached about a deal?'

'Nothing. The BG should be keeping their real identities quiet.'

'That's good. But somebody somewhere must have been approached.'

He turned the iPad so both of us could see the read-out. 'As far as we know, twenty-nine vessels held and six hundred and eighty-one hostages.'

The list was divided into countries, age groups and occupations. 'There's a lot of sea out there. Maybe they didn't make it back to the coast.'

That got me worried. 'Do you think they'll have been zapped?'

'Unlikely. They're merchandise. But that's not to say the BG didn't put up a fight and the three of them were killed – or they may have sunk. Those fishing skiffs they use aren't exactly on the Lloyd's Register.'

'What about the four Americans?'

'That was a total mess. The Somalis went to negotiate with the US Navy. The US Navy didn't believe them. They held them instead. Their friends on the captured boat thought they were being stitched up, so they killed the Americans.

'In general, if they've got them, they still won't kill them. Only when they stop being worth money do you have to get worried. If they don't have outside investors, they'd have to take a loan from their clan warlord to keep and feed the hostages. They might be using your three to pay off debts they owe the clan. Who knows? It's complicated out there.

'But if they are alive, even if they've been sold on, someone would start to negotiate, someone would make contact. Otherwise there's no point in keeping them.'

I nodded, and threw down some more Danish. 'You're sure they're not anywhere in that box of tricks?'

'Just a sec. Maybe I can work out which group took them. You said it was towards the end of last week?'

He logged onto a website, and I watched him enter his password. The page opened up on the Anti-piracy Environment Awareness Chart. It wasn't a chart at all, more a collection of big break-out boxes, with Google maps, pie charts and bar graphs. He expanded the page to show me something.

'Depending on the time of year, some areas are more swamped with pirate activity than others. These people are fishermen. They know the winds and tides. They know the sea. They know when they can go out there safely. They know when they can't – well, the successful ones do. Look.' He pointed at the screen. The Monthly Piracy Risk showed a satellite picture for each month of the year, and then dots where the attacks had taken place.

'See the difference between March and June?'

The Gulf of Aden in June had just a few dots on it, and the same past the Horn of Africa and out into the Indian Ocean. But March was a different story. The area was almost black with dots, as was the whole area east, north and south.

'It's because of the north-eastern monsoon. That comes down from India and Arabia, normally about December to March. The swell is only about two or three metres, so those small craft can use the wind to negotiate it, get clear of the coast and go out there looking for a mother-ship. If they strike lucky, they might hit what they want to hijack straight away.

'But June and October are when the south-west monsoon comes in. We're talking thirty-knot winds and swells of ten metres. That's the same size as the Japanese tsunami, Nick. They haven't a hope of making it out to sea without capsizing.'

'So piracy is seasonal?'

'Yes. And because we can predict winds and tides, we can have a good idea of where and when they're going to strike.'

I looked at the pictures. The yellow dots on the Google Earth map showed the 44 per cent of ships that had been approached. The green ones showed that only 18 per cent of those were actually attacked. They must have decided the others were too big or too fast, or maybe painted grey, with big guns. A bar chart showed activity by days of the week. I pointed to Friday and Saturday. 'Hardly anything happening there. These lads like their weekends, like everyone else.'

He chuckled politely. 'The British Navy takes the lead on anti-piracy at the moment. They use this to try and predict where the strikes might happen, so they can concentrate their resources. As I said, there's a lot of sea out there. If they don't get out a mayday, nobody knows what's happening.

'But what we do is put on an overlay that shows the information we're gaining from dealing with the clans and the kidnappers, to see which groups are active, who's done the lifting. So let's have a look at what's been going on around the Seychelles.'

Every time there was a dot, there was now an

overlay and a number between 1 and 19 that represented different groups. The numbers were random in all the areas for March. It looked like a free-for-all.

'Sorry, Nick. Sometimes the clans designate areas for their own. But it's open season out there in March. Prime time. If only the yacht crew had had access to information like this, they'd have known where to steer clear of. It's stupid going into those areas at the best of times. What was going on?'

'I haven't got a clue.' I sat back in the chair. He could see the worry on my face.

'Someone, somewhere, will know. If they're alive, the Somalis will have contacted somebody.' He pursed his lips. 'You know these three, don't you?'

'Yeah. One's a guy who used to be in B Squadron. The other is the widow of a dead mate. The child's from her new marriage.'

I got to my feet and picked up my black parka. I needn't have brought it with me. It was a lot warmer in London than where I'd come from.

'Tell you what, mate, as soon as this is over, and Anna's back, why not come over for a week?'

He stood up, and we shook hands again. 'Any help you need, Nick, you know where I am.'

'One more thing. Al-Shabab – they still active?'

He nodded. 'Don't even think about it. Go find your contact.'

I sat back down and couldn't do anything *but* think about it.

Al-Shabab, the hard-line Islamist movement, was Somalia's Taliban, even down to the suicide bombing and severed heads. They'd been bolstered by experienced fighters from Saudi Arabia, Egypt, Afghanistan and Pakistan, and now controlled most of the southern part of the country. If those fuckers discovered my three were high value, they'd be coming to lift them from the clans. Tracy, Stefan and BB would die in captivity, or be executed, because . . . Well, just because.

Jules was looking for something. 'The Gents. You know where?'

'Yes, mate.' I pointed. 'Let me have a look at that chart again, will you?'

He got it online and headed left of the counter.

4

Green Dragon Hotel, Hereford
15.00 hrs

The Green Dragon on Broad Street felt like it had been around as long as Hereford had been. It was the kind of ye olde tourist hotel where the Rotary Club met every Friday and Saga coach tours stopped for scones and tea.

The TV wasn't tuned in to RT, so I sat on the big flowery eiderdown and tapped Anna's number on the iPhone screen instead. It was a lot earlier than I normally called her, but I was going to have a pretty full day. I needed to catch up with Crazy Dave and then trawl the bars for Jan.

I'd already tried the last address I had for her, a flat in a three-storey pebble-dashed housing association joint on the Ross Road at the edge of town. She'd taken it over from her mum years ago. It was almost opposite where the old Regiment camp used to be. In her early husband-hunting years, she must have

171

thought it gave her pole position. There'd been no one at home, and I wasn't about to start knocking on doors to find out. Not yet, anyway. It was Friday. Unless she'd changed the habit of a lifetime, she'd be out on the town sooner or later.

The phone only rang a couple of times before she picked up.

'How's it going?'

'Better than yesterday. Where are you?' She was inside this time. I could hear Arabic TV in the background and no gunfire.

'Back in the UK, in Hereford. You OK to talk?'

'You took the job?'

'Maybe.' I explained. 'I'm banking on BB keeping them alive long enough for me to find out where they are. Any luck with Frank?'

'All I can tell you is that he was originally called Vepkhiat Avdgiridze. He's not Ukrainian. He's Georgian, from South Ossetia. It's been fighting for independence for decades.'

'I know. I was there a year or two before Putin went in.'

North Ossetia was part of Russia, but South Ossetia had always been disputed territory. Most South Ossetians carried Russian passports and wanted to break away from Tbilisi. They had declared it a republic in 1990 and the Georgian government had sent in tanks. A series of wars followed, until the Russians finally invaded 'to protect their citizens' in 2008. Well, that was one of the versions. Since then, it had been recognized as an independent republic by Venezuela and a handful of other countries that sucked up to Moscow, but the Georgian government still saw it as occupied territory.

'Where does Frank fit in?'

'He finances the South Ossetian independence movement. He helps them attack Tbilisi in any way they can. He's not short of cash. It looks like he has fingers in every pie. Oil, gas, real estate. He backed Putin when he reorganized things. He's no good guy, but he has class. He doesn't own a football club or run for provincial governor. He keeps himself to himself. For him, it's all about business, all about the deal.'

'Are you sure he's the one?'

'I'll send a picture.'

'What about you, Anna? You OK?'

'I'm fine. But, you know, I've been thinking . . . Maybe . . . Maybe I should stay a while longer. If Gaddafi retakes Benghazi, I should be here.'

'And maybe Bahrain, maybe Syria?'

I kept it light, but we both went quiet for a while.

'So when will *you* be coming home, Nicholas?'

'If they're alive, I'm going to have to go and get them.'

I heard an intake of breath. 'Yes . . . Of course.'

There was a pause.

'Nicholas, I have to go.'

'I'll call you tomorrow. But I won't have a clue what you've been up to because pointy-head TV doesn't show RT.'

She'd have no idea what pointy-head meant, but she started to laugh. I liked it when she did that.

'Be safe, Anna.'

'And you, Nicholas.'

The line went dead.

I sat on the bed, trying to make sense of our non-conversation.

My iPhone alerted me to the arrival of Anna's MMS. I opened it up. The photo was slightly fuzzy and taken from a distance as he got into a limo, but it was Francis Timis all right.

I juggled tubes of instant coffee, fired up the small plastic kettle and worried about Anna. It was becoming a bit of a habit. It wasn't just the danger she put herself in. I missed her. She was too busy saving the world for us to spend much time together. But I couldn't blame her. Whoever said war is a drug was right on the money.

I called Crazy Dave on the room phone. I was pretty sure he'd ignore a withheld number or one he didn't know, but pick up on a local call. I wasn't wrong.

'Dave . . .'

'What?'

'You about for a brew in, say, an hour?'

'If you want work, you can shove it up your arse. As of sixteen hundred hours today I'm retired.'

'Then get the kettle on for half three. You can still present yourself with a gold clock at four.'

'Yeah, funny. What do you want?'

'I'll explain when I get there.'

I was glad I'd caught him in a good mood.

5

The Green Dragon's car park was at the rear of the building. The garaging had probably once been filled with horse-drawn carriages. I checked out and drove my grime-covered 911 past Ascari's café and onto Broad Street. The sky was dark and heavy with cloud.

I used to spend a lot of my time-off in Ascari's, eating toast and drinking coffee. It was where I'd really got to know Crazy Dave. When I joined he was already a sergeant, something like three generations above me. He was in A Squadron, I was in B, so I didn't get to see him that much. But over coffee and scrambled egg, we're all the same. We both used to spend our Sunday mornings there, reading the supplements; him because he was trying to avoid his wife, me because I didn't have one. Crazy Dave didn't need to go there so much now. His wife had left soon after he'd got himself fucked up. His legs were useless, and as far as she was concerned, so was he. He was in and out of hospital like a yo-yo, and she didn't fancy joining him for the ride.

There was a bit of bad blood between us too. I'd felt sorry for him when we met up again in 2005 – but it only took me a week or two to start thinking two fucked-up legs weren't enough. A friend of mine from Regiment days tapped Crazy Dave for some work. He was in the early stages of motor neurone disease and wanted one last big pay-off so his wife would have a pension. So far so good, but Crazy Dave had found out and taken advantage of him. Charlie was so desperate he'd accepted only a fraction of what the job was worth, and Dave had trousered the rest.

I made him give Charlie's widow the lot. In return, I'd hold off telling the guys who came to him for work how much of a mark-up he liked to take, or telling the companies that used him that he had a quality-control problem – he didn't even check his workforce had fully functioning limbs.

The bit I'd enjoyed most was telling him that if he didn't get his finger out and have the cash in her account within twenty-four hours, I'd be straight over to separate his bony arse from his wheelchair.

Next time I saw him, a year later, that was precisely what I did. I'd needed some int, but I'd fucked up. Instead of just asking him for a favour, which would have given him a bit of a kick, I'd tried to blackmail him. He gave me the int, and told me we were all square. Then he told me that if I made the mistake of thinking otherwise, he had three hundred guys on his Rolodex who'd happily take a shovel to my face.

If only I could have left it at that.

There are times when you have to accept you've been fucked over, and that was one of them. But it pissed me off that he made so much money from scamming his own people, and something in me snapped.

I grabbed his right calf and started towards the door, dragging him and the wheelchair behind me. He screamed and shouted at me to stop, but I kept right on going. When we reached the door Crazy Dave couldn't hold onto his chair any longer and fell out on his arse. I dragged him through the rain and only let go when we reached his Popemobile. He flailed around on the wet tarmac, trying to pull himself along on his elbows, back towards the house.

To this day, I didn't know why I did it. It was immature, gratuitous and got me nowhere – but, fuck, it put a smile back on my face.

Unfortunately, I now needed his help again.

6

I turned right at the junction with Broad Street, passed the front of the hotel and headed towards the River Wye.

The only crazy thing about Crazy Dave was that he'd earned his nickname because he wasn't: he was about as zany as a teacup. He was the kind of guy who analysed a joke before saying, 'Oh, yeah, I get it. That's funny.' But then again, he wasn't trying to find work for a bunch of stand-up comedians – even if we sometimes thought we were pretty fucking amusing.

There had always been a broker knocking around Hereford. He had to be ex-Regiment because he had to know the people – who was in, who was getting out – and if he didn't, he had to know a man who did. When Crazy Dave left after his twenty-two years, he became an intermediary between ex-Regiment guys and the private military companies and individuals who wanted competent people. Dave got his cash by providing the right person for the right job. There's an HR department in any civilian organization, so why not in a military one? After all, it would be a shame to waste all those skills the taxpayer had paid for us to learn.

Dave's business was a perfect fit with Cameron's Big Society. We get the guys into the army; we pay for them to be trained; we pay them to fight, and then we let them go and use their skills in the outside world. Some of them even filed tax returns.

I was heading for Bobblestock. It had been one of the first of the new breed of estate that had sprung up on the outskirts of town when Thatcher tried to turn us all into homeowners. The houses were all made from machined bricks and looked as if they were huddled together for warmth. They all had 2.4 children inside and a people-carrier on the drive.

Crazy Dave lived on the high ground. He'd told me proudly that he'd bought into phase three of the build. The window frames were painted brown instead of white to distinguish it. Apparently that gave the houses a more substantial look.

I drove into the estate. Nothing had changed in the five years since I'd last seen him. I stopped outside his brick rectangle and got another chance to admire the garage extension, which looked as if it had been assembled from a flat-pack.

The house to the right had been called Byways last time I was round. Dave must have new neighbours. Number 53 was now called Rose Cottage. There was fuck-all cottage-like about the place. A net curtain twitched inside. Maybe they'd bought it recently and were still coming to terms with the guy in the wheel-chair next door having rough men arriving at his house at strange times of the day and night. They probably thought there was some sort of sex thing going on.

Number 49, to the left, was still called The Nook. Crazy Dave, of course, just had a number. How crazy was that? A '60'-plate Peugeot Popemobile was parked outside, the correct nine inches or whatever it's supposed to be from the kerb. The road was a dead end, so he'd even gone to the trouble of finishing his last trip with a three-point turn and aiming it in the right direction for a quick getaway.

The whole thing was rigged and ramped, even down to levers and stuff instead of pedals. I could see bags on the passenger seat and down the sides of the pope's throne in the back.

I walked up the driveway towards the concrete ramp that had replaced the front steps. I waved at the small CCTV camera covering the front of the house. The door buzzed. I pushed it open and let myself in.

The house was exactly as I remembered it. It still smelt like it'd been given the once-over with a couple of cans of Pledge. There was still a Stannah parked at the bottom of the stairs, and at the top, enough climbing frames to keep a whole troop of baboons happy. Down in the hallway, some shiny chrome bars had been stuck to the walls. A couple of dangle bars hung on nylon webbing. It looked like a gymnast's idea of heaven.

My Timberlands squeaked on the laminate flooring as I walked into the no-frills living room. There was a big fuck-off TV, and that was about it. The rest was open space. It wasn't as if Crazy Dave needed an armchair.

French windows opened onto the garden, accessed via another ramp. I followed a narrow path of B&Q's

best fake Cotswold stone up to a pair of doors set into the garage wall. The garage had been converted into an office.

Crazy Dave was sitting behind his desk, within easy reach of the two most important assets his business possessed: a pair of small plastic boxes stuffed with index cards containing the names and details of more than a hundred former members of Special Forces. No wonder the garage had drop-down steel shutters and weapons-grade security. To people wanting to know which companies were doing which jobs, those cards would have been worth more than a container ship full of RPGs.

I closed the door behind me. 'Better late than never.'

'What?'

'About time you got that thing paved. It was like walking through the Somme with that wheelchair of yours fucking up the grass.'

He wasn't smiling.

'Don't get up, mate.'

Still no smile.

I held up my hands. 'Dave, I want to call a truce. End-Ex. I'm sorry about what I did. I fucked up. Simple as that.'

'Yes, you did.' He hesitated for a moment. 'But you know what? Fuck it.' He slapped the arms of his chair. 'When you're in one of these fucking things you realize life's too short to get pissed off about stuff like that. So fuck you, and fuck the problem. What do I care? I'm living in a soap, am I?'

That was good enough for me.

Where the up-and-over door had once been there

was now a stud wall. There were no windows in here – just three sets of fluorescent lights. The brew kit still sat on a table against the opposite wall. The Smarties and Thunderbirds mugs were still going strong. I wondered if he'd saved the Easter eggs they'd come with.

He nodded at the CCTV monitor. 'Nice motor. You kill someone for that?'

'Yeah, I did.' I made my way to the desk. 'So, how've you been?'

The last time I saw Crazy Dave he was balding, with a moustache, like Friar Tuck in a 1970s porno. Now all the hair had gone, but the moustache was still hanging on.

'Fucked.'

'So I can see, mate. The Charles Bronson look ain't doing you any favours.'

He gripped the arms of his wheelchair, lifted himself a couple of inches out of the seat and held himself there, perhaps something to do with his circulation, or to stop pressure sores developing on his arse. 'Yeah, well, we've both got life sentences, haven't we?'

He careered round the desk in a maroon space-age chair. It looked as though it could use some go-faster stripes. 'But at least I can get out on the piss when I want to.'

'Can you do a wheelie in that thing yet?'

He reversed, jerked, and the front wheels came up. He grinned like Evel Knievel. But we both knew that was as good as it was going to get. Crazy Dave had been invalided out of the Regiment after a truck driver from Estonia bounced him off a motorbike on the M4 and forced him to take the scenic route. As if that wasn't bad enough, he'd borrowed my Suzuki 650. Six months in Stoke Mandeville hadn't sorted him out. His legs were still useless.

8

His next party trick was to get us both a brew.

'So – you come here with something you know, or something you want to know?'

'BB.'

'The principal's wife getting a seeing-to again, is she?'

'That's the least of my worries. Do you know who the wife is?'

He spun round to face me with a bag of sugar in his lap. 'I don't get involved at that level. The job's gone through about three or four middlemen before it gets to me. They wanted a BG for a mother and a child. I pick – I used to pick – the best available at the time.'

I shook my head. 'Mate, how come you were the only one—'

'To give him work?'

I nodded. 'He was even a nightmare on the tsunami job, when there wasn't anybody to shag. What's he got on you? Is he giving you one as well?'

He spun back round to the kettle and put the sugar down. 'Shit!'

'Touched a nerve, have I?'

The wheelchair raced towards the door. 'No – a shit, I need a shit.'

I followed him into the garden.

'Look, Nick. He finished that anti-piracy job after about six months. That was fuck-all to do with me. I gave him a job with the oil companies looking after the pipeline in Georgia. It was a good little number in Tbilisi. But he fucked up by falling out with the company over expenses.

'Then I gave him a job working for an American family in London, which he fucked up big-time. I think the husband was a computer mogul, downloads, some shit like that. While the husband was away, BB started thinking with his cock again. He reckoned that if he got in with the wife, she'd divorce the guy and give Wonderboy access to a big wad of cash.

'The problem was, he pissed off a lot of other people along the way. He was going round acting as if he was running the job. It was a big one. There were nearly thirty of them on the team, looking after the family in the UK, and the husband as he bounced around the planet selling his downloads or whatever the fuck it was.

'Anyone who got pissed off with him, BB would get her indoors to sack them. He didn't give a fuck about those lads, just had his eye on the money. Silly bastard, he thought all he had to do was keep his shagging quiet until the divorce, and then everything was going to come up roses.'

We got to the Stannah lift. Refusing my help, Crazy Dave swung out of the wheelchair onto the hanging frame, then manoeuvred his arse into position.

'BB's problem is, he doesn't understand that the main reason these guys have got so much of the stuff he'd like to dip into is that they're smart.'

Crazy Dave pressed a button. The motor took him upstairs with a gentle whine. I followed.

'So then what happened?'

'He found himself out in the cold. He had no money, and he had no mates because he'd been such a cunt to everyone. That lad can't seem to keep any distance between his cock and his head.'

We reached the landing. The stair-lift stopped and he grabbed another climbing frame. Bars hung at intervals from the ceiling all the way to the bathroom. He started swinging arm over arm, legs dangling, towards the far end of the landing. From time to time his feet scuffed along the carpet.

Crazy Dave didn't need to know the whole story. 'Mate, I have to know if he's still effective. When the shit hits the fan, has he got a brain? The principal has asked me to check him out. He's very concerned about the boy's protection. He wants the best available – and if that's BB, so be it. What do you reckon?'

The last of the hanging bars was his turning point above the toilet itself. He lowered himself onto his throne, complete with arm supports and a nice padded PVC seat.

'That's not a problem. He's good – he's a twat, but he's good. If he wasn't, I'd have gone out of business long ago.'

Crazy Dave was pulling down his grey tracksuit bottoms a lot quicker than should normally be required. He tried to rip off the Velcro fastening on his big boy's nappy with the other hand. 'Fucking things. Why don't they make the tabs bigger, for fuck's sake?'

The nappy finally came off, and he gave a sigh of relief.

'You know, everyone gives him a hard time because he was TA. Nothing to do with the shagging. I was TA, for fuck's sake, and I didn't do too bad, did I? Because he's a dickhead, no one takes him seriously as a player. But they're wrong. If the shit ever hits the fan, he'll look after the wife and kid big-time. He's more than capable.'

He looked up before letting rip. 'Now fuck off out of here.'

I closed the door but stayed close enough to know that his arse still worked, even if his feet and legs didn't. 'Hey, Dave, why's the council still saying no to a bog downstairs?'

He'd spent two years making application after application. He'd even shown up at the council offices in his wheelchair, but the same twat kept knocking him back. It looked like he still was.

He laughed. 'I got consent about three years ago, but fuck them. I've got used to coming upstairs. Besides, it's the only exercise I get.'

'You really binning it?'

'Yep, fuck it. You know what? I go for a drive every afternoon these days. And sometimes late at night. I just want a little freedom, like I used to have on the bike. I always wanted to do Europe on one, you know.

Go banzai on them *autobahns*. So about a month ago I thought, Fuck it, that wagon out there is going to take me all over, from this evening, and then I'm getting a fucked-legs wagon in Canada. Not exactly a bike, but so what? I've got to get it done before I die in that fucking chair. It's sixteen hundred hours and I'm off to Dover, so now you can really fuck off.'

I had to hand it to him. 'Good luck, Monkey Boy.' I headed downstairs.

9

I'd been hitting the bars in town, doing my best not to bump into anybody I knew apart from Jan. I didn't need the 'Oi, what're you doing here?' and 'What you been up to?' and all that sort of shit. I needed to keep moving. Only if push came to shove would I actively seek out familiar faces to try and track her down. Failing that I'd go back to her flat and sit and wait – and hope that she still lived there.

I'd already done most of the pre-gaming bars. The last hits had been the Barrels, the West Bank and the Hop Pole, and now I was heading to Saxtys. The wine bar had been in the city centre for decades in different incarnations. It also had a nightclub that was Jan's idea of a perfect Friday night out.

I walked through the glass doors into a wall of noise. The blow-heater blasted downwards across the threshold to keep it warm inside. The place was packed with pressed shirts, clean jeans, night-out

dresses. Colognes and perfumes filled the air. I eased my way through the wall-to-wall crowd. The club hadn't opened yet, but it was time enough for Jan to have booked herself a spot. Women like her who thought they were still sixteen were as much a fixture in this town as the cathedral.

And there she was. Right at the back of the crowd, at the bar, just before it opened up into the seating areas. She and two other mutton-dressed-as-lambs were standing around a small table, waffling away.

Time hadn't been as kind to Jan as it had to Tracy. Her sleeveless blue dress stretched just that bit too tight. Her bra straps showed, and the flesh overflowed each side of them. The hair was still the same, far-too-dark-to-be-natural brown and straightened beyond belief. Her mascara was laid on with a trowel, and she hadn't held back with the bronzer and eyeliner.

I moved towards the bar and into her line of sight, but she was too busy chatting to her mates. If they ever started shooting *The Only Way Is Hereford*, these three would be first in the audition queue.

'Jan!' I did my best to look surprised to see her. 'Jan!' I had to raise my voice. 'How are you?'

She gave me a fuck-off-whoever-you-are look. I wasn't in Friday-night clothes and I wasn't twenty-five.

'It's me – Nick.' I kept the smile in place, still bending, tilting my head down to her level.

Recognition finally dawned.

'All right, Nick?' Her expression brightened. 'How are you? It's been ages!'

The Hereford accent always sounded like soft Welsh

to me. Her arms came up for a bear hug and I got a noseful of Boots Special. She took a step back but kept a hand on my arm as she checked me out.

'Too long, Jan. Mong's funeral, I guess. You look . . . really . . . good . . .'

She liked that. She probably wasn't used to flattery from someone who wasn't after a shag. 'Oh, thanks, Nick. I've got to put a bit more slap on these days to cover the wrinkles, but I get by.'

Her mates melted away and started talking to a group of men with sharp creases down the sleeves of their Friday-night shirts. She hadn't introduced me to them. Code, probably, for 'fuck off'.

We had to keep close to make ourselves heard over the music. The Boots Special was starting to make my eyes water.

'So, you married again yet?'

She lifted up her left hand. 'Not right now. But I'm a four by four.'

'A what?'

'Four kids by four husbands. They're all grown-up now. Flown the nest. Gives me some me-time at last.' She gave me a sad smile. It told me that me-time was not quite as much fun as she was trying to make it sound.

'You still living on the Ross Road? In the flats?'

She reached down for a glass of what looked like spritzer and sipped from it until the ice slid down and hit her lips. 'What about you? You found a nice girl?'

'Why? You offering?'

A faraway look came into her eyes. 'Well, there's a thing . . .'

She started the general catch-up stuff. Have you seen this guy, that woman? All that shit. I didn't have a clue who she was on about half the time. This was no longer my world. When I'd left Hereford to go and work for the Firm, that was it. I wasn't coming back for weekend trips. Hereford was done. And after London, there was somewhere else, and somewhere else again. I'd moved out. I might even have moved on. The only thing I'd left behind was my account at the Halifax. I wondered how the recession had hit my £1.52.

'Seen anything of BB?'

Her expression clouded. 'No – fucking arsehole. He stayed at my place the night before the funeral, then didn't even bother coming to the service. What a wanker.'

I shuffled her towards the bar for another drink. There were still a few things this girl wouldn't take lying down.

'What about Tracy? Last time I heard, she was in France. She met somebody?'

There was no hint in her face of a drama. 'Yeah, she's OK. Some Russian or other. Lucky bitch. I wanted to go over as well, see if I could get one. She's in love. They've got a little boy. Stevie . . . something like that. I think he's about four . . . five . . . six, maybe. Don't really hear much from them.'

She didn't look too impressed with it all.

'That's great news, isn't it? That she's happy?'

The barman came over to Jan far earlier than our place in the queue deserved. She didn't even need to tell him what she wanted. 'What about you, Nick?'

'I'll just have an orange juice.'

Her eyes narrowed. 'You still looking to live to a hundred?'

'Nah. I just know a whole lot of other ways of killing myself.' I moved the smile back into place. 'You haven't heard from Tracy, then?'

'Not since she's been in the money.' She leant in a bit closer. 'You kept on telling her to leave, didn't you? Well, hasn't she done well for herself?'

Her nose wrinkled. It wasn't a pretty sight.

'You could go, try somewhere else. You said your kids have left home . . .'

The drinks turned up, and a brighter future was no competition for a long swig of spritzer. 'You were always good to her, weren't you, Nick? She used to give me some of the money you sent, just sometimes, when I was a bit hard up.'

'Oh, right. And I bet she still sends you a few quid, eh?'

I got a nod, but a disapproving one. 'Yeah, but not that much. And it's not like she couldn't spare it. I thought maybe she'd buy me a house, but no. It'd be pennies for her. But what do I get? Nothing. And I'm her *sister*, for fuck's sake.'

Jan took another slug. She'd made the mistake of thinking that just because people had money it was their duty to piss it away. She was jealous that Tracy had it, and angry that she didn't hand enough of it over. It wasn't Tracy's to give away in the first place, but that didn't seem to occur to her. All she wanted to do was grab.

'Listen, Jan. I've got to meet someone at the Market

194

Tavern. I'll try and get back later. But if I don't make it, what's your number?'

I pulled out my phone, still smiling so much my face was beginning to hurt. She opened her bag. I didn't expect to see house keys. She got so pissed she'd lose them, so she used to hide a spare set. But there they were. And I also clocked three mobiles.

'Jesus, Jan. You a dealer or what?'

She selected one and powered it up. 'Just a complicated life, Nick. Two men to manage, and you've got to keep them apart. I'm a bit old-fashioned like that.'

I gave Jan my number once she had worked out how to access her contacts file. 'This is my personal phone. I don't really like keeping anything on it. Not even texts or anything. You never know who might sneak a look while you're busy making yourself beautiful. That wanker BB would have been straight in there. He'd probably send texts from it to all his mates, to tell them what he was up to. If he had any mates.' She gave me hers. An O2 number. I tapped it in.

'Whenever you're in town, Nick . . .' She gave me a hug, phone still gripped in her hand. Then she switched it off. 'I hate these things.'

We parted with a quick kiss on the cheek. Her soapie mates were now getting chatted up by another group of guys with well-clipped hair and Friday-night shirts. She selected the one with a very tight blue-striped short-sleeved number, and was soon in the swing of things. Banter wasn't necessarily his strong suit, but he was keen to give her the full benefit of his tribal tats. He flexed his biceps by gripping his Bud bottle like it was the last one on earth.

10

I worked my way out of the bar and turned right along Widemarsh Street towards the Green Dragon.

Ant was the taller of my new pair of comedians, but seemed to think lighting a cigarette in the doorway of Marks & Sparks would make him invisible. He was still in his favourite overcoat. I didn't bother looking for Dec and his nondescript haircut. He'd be staking out the other side of the bar in case I chucked a left when I came out. The car they'd followed me in to Hereford was a C-class Merc, in case they had to keep up with the 911. But it wasn't in sight now. They would have seen mine in the car park. They'd assume I wasn't going anywhere for a moment or two.

They hadn't been on my flight, and the next one was four hours later. But they'd managed to pick me up outside my apartment after my meeting with Jules and followed me to Hereford. Frank really did take that knowledge-is-power shit seriously. He couldn't just let me get on with the job.

I left Marks & Sparks behind me and followed the

road round to the right, then went left onto Broad Street. I got online as I drove, checking for the default PIN code to access message services on O2 numbers. I found it on Google.

Once back in the hotel, I used the almost redundant payphone and called Jan's mobile. It was still switched off. If she'd answered it, I would simply have said, 'Hi,' and tried again in the middle of the night.

I pressed the star button as soon as it went to voicemail. I was welcomed warmly to the O2 messaging service. I tapped in the 8705 PIN code Google had given me, and was inside in less time than it had taken to defeat the electronic lock at the Ararat Park Hyatt.

An infuriatingly cheerful female pre-record told me that there were three new messages and twenty-four old ones. The voice prompt then invited me to press 2 to listen to them.

The first was three days old: a pissed-off Jock, honking that none of his calls had been returned on either of her phones and that he had found this mobile in her bag – so she could fuck right off, and by the way, he also wanted his iPod speakers back. The next one was the same guy, a day earlier. He'd just got back to H and he'd love to meet up and, yes, he knew about this number but he had missed her.

I cancelled them. I didn't want her to know they'd been accessed. This was the method a few journos had been using to hack into mobiles belonging to celebrities, royals and politicians over the last couple of years. And if you couldn't be bothered to change your PIN, what grounds did you have to complain?

The next message was four days old. 'Hello, Janet.

Greetings. My name is Nadif. You must call me.' The voice was deep, slow and resonant. 'This is very important. Your sister, her child and her friend . . . they are in great danger. I can help you. Please, you must call me.'

I reached for the stub of hotel pencil on the bedside cabinet, scribbled the mobile number on the pad, and cancelled this message too.

Then I called Nadif.

11

The phone rang for ages. I was on the point of giving up when the deep voice suddenly answered. He was guarded, probably because I'd withheld my number. 'Hello . . .'

I didn't fuck about. 'You left a message. I'm calling about Tracy – Janet's sister. My name is Nick. Are they safe?' I kept my tone even and respectful, not wanting to spark him up.

His, too, was measured. 'I'm trying so hard to keep them alive. Why have you taken so long? Who are you?'

'I'm a friend of Tracy's. A very old friend. Is her little boy safe?'

'They're all safe. But they won't be safe for long. Only I can save them. But I need your help. Please, you must help me. Will you help me?'

The world is full of chancers who pick up their phones after a kidnap, claiming to be the only ones who can get the hostage back. They collect a deposit, and then they're never heard from again.

199

I needed to know that Nadif wasn't one of them.

'Nadif, I want to help you, but before we can do anything I need proof that they're alive. Can you provide that? Can you prove to me they're alive?'

'Yes, of course. But the people who are holding them, they demand three million dollars. Do you have that? Can you bring them this money? If you bring this money, I can help you get them released. Do you have this money?'

My tone changed from positive and obliging to scared and concerned. 'No. I mean, yes, maybe – maybe, maybe. I don't know. I'm not rich – we're not rich people. But we will get the money together. I will try everything. I will do everything possible to get that money. I will get the money somehow. But, please, you must prove to me first that they're alive. Can I talk to them? Please?'

There was a pause.

'Nick, do you really, really want them to come home?'

'Yes, I do. I really do. I'll do anything I can to get them back.'

'That is very good, Nick, because only I can keep them from being killed in a very terrible way. Remember that, my friend. I will prove that they're alive. You will come to me tomorrow. You will do that, yes?'

I took up the pencil once more as he gave me his address in Bristol.

'Listen, I'm less than two hours away. Why don't I come now? We can start the process. Please, Nadif, I don't know what we'd do without you.'

He agreed, and I powered down the phone. I grabbed my keys and started down to the car park.

The one thing you've got to do with these people is be subservient. You must show them at all times that they hold all the cards. Right now it wasn't that difficult.

12

I drove past Ascari's.

Maybe it would have made sense to sell the 911 a month ago, but I couldn't bring myself to do it. I'd enjoyed fucking off the salesman when I bought it, and I still enjoyed the mere fact that I owned it. I'd wandered into the showroom in my stinking trainers and running kit and the fucker had sneered when I asked how much it cost. I'd pulled out my wallet and asked if he was OK with cash.

And, anyway, I wasn't too sure what was going to happen with me and Anna. Maybe she'd seen the light and was ready to fuck me off already. After all, I was punching above my weight and she wasn't in any rush to get back to Moscow. I wasn't too sure how I felt about that, so I immediately told myself: Fuck it, so what? I didn't own the woman.

But going back to a life of Saturday mornings on my own in a café? I suddenly realized I was too old for that shit.

At this time of night there wasn't much traffic once

I'd got out of town, especially on the route I was taking. Rather than use the main drags and the motorway, I was going to go via Pontralis, into Wales, and then on B roads to Chepstow, before crossing back into England on the Severn Bridge.

I knew I'd be able to get my foot down this way. The speed cameras had sprung up like dandelions over the last few years, but I had a detector. I could do this route blindfolded. I used to fast-drive it day in, day out, in another lifetime. Bristol was used as a training ground for covert operations in Northern Ireland. The little B roads were where we'd practised our fast-driving skills. Sometimes you could make it door-to-door in under an hour.

The roads were narrow and bendy, with high hedgerows each side. Ant and Dec were going to have their work cut out to keep up, though the geography would help them. Each time I went up a hill, they'd be able to see my full beams.

Now and again I saw headlights behind me as I hit a long stretch of straight. I didn't blame Frank. I'd probably have had someone following me as well.

13

I reached the Chepstow ring road, and then the bridge approach. The traffic was a little heavier as I re-entered England for the princely toll of £5.70. I took the motorway to Bristol and headed for the town centre instead of Nadif's address. I parked on the second floor of an NCP and took the stairs.

Leaving the car there had nothing to do with good anti-surveillance skills. I just didn't want to get Nadif all sparked up. A 911 outside his front door would say all the wrong things about the size of Tracy's bank account. I also didn't want to come out and find the thing up on bricks. If Frank's boys were about, they'd get the message as soon as they saw where I was going.

Bristol is a bit special on Friday and Saturday nights. It's a well-known venue for lads on the piss and, increasingly, girls keeping in step. My route to the ATM became a giant pavement slalom as I dodged and wove through discarded kebab wrappers and the odd splash of vomit. I maxed out for the day on my three cards and soon had fifteen hundred pounds in my jeans pocket.

A taxi rank served the Broadmead Shopping Centre and cinema. I joined the queue. Four or five groups of students were ahead of me. The girls' skirts weren't long enough to cover their goosebumps, and they weren't carrying coats because they knew they'd get nicked in the bars and clubs.

When my turn came I jumped into an old Renault people-carrier. The sickly aroma of vanilla air-freshener did nothing to disguise the smell of the roll-up the driver had blatantly just finished. He was in his mid-fifties, white hair greased back. He didn't need gel; not washing it for a month did the job just fine. His faded tattoos and big rough hands told me that, if it wasn't for the recession, he would have been more at home on a building site.

'Easton, mate. I'm after Barratt Street in Easton.'

'It's an extra fiver for a drop-off in little Mogadishu, boy.'

It was far enough from the centre of town to be a good fare, but even beneath the deep West Country burr I could tell he wasn't too pleased.

We used Bristol for training because it was close to Hereford and as segregated as Belfast and Derry. The safe areas were very safe; the rough areas were very rough. But unlike in the Province, the segregation wasn't religious. It was financial. A lot of places were in shit state. The local housing authorities used them as dumping grounds for the poor and disadvantaged. In the 1980s the St Paul's area, near the city centre, became notorious for riots and drug-dealing. It all boiled down to lack of opportunity.

Easton had become a Somali ghetto, and it was no accident. Bristol lads were the original slavers, and for hundreds of years the dockland was populated by Africans, Indians and Chinese. Some of the graves in the local cemeteries contain the bodies of black businessmen, and they date back to the first half of the eighteenth century.

My iPhone vibrated.

'I need to stop at a cashpoint, mate.'

He grunted something indecipherable in carrot-cruncher code but pulled over outside a building society. I added another fifteen hundred to the wad I'd taken out the other side of midnight.

14

The kebab wrappers and splashes of vomit gradually retreated as we moved into a more residential landscape. Every traffic light was red, but we were soon surrounded by terraced houses and little bay windows. They might have been nice and shiny when they were built during the Boer War, but Easton had definitely seen better days.

We followed the railway line, carried above us on a plinth of grime-covered brown brick. The roads were only just wide enough to take the people-carrier. They were designed for the odd coal cart to trundle up and down, not for the world of Grand Theft Auto. Vehicles were parked up on both sides, half on the pavement, half off.

We drove past three or four mosques and endless rows of dirty brown houses. All the old corner shops had become fast-food joints. Box-fresh knights sat astride rusty mountain bikes outside them, waiting to fulfil their delivery promise. But it wasn't late-night pizza these kids in their immaculate white high-sided trainers and ball-caps were in the business of bringing to your door. It was something even more addictive.

We stopped at a junction, and he pointed to our right. 'That's Barratt. I can't get down there.'

I paid my £17.50 with a twenty-quid note and told him to keep the change. A big old industrial building that had been converted into a gym stood on the corner. Lights glared from the first and second floors, but nobody was inside. I turned down the narrow and dimly lit street beside it.

15

There were no front gardens as such, just walls a couple of feet from the front windows. Some were slabbed, some had weeds springing out of broken concrete. One had a mattress decorated with Coke cans and McDonald's wrappers. Most of the cars and vans alongside them were at least five years old. I walked past a jazzed-up 1.2-litre Peugeot with the world's biggest exhaust extension.

I rolled the three grand as tightly as I could and shoved it down into the front pocket of my jeans.

All the windows had been fitted with plastic or aluminium double-glazing at some stage, the kind that meant you couldn't possibly escape if someone torched your house. That was just the cheapest way to do it.

Black wheelie-bins and matching Sky dishes lined every front wall.

I checked my Breitling. I'd had a little bit of a spending spree with Anna in Moscow and thought it was time to step up a notch. Funnily enough, it told me the same time as any other watch, but it still gave me a kick every time I looked at it.

It was 01.35.

I slipped it off my wrist and out of sight.

Nadif had told me to keep an eye out for Ali's convenience store. A car passed, stopped at the junction behind me, and then drove off. I was impressed. Frank's lads had done really well staying with me.

Now and again a TV blared and light flickered in the gap between the curtains. The only other noise came from trains rattling past the end of the road behind me.

Back in Queen Victoria's day, Ali's front window would probably have boasted neat displays of coal-tar soap and jars of imperial jam. Now it was full of Chinese pots and pans and offers of a thousand tea-bags for 99p. Peeling stickers announced it was a gas and electricity pay point, sold SIM cards, Mars bars, the *News of the World* and fax and photocopying facilities.

The only thing they didn't advertise was *hawala* broking services, but I had no doubt that if you wanted to send money to relatives in Karachi, Dubai or Mogadishu, Ali would be your man. You'd bring your cash along and give him a code word or phone number, which he'd pass to a broker at the other end. Your favourite uncle would turn up, say the magic word, and be handed a brown envelope of the local currency – minus commission, of course. The two brokers would sort that out between themselves.

Billions and billions of dollars had been moved all over the world in this way for decades. It's the money-movement method of choice for criminals and terrorists, for obvious reasons, and a law-enforcement nightmare. Not that any of the lads round here would be financing the next 9/11. They'd just be slipping a few bob to their families back home so they could eat.

The shop was closed, but it wasn't cut-price tea-bags I was after. It was the blue door to its left, which belonged to the flat above. The wrought-iron knocker was in the shape of a lion's head. I tapped it three times. I didn't bother checking whether Ant and Dec were breathing down my neck. I'd brief Frank as soon as I knew what he needed to know.

A light came on behind flimsy curtains on the second floor. The silhouette of a body moved across the room. A few seconds later, two lever locks were being turned and I had to step back as the door was pushed open. I soon saw why. There was an ornate wrought-iron security gate behind it, fastened through the first two bars with a D-ring bicycle lock.

I could tell the lock was an old one by its circular key well. It was probably another of Ali's bargains – and a complete waste of time. Before manufacturers wised up and introduced flat keys, me and a couple of mates used to supplement our rifleman's wages by nicking mountain bikes from Andover's sports centre when we were squaddies in Tidworth. We'd hire a van for the weekend, throw as many in the back as we could liberate, and flog them on the London estates.

A steep, narrow stairway with a threadbare brown carpet led into the gloom the other side of the gate. The woodchip wallpaper could have done with a few licks of paint.

My new best Somali mate stood at the bottom of the stairs, wearing the kind of smile that any vicar would have been proud of. A good six feet tall and slim, with fine features and high cheekbones, he really did come from the place where Africa meets Arabia.

'You are Nick.'

The voice belonged to a man about three stone heavier. Mr Lover Man back in Moscow would have given his right arm for a voice like that.

I nodded. 'Nadif?'

16

He checked left and right my side of the gate.

'Where is your car?'

'I took a cab.'

'You do not have a car?'

'It's nothing to shout about.'

'What sort of car do you drive, Nick?'

'An old beat-up Renault. Why?'

He nodded thoughtfully. 'Where do you come from, Nick?'

'I was in Hereford this morning. That's where Tracy comes from. Her sister, Janet – you called her, yeah? – she still lives there.'

He nodded slowly and undid the D-lock. The gate squeaked open. It looked like it had come from a garden centre. He was in jeans, cheap brown Burberry-check slippers and a grey hoodie with a faded black star across the chest, none of which matched his stature and his long, thin, delicate hands. This lad could have followed Jules down the Calvin Klein cat-walk. He'd never been near a building site or a fishing boat in his life.

I stepped inside. The stairwell stank of cigarettes and microwaved ready-meals. His eyes never left me as he closed both doors. I moved to the bottom of the stairs. He gestured politely. 'Please, after you, my friend.'

I didn't follow his invitation until I'd seen what he did with the keys. The double-glazing meant I wouldn't be able to jump out of a window if there was a drama. He slid them into his pocket, quite casually, like a man who didn't have six mates upstairs as a welcoming committee. If I was wrong about that, I'd soon be finding out.

The room above was a mess. It looked more like a boffin's bedsit than the HQ of a kidnap king. The only new bit of kit was the aluminium MacBook sitting on the cheap veneer table to the right of the door. Beside it was an old, steam-driven fax machine.

Back issues of *Newsweek* and estate agents' brochures were heaped on the floor. Two steel Parker pens lay on top of a pile of folded local and national newspapers. He was either going to read them later or have a crack at the crosswords. A couple of ashtrays, each with only one or two stubs in them, sat beside a velour armchair that was a bit short of velour. An equally moth-eaten TV showed BBC News 24 without the sound. In Bahrain, Saudi armoured vehicles were well and truly bedded in.

I nodded in the direction of the screen. 'Any news on Japan?'

'Not good, Nick.' He shook his head mournfully as he pulled a folding wooden chair from under the veneer table. 'But let us talk about other things. Please, Nick, sit.'

He waited for me to do so before he settled into his armchair. He rested his chin on his steepled hands.

'Now, Nick, tell me. Will you be able to get the money? It's the only way I can save that small child and the others too – Tracy and Justin . . .'

'I'll do my very best.'

'Nick, you have to get the money as quickly as you can. It's the only way I can get them out of that hell-hole. I worry so much about them. You are their friend, yes? Do you love them? Do you love them enough to help me free them?'

My chair creaked as I sat back. I caught a glimpse of the kitchen. Washing dishes obviously wasn't high on Nadif's list of priorities. The guy had bigger fish to fry.

'Yes, of course. I've been asked by Tracy's sister and Justin's family to ensure their safety. You'll have to help me, Nadif. Three million dollars is such a lot of money . . . It's going to take the families some time to raise it. They were on a nice boat but they are not rich people. I hope you can use your influence. A man like you, I'm sure you have much respect in Somalia . . .'

He liked that.

'But first I have to know that they're alive. Their families . . . everyone's really worried. We don't know the people who have them. Can you arrange for me to talk to them? Please . . .'

He glanced at the red Swatch on his wrist and lowered his hands onto the arms of the chair. 'Would you like some tea, Nick?'

'That'd be good. Thank you. Thank you very much. Then can I talk to them, please?'

He got to his feet. 'All in good time, my friend. Be patient. These things take time.'

He disappeared into the kitchen. So far, so good. He liked being thought the top banana – or, more probably, that I seemed to think I was smoking him like a kipper. These guys were far too smart to be taken in by flattery, however much it was part of the ritual. A Somali taxi driver in the UK had brokered the deal to repatriate the kidnapped British sailors, Paul and Rachel Chandler, after they were taken hostage on their yacht between the Seychelles and Tanzania in 2009. For all I knew, he might have been Nadif. Whoever it was, I bet he used the same gentle, sympathetic patter.

He brushed aside the crap in the sink enough to fill a kettle. 'Nick, my friend, how much money can you raise immediately?' His deep baritone resonated round the small room. 'I think we need to make a show of faith. But I also need to know I can trust you, personally, before we go forward and try to get your loved ones freed.'

17

As glasses and spoons clanked in the background, I leant forward and riffled through the paperwork around me. There was all kinds of stuff, but nothing that gave me a clue about where they were being held. The Savills brochures were for houses around the £500K mark, countrywide. School prospectuses invited dutiful parents to invest almost half that figure to ensure their kids got to wear the right kind of tie. Next to the Mac was a list of local papers Nadif had logged onto. Several were crossed out.

'Of course you can trust me, Nadif. That's why I'm here. We're desperate. Whatever I have to do, I'll do. I just need to be able to speak to them. I need to know that they're alive.'

'Tell me, Nick. Do you own a home? As well as your car?'

'I've just bought a flat in London.'

'What about the other families? Do they have homes?'

'Justin's family live in a council house.' I knew

fuck-all about them, but I wasn't going to admit it, and I needed to keep his expectations low. 'Tracy's sister rents her place. She hasn't much money. But don't you worry, Nadif. We'll find some way of getting there.'

Guys like Nadif didn't miss a trick. They're negotiators, the middlemen between the hostages and the clans. He was going to make it work both ends.

And judging by the contents of his archive, I could see he was a whole lot more than a broker. He was the spotter, too. During the negotiation he'd be looking to find out as much as he could about the payers. He had to make sure he was squeezing out every last drop. If a family claimed they were doing everything they could to raise the cash, he'd go round to the house and make sure it was up for sale. And if they couldn't come up with an interim payment, he'd be telling them to sell the BMWs in the drive. If they claimed that they were trying, he'd say, 'I didn't see any details in the local newspaper. Maybe it would be best to go to a dealer.' Or, with just the right degree of sympathy, 'Your three children are at Marlborough. Wouldn't they prefer to have their auntie back home with them?'

You could depend upon Nadif to do his level best to help.

I wondered for a moment whether the school prospectuses were for his own kids. With the sort of hostage numbers Jules was talking about, business must be good. This shithole certainly wasn't where he lived. It was a bedsit without a bed. He probably lived near the university, in a townhouse that would put anything that cost as little as £500K to shame.

18

'Nick, my friend, as a show of faith between us and the people who have your loved ones . . . an appropriate price would be ten thousand dollars, I think. Then I can talk with the clan leader, a very important man, without insulting him. I can talk to him right now, and let you speak to all three of your loved ones. But you must know these services cost money. I understand your concern, but I must talk of these things first.'

Unless he was bullshitting me, I now knew one thing: they had moved up the food chain, from the kidnappers to a clan. The kidnappers would have declared the hostages to their clan leaders. They'd probably have funded the whole thing with a loan from the nearest warlord. When their demands were met, the pirates would take their cut and repay the loan, plus interest and whatever percentage he demanded.

If there was no cash, or the hostages died, the debt still stayed in place. Maybe the guys who'd snatched Tracy had to pay off an existing loan. What the fuck did it matter? I was going round in circles, and I hadn't yet had any proof of life. That was all that mattered right now.

Nadif reappeared with a pewter teapot and glasses on a tray, just like he would have back in the old country.

'Nadif, I've been sitting here thinking about how to get that sort of money quickly. It's very, very difficult. But I have come with some money. I've got three thousand pounds on me – nearly five thousand dollars. Maybe that would be enough for you to let me speak to them now.' I paused. 'And whatever money is finally agreed, maybe ... maybe twenty per cent could go to you when they're released.'

I knew he'd be making about five per cent from the clan. And if he went the *hawala* route with the money, maybe he'd take another five per cent on top.

He sat down again and poured the tea, slowly and from a generous height. The oxygen it absorbed as it splashed into the glasses was supposed to improve the flavour. I smelt apples as the steam came my way.

Somalis are a cultured and ancient race. Even when they're living in shit, they show each other great politeness and respect. Centuries ago, they were pouring tea like this when we were still burning witches and gnawing turnips. At the same time, they could be savagely brutal – though I guess they saw it as no more dramatic than a lion killing an antelope. Not evil or malicious, just the way of the world.

I sat and waited for him to complete the ritual of the tea, and the ritual of making me wait for his answer. To be a demanding arsehole didn't work with these people. They were businessmen, and their business just happened to be trading in humans.

The pouring stopped. He offered me sugar. I shoved in three teaspoonloads and stirred. He did the same. And then, lifting the glass gently between thumb and forefinger, he offered a toast.

'I think that's a very good suggestion, Nick. If you pay me that cash now, I will make contact, and we can start getting your loved ones back. You can pay me in instalments as everything moves on. But can I trust you?'

'Of course you can trust me.'

'These people are very dangerous. You can't deal with them. Only I can get your loved ones out.'

'I know that, Nadif.'

I pulled out the roll of money and put it on the table. It sprang open and doubled in size. Seeing cash physically increase in value always focuses the mind on the deal.

We raised our glasses, clinked, and both took a sip of tea.

He looked at me. 'You know, my friend, I think we *will* get your loved ones back home, and safe, quite soon.'

I got some very sweet apple tea down my neck.

He took another sip and then got up. 'Please excuse me . . .'

He went back into the kitchen and I watched as closely as I could while he fumbled about under the sink. He conjured up a mobile, an old grey pay-as-you-go thing, like a rabbit out of a hat.

He checked his watch once more. Mogadishu is

three hours ahead. It would be very early morning there.

'Nadif, aren't you worried that the police, or the intelligence service, can hear what you're saying?'

He smiled as he dialled. 'Please do not be concerned. No one cares about being listened to. Nothing will happen. In Somalia, there are no police, no government, no army – no one. And here, why would they want me to stop? I am performing a service. I return people's loved ones to them. I help them. Your government, they do not. The Americans – they too can listen if they want to. Will they come back into my country after what happened to them last time? I don't think so, my friend.' I could hear the phone ring. 'You see, everything is fine. Please be calm.'

He brought it up to his ear. I caught a few syllables of Somali waffle. Nadif didn't bat an eyelid.

He turned and looked at me, phone still glued to his ear. 'Nick, it may be a little time until you can speak to them. They have been moved – for their own safety.'

I was about to open my mouth when his hand came up.

'It's OK. I will make sure they are not harmed. Trust me, Nick. Please, one moment.'

There was more waffle. He sounded as calm as if he was ordering a takeaway from the boys with the white trainers. Then he passed the phone across to me. 'It's a message for you, Nick. Don't talk, just listen.'

I put it to my ear. The line was terrible. In among the crackling I could hear birds sing. A vehicle rumbled past. Then I heard a woman's voice. 'Yes – yes, of course I will . . .'

There was a rustling sound, and then a sniff. 'In here?'

I couldn't help myself. 'Tracy, it's Nick . . .'

Nadif waved a hand. 'She cannot hear you, Nick. You are listening to a message.'

Her voice was flat and dull. It was obvious she was reading. 'Help me. I am very sick. My health is deteriorating markedly due to fever and dysentery. I need to see a doctor. They will not give any of us the medicine. I have a toothache. My tooth is badly broken and very infected and abscessed. I need help immediately. Please.'

It sounded like one of those Nigerian email scams.

She didn't stop there. 'My son has severe stomach problems. There is no one to take care of him. I don't want him to die here. Please do not let my son die here. I'm so afraid I will die of diseases if I don't get help soon. I don't know how much longer we can bear this. Someone, please help us. Please.'

Her voice quavered. 'The men who hold us are very serious and they say that, if the ransom is not paid, they will kill all three of us. But I'm telling you, our conditions are very serious right now and we could very seriously die of an illness. My son, Stefan, might die. Justin might die. We're very sick people.'

There were a few mumbles from whoever was holding the mike and I could hear the rustling as it was taken away from her. There was a click, and Nadif held out his hand. 'Please, Nick. Thank you.'

They exchanged a few more words and the line went dead. He put the phone down and sighed theatrically. He looked at me like he had the weight of the world on his shoulders. 'Nick, these are dangerous people. I can help you, but you must get the money. Somehow, please.' He put his hands together again, as if he was praying. 'My friend, I have done my part. I will make sure that you get to talk to her tomorrow. I will organize this. Are you now going to show some more good faith, Nick? I am helping you. Now you have got to help me. They must be paid so your loved ones are free.'

He stood up and rummaged in a pocket for a business card. Like Frank's, the only thing on it was a mobile number. Unlike Frank's, you could help yourself to twenty of these for two quid at your local motorway service station.

'I can help you, Nick. But you have to help me to stop those crazy people from hurting your loved ones. Go home and call me tomorrow at midday. I will have some good news, I promise.'

19

I found the number for a minicab firm outside the railway station. Fifty minutes later I was rattling round the ring road in the 911, following signs for the bridge. I hit the Bluetooth and synched up the iPhone, checking the occasional set of headlights in the rear-view.

I rehearsed tomorrow's speech to Nadif in my head. I'd be phoning with good news. I could raise maybe thirty thousand dollars within the next couple of days. How was that for good faith? Very soon, my very small flat would go on the market, even though I'd only just bought it.

I'd be able to make some money, I'd tell him, but I had a mortgage of just over £100K to repay. I should be able to clear another £45K, but the way the market was, it would take time. Maybe I could try to re-mortgage. Janet and Justin's families were working hard to raise money. I was showing trust; I was showing commitment. I would get the money together, come what may.

In the meantime, I really needed Nadif to keep them alive. I needed him to let me speak to them. A man with his influence must be able to help me do those things.

My Breitling had me coming out of the city and onto the motorway at just past five a.m. I dialled Frank, expecting him to be engaged. Ant and Dec would be phoning about now to say I was heading back towards Hereford.

I had to carry on managing his expectations. Apart from anything else, I didn't want him to go his own way. He was already following my every move. What else might he be up to? When people start fucking about with the system, hostages get killed.

It rang just twice before a voice barked from the speakers: 'Yes?'

'All indications are that they're still breathing. I've made contact with someone I think can broker the deal.'

There was a pause.

'Have you spoken to them? Arrange the exchange. I can have the money ready in—'

'Stop. It doesn't work like that. Where are you? We must meet. I need to tell you what's happening, and what to do next. I'm not going to do that on an open line.'

There was another pause.

'How good are the indications? Are you able to get them back?'

Either he hadn't heard or he wasn't listening.

'I'm not talking on the mobile. We need to meet.'

'I am in France. I will send my jet to London.'

'Can't you come to me? It'll be quicker. The clock's ticking.'

There was a long silence.

'There is something happening here that I cannot cancel. How long until you can get to the airport?'

'Three hours, maybe. Less if I get picked up at Bristol airport.'

'Where?'

'B-R-I-S-T-O-L. It's in the south-west.'

'Someone will call to arrange this.'

'One more thing . . .'

'What?'

'Call off your guys. You don't need to check up on me. I'm only letting them stay with me because they're yours. It'd be a lot easier for me if you lose them. I'm not going to let you down, because I'm not going to let her down. I'm not going to leave them in the shit. So just call them off, yeah? They'll only fuck things up.'

It took him a moment to digest this too.

'I have no one following you, Nick. Why would I? Why do you think I chose you? You say you can lose them, so do it. Whatever it takes. I do not want any of my enemies to interfere with this.'

He ended the call.

I pulled off the motorway at the next exit and headed back the way I'd come. I rang Nadif. His phone was turned off. At least, I hoped it was.

Frank's enemies were now my enemies. He probably wasn't short of them, but the only ones I knew about came from Tbilisi.

20

**Saturday, 19 March
06.40 hrs**

It was light by the time the taxi dropped me off. This time I got the driver to take me to the other end of Barratt, so I could walk the last three blocks. As we drove past the turning, I looked to my left. A couple of people in work clothes were getting into their cars.

'Just here, mate. This'll do.'

I paid him off and headed back towards Ali's place. I could soon see the shop front about thirty metres down on the left. What little sunlight there was glinted on the display window and the roof of a car parked beside it. There was no sign of any shiny rental C-class Merc.

I got out my iPhone and tried Nadif one more time as I turned in towards the blue door.

I grabbed the lion's head knocker to give it a couple of bangs, just to let him know I was there. The door opened towards me a couple of centimetres.

As nonchalantly as I could, I let go of the knocker and

stepped aside so I could see through the gap. I eased it further open with my finger. The D-bar was locked. I could see a little way up the stairs, as far as I needed to. A Burberry-slippered foot was just visible at the top. I hoped the rest of him was still attached.

I eased the blue door towards me until it looked like it was shut. A couple of brightly dressed African women came out of the shop laden with milk, bread and papers. They passed me, jabbering away in a dialect I didn't recognize. I stayed where I was, as if Nadif was just about to answer the door. A couple of trains passed each other at the other end of the street. Traffic whipped along the elevated section a couple of hundred metres away.

Once the women had disappeared, I stepped back onto the pavement and went into Ali's emporium. It was full of plastic stuff I hadn't known I needed: cans of dodgy-sounding fizzy drinks and cat food; plastic flowers and bottles of cleaning fluid with Greek labels. I went straight to the kids' section. For a quid, I picked up a twelve pack of felt-tip pens, a bit thicker than ordinary biros, in a plastic case with a picture of Shrek on the front. I grabbed some rubber gloves on the way to the till.

The woman behind the counter was deep in conversation on the phone about the trouble in Libya as she marked up front pages full of it for the paper rounds. Her brother-in-law's family lived in Benghazi and she was worried sick. I didn't interrupt. I put a two-pound coin on the counter with a sympathetic smile and loaded the stuff into a carrier myself.

As soon as I was outside, I ripped Shrek's head off

with my teeth and pulled out a pen. By the time I got to Nadif's door, I'd also pulled off the cap at the end opposite the nib. I didn't look around for Ant and Dec, or anyone else. I had to look natural. I had my back to passers-by. They wouldn't be able to describe anything about me except my height, hair colour and clothes.

I eased the door open far enough to expose the bike lock. There was no point mincing about. I jammed the open end of the pen into the circular key well. Gripping the bar with my left hand, I pushed the pen and twisted. Two turns and the lock fell apart.

I pushed the grille open and slipped inside. I closed the main door behind me. I looked up at the little I could see of Nadif as I put on the rubber gloves. The one contact I had was now history. I dropped the packaging into the carrier bag and shoved it down my sweatshirt.

Nadif's body, what was left of it, came into view as I moved up the stairs. He lay sprawled across the small landing. There wasn't that much blood on the carpet but his sweatshirt was covered with it. A tea-towel had been rammed into his gaping mouth, probably to stop him being heard as one of his steel ballpoint pens was forced through his right eardrum and driven into his brain.

The rooms had been ripped apart. My bundle of cash was scattered across the carpet, along with the papers, books and Mac screen. They'd been after something more important.

I checked Nadif's pockets for the keys and his mobile. Nothing. The rubber gloves were now wet and red as I lifted his right arm and turned him over. He had been punctured seven or eight times with a narrow blade into the lower stomach. Some of his gut had spilt out. Ant and Dec weren't fucking about. They knew exactly how to inflict maximum pain.

The second steel pen was embedded in his left eye. The eyeball was still in place but the vitreous fluid had drained out.

Why hadn't Ant and Dec locked the door? The keys were in his jeans pocket, in a thick pool of blood. They must have thought the door was on a latch instead of lever locks, and only realized once they had closed the D-lock. Or maybe they just didn't give a fuck.

I went and locked both doors. Because of the shitty double-glazing I didn't have any other way of escaping now, but if Ant and Dec decided to come back at least I'd buy myself a few minutes to reflect on how badly I'd fucked up.

Avoiding the blood, I climbed over Nadif. He didn't smell yet. But that wouldn't take long.

First things first. I checked the kitchen. The teapot wasn't on the tray, but the glasses were. They, too, went into the bag inside my sweatshirt. One of them carried my DNA.

I got to my knees and started pulling out the shit from under the sink that Ant and Dec hadn't already pulled out during their search. It hadn't taken Nadif long to retrieve that phone last night. It had to be close to hand.

I pushed at the panels round the sides and the back of the unit, then lifted the once-white Formica sheet at its base. I was rewarded with a Tupperware box containing three small grey mobiles and a charger. There were also five Lebara SIM cards, still embedded in their credit-card-sized plastic mounts. They're cheap. Immigrants use them to phone their families back home – or to call their clan leaders.

I hit the power button on each one in turn. They were SIMed up and had a bar or two of signal. I checked my iPhone and got ready with the numbers.

I called Crazy Dave on one of the phones. It rang several times before transferring to his messaging service. I cut away. I rang again. Still no answer.

I tried Jan next. That went straight to voicemail too. I cancelled.

Then I keyed in Jules's number.

It rang three times.

'Anything on those names yet, mate?'

He was even more hesitant than yesterday. 'Not yet, but I'm checking every day.'

'OK, can you keep on it? Got to go. Just thought I'd check.'

No point getting him sparked up for nothing. Ant and Dec didn't know about him. They hadn't been in-country in time to cover our meet at Cheapside. But they had been with me in Hereford. Even if they hadn't seen me with Jan, they would now have her number. It had to be on the mobile that was missing. They wouldn't have mine. It was a blocked number. But had they followed me to Crazy Dave's? They must have.

I hoped Jan was waking up in someone else's bed on the other side of town, and Crazy Dave was rattling down an *autoroute* in his Popemobile.

I pressed the tools on all three machines until I found Calls Made. They'd all registered international calls, and to one area. The code was 252. It had to be Somalia. I'd know soon enough, but right now I was looking for a call made at about two o'clock this morning. I scrolled down on the third and finally found it. 252 again.

I switched it off and slid it into my jeans, then fished out the carrier bag and added the other two to the Shrek and rubber-glove packaging. I had to tuck my sweat-shirt into my jeans to take the weight.

A baby screamed in one of the nearby houses and a mother screamed back just as loudly.

I took a badly stained, almost stiff tea-towel and wiped down the bike lock and the grille door. I felt sorry for Nadif. We'd only had one brew together, but I'd quite liked the poor fucker.

Ant and Dec wanted what I had. They appeared to be the only things of value in this shit-heap, now that the Mac had bitten the dust. I certainly wasn't hanging around to see if there was anything more. That phone number was all I needed.

I unfastened the security gate and unlocked the front door. I stood for a moment inside the threshold, listen-ing for voices or footsteps.

Nothing.

It was fuck-it time.

I opened the door just enough to slip through, relocked both barriers and wiped the outside as best I could. The tea-towel and washing-up gloves went into the carrier bag too.

Head down, hands in pockets, I walked back the way I'd come. I didn't know or care where I was going. I just wanted to be lost in the maze of terraces and alleyways.

21

Back in the 911, I headed across the Severn Bridge into Wales. A service station had fitted me out with a thin green fleece and a blue acrylic jumper.

The bag of goodies was on the seat next to me. The car was in Tiptronic mode so I could focus on sorting out the mobiles. I turned them both on, to identify which one I'd used to call Jan and Crazy Dave. I kept the one with the Somali number in my pocket.

I was soon through Chepstow and on the Pontralis road. The car swung from side to side. I needed to make distance but only had one hand on the wheel.

I rang Crazy Dave.

Still nothing.

I tuned in to Radio Wyvern. Hereford was now about nine miles away. I caught the nine a.m. news. No doleful announcements of the violent murder of a Hereford woman or a disabled man in the early hours of this morning.

I tried Crazy Dave once more. This time I got a dial tone. Non-UK.

'What?'

Simon and Garfunkel wailed in the background. Something about Cecilia breaking their hearts.

'Dave, it's Nick.'

'What?'

'Where are you?'

'I fucking told you, didn't I? What do you want?'

'Nothing, mate.'

'Well, fuck off, then.'

Jan's phone went straight to voicemail again. Perhaps she was doing what Cecilia had done.

I crossed the bridge towards Ross-on-Wye and parked up at Asda by the river. It was a five-minute walk to the flats. I'd done it a million times before the old camp at Stirling Lines had made way for an executive housing estate.

I redialled Jan a couple more times on Nadif's mobile, with the same result. If she wasn't at home, I was going to have to start searching.

St Martin's Church stood at about the halfway mark. Many of my friends were buried there. I always thought about them when I passed, but not today. I needed another word with Crazy Dave.

'What?'

'Dave, it's me again.'

Bob Dylan had taken over from Simon and Garfunkel.

'Yeah?'

'Jan? You know, Tracy's sister? You know where she works, or where she might be today?'

Dave didn't miss a beat. 'Who the fuck do you think I am? The fucking *Yellow Pages*?'

'What about her mates – do you know any of them?'

'I'm trying to have a new life here. Remember what I said?'

'What?'

'Fuck off.'

The flats, a collection of three-storey rectangular blocks, were on an uphill stretch to my right. The grass around them was neatly trimmed. The cream rendering looked in much better condition than I remembered.

Jan lived on the ground floor, far right, at the back. There was no C-class Merc in sight. I wasn't surprised. It would have stuck out like a sore thumb.

A couple of kids kicked a ball between them as their mum tried to open the main security door. She was laden with shopping and a pushchair, and had to use a knee. She called over her shoulder, 'You staying out?'

They didn't answer, just kept on kicking the ball. She got the message.

I quickened my pace but stayed out of her line of sight. A stranger entering the block would register.

I grabbed the steel handle as the door closed behind her and held it open a second or two to give Mum time to move out of the hallway.

I turned right down the corridor. I wanted the last door on the left.

The place had definitely had a facelift. Bright strip-lights showed off the newly painted walls. The 1960s doors with frosted panels had been replaced by solid wooden ones with on-trend steel furniture.

I gave Jan's a gentle knock. There was no bell. The

intercom at the front entrance did that job. There was no letter-box either.

I knocked again, this time a little harder and with my ear to the wood. The loudest thing I heard was a muffled shout from the two kids outside.

One more knock. Still nothing.

I walked outside. The footballers were sitting on the grass with the ball between them. I glanced around. There was nowhere out here she could have hidden a set of keys.

I followed the block round to the back. Her curtains were closed. There was no sign of life. Maybe she really had played away last night.

22

Among the forest of Sky dishes that had sprouted along the wall there were two small bird boxes. One was by her bedroom – or what I remembered as her bedroom.

I pushed my hand inside the hole, felt around inside and heard a metallic clink. Old habits die hard. One was a plastic fob to enter the security door, the other an ordinary pin tumbler.

The footballers looked ready to take an early bath. I walked past and pressed the fob. The door opened. I opened the flat door slowly. I didn't call out. As soon as I saw the state of the place I knew I didn't need to. The hallway was strewn with coats and newspapers. Every drawer of the sideboard she used to keep the kids' clothes in – the ones that didn't fit in the bedroom – had been tipped out.

I closed the door with an elbow and headed for the bedroom.

Her dress and underwear were on the floor, along-side her shoes. Next to them was a pair of jeans and a blue-striped shirt. Their owner was still in bed. The duvet he was lying on was covered with blood. He had puncture wounds in his neck and chest.

I moved on to the living room. It had been ripped apart. Jan was sitting naked on the floor, her top half slumped over the sofa. She hadn't been as beautiful as her sister for a good few years. Now she looked a whole lot worse. Her back was a riot of stab wounds and bruises. The carpet was soaked with blood. Like Nadif, she had been gagged with a tea-towel. Her face was black and swollen. There were splits in the skin above and beside her eyes. Part of an ear lay on the cushion beside her. The blood that had run down her neck and shoulders was dry.

Neither of them would have stood a chance.

I moved back into the bedroom and kicked at her bag to see if the phones were still inside. They weren't.

I went to the front door and checked the hallway before closing it behind me, using the sleeve of my brand new fleece.

Outside, the kids were nowhere to be seen. I turned downhill towards Asda.

How the fuck had Ant and Dec managed to deal with both locations? Maybe they'd followed me to Nadif's place, done him, then found out about Jan via his mobile. Or maybe they'd seen us together at Saxtys. It didn't really matter. What did was that they had both confidence and ability, and that made them dangerous.

I felt sorry for Jan, and even sorrier for Blue Stripes. All he'd wanted was a shag. The Jock on her voicemail was going to have a pretty hard time too. The police would find his pissed-off phone messages on Jan's other phones and he'd have a fuck of a lot of explaining to do. Another poor bastard dragged into this nightmare – but at least he was alive.

I pointed the 911 out of the city. I wanted to get into the countryside as quickly as possible.

I jumped out at a lay-by beside the mud flats, engine still running, and pulled apart Nadif's first two phones. They didn't have his two a.m. call in the memory, but they did have the ones I'd made. I took out the batteries and wiped them on my fleece. I clambered up the bank and through the hedge. I kicked a hole with my heel in the mud the other side, stamped the phones into the bottom of it and smoothed wet earth back over them.

I powered up Nadif's remaining mobile and hit redial on the Somali number as I got back in the 911.

It rang several times, then I was treated to a high-decibel crackle of the local dialect. The only thing I could tell from it was that the guy who'd answered was very old indeed. I waited for him to pause for breath.

'Do you speak English?'

More crackle. '*Italiano?*'

'No. English?'

There was a sudden explosion of invective. It sounded like everyone around the old boy was getting shouted at to shut the fuck up. I held the phone away from my ear. Then there was a rustling sound, as if the mouthpiece was brushing against facial hair. A new voice came on, much younger.

'Yes.' He paused. 'Where is Nadif? This is Nadif's

phone. Where is Nadif?' He had a soft American accent, more *Twilight* than *Friends*.

'Nadif has been killed. I don't know who did it, and I don't know why. I want to find out. But I need help. I need help from someone with power and influence. I want to pay for my friends to be released. Nadif was going to help me, with his powerful friend. Are you his powerful friend?'

'Yes. Only I can help you get your friends released. What is your name? Who are your friends?'

'I'm Nick. My friends are a man, a woman and a child – a little boy. Their names are Justin, Tracy and Stefan.'

He was straight down to business. 'Do you have the money, Mr Nick? Do you have three million American dollars?'

'I am trying to get it. Please can I speak to them? I need to know they're OK.'

And then it was as if we hadn't had the first part of the exchange. 'Nadif, where is Nadif?'

'Nadif is dead. I don't know who killed him.'

He thought about it for a while. I heard more rustling. 'You will call again tomorrow. Same time.'

The phone went dead.

I gave it thirty seconds and rang again. Nothing. He'd powered down.

PART FIVE

1

Courchevel 1850, French Alps

16.32 hrs

The skids of the Bell 222 settled on the tarmac and the pilot killed the engines. The stainless steel and fibre-glass rotors wound gradually to a standstill. I took off my headset and waited for the door to be opened.

The Bell could normally take eight passengers at a time on the shuttle between Geneva and Courchevel. Frank's people had booked it exclusively for my use. The pilot said his instructions were to wait as long as I needed him to. Then, as soon as he'd worked out I wasn't Russian, he started talking and didn't stop until we landed. Better thirty minutes of that, I supposed, than two and a half hours up the mountain by car, duelling with kamikaze Peugeot drivers.

Apparently it had been a very strange season. Winter had started a month early, with heavy snowfalls in October. Spring had also arrived way ahead of time. The sun had shone almost continually and there had been weeks of bizarrely hot weather. Then December had had some of the best snow of the season.

'But you know how I will remember this season most of all? As the one when the snow didn't fall. We waited through January, February and now this month for the big dumps of snow that never came. That's why we're lucky we live in the Trois Vallées.'

'Why's that?'

'Wise leaders who invested heavily in snow cannons, reservoirs and piste groomers.'

'Man-made snow doesn't sound very eco-friendly.'

'It's economy-friendly. Without it, the Russians wouldn't have brought their bling-bling.'

'Good for business, are they?'

'These days, they *are* the business.'

I stepped out into a landscape that looked white enough to me. The piste groomers must have been working their miracles.

I looked along just 525 metres of steeply rising runway. There was a vertical drop at the end. It was easy to see why Courchevel airport was rated one of the most dangerous in the world. There was no go-around procedure, the pilot had said. The hill was supposed to help to slow a landing aircraft.

'Does it work?'

'Not always.'

Add to that a hazardous approach through deep valleys that could only be performed by specially certified pilots, and often freezing conditions with black ice and heavy snow, and you had one of the most challenging landings on earth. Jets couldn't use it. Larger propeller aircraft like the Twin Otter and Dash 7 could, but they had been phased out. Smaller Cessnas and helicopters had taken over.

A driver in his early twenties greeted me and led me to a car. He was smartly dressed in a black suit, shirt and tie. His gold-rimmed Ray-Ban Aviators glinted in the sun.

I couldn't help smiling to myself as I climbed into the back. I'd listened to Talk Radio on my way to Bristol airport. The coalition's austerity measures weren't going down well. Prices at the petrol pumps were higher by the day. So was the number of un-employed. All in all, it had been another grey and gloomy day in Broken Britain. Yet in a parallel universe Frank's plane had turned out to be a G6 Gulfstream, more airliner than private jet, and I was in a black Merc limo with darkened windows on the way from the 'altiport' at one of the world's most upscale ski resorts to meet with one of the world's richest men.

According to a brochure I found in the Gulfstream, Courchevel 1850 was the highest and most famous of the resort's four centres, distinguished from each other by their height in metres. It was also the bit where the billionaires hung out. 1850 was in fact only 1,747 metres above sea level, but the good burghers were keen to shaft arch-rivals Val d'Isère. Everyone wanted a slice of Russian action, and the Russians always flocked to the biggest, highest, priciest – anywhere, in fact, with *est* on the end. With five-star hotels charging $35,000 a night for a suite, chalets at $190,000 a week and restaurants that boasted more Michelin stars per head of population than anywhere else on the planet, they wouldn't have been disappointed. If there was snow, they were here – if they weren't in Moscow making money, or in London spending it. And where the Russians go, the *nouveaux riches* from the emerging economies in Eastern Europe, Asia and South America follow.

I'd landed in Geneva and got straight on the Bell. The helicopter transfer company's choice of aircraft gave me a big kick. It had starred in *Airwolf*, one of my favourite TV shows as a kid. It looked much the same: navy blue, sleek and menacing as it flew low between the mountains.

There had been property brochures in the Gulfstream, too. As I drove in the back seat of the air-conditioned, leather-upholstered luxury bubble, I knew I was passing 'chalets' that cost upwards of $5 million. We were a world away from the shabby, peeling shit-pits I'd left behind me in Easton. No clapped-out Ford Focuses, either. All the other vehicles on the road were Range Rovers or Cayenne 4×4s. It seemed you could have any colour you liked as long as it was black.

We passed people out and about. They were walking little rat dogs wrapped up in Prada Puffas the same colour as their owner's. This was Bling Central, on ice.

Even my young driver looked too cool to need to breathe. His Aviators didn't have fingermarks; he never needed to adjust his short, wet-gelled hair. My own hair was greasy and my eyes felt so knackered they probably looked like they belonged to Vlad the Impaler. Fuck knows what he made of me in the back, contaminating his leather.

'Are you here for the party, sir?'

His English was clear and crisp.

'No, mate, just a quick visit. Whose party?'

'I'm not sure, but they say it's costing five million euros. Cirque de Soleil are being flown in all the way from Canada.'

'That's some party. Keeping you busy?'

I found myself doing the cabbie chat I normally saved for London.

'Three hundred people are coming, or so they say.'

'Not for the skiing, that's for sure.'

There was snow around the chocolate-box village, but it was dribbling down the mountain with every passing minute. Now we were lower, I could see large expanses of rock fighting their way into view.

He checked his sat-nav for the hundredth time. 'Not far now, sir.'

2

We stopped outside a massive, classic Swiss chalet that looked as if it had been carved out of the granite high ground behind it. Snow covered the gently sloping roof and wide eaves. The pathway had been freshly cleared.

'Are you the new owner, sir?'

I checked out the three-storey slice of paradise like I was trying to remember if I'd bought this one or the next, and dreamt a little before coming back to the real world. 'No, mate, not me. How much did it go for?'

'Twenty-two million dollars. Just last week. They say it has a pool.'

For that amount of money, I'd have demanded a bigger driveway as well. It only just fitted the gleaming black Range Rover with French plates and darkened windows.

'I'll tell you if it has when you take me back. You're waiting, yeah?'

'Yes, sir. I am booked until you want to leave. Same as the helicopter.'

I opened the door. The cold, crisp air attacked my face. I liked it. It woke me up a little. 'What's your name, mate?'

He swivelled in his seat, smiling under his sun-gigs. 'Jacques.'

I leant down. 'You new at this, Jacques?'

He nodded like a puppy. 'My third day.'

'Try not to speak to the guests, Jacques. These people don't like that.'

He flapped. 'Sir, I'm so sorry, I—'

I put up a hand. 'It's no drama with me, Jacques. You seem a good guy and it would be a nightmare to lose a job like this. Best to have fun using your eyes and ears. You might find out exactly what's going on around here, yeah?'

He let it sink in.

'The guy in that house, Jacques? He can buy that shit because he knows that knowledge is power. He told me so himself. So, if you listen, look and learn while you drive you won't have to depend on "them" to tell you what's what. They'll depend on you. Get it?'

He nodded.

'See you in a bit, then, Jacques.'

The huge wooden door was a few centimetres ajar. I pushed it wider. The hallway was empty. No one lived here. But it was far from a rustic ski lodge. The interior looked as if it had been ripped out of a Manhattan penthouse. Sleek, modern lines. A symphony of glass, steel and dark grey marble. The front of the house was all that was left of the original.

I could see now that the hall wasn't entirely empty. Mr Lover Man and his mate Genghis were hovering.

They didn't look fazed to see me. There was no reaction at all. Frank must have been giving them tutorials.

I nodded a greeting. 'Afternoon, lads.'

I didn't get as much as a blink in return. Genghis just pointed upstairs. I walked across the marble floor to the grand glass and steel staircase.

As I climbed, I began to hear the echo of excited, high-pitched voices. They spoke English with heavy French accents. They were enthusing about how beautiful the new colours would look. I reached the first floor and walked towards the oohs and aahs. I went through large double doors into a high-ceilinged room that could have doubled as a wedding venue. The tall panelled windows overlooked the dog-walkers up on the mountain path.

Swatches of material and big wallpaper folders covered the parquet floor. Frank was wearing jeans that had creases ironed into them, and a white open-necked shirt under a yellow golfer's sweater. He was staring down at the collections of colours and patterns strewn around his feet. Either this was about taking his mind off his troubles, or he was back in Terminator mode.

The high-pitched voices turned out to belong to a man and woman who looked like they should have been on one of those makeover shows. They were talking to each other as if they were the only ones there, and Frank was the film crew.

'Everything looks so wonderful in this light.'

Frank glanced up as I headed towards him. His face said he definitely wasn't as jacked-up about it as they were. Besides, the light was shit: the cloud made sure of that.

He was doing some serious weight training with that platinum Zenith Class Traveller on his wrist. I'd fancied one myself in the Moscow watch shop until I'd seen the price tag. It had no jewels, no glitter; it was just a practical-looking lump of metal with loads of little dials on. I wasn't sure how they justified it being £475K. For that price, it should be making the tea.

Frank followed my gaze. 'You know your time-pieces. I have a passion for them.'

He twisted it to and fro on his wrist. 'But, you know, they're easy to come by. Unlike decent houses under thirty million dollars in this place.' He looked around him. I couldn't tell if he liked it or not.

'You here for the birthday party, Frank? Or is it yours?'

He rested £475,000 worth of watch on my shoulder.

'If so, they say it's costing you five million euros. They also say Cirque de Soleil are being flown all the way from Canada to spin about on a couple of ropes.'

He nodded slowly. I still couldn't work out what was going on in that head of his.

'I'm just a guest. I'm part of the ten per cent of the population who own eighty per cent of the planet. You'd think we'd operate as individuals, but sadly we're just a herd.'

His hand left my shoulder and pointed at nothing in particular in the cavernous room. 'This? I eventually had to get one. We all do.'

He got big smiles from the two as they held squares

of wallpaper against the wall to ooh and aah at. They must have been interior designers.

This was getting us nowhere. I couldn't tell if Frank was putting on a brave face or was simply in denial. Either way, I had to shake him out of it. I needed answers.

I pointed to a door.

3

I led him out into a wide corridor with yet more marble beneath our feet.

'Where's the other Brit from Moscow?'

Frank looked around. He wasn't happy to talk here. To our right were ceiling-high doors that would open into rooms with views of the mountains, trees and snow. He hesitated.

'Does this place have a pool?'

He nodded and started to walk along the corridor. As I followed, my iPhone vibrated in my jeans, but the squeak of my Timberlands on the marble was louder.

At the far end of it we got into a glass and steel lift. He finally spoke. 'The other Brit has gone.' He pressed a button. 'I did not need him any more. He should not have got himself into such a position. Both of them were no good.'

We moved smoothly downwards.

'Why? You sent them to test me. They did.'

Frank stared at the glass wall as we passed the ground floor. 'But not well enough. If they'd been any good, you would have been picked up more easily.'

'But that would have meant I wasn't the man for the job.'

'Correct. But they should have killed you as soon as you put them in danger. Somebody has to lose. Somebody always has to lose.'

The lift stopped. Frank gestured for me to leave first. 'Just be happy it wasn't you.'

The door closed automatically behind him.

'Italian design, German hydraulics. Precision-built houses and Swiss watches, they are very nice things to have, Nick. But there are always better examples. There is always someone in more control than you are. Everyone has a superior.'

His jaw tightened, like he couldn't stomach the thought. Apart from that, his face was impossible to read. Talking about watches, lifts, even his HR concerns – it was like he knew what I'd come to confront him with and was doing everything he could to avoid it.

We walked along a short corridor. Our footsteps began to echo.

'So who's your superior?'

'Vladimir Vladimirovich Putin, prime minister of the Russian Federation, chairman of both United Russia and the Council of Ministers of the Union of Russia and Belarus. A truly powerful man.'

'And who's his?'

'People like me who buy chalets in this village. If he wants to be elected president again.'

As if on cue, Frank threw open another set of doors to reveal a wall-to-wall swimming-pool. It filled the entire footprint of the house. It had been carved out of the mountainside and finished to look like a South Pacific rock-pool. The water was crystal clear. The only evidence of humans ever being near it was a small table. On it lay a colouring book and a set of pencils, and a half-filled-in picture of a pink and yellow fairy.

Frank looked at it and then at me. 'For all that, I'm still being held to ransom by African fishermen. You have news for me, something you want to say.'

It wasn't a question.

'They could still be alive. I heard a recording of Tracy. It wasn't made for me. It was a generic message. "Help us, we're in trouble." This is good news. I could hear vehicles. It means they made it to land safely. But things have gone wrong.'

'How so?'

'The two guys who've been following me since Moscow. The two I thought were yours.'

I told him.

4

His face was stone as he took the information on board. Not even a flicker as I told him Tracy's sister was dead.

'What are you going to do about them, Nick? They are your problem. Mine is Stefan.'

'They Georgians?'

'Possibly. You have been working very hard to find that out about me. Enemies, they breed like rats.'

'So it's also your problem. They must know Tracy and Stefan have been lifted. They must be wondering if they can get to them before you do. Then they become their captives, to be used as leverage against you. No more supporting the south?'

Frank the machine stood still and listened, his eyes unfocused as he stared at the granite wall.

'They must be following me because they don't know which clan have them. They must be hoping I'll lead them to Tracy and Stefan – then they can jump in and grab them from me. That's what I'd do.'

He nodded very slowly.

'But that's not the important thing, Frank.'

He turned his head. His eyes narrowed.

'The important thing is, *how* do they know? Like I said, that's your problem. Was it the crew? The two lads you got rid of?'

He shook his head. 'The crew have been with me for years. They know their lives depend on their loyalty. The other two knew nothing.'

'What about the lads upstairs?'

'They are the only people I trust. They are also god-fathers to Stefan. No, that knowledge has come from elsewhere.' He jabbed a finger at me. 'But that can wait. How much do they want?'

'Three million US.'

He jabbed his finger again. His voice boomed around the granite walls. 'Give them what they want. I want Stefan back here, and safe. I want this ended before anyone else gets to them.'

'No, Frank. That's not how it works.'

His eyes burnt into mine. I wondered when he'd last heard the words 'No, Frank.' I had to get past this alpha-male shit.

He jabbed a third time, his face taut, a natural reaction when people are preparing to fight or just plain scared.

'Do what I say!'

He shouted again, this time so angrily he almost lost it. The sound reverberated like thunder round the pool-room. *'Do what I say! You will pay what they—'*

Mr Lover Man and Genghis pushed their way in, pistols drawn. Frank obviously never raised his voice unless there was a problem.

I stood stock still, arms out, presenting no threat. Frank waved his hands at them. Everything was OK.

They gently closed the doors behind them.

'Frank, I want them back too. Tracy was my best mate's wife. Her sister was my friend. I told you she's dead, but I didn't tell you how she died.'

I reached down and grabbed two of the colouring pencils off the table. I held them either side of his head. 'She had been tortured, Frank. Fuck knows why, because she didn't know anything. Maybe they did it for fun. But they took a pencil just like this and they rammed it into her ear. Right through her fucking eardrum. Can you imagine the pain? Can you imagine how loud she must have screamed? And then they did the same the other side. And when she didn't talk, because she had nothing to tell them, or maybe because they'd had enough fun for one morning, they hammered both pencils right into her brain. She must have died in agony, Frank. You wouldn't wish that on your worst enemy – let alone your son. But fuck this up, and that's what could happen.'

I didn't need to say more. All of a sudden, his imagination had joined the dots. His eye twitched. Well, it was something, I supposed.

He fought to find the words. 'Tell them . . . if they hurt my son, I will declare war on them. Tell them that.'

It was messages like that that would get his son killed.

'No, Frank. This ain't no Swiss watch. All the pieces aren't going to work perfectly. It's not just another deal. And, Frank . . .'

I let it hang as he fixed his eyes on his own reflection in the water.

'I need to know everything. I need to know if there is anything that might affect the negotiation, and so affect Stefan and Tracy. I need to know everything you know, Frank.'

He looked up slowly. Our eyes locked.

'The crew have told you about the two of them together?'

'No. Are they?'

'In all the houses. Even the boat. My shadows, they plant the cameras and collect the recordings for me. No doubt there will still be one on the boat. Knowledge, Nick, is power. Like you, I need to know everything that affects me.'

The chink in his armour was widening, and it wasn't Tracy.

'I want my son back. You do it your way. If it goes wrong, I will do it my way. I will have my son back. I will have my son . . . here . . . with me.'

'And Tracy? Where will she be, when Stefan's here? Does she still have a life if she comes back?'

He pursed his lips. 'I am not an animal, Nick. If I was . . . well, I wouldn't have a problem. Of course she will have a life. She is my son's mother. He has been her saviour.'

His hand came up, pointing back the way Mr Lover Man and Genghis had gone. 'Those two I trust with my life. Others, I pay for their time, nothing else. And you – I believe I can trust you with what you now know. Am I right to trust you, Nick?'

That didn't deserve an answer. 'We start with a

decent sum. Then we move at a slower rate, reducing the amount each time, until we get to around ten per cent of their demand. Say three hundred thousand dollars. No more than four hundred. Less than you paid for that watch. But it's not about the money. It's what they'll expect. If we go big-timing, the three of them are dead.'

I gave him another second. 'Do you have that property for me?'

His eyes were distant again. The machine in his head was telling him what I was saying was right. It just didn't feel right. He turned back to me. 'Yes. Today. You will have the details later.'

'I also need some money. USD.'

He nodded.

'I don't want it in my hand, I just want it available.'

'Whatever you need. When will you inform me what's happening?'

'When I've got something to inform you about.'

I was silent for a moment. 'Where does that leave Justin?'

Frank rubbed the bridge of his nose with his fore-finger and thumb. 'I don't even think about him. He's no good, just like the other two Brits that have worked for me.'

'No – this one's good at his job. He's doing the right thing. He's keeping you out of it and so keeping those two alive. If the Somalis knew who Tracy and Stefan were, it would be a whole different ball game. And if they do find out, they're going to be in even more danger than they are now – because if the Georgians get to hear, we're all in the shit. For now, Justin is keeping them as just another three quick paydays. So he should be paid up and fucked off when he gets back, yeah?'

The machine was a long time processing. I waited till his hand came down.

'Yes, of course. Now, you and I, we both have business to do. Different business.'

The £475K wrist rested on my shoulder again as we made our way to the lift. German hydraulics and Italian design carried us smoothly to the ground floor. His two shadows were waiting. He started leading me to the front door.

'The number you have for me – it will be exclusively for your use. I will always answer.'

We got to the threshold and shook. He turned away. I was to let myself out. He headed for the stairs with Mr Lover Man and Genghis.

I pulled out the mobile. The missed call was from the estate agent I'd bought my Docklands flat from a couple of years ago.

I opened voicemail. 'Mr Stone, it's Henry. Got the message you left mega early about us selling a small apartment of yours. That would be a pleasure. Could you please call me back to discuss?'

By the time I'd finished listening, I'd opened the door. I stepped outside. It was colder. And Jacques was waiting.

5

I jumped into the warmth of the Merc. Jacques was facing the front, being very professional. Mouth shut, both hands on the wheel.

'Tell you what, mate. Drive me down the hill to the town and I'll tell you if the place has got a pool or not. Might as well have a quick look round before I leave – might see something I fancy.'

He nodded. We headed down towards the centre. There was high ground around us; nothing but snow-capped Alps as far as the eye could see. No fast-food joints. No hire shops offering gloves included. The retail names were all the same as in GUM: Prada, Gucci, Versace.

We passed parking areas with coin-operated telescopes on steel stands. In days gone by, the tourists would have looked at the distant peaks or skiers on the pistes. These days they probably gawped at the multi-million-dollar houses and the Russians who stayed in them. That was what I was going to do, anyway.

'Park up here a minute, Jacques. I'll get one last look at the place.'

He pulled into one of the lay-bys and I spilt out. I checked the coin slot. It was two euros for two minutes.

'You got any cash, mate? I'll pay you back when I've been to a bank.'

He pulled out a large plastic bag from a side compartment. 'The parking's very expensive here.'

He passed me the whole thing. Now I knew what the Royal Family felt like when they went walkabout. I threw in ten minutes' worth.

That pink and yellow fairy picture couldn't have belonged to a boy. And if it did, Stefan needed to start playing with Action Man or some shit like that. So there was probably a little girl. And if there was a little girl, there was a mother.

I cast about in the general direction of the chalet. He'd looked bored with the designers. He'd be on the move before long. I moved up the road to the high ground. Chances were, he wasn't down here in the village. This area was for the rich. The super-rich, like everywhere else on the planet, took the high ground – and on the side of the valley where the sun liked to come and stay.

I moved it about until I hit the chalet we'd just left. The Range Rover had gone. Eyes away from the optic, I checked the road left and right. The black blob was heading towards the altiport, contouring one of the higher roads. I shoved in more cash to make sure and followed the road upwards until the Range Rover came back into view.

It disappeared intermittently behind chalets, rocks and trees this side of the road.

It passed a row of four large chalets and this time it didn't reappear. The chalets were monolithic. Their roof overhangs almost came down to the ground. Their gardens sloped downhill towards me.

There were three bodies in the white expanse of garden at the second chalet from the right. Two small figures in pink all-in-one ski suits. I couldn't make out their faces. They jumped on a sledge near the top of the slope. Waiting for them at the bottom was an adult in a white all-in-one. She had long dark hair.

I scanned the four chalets and back along the road to the left. Still no black blob.

The sledge reached the bottom of the hill. The woman started dragging it back up. The kids scrambled behind her in the snow. She stopped in her tracks. I focused on her. She was looking up the hill. She waved. I swung the telescope to follow her gaze. A man in jeans and a red jacket was waving back to her from the veranda.

The kids came into view. They scampered past the woman and up towards the man.

I refocused on him. It was Frank.

The two pink all-in-ones were soon running onto the veranda. Big hugs and kisses followed. The white suit climbed onto the veranda and approached him. She kissed him on the mouth.

The two kids bomb-burst past them. I moved the telescope. Mr Lover Man and Genghis moved into the frame. Genghis pretended to box with them as they jumped up at him.

I now knew the other reason Frank didn't want anyone to know about Tracy and Stefan – including his wife. I'd traipsed around enough galleries and checked out enough Russian family portraits during my culture fest to know about male primogeniture.

The State Tretyakov Gallery was the first place Anna had dragged me to. Sixty-two rooms, 150,000 works of art. That was a week I'd never get back. Most of it was a blur, but it was impossible not to notice that it was all about the boy. The first-born male was top dog, the only one that mattered. The girls could only inherit if there were no males in the way.

Stefan's job would be to continue Frank's newly founded dynasty. He'd be the first of a new generation of Russian billionaires who wouldn't know a lot about the journey their dads had taken out of old Russia, just as the old American robber barons, like the Rockefellers and Vanderbilts, had drawn a veil over what they'd done to trouser their fortunes.

I watched as they disappeared into the chalet, then waited a couple of minutes, but nobody came out again. I jumped back into the Merc and pointed towards the high ground. 'Those chalets up there – are they the rented ones?'

Jacques turned in his seat. 'Yes. For the party. Every hotel in Courchevel is full.'

'Let's get back to the helicopter. But not the way we came. Through the town. Does that work for you?'

'Yes, of course.'

He drove further into the resort.

'By the way, Jacques, aren't you going to ask me?'

'I have a new rule, sir. I only speak when I'm spoken to.'

'Go on. Just this once.'

'Thank you, sir. So, does it have a pool?'

PART SIX

1

Monday, 21 March
15.17 hrs

The din from the Cessna Cargomaster's 675h.p. Pratt & Whitney engine we were almost sitting astride engulfed the cockpit. If it hadn't been for the headphones I was wearing, I wouldn't have been able to hear a word of Joe's rant.

The Indian Ocean was six thousand feet below us. We had another twenty minutes of it at 125 knots before we hit Mogadishu. We'd been following the surf line of the Somali coast north. The country was only a little smaller than Texas, but it had more than three thousand kilometres of coast, about the same as the whole eastern seaboard of the USA. Plenty of space in which to park hijacked shipping, and there was enough of it below. Oil tankers and cargo ships wallowed in the swell. Skiffs were tied up alongside. Rusted wrecks lay on the beach.

The lushness of the Kenyan landscape had been left

behind more than an hour ago. Almost the moment we crossed the border, the terrain had turned to dust. There was nothing but sand and rough old brush as far as the eye could see. Further west was Ethiopia, and more of the same. To the north of Somalia was the Gulf of Aden. The country had a lot of unexploited iron ore, gas and oil. So far, the clans had been too busy making money from the sea, but I was sure it was only a matter of time.

The single-prop Cessna was essentially a flight deck with a great big cargo hold up its arse. FedEx used them in this part of the world because they could handle the rough terrain. Guys like Joe also used them to fly in and out of the worst places in Africa to pick stuff up or drop it off. But unlike FedEx, Joe would never be asking for a signature.

In my door compartment there was a headset extension lead that must have reached all the way down to the aluminium roller shutter that doubled as a cargo door. The shutters were originally devised for freefalling; they were easy to open in flight. So Joe not only dropped off things and bodies, he dropped them into places where landing was clearly a bad idea.

He was from Zimbabwe. His accent was as hard and leathered as his skin. 'Malindi – fucking great, man. I've been there ten years now. Fucking Mugabe is a fucking madman. My farm's been cut up for war veterans. They're kids, man. Never seen a fucking war. They don't even know how to grow shit, let alone fight. I'm fucking glad I'm out of there.'

The rant was just fine. But he'd taken both hands off the stick to add emphasis. At least this particular time he kept one finger fucking about with the instruments.

Joe was heading towards sixty, and small – about five foot five – but with hands that were far too big for the rest of him. Too many years in the sun had given his face crevasses wherever there should have been creases. The chest hair that poked out from the top of his green polo shirt was grey, but the hair on top of his head was jet black. It matched the Ray-Ban Aviators he wore to protect his eyes from the glare bouncing down onto the ocean and back up again.

Malindi is on the Kenyan coast. Europeans used to flock there for their holidays until a couple of years ago, when inter-ethnic violence left a hundred people dead just down the road in Mombasa. Now the hotels were empty, and only people like Joe lived there.

His hands came off the stick again. 'Yeah, man, fuck, I wish I'd left Zim years ago.'

It was the third time he'd said that in the last hour and ten minutes. His wife had wanted to stay, even when Mugabe's heavies were beating up the owners of neighbouring farms. Her roots were in the old Rhodesia. She was fourth-generation white African. Then one day last year Joe had gone away on a work trip and come back to find her dead. It wasn't murder. She'd died of some disease I'd never even heard of. Either that, or Joe had made it up.

He'd finally left the wreckage of Zim, but only with what he stood up in. Life in Kenya was hard to start with, he said, but he was a happy bunny these days. He was one of the vanilla guerrillas, ex-pat white lads who shagged the locals for the price of a beer and something to eat. And going by the condition of the aircraft, his bar tab was bigger than his maintenance bill.

Joe finally got both hands back on the stick and had a look round to make sure there were no other aircraft in the sky. At least that bit seemed professional. Taking off from Malindi, we'd taxied down the apron, but hadn't paused at the runway. There was no revving of engines or testing of flaps or any of that shit. He didn't even appear to consider wind direction. As soon as he was on the strip he just got us the fuck into the air without looking back.

'You been to Mogadishu many times, Joe?'

'Too many. But never in the city, man. I leave you kidnap guys to do that shit. I stay on the pan and don't leave the aircraft. The flip-flops there, they'd pull it apart in an hour.' He leant across to me as if he was about to shout, which he didn't need to because of the intercom. 'You're a fucking madman. Why don't you take a weapon?' His left hand tapped the AK sticking up between our seats, on top of the emergency box that contained distress flares and all that sort of shit. 'Buy mine, man. Three hundred dollars. A fucking bargain, man.'

I laughed. 'It doesn't work like that. I can't go in there mob-handed. I'm supposed to be the nice guy in the middle.'

That was all Joe knew about me. I was just another negotiator he was taking in to rescue yet another hostage. Frank had organized him. Frank had also promised to send some guys with money. They'd be waiting in Nairobi once I'd contacted the clan or sub-clan, whoever the fuck they were, and struck the deal. The money would be handed over anywhere I needed it to be. The clans had people in Nairobi. It could be handed over there, or brought to Mogadishu. Wherever, it didn't matter to me.

Joe was well into war-story mode. 'Last year I picked up some Canadian woman. She couldn't even drink water, man. She was broken. Her hands never stopped shaking. They fucked her up big-time.' He grimaced. 'Fucking flip-flops, man. They're animals. If they don't have anyone else to fight, they fight each other. They just love to fight. It's the clan system. They're fucking mad.'

He eased the stick forward a bit and we were buffeted about as the white sand below us got closer. The ocean was gleaming teal. Breakers formed white crests parallel to the shore.

'Do you know the flip-flops? Do you know the clans, man?'

'I know a bit.'

'They got this saying, man.' His right hand went up into the space between his head and the screen so his fingers could make quote marks. 'My full brother and me against my father. My father's household against my uncle's household . . .' He turned to me and shook his head. 'Our two households against the rest of my kin. My kin against my clan. My clan against other clans. And my nation against the world.'

He laughed to himself. 'It's like the fucking *Sopranos*, but with these fucking things.' He tapped the mag of the AK. 'Go on – two hundred and seventy-five bucks, man.'

'I wouldn't even know how to use it.'

275

He looked ahead. We descended more. He laughed. His left hand waved me off. The crevasses around his cheeks disappeared behind the sun-gigs. 'Fuck off, man. I've seen enough of you guys coming in and out of Nairobi. Don't give me that shit.'

Joe had picked me up in Nairobi. We'd headed east back to Malindi, refuelled, then chucked a left at the coast and headed up towards Mogadishu. He didn't know who I was going in to meet; who I was going in to pick up. And he didn't want to know. That was fine by me.

I reached for the stainless-steel Thermos and unscrewed the top. The coffee was instant, condensed-milky and sweet. I poured a cup and offered it to Joe. He shook his head. He was talking to somebody on the radio and concentrating on the approach.

I rested the cup on my chest while the Cessna shuddered. I closed my eyes, trying to get a little rest. It had been a busy couple of days and the next few were probably going to be worse. I took a sip of coffee as soon as things calmed down again.

It was the second day of Allied air ops over Libya. I'd called Anna from Nairobi to let her know what was going on, and to check she was all right. Everywhere had been bombarded. Syria had been sparking up. I was expecting her to say she wanted to stay on even longer and take in Damascus.

2

The aircraft took another pounding from the wind and Joe sparked up in my headphones. 'It's like a fucking cesspit, man. Look at it.'

I opened my eyes. To the left was desert. To the right was ocean, gleaming in the sunlight. It could have come from a far-away holiday brochure. Unfortunately, stuck between the water and the sand, there were the ruins of Mogadishu. The city looked like a massive black scorch mark. A haze of smog hovered above it.

The airport was at the southern end of the city. The runway was parallel to the sea and almost in it. As we came down through the heat haze I could see that the buildings were all low level, with roofs of Mediterranean tile and rusted tin. Only the mosques seemed taller. Mogadishu, Joe said: the world capital of things-gone-to-rat-shit.

Joe punched a few buttons and flicked a few switches in response to the waffle from the tower. Not that he seemed to be listening. 'Over a million fucking people, man, and every one of them kicking the shit out of each other. Did you know the Brits and Italians ran this place? It was supposed to be beautiful, man. Guys in Malindi remember when it was paradise.'

The area beyond the runway couldn't have been called heavenly. The crumbling grey remains of a concrete pier jutted out into the sea. Ships were anchored behind it for protection. Rusting hulks stuck out of the beach like rotten teeth. Further inland, a shanty town had sprung up. It looked like the world's biggest scrapyard, but not just for the steel.

The aircraft veered left and right as Joe sorted himself out for the landing. Surf broke on beaches that were covered with shit. It reminded me of the ones in Libya. The sea might look inviting but this was no holiday destination. The shoreline was there to launch boats from, but that was it.

I knew a bit about Somalia's history. I knew it had got its independence from Italy in 1960. Power was transferred from the Italian administrators and it became the Somali Republic. There was a lot of socialism going on in Africa in the 1960s. The continent was a proxy area for the Cold War. East and West fought each other for domination. The Soviet Union already had a foothold in the Somali Army, and became the dominant foreign influence in the 1970s. It armed, trained, and gave development assistance. Somalia became very pro-Soviet, as so many other African countries did during that time.

The relationship with the United States was fucked. They suspended aid. Then the infighting began. The Somalis couldn't seem to get away from the model Joe was on about, with everybody at everybody else's throat. There was fighting between clans, between government troops and guerrilla movements, and between the whole country and neighbouring Ethiopia. The war spilt over into northern Kenya. Ineffective government and rampant corruption had put the tin lid on it.

By the late 1970s, the Soviet Union had binned Somalia as well. All of a sudden it had nothing, and people were starving. They had to come creeping back to the West for help. The government was completely fucked. After another round of infighting and civil wars the clans had taken over in 1991. No sooner had they done so than they started to fight each other. In that year alone, hundreds of thousands of Somalis had died. Violence, disease and famine were relentless enemies. Half the children under the age of five died. Forty-five per cent of the population did a runner into neighbouring countries. Of the remaining 55 per cent, a quarter were on the verge of starvation.

Then, in 1992, the USA had stepped in. Operation Restore Hope was where it all began. The infamous Black Hawk Down incident was where it ended. After that, the US withdrew completely and left the country with no hope at all. The clans carried on fighting each other, and I supposed they'd continue until no one was left.

The aircraft bounced across a stretch of dirty, rubber-stained concrete. The sea crashed against the rock defences to my right. Goats tried to pull berries off some scrub to my left.

The terminal was ahead, with the airport's one pan

immediately in front of it. It looked exactly as I was expecting – a low-level, two-storey Soviet-style concrete block. What I wasn't expecting was for it to be in such good condition. The white paint and fields of glass gleamed out at me.

Joe had been waiting for my reaction. 'I know, man – great, isn't it? Until last year it was like the rest of the city. But the UN paid for the place to function.'

A banner below the control tower read: *SKA. Doing a difficult job in difficult places.*

I knew SKA. They were based in Dubai, and also had the contract to try and make Baghdad and Kabul airports function too. I liked the understatement of their message. It was a bit more subtle than *Where there's muck there's brass*, or *Give war a chance.*

I could make out more of the runway once we'd turned and faced back along it. What I'd thought were rocks protecting the edge nearest the sea turned out to be concrete that was crumbling into it. Maybe that would be the next phase of the build.

We taxied closer to the terminal. A ropy-looking Russian airliner stood on the pan. A mass of people huddled with loads of luggage in the shade of the wing. I didn't know if they were getting on or getting off.

Beyond them was an old military hangar. The metal sheeting had been ripped off. The frame was rusty. Inside was an equally rusted-up MiG fighter from the 1960s with a big circular intake at the front. It had probably fought the Americans over the skies of Vietnam. Now it rested on blocks as if the wheels had been stolen.

The revs dropped and the prop slowed as we turned onto the pan. Joe looked around in disgust like it was the first time he'd been here. 'See what you're going into, man. This is the most dangerous city on earth.'

'I know, mate.'

'You sure you don't want the AK? I'll give you the fucking thing. You'll be dead without it.'

I shook my head. 'I'd be dead with it.'

The propeller did its last few revolutions and shuddered to a stop.

'You definitely got my number, man?'

He'd given it to me on a card, made me put it in my iPhone, and even wanted me to hide it in a plastic capsule up my arse.

'Yep, got it.'

'This fucking shit-hole has nine fucking mobile networks. You can call from anywhere in this fucking country, man. Can you believe that? These flip-flops, they can't stop fucking talking, man.'

He nodded at something behind me. 'Good luck.'

I turned to see what he was looking at. Three technicals, two with 12.7mm heavy machine-guns mounted on the flatbeds, were heading our way.

'I've got to pay these cunts three hundred fucking dollars just to land here. My tax to the clan.' He pulled out a brown envelope and passed it to me. 'You give it to the bastards. I hate talking to them. Hopefully see you soon, man. Just remember, don't piss off the flip-flops.'

3

There were six or seven bodies on the back of each wagon, their legs dangling over the sides. A couple of them stood up, manning the machine-guns. The equivalent of our .50 Browning, they could penetrate light armour or the engine block of a truck and punch a hole the size of a man's head in a wall at a thousand metres.

These things were the stock weapon for Africa, South East Asia, Iraq and Afghanistan. The Russians started building them in the 1930s to take Vickers' machine-gun ammo. We'd donated millions of rounds to them during the Second World War to hammer the Germans. They'd carried on making them until the 1980s. Some donations you live to regret.

The sun burnt through my long-sleeved T-shirt and roasted the back of my neck. The Cessna's engine exhaust turned the oven up a few more degrees, as well as filling my nostrils with the stench of Jet A1.

I retrieved my day sack. There was nothing in it but a toothbrush, a solar Power Monkey I'd bought in

Millets, and a plug-in mobile charger. All I had on me was my passport and two thousand dollars in fifties, my goodwill and escape money. I'd taken to wearing my passport and cash like an American tourist in Mexico, in a waterproof pouch around my neck. It made sense. I could always feel it, and never had to worry if my sweat was going to make it soggy.

Joe was still worried. He leant over and shouted, 'You sure you don't want an AK, man?'

I shook my head.

'I'll be standing by for your call. But, fella, be quick making that deal if you want to stay breathing.' He pointed down at the weapon. 'Last chance . . .'

This time I just raised an eyebrow.

'Fucking crazy, man. Good luck!'

I closed the Cargomaster door and he taxied away towards the fuel truck. The driver was beckoning him urgently, like a shopkeeper in a souk – as if Joe had anywhere else to fill up.

Now the smell of engine fuel had gone, another took its place: the sulphurous odour of rotting garbage and burnt rubber. Combined with the heat, it was so minging I could almost taste it.

The technicals were black or maybe blue. It was hard to see under the layers of rust and dust. Arabic music moaned and shrieked out of the two wagons packing the 12.7s.

Most of the heads bobbing around in the back were swathed in multicoloured headscarves, LA-gang style. Some of the legs hanging over the sides were jeaned, some trousered. Others were just bare, with white-chapped knees and scabs. The footwear ranged from trainers to plastic shoes and flip-flops. A mixture of T-shirts, football shirts and charity hand-outs from the disco era completed the cutting-edge Mogadishu look. Some wore canvas chest harnesses over their AC Milan or Newcastle colours; others had just shoved a spare mag into a shirt pocket. Backpacks bristled with RPG rounds.

These lads seemed keener to give each other a hard time than to give me one. There was lots of tooth-sucking and flashing eyes. It took me straight back to my own schoolyard – on the days I bothered to turn up. They weren't happy memories. I used to ask Sharon King out at least twice a week. But I didn't stand a chance. I was white and a minger.

Back in the real world there were two items that they all had in common. The first was an AK. You name the variation and the style, they had it. The second was a pair of outrageous sunglasses. Mirrored, star-shaped, wraparound or John Lennon, China's rejects had found a home here. Elton John and Edna Everage would have been green with envy.

A fair number of them were gobbing off into hand-held radios. Joe was right. They did like to talk. A 1990s Nokia ringtone came to join the party.

Not one of these guys was older than twenty-five. It wasn't because they were early achievers: most of the older ones were probably dead. And they were grinning like idiots. Either they were happy to see me, or high as fucking kites.

What worried me most was that their nervous energy came not from a lack of bravery but too much of it. Their teeth were stained black and orange from a lifetime's *khat*, the chewing leaf of choice. They were probably paid in food and drugs, just like the insurgents in Iraq – or anywhere that needed its warriors to be fed, fearless and fuckwitted.

The boys went quiet as the passenger door opened on the technical nearest to me, the one without a heavy gun. A pair of real leather shoes emerged, then trousers and a clean blue shirt, tucked in but unbuttoned like a 1970s porn star. Their owner unhooked his wraparounds and welcomed me with a Colgate smile and a warm handshake. His fingers and right thumb were ringed with chunky gold.

'Ah, Mr Nick. It's me, Awaale.'

The guy giving a welcome as if we were old mates was about the same height as me, but skeletal – rather in keeping with the *Twilight* accent I'd heard on the mobile. He had deep, hollow cheeks, a goatee perched on his narrow chin, and the air of a man who might have been around since the sixteenth century.

I took my shades off too as he brought his other hand out towards me, but not just to shake.

'Do you have the airport tax, Mr Nick? Otherwise your friend can't take off.'

He held out his left while still shaking my right.

I'd made yesterday's call from Nairobi, something Awaale wasn't expecting. I told him I was sure none of us wanted to waste time, so I would come to Mog and do the deal. He rang back after talking to the boss. He liked the idea. So here I was. What he didn't know was that I was coming to get them out anyway – with or without a smile and a handshake. But this way was better and safer for all of us.

I handed over the envelope. He let go of me so he could open it and start counting. No one was going anywhere until he had the right money. The lads behind him passed around cigarettes and started to waffle into their radios all over again.

There was a burst of automatic fire in the mid-distance, followed by a loud bang less than a kilometre away. The birds jumped out of the trees, but nobody else took a blind bit of notice.

He finished counting and gestured to the double-cabbed technical he'd arrived in. 'It also means that you will not require a visa today.'

I nodded my thanks. 'Am I going to see them now?'

He echoed my smile and patted me on the back like a long-lost mate. He opened the rear door for me. Cold air hit my face.

'Soon, Mr Nick. First we will drink tea and discuss their freedom. You have the money?'

'Some of it. I'm doing my best. The families are doing their best. We've got some money together.'

His grin widened. He knew I was bluffing. There was going to be no three million. We were both playing the game.

I stepped up into the air-conditioned cab.

'Is this the first time you've been to my country, Mr Nick?'

'It's not got the best reputation as a holiday destination, has it?'

He laughed. Shouting at the crews in local, he jumped into the front. The driver wore a green military-style shirt. He turned the wagon in a wide circle and tucked in behind the first technical as it headed past the terminal. The other lads fell in behind us. We had ourselves a convoy.

The dash and steering wheel were covered with cut-to-shape felt to stop them melting in the African sun. The whole cab reeked of cigarette smoke. Every surface was caked with dust and nicotine.

Awaale spoke without looking at me. He just leant back a bit in his seat so he could make himself heard above the music.

'I think you're wrong, Mr Nick. I think we have much here to delight the tourist. I'll show you.' He slapped the driver's shoulder and waffled away in local. The two of them had a good laugh.

'Will I be seeing Tracy, Justin and Stefan today? I need to know they're OK.'

He put up his hand. 'Yes, of course. No problem. But later.'

I leant forward. 'Are they OK? On the recording Tracy said she was ill.'

'Yes, everything is OK. You bring the three million, and you take them home to their loved ones. Easy.'

He planted the mobile in his ear and started waffling. The happy tone had disappeared.

4

The moment we left the airport compound, all I could see was dust, decay and destruction. Even the exit onto the main road was just a bunch of breezeblocks and a pile of sandbags. A couple of lads lazed against them. One sat astride a crumbling wall. All the signs were hand-painted, even the one that said *Security*. Nobody gave a fuck.

We turned onto a wide boulevard. I couldn't tell which side of the road they drove on here. Nor could the driver. We bumped over the remains of the central reservation and continued into the face of the on-coming traffic. Mountains of festering rubbish and the rusted remains of burnt-out vehicles lined each edge of the crumbling tarmac.

Coming towards us were four green Russian BTR armoured personnel carriers, their massive petrol engines belching out clouds of exhaust. Lots of helmeted heads stuck out of the tops.

No one gave the eight-wheeled monsters a second glance as they moved off to the side of the road and stopped. We carried on past. The black stencilling on the sides told me they were UN troops from Uganda. Not that I could see any troops any more. The helmets had dropped down into their APCs, only popping up again once we had passed.

Awaale tapped my shoulder as I peered back through the cab's rear glass. 'They are no trouble, Mr Nick. They just want to go home to their wives and not die in the dust.'

He sat back and he and the driver had a laugh at Uganda's expense.

Any building that was anything more than a shell or a heap of grey rubble looked like it still had people living in it. The ads on their walls had either faded or been shot away by AK and 12.7 rounds.

Every open space was clogged with makeshift shelters, round stick huts covered with layers of rags, or shacks made of scraps of wood and rusted wriggly tin.

I saw now where the smog came from. Tyres were burning everywhere, sending plumes of black smoke over the low rooftops.

The pavements were filled with people just lounging about, doing nothing. What was there to do? Most of the women were *burqa*'d up in black or bright orange, with scabby kids at their heels. Old men in loose cotton skirts and worn-out plastic sandals crouched in the uneven shade of the acacia trees. The Italians must have planted them years ago, and they still hadn't quite given up the struggle. Telephone poles leant at crazed angles, with a metre or so of wiring hanging loose.

There were a few vehicles on the road but nothing to slow us down. A wagonload of goats had nothing on a 12.7mm machine-gun. Every single wall was pitted by strike marks from RPGs or rounds. After years of fighting the government, the Americans and finally each other, the whole place was shot to fuck. And the red desert continued trying to reclaim the city for itself.

Awaale was still gobbing off into his mobile. He was happier now. I could see the old smile on his lips in the rear-view mirror. Before long he placed a Marlboro from the pack in his shirt pocket between them and lit up. The wagon bumped up and down, almost in time with what sounded to me like the same never-ending song on the radio.

Cars and pickups suddenly crammed the streets. Rusty trucks leaking diesel and minging old French saloons from the 1970s rubbed shoulders with brand new Mercs. Famine or feast: this was more like the Africa I knew. Kids darted down alleyways, their runny noses clogged with dust. Meat hung from street stalls, swarming with flies. Bored-looking men and women squatted beside piles of bruised fruit at the roadside. One guy under a beach parasol sold nothing but batteries.

The buildings were in better condition here, and slightly more substantial: two, three and four floors, with air-conditioners humming on the outside walls. Water streamed from the units, staining the already badly stained white paintwork. It wasn't the only clue that this part of town was where the money hung out. The ads here weren't faded and the latest BlackBerrys and iPads were on display in the shop windows.

Metres from the brand new Mercs in the traffic, guys sat in old armchairs with weapons across their knees. They were probably guarding the *hawala* brokers. Most people here depended on money from relatives overseas to survive. A million Somalis had fled the country. Between them, they sent home about two billion dollars a year to the poor fuckers they'd left behind. I wondered whether Ali in Barratt Street had a slice of this action.

The lads in the armchairs weren't short of competition. Every man in sight was toting some form of eastern-bloc AK or light machine-gun. The really flash boys carried RPGs in their ancient canvas day sacks.

5

Stopping and starting every ten seconds, we ground our way through the chaos. The driver of the technical in front eventually got bored and his gunner, who had the best sun-gigs of all – massive blue mirrored stars with white frames – raised the weapon and loosed off two long forty-five-degree bursts. The moment people realized they weren't under attack they just got on with their lives again, but the birds didn't come back in a hurry.

We bounced from pothole to pothole. My head shunted left and right. Awaale closed down his phone and slid it under his Marlboros. His eyes scanned left and right as we picked up speed.

'Where are you from, Mr Nick?'

'London. What about you? Where did you learn such good English?'

'With my father.' He pointed beyond the huge snake of illegal wiring that hung from pole to pole across the street, towards a five-storey building with shuttered windows. The wall facing us had a large painting of a TV, and next to it the words *VIP Institute*.

'Look, Mr Nick. Do you know what that building is?'

'I guess it must be where we're going to meet Tracy and the other two.'

He tilted his head towards the driver and told him of my stupidity. He had to shout over the music. They both had another chuckle.

'No, Mr Nick. That's the Olympic Hotel. Black Hawk Down – have you seen the movie? My father – he's famous.'

'I haven't, but I know the story.'

We came level with the building. A leaking pipe had filled the ruts in the road with water. Dogs lapped at it like they hadn't drunk for days.

'This is where the attack started. The Americans came to capture General Aidid, but it was a trap. The general was a great man.'

The driver had started scanning left and right as well. The lads on the back were edgy. Everyone was on his toes.

'You know about General Aidid and the trap?'

I nodded. General Mohammed Farrah Aidid hadn't actually been a general but the clan warlord who'd controlled the city back in 1992. Operation Restore Hope hadn't been designed as America's biggest gangfuck since their failed attempt to rescue hostages from their Tehran embassy in 1980. It was intended to relieve the famine by securing a corridor for the aid to get through. The clans had carved up the country for themselves. With no overall government or structure, the whole country was dying of starvation. The aid convoys were hijacked. The clans fed themselves and their machine, just like Joe's mate Mugabe was still doing in Zimbabwe. Control the food and you control the people.

The Americans began to make headway. By 1993, the famine was winding down. George Bush Senior came to witness their success for himself. US forces were looking to leave, and undergoing a lengthy hand-over to the UN. The Pakistani Army and a handful of others flew in, ready to continue the good work. But there was a problem. Aidid was pissed off at being marginalized by the rest of the clan leaders. He decided he was going to show everyone who was boss. In June that year twenty-four Pakistani UN soldiers were ambushed and massacred. Some were disembowelled; others had their eyes gouged out.

Suddenly the Americans were no longer on a humanitarian mission. They were at war. The soldiers who'd come to feed the hungry were back in combat. The next few months became one long street battle. Casualties on both sides were high.

The US's resolve weakened. They looked for an exit. On 3 October they thought they had the answer. They'd received information that Aidid was holed up in the Olympic Hotel. Delta Force – the D Boys – assaulted the building. It was an ambush. Two Black Hawks were taken down by RPGs in the middle of the city. Firefights kicked off as US forces tried to extricate the aircrew. Nineteen US soldiers were killed and eighty-four wounded, along with an unconfirmed number of clan fighters. The Americans said more than a thousand; the clans said 113.

The world didn't see the street fighting and the casualties. They saw a Black Hawk pilot being dragged through the streets in his underpants with ropes round his ankles. It played for days on CNN and all the national outlets. Bill Clinton had taken over from Bush Senior. He couldn't understand how a humanitarian operation had turned into a complete disaster. He ordered US forces out. And he was wary of helping anyone again. That was why the Rwanda genocide was allowed to happen in 1994, and the Srebrenica massacre in 1995. Nobody in the White House wanted another dead American dragged through the streets of a foreign city.

We bounced past the hotel and off the main drag, through a rotting labyrinth of muddy stone rag-covered huts. Hundreds of thousands of human beings existed here and mangy dogs skulked in the shadows. Kids with misshapen heads and contorted limbs haunted the irregular dirt streets and cactus-lined paths, massive growths hanging from their bodies.

High-voltage cables sagged dangerously low across the gaps between tin-roofed dwellings. The whole place was strewn with rubble, fetid rubbish and, of course, burning tyres.

Rubble, rubbish and yet more smoking tyres lay around a large man-made mound about two hundred metres away, on top of which stood a lone shack with a cart outside. The king must have lived there.

The locals melted away as soon as they saw the technicals screeching to a halt. Faces appeared at the grilles of old steel doors. A dog barked at the tailgate of the wagon in front of us and was soon kicked away by one of the lads in trainers.

Awaale leapt out. 'Mr Nick, come.' He motioned for me to follow. Kids screamed on either side. We walked down a narrow alley. The traffic noise became a distant hum. Birds twittered. It was almost like a Sunday stroll, until a distant burst of automatic fire broke the spell.

'Where are we going?'

'I want to show you what the tourists are missing.'

6

We found ourselves beside four single-storey houses that had been blasted and burnt out years ago. In their midst stood a copse of bright green cactuses about the size of a tennis court. They were just over head height, some with bright red flowers.

Awaale stood there proudly. 'This place, my father made it famous.'

I knew I should have been admiring his dad's cactus allotment, but I couldn't help myself. 'You think tourists would flock here to look at this? Awaale, I don't have the time, mate. I really need to see Tracy and—'

His hand came up.

I was pissing him off. I needed to wind my neck in.

'All in good time, Mr Nick. Look more closely.' He bent from the waist and I followed suit. He pointed. 'Lower.' It was definitely a command, not a request. I knelt in the sand. Under the canopy of spikes I could now see curls of razor wire, guarding a profusion of twisted metal shapes. Then I spotted US Army initials, black on dark green.

The carcass of a Black Hawk.

'Your father . . . ?'

'My father shot this down. It was the first. My dad is famous.'

He turned and shouted, and one of the lads came running over with an RPG launcher.

'He used one of these.' He rested the weapon on his shoulder and pointed it at the sky. 'My father – a great man.'

I looked back at the wreckage under the cacti. A multi-million-dollar machine, taken out by a $310 kick up the arse.

The Black Hawks had flown low over the city with snipers on board to support the attack on the Olympic Hotel. The intelligence guys had determined that RPGs did not represent any air-defence threat. They thought that if you aimed the weapon into the sky, like Awaale was doing, the back blast would hit the ground and take out the firer – and no way would the clans fire it from a rooftop because they would be spotted immediately and hosed down. But Aidid knew better – and he knew that the best way to hurt the Americans was to shoot down their helicopters. The Black Hawks were like the Apaches in Afghanistan – the symbol of the US's power and the clans' helplessness.

Aidid had planned his ambush well. He had smuggled in Islamic fundamentalist soldiers from Sudan who'd fought against Russian Hind gunships in Afghanistan. They showed men like Awaale's dad how to modify the RPG so they could fire from the street. All they had to do was weld some curved piping on the end to deflect the back blast – adding that extra ten dollars to the original $300 cost.

Something else. RPG grenades burst on impact, so it's hard to hit a fast-moving target with one. The 'advisers' fitted the detonators with timing devices to make them explode in mid-air. That way, they wouldn't need a direct hit to bring down a Black Hawk. The *mujahideen* also taught Awaale's dad and his mates that the heli's tail rotor was its most vulnerable spot. They taught them to wait until the Black Hawk passed over, and to shoot up at it from behind.

The whole operation to capture Aidid from the Olympic Hotel had been supposed to take no more than thirty minutes, a typical enough time for an SF op. Instead, once this Black Hawk had come down, it had spiralled into eighteen hours of urban combat, as US units tried to fight their way in to rescue the crews and shooters. Then another $310 dollars' worth brought down a second Black Hawk, and the nightmare was complete. Two posthumous Congressional Medals of Honour, the equivalent of our VC, were awarded for that night's action. Aidid wasn't touched. It wasn't until three years later that he was killed in the city during a clan battle.

I stood up and brushed the sand off my hands. 'Where's your dad now? Is he still alive?'

'He's a taxi driver in Minneapolis.'

'You went with him?'

He nodded.

Now I knew where the accent came from. The US had stopped their aid to Somalia, but they hadn't turned their back completely. As the cactus allotment sprouted and grew, the US had opened its borders to refugees, especially the educated or moneyed ones. The vast majority of them joined their mates in Minneapolis. Before long, it was the biggest Somali population on the planet outside Somalia itself. Even Easton couldn't compete.

I stood there as the RPG was handed back. If Awaale was telling the truth, the guy who took down the first Black Hawk was now driving Americans home from the airport. I guessed his war stories weren't part of his cabbie chat.

'Why are you smiling, Mr Nick?'

'You must be very proud.'

'Sure I am.'

There were shouts. He looked away sharply. The smile dropped from his face. He shouted back.

'We have to go, Mr Nick.'

He didn't wait for my answer. He was already legging it towards the technical. I didn't need to know what the fuck was going on. All I needed to know was that if he was running, then so was I.

7

The crews were getting sparked up, but it wasn't because they were scared. It was worse than that. They were almost hyperventilating with excitement.

I heard screams and wails from inside nearby buildings. The people who'd run back into their homes knew what was about to happen.

We jabbed down a series of narrow alleys. He was too busy yelling at his crews to pay any attention to me. None of them was taking cover.

The shadows from our left were lengthening, but I could still just about see what was happening in the gaps between buildings. There was around an hour until last light.

The crews were more sparked up by the minute. They hollered at each other and into their radios and mobiles. Whoever it was they were talking to, it was one big frenzy of *khat*, adrenalin and testosterone.

I had to shout over the din: 'Awaale, what is happening?'

I'd ducked into a doorway on the left-hand side of

the alley, for all the protection that was going to give me. I banged my back against a steel door that was well and truly bolted.

Awaale waffled away on his radio on the opposite side of it. He raised a hand to shut me up.

A technical that I hoped was ours stopped two blocks down, at the junction with what was left of a real road. Its gun pointed down the main drag left and started to pump out rounds.

Everybody jumped about and took up very bad fire positions on the crossroads. The whole world went noisy. The crews stuck their weapons round corners and brassed up who knew what. They were spraying half of Mogadishu.

Some of the lads darted across the road, firing from the hip. One tripped, lost a flip-flop, rolled, fired, got up and carried on running. The home team whooped and cheered. One even took a picture with his camera phone. I wondered if it would turn up on Facebook. Another couple of boys got into decent firing positions on the building corner, loosed off a burst each, then stopped and pulled out the Marlboros. They took a few drags, stuck their weapons round the corner again, and had another cabbie.

Fuck knows where the other two technicals had gone. With luck, they'd stayed close. I needed them to get me to wherever Tracy and the others were being held.

A guy with an RPG tube jumped off the back of the technical I could see. He stepped out into the open ground of the junction and fired, then came running back. Everyone else just watched and smoked. Why he couldn't fire from cover, I wasn't sure.

I heard a rumble, very close, followed by the rattle of a 12.7. I hoped it was one of ours.

Over to my half-left, a green tracer round bounced off the concrete and spun up into the air. I watched the propellant burn out. They were firing at something, but I didn't have a clue what. The noise was deafening. Both the technicals opened up again. Another RPG whooshed away.

I ran across to Awaale. 'We've got to go, mate. I've got people to see. We can't make them wait for ever.'

He took no notice. Everyone was gobbing off on the radio, shouting and pointing at everybody else.

The second technical appeared. It drove up the road towards us, inches of clearance each side, braked and reversed back. The lad cracked off with the gun down one of the alleyways. Total fucking chaos. No one in control. Everyone was doing their own thing.

But we had incoming for sure. Strikes were tearing the rendering off the buildings around the junction.

There was another loud whoosh over to my far left. An RPG round piled straight up the main drag, passed the junction and kicked off into something further down. There was the mother of all explosions. A cloud of dust and debris plumed a couple of blocks away and rained down on the wriggly-tin roofs.

There were whoops of laughter.

'Awaale, what the fuck are we doing?'

He looked at me like I was a madman. 'We're fighting, Mr Nick! We're fighting Lucky Justice. We must always fight his clan. This is our city. This is the general's city. My father is famous here.'

All well and good, but Awaale's dad, very sensibly, was eight thousand miles away.

I ran over the sand gap and grabbed Awaale, pulling him into a doorway. A dog went ballistic the other side of the steel. I gripped Awaale to make sure I had his attention. If the crews wasted much more ammunition and Lucky's didn't, this wasn't going to end well.

'You can fight them whenever you want, mate. I need to see my friends. I need to pay you some money. That's why we're here, remember? We've got to move on.'

Awaale was too busy playing field commander. 'Yes, yes. Soon.' He got straight onto his radio. Fuck knew if anybody was listening.

The air was suddenly full of ringtones. The lads reached for their mobiles. Four of the crew were running from the left of the junction. They must have been from the third technical. They were carrying a body. It was a waste of effort. Even from where I was, I could see he was dead.

8

A couple of guys loosed off more RPGs down the road. They weren't exactly aiming with pinpoint accuracy. They had them on the shoulder for less than a second. They just stepped out of cover and pulled the trigger.

The 12.7 had now moved into the open and was static at the junction. The gunner couldn't control it. Tracer rounds started horizontal, then shot into the air, arcing towards an imaginary Black Hawk.

More of Awaale's boys took up positions behind the vehicle. If the general had taught them all they knew, no wonder he was dead: that just concentrated fire; the enemy had something to aim at. If these jokers reckoned 10mm of steel was going to stop them, then the *khat* must be even stronger than I'd thought. Vehicles give cover from view, not cover from fire.

More rounds ripped up the road towards the technical, striking the buildings around the junction. An RPG followed, this time much higher. Its smoke trail was three metres above the technical. Then another. No one took cover. I watched it bounce and skid across the road before exploding just out of sight.

Our technical decided to come back into cover. I didn't have a clue where the other two were. I gripped Awaale again. This was a Mexican stand-off, but without the Mexicans. 'Awaale, are we going to stay here until we run out of ammunition? Or we're all dead? How's it work, mate?'

He gobbed off into his radio yet again. No one answered. The dog was going ape-shit behind the door. His claws scrabbled at the steel like a maniac's. A radio playing Arabic music was turned up to full blast.

'Awaale, mate. Stop. Look at me. I can help you. Do you want to show what a great fighter you are? Like your father?' I didn't wait for an answer. 'Let me take a machine-gun up there.' I pointed behind the house, to the high ground beyond the Black Hawk Down site. 'I'll go and find out exactly where Lucky's crew are. I'll tell you – then I can give you covering fire so you can move round and get to them. OK? So we can get this over. You can slot them, then we can move on.'

His radio moved down to his chest.

'Come with me.' I got on my knees. Now we were level with the dog, it went berserk. 'Look, this is how we can do it.'

'How – how?'

I smoothed out a patch of sand and traced a cross with my finger to show the junction. I jabbed it at the left-hand end of the horizontal line. 'That's where we are now, yeah?'

'OK.'

'And Lucky's somewhere up here . . .'

'Sure. We're going to kill him.'

I outlined my plan of action and explained how we should each stay out of the other's arcs of fire. He looked at me like I'd shown him the secret of the universe. 'Mr Nick, this is so good.'

I nodded. 'But we must go before it gets dark. Give me a radio that works. Give me that one. You grab another one off one of the guys. Bring the technicals here. Tell them I'm in charge of this one, OK?'

'OK, OK.' He sprang up, ready to swing into action.

I grabbed his leg. 'Do the drivers know where to go next? I need to get those hostages home.'

'Yes, yes.' He was out of my grasp and running.

Great. If this all went to rat-shit, at least I'd have a wagon to take me to the meeting. Now I just wanted to get on with it, one way or another, before we were here all fucking night.

9

It wasn't long before the technical that had been firing hurtled towards me. The gunner held on for dear life as it lurched across the potholes, sending up a huge cloud of dust in its wake. I couldn't even see the junction any more.

I waved it down just in time. It was going far too fast. By the crazed expression in the driver's eyes he wouldn't have stopped much before Malindi.

I opened the door. 'Speak English?'

The guy was totally off his tits. I checked behind. The gunner was much the same. I showed them Awaale's radio. 'Let's go.'

The driver's eyes rolled. 'Radio, radio!' He pointed down. There was already one in the foot-well, another 1990s job, the size of a house brick. Maybe Awaale had thrown it in.

I pressed the red tab on mine. 'Awaale, Awaale . . .'

Whoever was at the other end clicked on and the line went live with gunfire. Awaale shouted in the background and I heard giggling. Then it clicked off.

I tried again. 'Awaale!'

There was a rustling sound. 'It's me, Mr Nick. I'm here, I'm here.'

'Good man. Wait until I get up into the high ground. As soon as I start firing, you get your crew to move to the left of the junction and come up level with them. Once you're there, you tell me, OK? Do you get that, Awaale?'

'Yes, yes, Mr Nick, no problem.'

'Good.'

'Yes, yes. OK.' The radio went dead.

I motioned the driver out of the way, into the passenger seat. 'Come on mate.' I smiled. 'Chop-chop.'

I piled back down towards the Black Hawk monument and up the track behind it, towards the little shack on the high ground. The sun was low, casting really long shadows. Half an hour max till last light.

I slowed as I neared the top of the mound. Fuck the other technical. It was too complicated with these guys out of their skulls. I had one vehicle: let's get on with it.

I started to crest the mound. I wanted to see just enough of the ground below us for the 12.7 to have muzzle clearance with nothing else exposed. We'd present too good a target otherwise.

I manoeuvred into position to the right of the shack, jumped out and moved forward in a crouch.

I pressed the red tab. 'Awaale, Awaale, I've got them. I can see where they are.'

'Where are they? Where are they?'

'Whoa . . . Where are you?'

'We're at the junction. We're waiting.'

'OK. Can you hear me clearly, Awaale? Can you hear me?'

He was shouting over the gunfire. I could see muzzle flashes in the distance as Lucky's gang kept giving it some in the ever-darkening gloom.

'I hear you.'

'OK. From the crossroads, if you go up five blocks – repeat, five blocks – you'll come to another intersection, and that's where they are. I can see one technical – repeat, one technical – with a heavy gun onboard. But it's not being used, Awaale. It's just parked up. I'm just seeing small-arms fire. Do you understand that?'

I got nothing back.

'Awaale? Awaale?'

'Yes, I understand, Mr Nick.'

'OK. As soon as I start firing, you start to move on the left-hand side of the road. They're five blocks away.'

No reply.

'Awaale?'

No reply. Fuck it. I went to the wagon, jumped onto the back and started shouting at the gunner. I pointed down to the thin green tin boxes of ammunition. 'You load, yeah?' I mimed putting one onto the weapon.

The boxes held about fifty rounds each. That was what they normally came with, anyway. Fuck knew what was going on here. There were about twenty-five rounds hanging from the weapon and onto the steel floor. Empty cases were scattered all over the place. I kicked them out of the way with my Timberlands so I could get a firm, stable firing platform.

The firing mechanism was a really old one: two

wooden handles on metal frames with a paddle in between. I didn't bother to check if the safety was on. For sure it wasn't.

The circular spider-web sight was the kind normally fitted for anti-aircraft work. I lined it up with the foresight on the junction five blocks up. I caught a couple of muzzle flashes and kicked off a three-round burst. The rate of fire was slow. The gas regulator must have been closed down too far. Or, more likely, clogged up with carbon because it was never cleaned.

The next burst included two tracer. They zinged into a wall just left of the junction, where I'd seen bodies taking cover. I quickly checked the belt. It was running fine. The green tip on every fifth round was tracer.

I kicked off at the junction itself. Five-round bursts, trying to control the amount of ammunition I was using, and also to keep the fucking thing on aim. The mount wobbled; it wasn't bolted in properly.

Pointing down at the next ammo box, I swivelled the gun left and right. I couldn't see any movement.

I got on the radio as the lads started to load it up. 'Awaale?'

Still nothing.

'Move, mate. Awaale, move.'

Two or three seconds later I heard the scream of engines. A cloud of dust billowed above the sea of wriggly tin and moved towards the junction. If Lucky Justice hadn't known where our technicals were, he did now. All Awaale needed to throw in was a bugle call and the fucking cavalry charge was complete. None of this stealth, getting right on top of the target nonsense: they were just going for it.

10

The leading technical, flatbed heaving, came briefly into view through a gap between the shacks. At least they were outside my arc of fire. I lost them again almost immediately. Every time I saw muzzle flashes, I'd put in a three- to five-round burst. I watched the tracer's gentle arc towards the target, 350 metres away at the most. I put another five rounds into the junction. And then another.

'Mr Nick, Mr Nick?' Awaale was back on the net.

I couldn't respond. In all the excitement, he'd kept his finger on the pressle. All I could hear was his engine gunning. I had to wait for him to release it.

'Mr Nick, Mr Nick?' This time he remembered.

I hit the red tab. 'Yes, Awaale, yes. Where are you?'

The driver had jumped out, and he was having a go at the targets with his AK. He fired big long bursts, which kicked off in all directions, mostly into the air. He didn't give a fuck: he was just going for it.

'Where are they, Mr Nick? Where are they?'

I peered into the gloom. He could be anywhere. There were dust-clouds all over the place.

'Stop, Awaale. Stop. Can you hear me? *Stop.*'

I clicked off.

'OK, we've stopped. Where are they? Where are they?'

'Calm down, mate. Wait, wait . . .'

I wanted him to take a breath, and then we could move from there. 'Where are you, Awaale?'

'I don't know . . .'

They'd gone careering off without a clue.

'OK. Fire your machine-gun in the air. When I see your tracer I can direct you.'

I got nothing back.

'Awaale?'

Five or six tracer suddenly blossomed fifty metres short of the junction, three blocks in on the left.

'Good. I want you to turn directly towards the road. They're very close to the junction. Is that clear?'

I had to shout so loudly I almost didn't need the radio. The gunner was going ape-shit on the 12.7. The driver was going ape-shit on his AK. Three empty magazines lay at his feet. Only he knew who or what he was aiming at. If, indeed, he was aiming at all.

I looked up. There was another *whoosh* from the junction. I could see the smoke trail heading our way. I threw myself to the ground just as the thing exploded. It had landed in front of the shack. An old guy burst out of the door, screaming like a banshee. He legged it down the other side of the mound and kept on running. I didn't blame him.

Dust and stones showered down on us.

I got back on the radio. 'Awaale?'

'Yes, Mr Nick.'

I could hear the engines gunning; everybody shouting.

'Awaale? *Awaale?*'

Nothing.

'I'll keep firing until you get to the crossing. All right? I'll fire until you get to the road. Awaale? Can you hear me?'

There were shouts from the two lads behind me. I jerked my head round and scanned the junction. A couple of bodies were sprawled in the dust. They'd got a couple of kills.

I bunched my fists, as if gripping the firing handles. 'Keep going, boys, keep firing . . .'

I sparked up the radio again. We just needed the Benny Hill music for this performance to be complete. 'Awaale?'

Tracer stitched its way across Lucky's position as Awaale's team blasted straight through the intersection like a demented cavalry charge, bouncing over the two bodies as they went.

I jumped back onto our flatbed, took over the gun and directed rounds towards Lucky's side of the junction, into walls and roofs and the shells of ruined buildings, wherever I saw anything moving.

Lucky's technical emerged from cover to take Awaale head-on. Awaale's driver spun his wheel so the boys behind the cab could lay down fire without zapping him and the boss if their barrels dipped.

I punched three-round bursts into Lucky's metalwork from my vantage-point. The tracer burrowed into the dirt, burning for a couple of seconds until it died. His gunner didn't hang around. He leapt off the back and legged it before he got the good news. The driver slumped motionless against the steering wheel.

I gave it one more burst in case any of his mates were still inside. Fuel must have been leaking from a ruptured tank. The tracer ignited it. The whole area was suddenly a riot of yellow and orange. Lucky's infantry turned and fired back from the flickering shadows.

Instead of standing back in case they were needed, Awaale's second technical rumbled forwards and kept right on going. The only area that didn't get raked with fire was the ground beneath the gunner's feet.

I kept my fire to the right, taking on any hint of enemy movement. There was shit on down there but no one cared. Both sides fired like gangsters, side on, with their AKs in the air. I stopped and let them get on with it. My nose filled with the stink of cordite. The barrel was smoking hot.

I clambered down and waved at the driver and his sidekick. 'Let's go, lads. Chop-chop.' I clapped my hands. We had to move on. I had a meeting to go to.

I climbed into the cab. My two new recruits hauled themselves onto the flatbed.

We thundered down the hill. It was well past time to get the fuck out of there and get on with my day job. We closed on the killing zone. I drove past the door-way where I'd gripped Awaale. I made a left turn at the junction, slow and wide enough to make sure the gun had enough play to point where it was most needed. I thrust my hand out of the window and gesticulated wildly. 'That way, mate. That way.' I doubted he'd hit anything, but at least he wouldn't be aiming at me.

We spotted his crew almost immediately. They were dragging three bodies from behind a wall. They shared the cigarettes they'd lifted from the dead men's pockets and loaded Lucky's weapons onto the unarmed technical.

Awaale was nowhere to be seen. I started flapping. If I lost my English speaker, I was fucked. I picked up the handset. 'Awaale. Where are you, mate? We're back at the junction. Where are you?'

Silence.

'Awaale?'

Then I heard my own voice coming from the burnt-out shell of a building.

11

He clambered out of what had once been a window. He was a very happy boy. 'We killed some, Mr Nick, and the others turned and ran. No Lucky Justice, but this is still a good day. We'll do this again. And again. Lucky's crew will get the message. The general's crew are back in town.'

He thrust up his bloodstained palm, inviting me to give him a high-five through the window. I fucking hated high-fives.

'You're right, Awaale. If Lucky's still alive, you can see why he was given the name. Now, can we go and see my friends? I really need to know they're safe.'

His boys were busy mutilating the bodies with knives, rocks, and then a burst of AK for good measure. The corpses were left behind; they were the message Awaale was talking about.

I slipped into the back of Awaale's technical. Awaale wiped his hands clean on his trousers and resumed his place in front. Music blared from every cab. AK rounds stitched another message into the sky. Every mobile within reach sparked up, in case anyone hadn't already heard the news.

As the lead wagon joined the celebration, green tracer snaked from the muzzle of its 12.7. The gunner lost control as they bounced back through the potholes and pummelled the buildings 400 metres away.

Awaale didn't seem to mind. 'Mr Nick, that was good, yes? We kicked the ass, oh, yes indeed.' He pulled the Marlboro pack from his sweat-soaked shirt and offered me one. When I shook my head he slapped the driver gleefully on the shoulder. He laughed, and his white teeth gleamed.

Everybody had had a great night out. Well, apart from the lad whose body now lay on the flatbed behind us. There was a curious innocence to their violence. There was no anger. They seemed to bear no hatred towards Lucky's crew. Killing and maiming wasn't an outrageous act to them. It was what they did. It was all they knew. They had no boundaries. And that was what made them so dangerous.

I leant forward. 'You did really well, Awaale. I think your father will be very proud of you.'

'I know. I know he will be.'

He pulled out his mobile, hit the speed dial and was soon waffling away. He sounded as excited as a child. I didn't need to be a Somali speaker to understand the facial expressions and the *boom-boom-boom*. There were nods of agreement from the driver, and I twice heard my name.

Awaale turned to me with the world's biggest grin and handed me the phone. 'It's my father, speak to him.'

'What's his name?'

He looked puzzled. 'Awaale, of course.'

Of course.

To start with, I could just hear a female voice announcing that the Northwest flight from Chicago had been delayed. Minneapolis was eight hours behind. It must have been about midday there.

'Hello, Mr Nick. My son tells me that you have helped him to do great deeds today. You've made me a very proud father.'

'Thank you.'

'You're there to buy back your loved ones, yes?'

'Yes. I'm hoping your son will be able to help me. Maybe you can too. One of them is the wife of a dead warrior. One of them is a small boy, a little boy. I know you're a brave man, a famous man here in this city. Will you be able to help me?'

The Tannoy came to his rescue. The Jet Blue from LaGuardia had landed.

'Mr Nick, I have to go. My passenger has arrived. Please tell my son I love him.'

He rang off. I passed the phone to Awaale. 'Your father says he loves you.'

'I know. I love him too. He's a great man.'

It was smiles all round in the front of the cab as we drove past the Olympic Hotel. The streets came alive with movement and light. Everybody had a weapon. It was like we'd just come back from a carnival, all on a high, and we were the three winning floats.

12

We were soon passing the airport. The same guards sat on the wall and smoked under the hand-painted sign. They didn't even look up as our convoy drove by. See no evil, hear no evil, speak no evil was the secret of survival round here.

Only the shells of once-great buildings remained each side of the boulevard. In this part of town, even the trees were fucked. Maybe this was what the Italian Riviera would have looked like if it had been carpet-bombed in the Second World War. This had to be the old city, where the Italians and other ex-pats had hung out on the beach in their all-in-one bathing suits in the 1920s. Now there wasn't even a dog to be seen. It was a ghost town.

We bounced over mortar craters and potholes, slaloming to avoid big lumps of concrete picked out by our headlamps. They provided the only source of light in this part of town.

Awaale started gobbing off on his mobile again. I wasn't sure how anyone would hear anything that was being said. The driver waffled away. The music blared. Awaale closed down and shouted, 'Nearly there, Mr Nick.'

We bumped over what was left of the central reservation, down a side road and into a large square with an empty concrete plinth at its centre. It would once have borne a statue of a Somali puppet dictator or an Italian general with a hat full of plumes. Bodies were silhouetted against the flames of a fire beside it.

As we got closer, I saw we were inside a compound of sorts. Stacks of tyres filled the missing doors and windows of a large colonial building. There was movement inside.

There was no gate. There wasn't even a barrier into what looked like the coach entrance for this grand building. The wagon stopped next to four or five other pickups and cars. Burnt-out vehicles littered the area.

Awaale was already out of our wagon before the technical behind us had stopped. He sounded excited. 'Come, Mr Nick. Now it is your time. Come.'

I followed him inside. It must have been a hotel once. A lobby the size of a football pitch opened onto a pair of sweeping staircases that, like everything else around here, had seen better days. The place had been stripped of everything that wasn't nailed down. The glass in the windows had gone. Wiring had been pulled. There wasn't a door in sight. Everything transportable had probably been sold as scrap or used to build the shacks we'd spent the afternoon beside. I was getting used to the smell: decomposing rubbish and burning rubber were once more the order of the day.

The staff and customers had been replaced by legions of young guys off their tits, eyes glazed behind their Elton Johns. Their smiles were gold-toothed and *khat*-stained, and that worried me all over again. I knew they couldn't be controlled; I'd now seen it up close and personal. This was *Mad Max* country. I was in the Thunderdome.

Awaale led me into a ballroom. The whole environment changed. I could hear the hum of a generator somewhere. Arc lamps had been hammered onto the walls. The room wasn't completely bathed in light but there was enough. Four young guys in Western dress were hunched over ancient PCs. One of them was keeping up to speed with Facebook. Another was admiring a picture in an online brochure of a happy couple at the big wheel of their even bigger yacht. This was Mog's answer to GCHQ.

I followed Awaale to where two minging old brown settees sat either side of a US Army aluminium Lacon box the size of a coffee-table. The green paint was worn away and the metalwork looked like it had been dropped out of a helicopter.

'Sit here.' He pointed to one of the settees. 'Not long now.'

Dust rose and caught in my throat as I followed his instruction. I shoved my day sack on my lap.

Awaale moved away. He gobbed off to one of the PC geeks and then checked everyone's screen.

A minute or two later an old wooden tray arrived and was deposited without ceremony on the Lacon box. A pewter pot and two empty glasses took pride of place. Another glass contained sugar and a plastic spoon. I caught the aroma of mint as a man in his mid-sixties – seriously old for this place – sat opposite me. Awaale came and stood between us.

'Mr Nick, this is Erasto. He will help get your loved ones released.'

Erasto wore a cotton skirt with a black and white check shawl around his shoulders. His feet, which stuck out of a pair of old flip-flops, looked like they were covered with elephant skin. An Omega stainless-steel Seamaster glinted on his left wrist. It was one of the watches I'd looked at when I bought my Breitling in Moscow. It had been way out of my price range.

Awaale handed him the envelope containing Joe's airport tax. Erasto shoved it under his leg without taking his eyes off me. I felt like I was under a microscope.

Awaale poured the tea, just like Nadif had done in Bristol.

13

Erasto continued to stare at me. *'Parla Italiano?'*

The sandpaper voice sent me into a time warp. 'No.'

He looked as disappointed as he probably had when we'd talked on Saturday morning. He turned to Awaale and waffled away in Somali. Awaale passed him a glass of hot water that smelt strongly of mint and nodded so much I thought his head might fall off.

'Erasto wants to know who killed Nadif.'

The old man's deep-set eyes bored once more into mine.

'I don't know.'

Now wasn't the time to complicate things. I was talking to someone who might have the three bodies I was here to collect. That was all that mattered to me.

Awaale translated.

Erasto sat for a while, deep in thought. Then he fired off another question.

'When will Erasto have his three million dollars?' Awaale handed me a glass.

I watched Erasto's thumbs roaming over his iPhone screen.

'Erasto, your expectations of me, your expectations of Tracy's family and Justin's family are just too high.' I kept looking at him. I was talking to him, not his interpreter. 'We are not the people you think we are. We do not have the sort of money you're asking for. Erasto, we will never, ever, have that amount of money.'

Erasto's thumbs got busy again. By the look of it, he was starting to text. All I cared about was that Awaale was passing on exactly what I had said.

Erasto looked up at him, then shrugged and gobbed off as if he was turning down a dodgy piece of fruit from the market.

I heaped a couple of spoonfuls of sugar into the brew and got a mouthful down my neck.

Behind me, one of the geeks started playing what sounded like a YouTube clip. A group of women sailing round the world were telling their mates – and any strangers who felt like listening in – that they were on the way from Oman to Zanzibar. Fucking good luck to them. That might be the last video blog they posted for a while.

Awaale nodded. I watched Erasto as I listened to his response.

'Erasto says that unfortunately, if you do not have the money, he cannot do anything to help you. You must pay him. This is the only way your loved ones can go free. He wishes to help you, but this money must be paid. When you spoke to us before coming to Somalia, you said you had the money. So how soon can it be delivered?'

Erasto took a sip of tea and tucked the iPhone beside his ear. He mumbled away as if we no longer existed. I needed to be respectful, but I also had to make sure I was expressing myself extremely clearly. Any fuck-ups should stem from a crumbling negotiation, not a fundamental misunderstanding. I looked him in the eye. He fixed his on me for a second, then carried on with his waffle.

'Erasto, I think we may have a misunderstanding. When I spoke with Awaale, I said the families were getting money together. We have managed to raise three hundred and nineteen thousand dollars. But you must know we will never be able to get one million, let alone three.'

I waited for Awaale to pass Erasto the news of the 'misunderstanding'. The old man closed down his iPhone and continued drinking his tea. But I knew I had his full attention now.

'Three million is an impossible amount for us. I believe that was a misunderstanding on my part, and I apologize.'

Erasto leant forward, placed his glass on the tray and allowed Awaale to refill it until he indicated that he wanted no more. He examined the tea minutely.

Awaale splashed some more into mine.

'Erasto says that if you deliver the money now, you can have the boy first. The price is three hundred and nineteen thousand dollars each.'

I bent so low that Erasto had no choice but to renew eye-to-eye. I didn't see a flicker of emotion, not even a hint of what was going on in that head of his. Erasto and Frank must have come from the same gene pool.

'I'm sorry, Awaale. I can't negotiate for individuals. The price must be for all three.'

Erasto sat back with his brew. He didn't need Awaale to translate. He cut him off mid-waffle. Awaale faced me again.

'Erasto wants more than you offer, and he wants it quickly. He's willing to negotiate. He understands how important it is to get the family home. Can you get more money quickly, Mr Nick?'

'I can arrange for the three hundred and nineteen thousand dollars to be here tomorrow. I will try and get more, but it will be difficult.'

The lack-of-cash story seemed to be holding. I was expecting Erasto to ask why, if everyone was so poor, they were on such an expensive boat. BB must have done a good job of smoke-screening. 'But to raise more, and to bring the money to you, to ask the families to do this, I must know that they are safe.'

Erasto picked up his airport tax and got to his feet. He rattled off another set of instructions to Awaale. I wondered for a moment whether the *Italiano* question was just part of his performance. I wondered if he needed an interpreter at all. My iPhone vibrated in my jeans as he left the room.

14

Awaale motioned me over to the nearest PC. 'Erasto
says if you can find some more money then you can
see them. But he wants the money here quickly. Then
you can take them home, maybe tomorrow, maybe the
next day. If you come up with more money, Erasto will
help you. But come, I will now show you that your
loved ones are OK.'

The screen was covered with dust. There was a grinding sound as he tapped the keys. I watched a video clip
upload. 'See, Mr Nick, we are looking after them.'

Tracy and BB sat on a patch of filthy concrete with
Stefan between them. Tracy was wearing a red *hijab*.
Only her face was exposed. It was clean and
unmarked, but her holiday tan couldn't hide the fact
she was in shit state. Her eyes were red and sunken.
She looked nervous and worried. She had her arm
around Stefan. He clung to his mother. He was dressed
in blue-striped shorts and a blue T-shirt, with nothing
on his feet. They were black with grime. His legs were
covered with insect bites.

It was BB I most wanted to see. He sat cross-legged and kept his eyes to the floor until a flip-flopped kick in the back encouraged him to look up. His message to the camera lens was extremely clear: 'You cunts . . .'

This video wasn't recent. He had less than a week's stubble.

The sound of traffic and birdsong filled the background, as it had in the phone message. Their captors, in ski masks or *shemaghs*, filled the screen behind them. They all had weapons clutched across their chests, and belts of linked ammunition around their hips.

Awaale wagged a finger. 'You see, Mr Nick? You find some more money for Erasto and your loved ones will be home before you know it.'

I turned to face him. 'I'll try, Awaale. I'm doing everything I can to help you. You know that. Your father knows that. You both know I risked my life for you and your friends this afternoon. But I must see Tracy and Stefan first. Really see them. Speak to them before any money changes hands. Can you make sure that Erasto understands that?'

He placed a hand lightly on my shoulder. 'I know these things, Mr Nick. But this is business. Erasto's business. You need to make calls, Mr Nick. I will take you to see your friends tomorrow. Now, you have a cell? You can use mine . . .'

'No, I have one. Where am I staying? This could take a bit of time.'

Awaale's brow furrowed. 'Staying? You will stay *here*, Mr Nick. You cannot leave. It is dangerous. There is nowhere to go. You must stay here until you have got Erasto some more money.'

I knew this had more to do with keeping me until I came up with the cash than with my personal safety. And I knew the unspoken threat that I could be Erasto's next fund-raising opportunity was hovering at the edge of our exchanges.

'Can I charge up my iPhone from whatever the PCs are running off?'

'Sure. Why not? Then please, make your calls.' He pointed back at the settees. 'Do not leave this area. I do not want to see you killed.'

As if on cue, there was a burst of machine-gun fire in the city and tracer disappeared into the night.

He headed out the way he had come, waving his hand. 'You see, Mr Nick, we must keep you close.'

I'd suggest another thirty-one K. If Erasto didn't go for that, I'd come back with a further nine. I wanted him to understand that it was time to take the money and run. Why keep them any longer if the next tranche was going to be even less, especially if they were starting to get ill? BB didn't look too good. If they died before we shook hands there would be no deal. Maybe that was why Erasto was in such a hurry.

Back on the settee, I checked my iPhone. Jules had rung. He'd also left me a text.

Call me. It's important.

It still freaked me out that even in a shithole like this I could talk to anyone, anywhere.

The phone buzzed twice. Jules didn't hang around.

'I think I've found them. All three of them. But it's not good. The int says that al-Shabab have three whites: an adult female, a young male, who we think is her son, and an adult male. They were lifted from a

330

yacht just over a week ago and sold on by the clan. It has to be them.'

I kept my voice down, my hand covering the phone. 'I'm in the city. I'm with the clan now. They're claiming they still have them.'

'Jesus, Nick, why didn't you call? Have you seen them?'

'No. But they want money fast. I guess we now know why.'

'I don't think they've got them, Nick. Not any more, anyway. They must have sold them on. Or the clan had a debt to AS, and faced a zero option. Either way, unless you've seen them, it looks like AS are now in control.'

'Do you know where?'

'As of yesterday, Merca. South of the city. That's all we know. AS control most of the south. If AS do have your three, you must get the boys you're dealing with to start telling the truth. Like I said, when it's not about money, it's time to get out your worry beads.

'They use hostages to control the locals. The message is, they're white pigs who don't adhere to Sharia law. This is the punishment they deserve. In other words, if you don't shape up, this is what'll happen to you.'

There was a peal of laughter in the next room. I asked Jules to keep in touch and hoisted my day sack onto my shoulders.

15

I wandered out into the darkness.

Awaale was by the empty plinth in the courtyard. He'd joined his crew around the fire. They were chewing *khat* and drinking from big litre bottles of Haywards 5000 as they relived the events of the day. That was one ship that would never be hijacked: the beer boat from India.

A few women had joined the group. They were young and attentive – to anyone who would give them a swig of lager and a mouthful of the flat bread that was piled up with lumps of veg on a nearby tray. Awaale tore himself off a piece, wrapped it round a tomato, and took a bite.

'Ah, Mr Nick.'

'I need to talk to you, mate. I've got some good news.'

I stopped about two metres from him. The others looked up and cheered. Their eyes were wide, dilated pupils shining in the firelight. I guessed they were busy telling a couple of the girls how they'd kicked

Lucky Justice's arse, the sort of stuff that made us all look good.

'Excellent, excellent.' Awaale jumped up, wiping his hands on his jeans. 'Very excellent, Mr Nick.'

I started towards the technicals. 'Let's go somewhere quiet, mate. How about over there?'

We headed past the back of the technical we'd been in today. The captured AKs and the body of the lad who'd been zapped still lay on the flatbed. He looked like a rabbit that had been tossed aside on a night shoot. He couldn't have been any older than fifteen.

I carried on waffling encouragingly as we went further into the shadows. 'I got the OK to offer more money. But one thing I need, mate . . .' I put a friendly arm round his shoulder – then grabbed him and spun him round in an arm-lock, tucking the back of his head into my shoulder. I squeezed my right arm tighter and slapped my left hand over his mouth.

His legs trailed behind him as I dragged him into cover. I could feel moisture on my hand as he tried to shout. His heels kicked up sand as he tried to keep control of his legs. I kept moving fast enough to stop that happening, then hooked them out from underneath him. I went with him, keeping the arm-lock in place as we fell. He took my full weight on his back, losing all the air from his lungs.

We were about forty metres from the fire. Girls giggled. Bottles clinked. The lads carried on with their banter.

I turned Awaale's head just enough to see the side of his face. I made sure he could see mine. He'd be getting very little air. He'd be feeling the strain on the vertebrae in his neck. He'd think his brain was about to explode.

I made sure my mouth was right up close to his ear. 'All that matters to me are my friends. You mean nothing to me. If you make a noise, you will die just before I do. But I will die a man, because I'm going to fight. You will die like a dog, here in the dust. So honour your father, and stay alive. Stay alive to fight the battles he fought. Do you understand me?'

Awaale just about managed a nod.

'All right. Keep quiet, keep safe. Do you understand?'

He gave another twitch.

I lifted my hand a fraction from his mouth.

He nodded hard.

I tightened my grip again and pulled the arm-lock into my chest. I needed him to know how quickly I'd be able to squeeze all the breath from his body. His throat contracted. His eyes screwed up in pain. He got the message.

I released him again, just enough for him to be able to talk.

'I know they're in Merca. Where in Merca are they?'

His head shook, as if he was denying it. I pushed my hand over his mouth again and tightened the lock. His Adam's apple bobbed against my biceps. He let out a whimper. His hands scrabbled in the sand, as if that was going to take the pain away.

I released him again. 'Awaale, I don't have time to fuck about. I'll find out what I need to know from you, or I'll kill you and find out from someone else. Do you still have them?'

He went completely still, but I could feel his heart pounding in his chest.

'*Tell me.*'

The hilarity around the fire was at an all-time high. The lads didn't seem to be missing Awaale one bit.

At last he spoke. 'You will see them tomorrow. I promise. Just let—'

'Fuck it. I'll ask Erasto instead.'

I squeezed the vice even tighter. I leant further forward for good measure, until my chest pushed down on the side of his face.

His legs jerked. His hands came up.

He bucked and kicked and his thumbs searched in vain for my eyes. His nose and throat rasped. Snot and saliva oozed through my fingers.

Then he went still once more. He patted my shoulder in submission.

I raised my chest and looked down at him. I wanted to see the surrender in his eyes. They were red and bulging like he'd had a kilo of *khat*. His arms just trembled now. He was starting to go.

I released some of the pressure. He fought for oxygen. His Adam's apple would feel like it was stuck in the back of his throat.

I let him have just enough air to stay conscious.

'Where – are – they?'

At first he just gulped.

Then he whispered a word.

'Again.' I moved my ear closer to his mouth.

'Merca.'

'They're in Merca?'

'Yes, they—'

I didn't let him get the last bit out. I drew back and punched him in the face. I didn't want him to make the mistake of thinking we were new best mates. 'Who has them?'

'Al-Shabab. The—'

I punched him again. 'You know where they are?'

His head shook. 'No, no.'

'Then you're no good to me.'

I retightened the vice momentarily to make sure he knew this was a tap I could turn on and off at will.

'I do! I do know! They have them in the town. Please, Mr Nick.'

The lads round the fire were really going for it. Bottles were smashed and the girls swayed against the flames. Sweat dripped off my nose and chin and dropped onto Awaale's face.

'Why have they been taken?'

'We had no choice. We have to pay them not to come into the city. They wanted the whites. It was a good deal for us. Erasto had another buyer, I don't know who. But this was better for us. To keep al-Shabab away from the city. We don't want them here.'

The girls were really going for it, gyrating their arses in front of the lads, hoping to get more than another bite of flatbread.

'So Erasto was getting me to pay up for nothing?'

'It's business, Mr Nick. Erasto still needs payment for the boat. Al-Shabab have the boat. He wants payment for it. He wants money for the work.'

'What about the video you showed me?'

'I shot it before we handed them over. And recorded the message. Erasto wanted payment for the boat.

336

They wouldn't give him anything for the boat. We thought we'd get payment this way.'

A couple peeled away from the group and headed towards us, laughing and joking. I could smell the smoke on them as they came closer. I gripped Awaale.

They weren't interested in us. They clambered into the back of a 4×4 and music soon sparked up in the cab. The laughter and clink of bottles back at the fire was soon drowned by moans and groans and heavy breathing. The wagon started to rock.

'Give me a number. I want to talk to them.'

'It won't work, Mr Nick. They will not listen. This is not about money.'

'Then you're going to take me there and I'm going to get them out.'

I got up and pulled him to his feet. 'You make a noise, you go down again, OK? Remember, you can die like a man or you can die like a dog in the sand.'

I dragged Awaale past the 4×4. Its suspension was now taking a serious pounding. I picked up a blood-stained AK from the back of the technical. I turned towards the glow of the fire and pulled the cocking handle to make sure there was a round in it. I motioned for Awaale to take the magazines off all the weapons and put them in my day sack.

I kept a grip of him and steered him towards the nearest technical with a 12.7. The 4×4 kept on rocking.

'Mr Nick, they'll know that we've gone.'

'Just do it.'

I shoved him into the driver's seat and sat opposite with the AK on my lap, the muzzle pointing towards him. 'Merca. Let's go.'

337

He had both hands on the wheel. 'Mr Nick, you don't understand. Maybe Erasto can talk to them. Maybe he can—'

'*No*, Awaale. *You* don't understand. If you don't do what I say, I'll do it myself, without you. And that means I will kill you. Now turn the engine on. Chop-chop.'

He did as he was told. He breathed heavily as I checked the fuel gauge. It was just under half full.

'How far is it?'

'It's so far, Mr Nick. We'll never get there. The roads are dangerous. Al-Shabab have checkpoints.'

'Just get on with it. Start driving.'

We rolled past the party boys, who threw a couple of bottles at the wagon for a laugh. The girls wiggled their arses.

We bounced on through the darkness of the square, heading for the main. I sparked up my iPhone.

'Awaale – stop here. Turn off the lights.'

He did so.

I dialled Jules. It didn't ring for long.

'Nick?'

'AS do have them. Have you any contacts? Will they negotiate? Any way I can get hold of them?'

'We've had no negotiations with them. Ever. No success liberating anybody from AS.' He went quiet for a moment.

'How far is it by road to Merca?'

'Nick, it's dangerous. Please, think about this . . .'

'How far?'

'Maybe a hundred kilometres. You'll be dead by morning. It's crazy.'

'So what's new? I've spent most of my life thinking I'll be dead by morning. Jules, I'm going because I made a promise to a mate.'

'But, Nick – think of Anna . . .' There was an edge of desperation in his voice.

'Jules, listen. I made a promise to my dead mate that I'd look after his wife. So that's what I'm going to do.'

'Nick, hang on – we need to talk.'

I closed down, and got straight through to Frank. 'Are your boys in Nairobi? Will they be able to get hold of cash within a couple of hours?'

'Yes. The pilot is at the ready. Your problem . . . the problem you had in the UK. Did you lose them?'

'Dunno. I'll call again when I have something solid to tell you. Stand by.'

Awaale sat there, trying to make sense of it all.

'Right, we're going to Merca. You're going to stay with me. I need a local speaker, and I need a black guy. And that means I need you.'

He flapped his hands anxiously in front of me. 'But, Mr Nick, the roads – please . . . It's so dangerous . . .'

He slapped his cheeks. 'No face hair . . . and you, you will not make it. Erasto can help you. Maybe he—'

'Stop. It ain't going to work. Dangerous roads?'

'Yes, they are dangerous. But Erasto—'

'Awaale, shut up. We're not going to take the roads. Let's go.'

'Where?'

'Erasto's a fucking pirate, isn't he? We're going to get ourselves a boat. Come on – chop-chop.'

16

Flames flickered behind crumbling walls each side of the deserted streets. It reminded me of Aceh, only here the devastation was man-made.

'Where are we going now? How far?'

Awaale hit the airport road and followed the unlit strip around the perimeter beyond the terminal. 'We take the boats from the beach, Mr Nick.'

'The pirate boats?'

He nodded.

That was good. If they could travel five hundred miles out to sea in those things, hugging the coast would be a piece of piss.

'But Erasto, he will be very, very angry, Mr Nick.'

'No, he'll be very, very happy – because I'll pay him when we get back.'

I studied Awaale's face in the glow from the dash. His sensitive, intelligent features didn't belong in a place like this. 'Why did you come back to Somalia? Things must have been a lot better in Minneapolis. You're an American citizen, aren't you?'

'Yes.' He shrugged. 'But I am young, and I am a Muslim. It doesn't matter what passport you hold. My father wanted me to stay, to keep on trying. Even a McJob . . .' He looked at me and smiled. 'It may not look like it, but it's better here. I send money to my father, he sends it to others in Minneapolis who need it. It's better here.'

Our headlights splashed across the line of decaying hangars and dilapidated Soviet fighters on concrete blocks. Soon we were in the world of sand and rusting hulks that separated the top of the runway from the docks. A shanty town had grown up around the large commercial ships that had long since been run aground. The closer to the beach we got, the deeper the rusting wrecks had settled into the sand. Threadbare men huddled around the small fires that glowed in the darkness. Keeping a firm grip on their bottles and AKs, they shielded their eyes from our main beams as we passed.

Awaale pulled up alongside one of the groups and tilted his head at me, looking for permission to jump out. I nodded. He stepped down onto the sand and rattled away in Somali. Erasto was mentioned more than a couple of times. The locals didn't rush forward. I couldn't work out if they were being cautious or frightened.

'Mr Nick, this way.'

I also didn't know whether Awaale was basically just a very good guy, or if the mention of payment had made all the difference to our relationship. It wasn't long since I'd been threatening him with the AK; now he was leading me willingly to a row of skiffs. I could

341

just make out their shape a few metres short of the surf.

We waded into a foot of water. It was warmer than I was expecting. The wooden craft were maybe five metres long and a couple of metres wide. A Mercury 150 outboard was bolted straight into the wood at the back of the nearest one. There were no fancy fuel bladders or metal tanks, just three white plastic twenty-litre drums. A hole had been drilled into the black screw caps to accommodate the fuel line.

There was a rubber squeeze pump about halfway along the pipe to propel the fuel into the engine without an air blockage, and that was it on the technology front. The three containers were tied together but not secured to the boat. Sixty litres, I reckoned, would equate to about a 150-kilometre round trip. That should be all right. And it could easily take five of us.

I shouldered the AK alongside my day sack, and helped Awaale pull the boat fully into the water. A light breeze brushed our faces. 'Do you know exactly where Merca is?'

'Sure. It's the first town.'

The last foot or two of keel cleared the sand and the skiff bobbed up and down at chest height beside us.

'We can't miss it?'

He stared at me. '*We*? No, Mr Nick – I have to go back. The technical, I have to—'

I heaved myself over the side and onto the worn wooden deck. There were two cross benches, one at the back by the engine, and one mid-ship.

'No, mate. You're coming.' I grabbed the shoulder of his shirt and gave it a tug. 'Come on.'

He was suddenly very concerned about the mobile and cigarettes in his shirt pocket. 'But, Mr Nick, I *must* go back. They will miss me . . .'

'Tough shit, mate. You're coming.'

I pointed to the fuel pump. 'There you go, get squeezing.'

I released the retaining lever that kept the propeller clear of the water. As I tilted the engine down, the boat swung side on to the incoming waves.

There were no electrics on this thing. Opening up the choke, I tugged the rope starter cord until the outboard kicked off. I twisted the throttle on the tiller, turned the choke down to halfway, and revved some more. The stink of fumes washed over us; smoke must have been billowing from the exhaust. I let the revs drop, pushed the gear lever to forward and started turning back offshore.

I wanted to get beyond the surf before chucking a right. We should be in Merca in about three hours. Awaale sat forward of me. He just wanted to be back on the beach. The breeze was still warm, but his arms hugged his chest like we were in the Arctic.

'Calm down, mate. It'll be first light soon. Then you'll wish it was cooler.'

His head dropped. I throttled up and headed south. I needed to keep the shore to my right. It would be all too easy to wander off to the east as the lights disappeared.

17

We passed where the runway jutted out into the sea. Whatever lights were there began to fade. We powered on into inky darkness. There were no points of reference. As long as we kept to the phosphorescent line where the surf started to form, we should be OK.

I checked the time on my iPhone. I'd left the Breitling with the 911. We had about four hours until first light. In this part of the world, sunset and sunrise were fairly consistent events, give or take ten minutes, at any time of the year. It was up at six and down at six. If we were still going by first light and the sun was directly to our left, we'd have overshot. We'd be on our way to Kenya and Tanzania. If the sun came up and we were facing it, I'd have seriously fucked up. We'd be heading east: next stop the Seychelles or, worse still, India.

I left Awaale to his own devices and checked the iPhone. I still had five full bars. Reception was better here than anywhere in the UK. It was another good indication that the coast was within sight. If I started drifting east I'd be losing signal.

I sparked it up. Anna took a while to answer.

'Nicholas? Where are you?'

'On a boat. I've just left Mogadishu. I think we've found them.'

'Wait – when did you get to Mogadishu?'

I explained everything. I couldn't really tell what she thought about it. 'Jules thinks they're in Merca. So does my Somali friend. I've got nothing else to go on. So that's where we're heading.'

Then it became very clear what she thought. She was angry. 'Nicholas, AS, they're dangerous. Even al-Qaeda won't deal with them. They'd get taken hostage too. They don't bargain. They don't negotiate. Why didn't Jules warn you?'

'He did. But I don't have a choice, Anna. I made a promise.'

'What promise?'

'To a mate.'

Her tone changed. If I'd had a mother who cared, she would probably have sounded like Anna. 'Nicholas, I'm worried sick. Please think again.'

'What would you do?' There was a pause. I heard gunfire in the background. We both knew that was the answer. 'You OK up there?'

'Everything's fine. It's just anti-aircraft fire trying to hit the French bombers.'

'Where are you?'

'Mistrata. We got a lift on one of the casualty ships from Benghazi. Gaddafi's navy is attacking the port. The US Sixth Fleet are firing on them. The French are

345

bombing from the air and the rebels are fighting street to street. It will be a long battle. But, Nicholas ... Please, please, *please* be careful. You need to stay alive. You really do.'

'What for? For you?'

There was a pause. 'Of course.'

'Well, in that case, you've got to stay alive as well, for me. Deal?'

'I need a call from you every day, OK?'

'OK.'

'Promise me? Every day?'

'Yes, I promise. Every day.'

Awaale had curled up below the bench. He really was the eternal optimist. He was never going to get comfortable down there as we bounced through the water.

'You all right, mate?' I had to shout over the wind and the roar of the engine.

'The sea ... it makes me very sick.'

'Sick? You're supposed to be a pirate!'

Awaale gave a groan.

'Get up, mate. You're going to feel a whole lot better sitting up.'

He wasn't listening. 'These people – Tracy and the child. They're not your friends, are they? You've been sent to take them home.'

'It's a bit of both, mate.'

I left him to his misery and tried not to think about sleep and food: I needed both. But they were going to have to wait. To my half-right, in the distance, I saw ribbons of light.

The iPhone told me it was four thirty – about

another hour and thirty before the sun came up. I wanted to get there in time to check that it was Merca and be able to get away, if it wasn't, under darkness.

18

Tuesday, 22 March

The place was crawling with lights. There were thousands of the things – not just the ribbon of cooking fires and lanterns I'd been expecting.

I kept the skiff as close to the shore as I could. As we were thrown about by the surf the *adhan* for Fajr prayers, the first of the day, kicked out from mosques all over town. I checked behind left, to the east. A thin ribbon of light was starting to stretch across the horizon.

The engine howled as the propeller momentarily left the water. Awaale was now sitting on the mid-ship bench, a hand either side of him, gripping it tight. He still wasn't enjoying this one bit.

'Is this Merca, Awaale? Is Merca this big?' I leant forward, keeping one hand on the tiller. 'You sure this is it?'

'Yes, this is it. I'm sure.'

I checked my iPhone. I still had three bars of signal.

It was a quarter to five. About the time I'd expected to be here.

I pushed the tiller sideways as we bounced over the surf line. The skiff slewed and powered back the way we'd come.

Awaale spun round. 'Back to Mogadishu? That would be much better, Mr Nick. This is a very dangerous place.'

I raised my free hand. 'Watch and learn, mate. You lads need skills if you're going to go up against Lucky Justice. Otherwise, you're all going to end up dead. That's an end to the parties and women, and al-Shabab will come straight in and take over the city. That wouldn't be good, would it? You've got to learn a few tactics.'

He nodded slowly. 'You're going to teach me?'

'As much as I can. But tell me this. Why don't you team up with Lucky to fight al-Shabab?'

He looked at me like I was mad. 'No way. We must kill Lucky first.'

'It's up to you, mate. Sometimes you've got to look at the big picture. You've got to think about the way you're doing things. That beach we've just turned away from is in the middle of the town, isn't it? So what would have happened if we'd just landed and wandered round looking for them?'

We'd now cleared the surf and were paralleling the white line of breakers. The lights of Merca were over my left shoulder as we headed north.

'You would fight and you would get your friends out.'

'No, I would lose. I have no idea what's in there. Do you?'

'Yes. There are guys from Pakistan, Yemen, Saudi.'

'Exactly. And they've all got weapons. I'd be dead, and the three I've come for would still be prisoners. So I'm not going to do that. I'm going to use my head. First, I make sure that this thing is hidden up so we can escape.'

He thought about it, then nodded.

'The next thing is to find them. Do you know where they're being held? You've been to this town.'

He looked at me again like I was mad. 'They'll be with all the other prisoners. The thieves. The adulterers. The cheats.'

'So there's a jail?'

He nodded. 'The Russians built it. Before I was born.'

The lights of the town were about a kilometre behind us. A light grey arch was growing out of the sea to our right. The sun itself wouldn't be far behind.

I could just make out the shapes of vessels parked further out on the swell, maybe five or six of them. Dozens of skiffs lined the beach, pulled up away from the water line.

I swung the tiller to take us in. Beyond the skiffs I could make out a procession of scrub-covered dunes, punctuated from time to time by small, dried-up wadis. We could drag the skiff up there and hide it in the dead ground. If it wasn't there when we got back, or had been compromised, I'd lift a technical or another skiff. Fuck it – I'd worry about that later. I had plenty to do first.

The propeller guard scraped along the bottom. I tilted up the 150 as the bow dug into the sand.

I slung the AK over my shoulder, jumped out and splashed water at Awaale. 'Come on, mate. Get out and push.'

He clambered out reluctantly. The skiff moved easily up the sand, like a sled. The wadi we pulled it into looked like a golf-course bunker.

Awaale collapsed alongside it. Like mine, his Timberlands and the bottom of his jeans were wet with seawater and crusted with sand.

'What are you going to do now, Mr Nick?'

'I don't know yet. First I want to confirm they're in that jail. Then I'll work out how to get them out. Maybe I'll do a deal.'

His head shook. 'It won't work. Sharia law, that's all that matters here. They have the freedom to do what they want. The Pakistani guys? As far as they're concerned, even the Taliban aren't true Wahhabis.'

I knew those guys. They were hard-core. They made the Taliban look like kindergarten teachers.

'What are you – Sunni?'

'Everyone is. Even in this town they are. But al-Shabab are here. So they're all Wahhabis.'

I made sure my day sack was fastened and the magazine clipped into the AK. 'OK, let's go.'

Awaale stayed put, his hands up in front of him like he was begging for food. 'Mr Nick, please, I do not want to go. We will be killed. Even I will be noticed. I don't belong here. Look . . .' He kept pointing to his lack of facial hair. 'I'll stay and look after the boat.'

I took two quick paces and stood over him. 'We –

that's you and me – are going in there, one way or another. I need your help. You put my friends in the shit, so you're going to help get them out. Listen, Awaale, I like you, but don't fucking push it, mate.'

I stopped. This wasn't going to help. It might piss him off so much he stitched me up with al-Shabab or dropped me in it by running away. Or it might make him too frightened to function. Neither was going to help me.

'OK, Awaale, listen. I'll pay you. I'll pay you twenty-five thousand US if you help me get the three of them to Mog airport. That's all you need to do. Just help me and do what I ask.'

Now I had his attention. His expression changed immediately.

'Fifty.'

'No. I said twenty-five. That's a lot of cash to send to your dad, isn't it? More than you'd ever earn back there in McDonald's – and more than the cut you get from Erasto.'

'Thirty-five.'

'I've told you. Twenty-five. Take it or leave it. I'm going in, mate, and you're going to be with me, one way or another. Decision time.'

I still had the iPhone in my hand. I started to dial Frank.

It rang just once. I hit the speaker-phone and jumped in before Frank could say anything.

'I need you to guarantee twenty-five thousand dollars for some assistance. I've got a guy here. I need his help. Explain how it would be paid. He's listening.'

Frank didn't even take a breath. 'Twenty-five

thousand US, guaranteed. It will be flown into Mogadishu airport in time for the hostage exchange. Now, are we done?'

I took it off speaker-phone and brought it back to my ear. 'Yes, we are. I'll call you when I have anything.'

I closed down the iPhone and tucked it back into my day sack. 'You ready?'

He stood up. 'I would have come with you anyway, Mr Nick. I just needed you to know how dangerous it is.'

'Do you want to pray before we go? We've got a couple of minutes before sun-up.'

He thought about it and nodded. He turned towards Mogadishu. *Qibla* was north in this part of the world.

Awaale stood in his Western gear and bling and raised his hands up to his shoulders, feet slightly apart, in preparation for *takbiratul ihram*. He mumbled away gently to himself. Maybe he did it every day, in between the beer and the girls, or maybe he was just getting a quick one in to hedge his bets.

'*Allahu-akbar.*'

God is great.

Maybe. But so was the AK on my shoulder, and I knew which one I trusted more.

19

My Timberlands sank into the sand. Awaale was slowly catching up.

'Why are you scared, Awaale?'

'I'm not.'

'That's good. We have work to do. A lot of work.'

He took a couple of quicker steps to draw level with me. I kept my eyes on the way ahead. I was a white man on the East African coast. That kind of news would travel like wildfire if I was spotted.

'The man on the cell, Mr Nick?'

'He's the one who sent me. Like I said, I'm here partly for friendship and partly for work. The mother and the man who's in there with them – I know them really well.'

'But who is he? On the cell?'

'He's the father of that child. So that's how it works. I must help them. And I'm getting paid, like you.'

'The man with them is not the husband?'

'No.'

With the sun now up I could see more clearly. Four

big commercial cargo ships rode at anchor, dwarfing even the largest of the yachts beside them.

We started moving through scrub. The sand here was mixed with sticky seed pods and bits of twig and stone. As we approached the outskirts of Merca I went into a stoop, using the brush as cover. The town was waking. Cockerels went berserk. Dogs barked. Nearly all the buildings were one-storey concrete or breeze-block structures with tin or flat roofs, arranged on a grid. There was a lot of cobalt blue going on, on the roofs and walls as well as the clothes-lines.

Long shadows appeared as the sun rose from the sea. The narrow streets would keep the shade for a while longer. Nearly every dwelling had its morning fire burning. Smoke curled from stubby chimneys. High walls sheltered the compounds. Some were crumbling, but so far everything here seemed in much better nick than in Mogadishu. The sand tracks between the houses were compacted by years of foot and vehicle traffic. There wasn't a scrap of litter in sight.

Sunrises in this part of Africa are brilliant and come on fast. The eastern sky had turned tangerine above low grey night clouds. The sun burnt the left side of my face. We walked down into an area of dead ground and up the other side. Ahead, a short, open stretch led to the edge of the town. I lay down in the cover of the last of the thorny scrub.

I kept my eyes screwed up and shaded with my left hand as Awaale collapsed beside me. 'Over there . . .' I indicated our half-right. 'Third house down, about forty metres. See the clothes-line?'

He nodded.

'We need the *burqas*. The blue ones.'

Awaale's head jerked round. He squinted in the sun. 'Steal them?'

'What else? Go into town and buy a couple?'

'It's not that.'

'It's no drama, mate. Just put the fucking thing on and walk like an old woman.'

'Do you know what happens to people who steal, under Sharia law?'

I managed not to laugh. 'Mate, if we get caught, having your hand chopped off is the last thing you'll need to worry about. Go and get them, there's a good lad. We need to get ourselves to that jail.'

He didn't budge.

'We must pay for them.'

'You can't start talking to anyone. It'll compromise us. Just go and get them.'

'No, Mr Nick. Women who do not wear *hijab* in al-Shabab areas are not allowed to leave their homes. No part of their body can be seen in public. *Jalaabiibs* and *burqas* cost at least fifteen dollars. If these women don't wear them, they'll be punished. They stoned a thirteen-year-old girl for this, even though she was not right.' He tapped his temple with a finger. 'She was walking in the main square. They stoned her to death. If these women don't cover up, they can look for their head in the sand. We cannot just steal them, Mr Nick. We have to pay for them. These people cannot afford to buy these things.'

I rolled over onto my side and dug in my American tourist pouch for the fold of goodwill cash. 'Here's fifty. I don't care how you give it to them, but be quick. Shove it under the door or some shit. I don't care. Let's just get these fucking things on and get moving.'

In the mid-distance, heading away from us down one of the wider streets, I could see three men patrolling, with black and white *shemaghs* and wild beards.

I grabbed Awaale's ankle. 'Make sure they're big ones.'

20

I watched him set off across the open ground. As he approached the building, chickens bomb-burst out from behind a wall. He walked past a big cone of dried ox-dung cakes. It kept their ovens burning. I wasn't sure what it did for the food. He knocked on the door.

For a long time nothing happened. A woman would never appear at the threshold. Maybe the men and children were out. He knocked again. An old guy in a grey *dish-dash* finally appeared. His grey hair was as long as his beard. Awaale gestured at the clothes-line. The old man stared at him for a long time before answering. There was more chat and the old guy kept stroking his beard. Awaale kept nodding away, reached into his jeans pocket and handed him the cash. The old man took it, turned back into the house and closed the door behind him. He reappeared in the back yard seconds later and took two *burqas* off the line.

The sky was now dazzlingly blue, with not even a hint of cloud. The sand around me was already almost too hot to touch. The sun burnt through my long-sleeved sweatshirt and onto the back of my neck. I felt like I was stuck in a toaster.

Awaale came back with the two blue *burqas*. *Hijabs* wouldn't have worked for us. They'd have left our faces uncovered. I waited for him to get to within a couple of metres of where I was lying. 'Pass me, keep walking. Don't look down. Just carry on down into the dip where we can't be seen.'

He did as he was told. My sweat-soaked clothes were soon caked in sand as I slithered back and followed him. Even the AK was covered with the stuff, from the perspiration on my hands.

Awaale had our purchases over his shoulder. I took off my day sack and boots. My socks would have to stay on. 'Get your rings and watch off. Have nothing on your hands or your wrist. Old women don't wear that shit.'

He started licking his rings and pulling them off. Women's hands in this neck of the woods are every bit as work-worn as men's, sometimes even more so, but round here they wouldn't wear decadent jewellery. I thought about how they must feel under their *burqas* in this heat. Hard-line Islam was alien to most Somali women, especially those in rural areas who worked the land or herded goats, sheep and cattle under the scorching sun. Wearing this shit must make their already difficult lives almost unbearable. And they had to slave away for longer to pay for the fucking things.

My Timberlands went into the day sack. 'What did you say to the old guy?'

He tucked the bling into his pockets. 'I said I needed

them because my wife and her mother were waiting in my boat, and we had to visit my wife's sister in town. I told him she is ill and we needed to go to her immediately. I had no time to run around the town.'

I hung the day sack over my chest like a city tourist and we pulled the *burqa*s over our heads.

'Shoes as well, mate. Shove them in your belt. Get your feet covered in sand and shit.'

He wasn't convinced, but did as he was told.

'Just think of the cash, and the war stories you'll be able to tell next time you're round the fire.'

I looked through the triangle of blue mesh as I waited for him to sort himself out. I felt my breath against the material, making me hotter and more claustrophobic by the minute. The previous owners deserved a whole lot more than fifty dollars for having to wear this shit.

I knelt and rolled up my jeans so just my socks would be visible if the hem of the *burqa* rode up.

'Do the same, mate. Roll them right up so they don't fall down when we start moving.'

Stooping *burqa*s don't get a second glance. They meant age, infirmity or illness. No one would want anything to do with a couple of old birds like us.

I slid the AK under my right arm, the butt nice and tight in the pit, the barrel down my side, the magazine cupped in my hand. The metal was so hot it seared my skin.

I turned and started towards the sea. 'Remember, mate, we're old women. We walk slow – bend over a little. Never put your head up.'

He looked like a blue pepper-pot. The top of it nodded away at me.

'Is your mobile off?'

His hand fiddled around beneath the material. 'Yes, it is, Mr Nick.'

'Right. If anything goes wrong, do exactly what I say, when I say it. You sure you know the way to the jail?'

The top of the pepper-pot nodded again.

'OK. We'll go back and walk along the beach. It's less exposed. And it'll get the bottom of these things nice and dusty. Then we'll move into the town. If anything happens and we get split up, we meet back at the skiff.'

Even under the *burqa* I could tell he still wasn't too impressed. And a lot less gung-ho now he didn't have a weapon.

'Awaale, I'm not going to do anything to put us in danger. I'm here to rescue them, not get into a fight. I'll just be looking to see how I can get them out. You take me there, and maybe I won't need you until we leave. Maybe I can do everything myself – but I won't know until you get me there and I see where and how they're being held. You'll do that for me, yeah?'

The top of the pepper-pot nodded once more. I turned towards the beach. 'OK, let's go, then.'

The heat really was unbearable under this thing.

21

We passed skiff after skiff along the shore line. Some bobbed up and down in the waves. Others had been dragged up onto the sand. In the distance, cargo ships and yachts were silhouetted against the horizon.

I moved closer to Awaale. 'Is one of those the *Maria Feodorovna*?'

The top of the pepper-pot swivelled. His breath rasped as he laboured to speak. It was like a sauna inside these things.

'The white one, on the far left.'

'What happens now? They just sit there?'

'AS – they will sell them to pirates. They offered it back to Erasto. But why would he want it? He can go and steal another one. They'll stay here until someone buys them.'

'Will they?'

'No.'

'So they stay there until they rot?'

Awaale didn't need to answer. He waved an arm. We'd come to an area of rusting hulks and the remnants of boats that had broken up in storms and washed ashore.

Awaale went to move on but I held him. 'Where is the jail from here?'

'We stay on the beach for a while. But then we must go into the town. I'll take you, Mr Nick, and then we leave and you work out how to free them, yes?'

'Yes. Just as I said – and, yes, you will be paid if you help me get them back to the airport.'

He turned, no doubt relieved.

'One more thing, mate. Why did Erasto want to know who killed Nadif? Why did it matter to him? It's not as if you lads worry too much about that shit, is it?'

His voice dropped. 'Nadif was his brother, Mr Nick. He was family. Erasto will find who killed his brother, and then he will kill him.'

22

Dung fires spilt a sweet, almost herbal smell from the chimneys as we made our way into the town. The main drag was about twenty metres wide. People were already out and about. They'd want to get their business done before the sun was at its fiercest. After midday, they'd bin it until last light – which would just leave the mad dogs and Englishmen to go about their business uninterrupted, with any luck.

Like everybody else, we kept in the shade. All the women were covered up, in one way or another. Most of them carried large empty plastic containers. On the way home they'd be full of water for the day's washing and cooking.

I caught a glimpse of some al-Shabab hard men in tribal *dish-dashes* and *shemaghs* down a side road. Long, wild beards on top; bare feet and sandals beneath. They carried AKs or RPGs. I stooped even further and kept on shuffling.

I thought about the old guy at the house. Fuck knew what he thought about Awaale coming to knock on his door to ask for a couple of *burqas*. I hoped they weren't distinctive in any way. I didn't want one of their mates to come rattling over for a chat.

This looked like the newer part of town. It would have been built at the same time as the Soviets were installing a missile facility at the port of Berbera in the 1970s and transforming Somalia's 17,000 armed forces into some of the strongest on the continent.

The bottom metre or so of the palm trees had been given a lick of white paint a few years ago. They were all bent away from the sea. The monsoon winds would have done their best to flatten them each year. I could have done with a bit of a breeze today, although I didn't want our *burqas* to do a Marilyn Monroe.

The same photocopied A4 flyer seemed to be pinned to every door and fence. I kept my speed down, but didn't move so slowly that I drew attention to myself. I bent forward, concentrating on the AK. I gripped it hard against me to stop the steel mag slipping out of my hand. I was sweating so much under this thing the skull band must be soaked on the outside. The mesh slit was a nightmare to look through. Even so, I could see this place was totally different from Mog. There was no grime, no burning tyres. But in other ways, it was scarier. Everyone looked anxious and uneasy.

On the other side of the road, four more AS sat in old armchairs under an acacia. They were smoking, and had a kettle boiling away on a little fire. All of them had AKs resting across their thighs. Two had canvas chest harnesses stuffed with mags. The other two had belts of 7.62 short slung over their shoulders, Mexican-bandit style. I couldn't see any machine-guns, just AKs.

All of them wore traditional cotton *dish-dashes* down to their knees and matching baggy trousers beneath them. They all had black and white checked *shemaghs* round their necks and multicoloured skull-caps. Their watches glinted in the sun.

They laughed and shouted to each other.

Awaale coughed just behind me. It was a flat cough, one I'd heard many times this morning as he tried to control his breathing. I knew the feeling. He had little or no control of the situation, and no weapon to react with if everything went to rat-shit. I switched off in these situations. I was going to walk down the road; I wasn't going to turn back. I was committed. There was nothing to worry about because there was nothing I could do about it.

We came level with the AS. They were just five metres away, on the other side of the road. My eyes flicked to the side; I wasn't going to turn my head. A couple of them glanced across at us, then away. One, darker-skinned and taller than the rest, perhaps a Pakistani, looked over, took two or three seconds to register what we were, and got back to the banter.

Two technicals came down the road towards us. One had a heavy gun mounted on the back. The other was weapons-free. Dark brown- or grey-cottoned legs and sandals dangled over the sides. I looked straight ahead and kept on walking. The wagons drove past and dust and shit swirled through the mesh of my visor. Behind me, Awaale had a coughing fit.

I steered us left at the first available turning.

23

It was an alleyway a couple of metres wide. Awaale shuffled alongside me, clutching one of the flyers. His head was inches from mine.

'Mr Nick, they're not in the jail.' He lifted the sheet of paper. 'This is not good, Mr Nick. We must hurry.'

I followed him across the road. He passed the four fighters and carried on down another alleyway. Two small boys were coming the other way, each leading an old man with a big grey beard and skull-cap, bent over much more than we were, their faces creased with age. As they got nearer, I realized the boys weren't looking after the men, it was the other way round. The kids' eyes were milky, clouded by what looked like cataracts. They could have been sorted out for a couple of dollars elsewhere – or for nothing if Somalia hadn't been too dangerous for the NGOs and MONGOs to pour into. As for the happy-clappy hospital ships, I'd have liked to see what happened if they'd parked up and offered Jesus along with a couple of plasters.

We stepped into the burning sun so they could pass

us in the shade. The boys were well into the Wahhabi way of things. They didn't even acknowledge us. I kept looking down into the dust, where we belonged.

When they'd gone, I moved nearer to Awaale again. 'What the fuck is happening? What does that bit of paper say?'

'I'll translate it for you, but not now. They could be moved any minute. You need to see them while you still can.'

He shuffled on and I followed. Babies cried in the buildings either side of us. We reached the end of the alley and emerged into what was clearly the older part of town. Plaster over stone or brick, the buildings looked like the colonial, Italian area of Mogadishu, but on a smaller scale. They had seen better days, but looked habitable. Most had first-floor balconies. Many boasted parapets; they looked like small medieval forts.

We were in a square, in the middle of which stood an octagonal obelisk that resembled a small lighthouse. Each face was painted alternately black and white.

A gaggle of kids dressed like miniature al-Shabab, but so far without weapons, ran into a building to our left. Facing us, the other side of the obelisk, was the largest of the buildings. It might once have been the town hall, years ago, when the Italians ran the place and there was law and order. The sun bounced off the ocean a couple of hundred metres down the avenue to its right. I could see what looked like old harbour walls.

Awaale paused for a moment. 'You see the red gates, Mr Nick?'

I followed his gaze to the left of the town hall. Solid metal at the bottom, vertical bars at the top, they were set into a low, once-whitewashed wall, topped with a security fence. Behind it was a single-storey colonial building that might have been a coach-house.

'They're in there, Mr Nick.'

'That's what the paper says?'

'They're being put on display. AS – the fighters, the mullahs – they live in the big building. It is now the Islamic Sharia Court. Not a good place.'

A gang of kids had stopped just to the right of the gates. Some were so deformed they were almost unable to function; some were being dragged about by the others. They were peering through the bars as I approached. I didn't know if Awaale was behind me or not. It didn't matter.

A couple of bodies moved around inside the compound: AS, armed and smoking. They picked up their wooden chairs and shifted them to a new vantage-point now the sun had moved. The kids shouted angrily, pointing down into the dead ground the other side of the wall. Locals lined up on both sides to get a better view.

To the right of the kids, close to the wall, a row of holes had been dug. The spoil was piled up alongside them. Arc lights had been mounted on the court-house walls. The wiring hung loosely from windows at the top of the building.

Five Somalis, three men and two women, were in the compound. But all eyes were on the three white prisoners.

24

Tracy, BB and Stefan were huddled in the shade of the wall to our left. They looked exactly as they had in the video. Tracy was wearing the same *hijab*. It was grimy and covered with dust. She lay on her side, Stefan in her arms. She stroked his hair, trying to comfort him. His eyes were closed. His legs were raw and red with the insect bites.

The three Somali men were in rags. Two lay down; one sat back against the wall. Their faces were blank; the abuse from the kids no longer registered.

BB sat on the far side of them. He also had his arse in the sand, his back to the wall. Elbows on his knees, his head rested on his hands.

The two Somali women were stuck in the corner, on their own, squatting on their haunches. One of them was crying. Her head jerked with every sob. The other, sobbed-out, simply looked down at the ground.

I moved along the wall to get closer to them. I was soon only a couple of metres away from Tracy. I could hear her singing gently to Stefan. 'Three Blind Mice'.

He still had his eyes closed. She sensed somebody above her. Maybe she'd become aware of my shadow on the sand. She looked up at me, tears in her eyes.

'Help us . . . please . . . help us . . .'

Her tears carved tracks through the layers of sand and dust on her face. Her lips were cracked and baked, but she was still beautiful. 'Please . . . help my son . . .' She reached up towards me.

All I could do was look. I turned my head towards BB. Was he in any condition to fight his way out?

He looked at Tracy as he heard her begging, then stared straight at my blue mesh.

The kids found something new to howl about.

He stayed completely focused. 'Why don't you shut the fuck up?' he said to them. 'And what are you look- ing at, you fucking bitch?'

Tracy struggled to her feet. Her hands gripped the bars less than a foot away from my face.

'Please help us . . . my baby . . . my son . . .'

I didn't want to look at her directly. We were too close. She might see my white skin through the mesh. As I looked away I could see why the kids had gone noisy again. Ant and Dec were being dragged out of the building to be put on display with the rest of them.

Both had just a day or so of stubble, and were in much better condition than the others. That said, they'd still had a good kicking. Ant had cut and swollen lips. Dec had a black eye.

Their AS escorts pushed them hard into the dust. The kids laughed, then screamed like banshees. The older locals were silent. I had the feeling they'd seen it all before.

Tracy's hands reached through the bars to try and grab me. I jerked back. She missed me by a couple of inches, then turned her attention to Awaale.

'Please help my son . . . please . . .'

She collapsed sobbing as the truth dawned. We weren't going to help. Nobody was. Her hands slid back through the bars.

The two AS hard men had had enough. They got to their feet and shouted at the kids to fuck off. Then they headed our way. They grabbed Tracy and flung her back onto the ground. Stefan was curled up in his own little world. It was like he'd pulled the duvet over his head and was praying the monsters would go away.

BB couldn't seem to decide whether he hated the AS or the audience more, so he turned on both of us. 'Yeah, go on, fuck off! Cunts . . .'

One of the AS lads picked up a handful of sand and stones and hurled it at us.

We got the message. We moved away. The kids ran off to join the others going into the *madrasah*, dragging their deformed mates with them. Hundreds of years before the Christian West switched on to the possibility, Muslims had figured out the world was round. They also knew the distance to the moon, and that the earth moved around the sun. Islamic schools were set up to teach mathematics, astronomy and philosophy as well as the Koran. I somehow doubted that this particular school was keeping up the good work. Judging by their performance a few minutes ago, they'd had the Koran drummed into them word for word, and been taught the hard-line AS interpretation of the text. Their generation of Somalis would know nothing else.

Awaale followed me past the court-house and down towards the harbour. Once I got there I'd turn left, back to the skiff. I needed to gather my thoughts.

It had all the makings of a weapons-grade gang-fuck, but at least BB sounded up for a fight.

25

The skiff was still where we'd hidden it. There were no new footprints coming towards it or going away. The surf had washed away the drag marks.

I'd moved out of the bunker and far enough into the scrub so we wouldn't be connected with the boat if it was found. Awaale and I were sixty or seventy metres away from the cache, but still close enough to the shore to see anybody coming up the beach towards us.

I took off my *burqa* and draped it between two spiky bushes to create some shade. I wasn't talking. My throat was dry. My body needed food and sleep. But all that still had to wait.

Awaale followed my lead. He whipped his *burqa* off and made a shelter next to mine. I stretched out in the sand. Within seconds my clothes were riddled with thorns and bits of brush. Awaale joined me. His shirt was soon covered in shit as well. He panted for breath as he reached for his cigarettes. The packet was soaked through. He stared at it in disgust and tossed it to one side.

I dug the Solar Monkey out of my day sack, opened the clam-like device to expose the photovoltaic cells and pushed it out into the sunlight. Awaale watched. He was attempting to reconcile himself with having to go without nicotine as well as water. I wiped my eyes, trying to avoid filling them with sand. It was fucking miserable.

'Check my adaptors. See if you can charge your phone up as well.'

I lobbed him the bag of jacks that had come with the thing. Mottled with sand, my hand looked like I had some kind of skin condition.

'Awaale, why are so many kids here malformed? They're everywhere – the lads near yesterday's dust-up, and now the ones outside the *madrasah* today. What's wrong with them?'

'I will tell you what's wrong with them, Mr Nick. They are diseased – they have a disease that comes from your world.' His face clouded. 'We have no government. Our coastline is unprotected. Most importantly for your people, it is unmonitored.' He waved towards the beach, to where the surf came crashing onto the sand. 'It looks like a holiday brochure. But the water is polluted. It has become the dumping ground for your toxic waste. Of course there will be no successful prosecutions of your big companies for this. So our children are born . . . the way you see them. You, the West, have done that.'

There was a deep sadness in his eyes. But also, for the first time since I'd met him, I saw the rage in his heart.

'Your factory ships sucked all the fish out of our sea.

Your toxic waste killed everything else. So our fishermen became pirates to feed their children. To feed their children who are born like sick goats and die before their time.'

He busied himself finding the jack he was after, allowing his anger to subside.

'Mr Nick, my job is done now. I'll wait here for you. I'll get you back to the airport. But what can *you* do? You have so little time before your friends are killed . . .'

I sat up, like he'd just given me the good news with a cattle prod.

He pulled a shoe from his belt and extracted the folded sheet of paper. 'Tonight, it says, the criminals will be punished. After Maghrib. The Wahhabis – the advocates of Sharia law – they're very strict.'

He started reading. 'The Islamic Sharia Court of Merca District confirms that one man will lose his hand for stealing from another man's house. Two men and two women have committed *zina*.'

'Adultery?'

'Yes. But it's not like you think. Having sex with someone and not being married to them, that's adultery to the Wahhabis. All of them will get *ramj*.' He hesitated. 'Do you know what that means, Mr Nick?'

The sweat on my chest and back went cold. I suddenly knew what those spot-lit holes in the ground were all about.

'I can give it a fucking good guess.'

'They'll be stoned to death. They'll be buried up to the neck, and then stoned.'

'Tracy and Justin too?'

376

'The same. They too have committed *zina*.'

The film on the memory chip replayed itself on the screen inside my head. 'They think they have committed adultery . . . ?'

'She has another man's child, Mr Nick. The Wahhabis. They're crazy people.'

'What happens to the boy? There are only six holes . . .'

'He will live at the *madrasah*. He will become al-Shabab.'

'What does it say about the other two white guys?'

'Nothing. Do you know them?'

'They came to do what I came to do – get the three of them out. But you were right. There's no negotiating with these fuckers.'

Ant and Dec must have been linked into the same int as Jules had.

'It gives me no pleasure to be right about that, Mr Nick. What is to be done? The *ramj* is tonight, after prayers.'

I took a breath; gathered my thoughts. 'OK. Here's the deal. You call Erasto. Tell him I need help to free my friends. Tell him I need as many men as he can send.'

He shook his head. 'No, Mr Nick, it won't happen. These people, they are not just crazy. They are *very* bad people. Erasto pays to keep them away. He will not—'

I pointed a finger at him. 'Tell him I'll pay him to fight them.'

He still shook his head. 'No amount of money will persuade him.'

'Tell him he can have the yacht as well. Fuck it, he can have every yacht out there, if he wants.'

'Mr Nick, it wouldn't be worth it to him. It would be war.'

'So what have you got now? Peace?'

Awaale turned onto his side. 'I am truly sorry. You're going to have to do this thing yourself. I will wait here. I will make sure the skiff is ready to take you back, to collect my money. But Erasto will not help. He wouldn't even listen to me. I am not my father.'

I glanced at the little red light on the Solar Monkey. 'Well, get him on the phone then. Call your dad.'

'My father?'

'He's got the pull around here, hasn't he? Get your phone out, for fuck's sake. Call him.'

I left him to it as I scrambled out of the shade. I didn't want Awaale to listen in on my next conversation.

26

Frank, as always, answered in two rings.

'I've found them. They're alive. But there's no way I can negotiate. If we don't act now, they're going to be dead by this evening.'

If Frank's heart missed a beat, he wasn't giving any sign of it. Part of me was starting to admire this guy. 'How much?'

'Three million, one hundred thousand dollars. In hundreds. I want the one hundred thousand separate from the rest, so when the three million's handed over, it won't be spotted.'

'OK.'

'I want it at the airport, soon as. Keep that aircraft on standby. It needs to be fuelled up, ready to go.

'I'm trying to get the clan to help us. If you don't hear from me by first light tomorrow morning, then I've fucked up.'

'OK.' He said it like he was agreeing to a pizza delivery.

There was a silence. I'd said all I needed to.

379

Frank filled it. 'You've seen Stefan, yes?'

'Yes, Frank. I told you. He's alive. Get the money to Mog so I can keep him that way.'

'Is he hurt? Is he ill?'

'As far as I can see, he's all right. He was with his mother. She's looking after him. She's comforting him. She's thinking only of him.'

I let the message sink in for a moment.

'There's one more thing, Frank. If all goes to plan, I'll find out what our problem was in the UK – who the guys were, the ones following me.'

I might have heard him sigh. 'That would be good, Nick. Thank you.'

'It's not only for your benefit. I don't want Tracy and Stefan lifted again, do I? I don't want to go through this shit again.'

I closed down the phone. I still had to manage Frank's expectations. And I still didn't know which way the arch poker player was going to jump. For all I knew, he might choose to fuck over Tracy and BB and lift Stefan from the *madrasah* later. That wouldn't be good enough for me. I had a promise to keep.

I dialled Anna. Things were about to get busy.

It didn't even go to voicemail. A female voice waffled at me in Arabic. I knew I didn't have a wrong number, so she must have been telling me that Anna's mobile either didn't have a signal or was switched off. I closed down. It had to be out of signal. Anna's mobile was linked into her bloodstream.

Back in the bunker, Awaale was talking to his father. 'He's come back.'

I crawled under the *burqa* and got the sweat-covered mobile to my ear.

'Mr Awaale?'

'Mr Nick, you are—'

He sounded half asleep. There was no time to fuck about.

'Your son has told you that I need some help?'

'Yes, but—'

'Mr Awaale, with respect, please listen. Hear me out. See if what I say makes sense. If it does, I need you to talk to Erasto. Persuade him that helping me helps him. And for your time, I will pay you twenty-five thousand dollars, the same as I will pay your son. He can send it to you. You have my word.'

I heard him rustling about. Now that I had his attention, he was probably sitting himself up against his pillows.

'Mr Awaale, I can offer Erasto two million US if he sends all of his guys to Merca today to help me rescue the three people I've come for. Erasto knows who I'm talking about. Whatever commission you need to share with him is up to you.'

There was silence as some serious thinking went on in Minneapolis.

'Mr Nick, it will cost you more than that. This is very, very dangerous.'

'There will be more. Erasto can take back the yacht that al-Shabab stole from him. Tell him there are also three pleasure boats here, as well as several cargo ships. He can take as many as he wants. Tell him that if he keeps paying al-Shabab, he's only delaying the inevitable. He's going to be fighting them at some stage. They will not want to stay out of his part of the city for long.

'So why not carry the fight to al-Shabab? Why not show what great fighters and strategists he and his men are, with a pre-emptive strike? Hit them where they feel safe. Show them that he won't stand for them coming in and taking over the part of the city that belongs to Erasto.

'I can make that happen, Mr Awaale. I can help your son here plan the attack, like we did yesterday. He will be a hero, just like you. Maybe one day he'll become head of the clan, because he knows how to carry the fight to the enemy. He can show the clan, again, today, what a great fighter he is. And Erasto's part of the city could be his, one day.'

I waited for him to mull this over. Or maybe he was playing with me. I didn't really care which: I just needed an answer.

In the end, I filled the silence for him, as he probably wanted me to. 'All I need is help to get me and the prisoners back to the airport. We will exchange cash for them there and then. It will be very, very easy. And I have one more thing, one more very big thing, to offer Erasto.'

'What is that?'

'I can give him the two men who killed Nadif. I can do that at the airport.'

'Nadif? Nadif is dead?'

'Yes. In England. I found him. He had been tortured first. I'll hand over the two men who did this, as part of the deal. They are here in Merca. But I'm going to need five minutes with them myself. I will not kill them. If there is no deal, I will kill them here in Merca, before I leave. Erasto will have no satisfaction, no revenge.

'Erasto needs to make a stand against al-Shabab. He's going to have to do it one day. Now is the perfect time. And he'll make a lot of money. So will you. I need Erasto's help, Mr Awaale. I need it now. Not later tonight, not tomorrow. Now. I need to know how many people he's going to send, so we can prepare. I need to know, one way or another.'

He had certainly woken up now. Money. Revenge. Fame for his son. Joe was right. *My brother and me against my father. My father's household against my uncle's household. Our two households against the rest of my kin.* Even Nadif had taken the side deal with me, against his brother. It was *The Sopranos*, with *shemaghs* and AKs.

'Please, Mr Nick, hand me back to my son. We will try to get your loved ones home safe. I will talk with Erasto. I will earn twenty-five thousand US for talking to him. Is that correct?'

'Correct.'

I handed Awaale the phone. As I did, I gripped his sand-covered hand. 'Make sure you tell your father that it *must* be now. Remember the stoning. We must take action *now*. I need to know.'

He nodded, and started mumbling into the phone. I lay back, marshalling my thoughts. If this didn't work, I had a ton of shit to do before last light.

Ten minutes later, I rolled onto my elbow and flattened out a patch of sand between us, so I could at least show Awaale what I had in mind. For now, it didn't matter how many men Erasto might send, so long as Awaale had the basics of the attack in his head. With all this talk of heroism, he was coming with me whether he liked it or not.

Once we found out whether or not Erasto was up for it, we could start fine-tuning. And, with luck, we'd find that out extremely soon.

PART SEVEN

1

Both of us were sweltering inside our pepper-pots once more. We were hidden behind a couple of upturned skiffs on the beach next to the harbour. The stone pier was a continuation of the road that came down from the court-house square. It jutted out to sea for about a hundred metres, and then did a dog-leg to our left and continued for another fifty. The stonework was crumbling badly. Maybe that was why no boats were moored anywhere near it.

From where we were, the court-house was at the top of the road on the right. The compound was to the right of that. A small alleyway divided them. The long shadows cast by the buildings behind us were fading fast. Awaale still had his mobile stuck to the blue material covering his ear.

He looked at me and shook his head. 'Still nothing.'

The fucker. I knew Erasto's skiffs were out there, in the dead ground behind the cargo ships. We'd watched them come along the coast and take cover about two hours ago. They also had a mobile-phone signal. Awaale had been chatting to them regularly, giving his orders for the attack like the true leader he was.

Now they were silent, just like Anna. I'd tried her twice since the first beach call. All I'd got was the Arabic pre-record. The message was so fast and loud it sounded like she was giving me a bollocking.

I checked my iPhone as *adhan* kicked off from the mosque's speaker system. It was four minutes past six. It wouldn't be long before *igama*, the second call to line up for Maghrib. We needed to be on target by then.

This wasn't good. The skiff crews should be answering their mobiles. Awaale needed to give them the order to move into the harbour. They should be on their way in by now. Erasto was getting enough fucking cash. Or maybe he thought there was more where that came from, and all he had to do was bide his time.

There were five skiffs, but I had no idea how many crew between them. Awaale said it was going to be no problem, he'd got it sorted. They were supposed to come from the other side of the cargo ships and hold position beyond the stretch harbour wall that ran parallel to the beach, covered from view and from fire. Those boats were our way out.

We'd RV with them down there. We'd get on board, have one final brief, and arrange the fire support group. Awaale liked the phrase 'fire support group'. He'd been saying it all day, shoving it in between the Somali waffle as he spoke to the crews on his mobile.

The fire support group would stay with the skiffs, to protect them and cover our move back down the road from the square. Awaale would take the rest of the crew with him. This assault group would split into two. One would pound the court-house with RPGs, machine-guns, everything they had, killing anyone running out of it and any AS who decided to leg it from the mosques and back up their mates. As that kicked off, Awaale would take me and the rest of his guys around the back of the court-house, along the dividing alleyway and into the compound. The locals would be at prayers. The one rule was: no zapping civilians. Apart from anything else, we'd be in enough shit if we were captured without having that hanging round our necks.

There had to be AS in the court-house, even at prayer time. And the prisoners next door had to be guarded. I'd seen six hard men in the compound an hour ago, sitting in the shade while the prisoners found shelter where they could. The new lot were the group of four we'd passed in the street earlier this morning, headed up by the tall Pakistani.

All I was going to do was scream into the compound and tell everybody to take cover before Awaale's team got busy with the RPGs. The crew's orders were then to kill any AS they saw, while I went and dragged the five of them out. Simple as that.

I'd steer them behind the court-house while Awaale kept giving us fire support – and then we'd get our heads down and leg it along the road to the skiffs. Awaale and his crew would then withdraw, and we were off. In and out in ten minutes.

That was if the fuckers answered Awaale's call.

2

Adhan was still being called. The muezzins' wails drifted from minarets all over town.

I nudged Awaale. 'Try again. If there's nothing, we're on our own.'

I gripped the AK under my *burqa*. Even if these fuckers let me down, at least it looked like BB was in the mood for a fight. And if Ant and Dec had two brain cells between them, they'd throw their lot in with us as well for their own survival. I'd worry about what to do with them once we were out of this shit. If they didn't want to help, that wasn't a problem. I'd just do what I was there to do.

Now *igama* was being called. Time to cut away from Awaale.

I pointed at the upturned skiffs. 'I'll meet you back here. Try and get one of these fucking things into the water. If you can't, we'll chuck a left and get back down the beach. We'll just have to take our chances.'

His mobile rang.

I dropped back to my knees. 'I told you to turn that

fucking thing off.' I poked his shoulder with my finger. 'Keep it on vibrate. We're not supposed to be here, are we? We should be praying.'

'Sorry, Mr Nick.'

He answered the mobile with a voice that was a lot quieter than the ring. I could tell by his tone that he wasn't getting any good news. The arc lamps in the square made the place look like a football stadium. I could just about make out the shape of his pepper-pot head in the ambient light as he stared at me through the mesh.

'Erasto . . . He wants more money. He wants four million.'

'He can have three. And I want an answer, yes or no, right now. If he delays this deal, it isn't worth a thing. It's going to be too late because they'll be dead. Tell him three million, yes or no. I've no time to fuck about.'

He put his hands up. 'Yes, yes, yes.'

Erasto must have heard me. I fucking hoped so. Awaale mumbled into the phone as I got back to my feet. He brought it down from his ear, and I saw the screen light dim.

'He's thinking.'

I leant closer to him, keeping my voice low. 'Well, while he's thinking, they'll be dying. I'm going up there now. He's fucking playing me, isn't he?'

The pepper-pot nodded, almost imperceptibly. 'You were expecting that, no? This is business. I heard your call today.'

'If you still think this is business, Awaale, you're missing the point. There are two kinds of people up in that compound: my friends, and your enemies. He's not going to get more money out of me, so fuck the lot of you.'

I heard a shout from where the road met the harbour wall. A male voice, and angry. An AS fighter strode towards us, yelling the same word, over and over. I didn't know what it was, but didn't need Awaale to translate. We were in the shit and getting a bollocking, big-time.

AK slung over his shoulder, he gesticulated furiously at us as he moved closer. We stayed on our knees, kept our heads low, acting subservient. The AS kicked sand at us. I hoped he was just asking why the fuck we weren't at prayers.

Awaale mumbled something in a high-pitched voice. It was pathetic. He shouldn't have done it. Luckily the AS was too busy shouting and kicking sand to be able to hear. We tumbled to our feet, but kept submissive. Awaale started to walk away, back along the beach. I followed.

I glanced back. The AS picked up a couple of rocks and came after us, still yelling abuse. He hurled one of his freshly gathered missiles towards us. It missed me but hit Awaale square between his bony shoulder-blades. It must have hurt like fuck. I heard a grunt, then felt a kick on my left thigh. His sandal made contact first with the AK under the *burqa*. The magazine rattled. The sound was unmistakable. And I knew he would have felt the solid wooden stock.

He unslung his own weapon and stepped back. I started to raise my AK, but I knew I was a nanosecond behind the curve.

Awaale rushed past me, hand held high in the air. He brought the rock down hard on top of the AS warrior's head.

The AS went down. Awaale dropped to his knees in the sand and the rock rose and fell again and again and again.

Awaale's mobile started to ring.

The screen glowed in the sand. I picked it up.

'Erasto? It's Nick. *Si o no? Si o no?*'

Awaale stood over what was left of the AS, fighting for breath. He dropped the rock, knelt briefly beside the body and wiped his bloodied hand on the dead man's *shemagh*.

I passed him the mobile. There was about fifteen seconds of waffle. He pulled off the head of his pepper-pot and threw it on the ground. 'Erasto says yes.'

He began to fish his rings out of his pockets to put them back where they belonged.

I grabbed him with my spare hand, making sure I kept the other on the weapon. 'Mate, I'm going *now*. By the time Erasto's lads get here and you've sorted them out, we might have run out of time. If they do make it, remember this: the crew looking after the skiffs, the fire support group, they must *not* fire at anything coming up or down the road that leads to the harbour wall. Do you get that?'

'Yes, Mr Nick. I know. They know.'

'Tell them to fire left and right, if AS are following us. They can drop anything that moves left or right of us, but not down the middle.'

'Yes, of course. No problem. Trust me. It will be a great victory.'

'Good. Now keep the fucking noise down, and put your mobile on vibrate. Remember the diagram in the sand. Even if I'm too late to lift them, you must still come up, you must still support me. The fire support group down by the skiffs, they will still support you. All clear?'

'Yes, Mr Nick. I have everything under control. We're going to kill many, many al-Shabab.'

'First we will rescue my friends. Killing al-Shabab is a bonus. You'll be able to tell your war stories, but only if you keep your head. This is a rescue mission. This is the reason we're here.'

'Yes, yes. I remember. No problem, Mr Nick.'

His mobile vibrated. He answered. I didn't wait to find out who it was. If Erasto had changed his mind, well, fuck him. I had to get up to the compound. With or without the crew, it was happening.

I skirted the body in the sand. The harbour wall was soon behind me. I faced the road that ran uphill. The light in the square sat like a glowing bubble in the inky black sky. Shadows danced in the dust. Bodies milled around. The faithful had finished their prayers.

I picked up my pace, the weapon back under the *burqa*, firmly by my side.

My iPhone vibrated in my pocket.

Fucking Awaale. He could really pick his moment.

I ducked into a doorway and pulled it from my pocket.

My eyes stared through the mesh towards the bodies at the top of the road. They were no more than a hundred metres away.

I muttered into the mouthpiece, 'Just get on with it, for fuck's sake.'

'Nick? It's me, Jules.'

'It's OK. I've found them. I—'

'No, no. It's not that, Nick. It's Anna. She's been shot.'

3

I leant heavily against the planks that made up the door. For a split second I felt nothing. Then a wave of dread surged through me.

'How bad?'

'Not sure yet. She's on a casualty boat out of Misrata. They're taking her to Benghazi. To the hospital at Al-Jaraa.'

'They?'

'The French. Benghazi is as far as it's safe for her to be moved.'

'I can't do anything, mate. Can—'

'Nick – stop. I'll take care of it. She just wanted you to know.'

'She called you?'

'She didn't want to worry you while you're on the ground. Where are you now?'

'Merca.'

I cut off. I couldn't do anything about her at the moment. All I could do was try to speed things up this end. Get it done, and get north.

I headed towards the square. The arc lamps were blinding. Centre stage, above the holes, more spotlights strung along the fence made sure the punters wouldn't miss any part of the drama.

The gates were open. I couldn't see anyone in the compound. All I could see were four old wooden wheelbarrows beside the holes. They were full of rocks the size of cricket balls, all ready to go. It didn't matter where my three were. They'd be coming out here any minute to face their punishment.

Crowds of people kept spilling out of the mosques. There were a lot of women dressed like me. There was no cheering; no raised voices. It was all very sombre. Only the *madrasah* kids, a hundred or so of the little fuckers, were getting sparked up. The mullahs were busy herding them towards the ringside. Even the two old guys we'd stepped aside for this morning had dragged their kids along for the show. Everyone else seemed almost scared.

I eased my way through the heaving mass, careful not to clip anyone I passed with the AK. I needed to be up close and personal, just like the blind kids. Bodies steamed around me. Flies and mosquitoes buzzed around the lights.

I got as near to the gate as I could. My eyes drilled into the compound. AKs slung over their chests, AS hard men herded us with thin, whippy sticks. We moved like a shoal of fish as the square continued to fill.

The door opened into the compound. A gasp rippled through the crowd.

Two AS brought out one of the three Somali men I'd

seen hiding from the sun this morning. Behind him, another two AS, one of them the Pakistani, hefted a wooden table.

A guy in a white skull-cap and ginger beard appeared. A murmur spread through the crowd. This guy was feared. He followed the procession towards the gate.

The Somali wasn't happy. He kept shaking his head, his hands joined in supplication. If he was expecting sympathy from Skull-cap, he was about to be seriously disappointed. The AS turned him back, shoving him on with bunched fists. They halted him just short of the holes. The table was put in front of him.

Skull-cap was dressed in a brown *dish-dash* and cotton trouser combo, with a pair of rubber flip-flops. His ginger beard rested on the black-and-white check *shemagh* wrapped around his neck. A machete dangled from his waist. He was young, no more than early thirties. Smooth-skinned. Really hard eyes that glinted in the harsh light. Pupils dilated. He shouted at the crowd, pointing at the trembling wreck who'd been selected as the warm-up act.

There was no ceremony. The Pakistani forced the Somali's exposed arm onto the tabletop. Skull-cap drew his machete, raised it high and brought it down. The blade took off the Somali's hand and half his fore-arm. The Pakistani released his prisoner and he fell to the ground, at first numb with shock, then screaming with pain. The arm rolled off the other side of the table and fell onto the sand.

Skull-cap bent down and picked up the severed limb by the thumb. He held it up to the crowd as the clothes-stealer was led away towards the school. The kids parted like the Red Sea for Moses. They stared open-mouthed at the mess that was left of his stump and the blood it dripped into the dust.

The oldest of the mullahs, stern and grey, slapped the miserable offender across the head with his shoe. He then beat the sole across his back as he was dragged towards the school. This lad was going to be taught the error of his ways, Wahhabi style, before he received any medical treatment – if he ever did.

The other mullahs sorted out the kids and herded them back into the pack for the main event.

4

Skull-cap screamed and shouted as the Pakistani led his AS team back inside. He wasn't shouting to them, but to the crowd. He pointed at us, then jabbed his finger skywards. His words were rapid and aggressive.

A different kind of murmur swept through the crowd as the two Somali couples were led out. This time it was disapproval. Some hissed.

All four moved very slowly. They didn't have to be pushed. Their heads were down. They'd given up hope. The women had their heads covered but their faces showing. As they made their way through the compound they displayed no emotion, not even fear. They were led to where Skull-cap waited by the blood-stained table.

I couldn't believe they wouldn't at least try to run. They stood in front of their allotted holes, heads down, eyes half closed against the light.

Still screaming at the crowd at the top of his voice, Skull-cap thrust his hand under the chin of each prisoner, lifting the head for all to see.

As he passed each victim and moved on to the next, the Pakistani pushed them into the holes. They had to kneel, with only their head and the tops of their shoulders showing above ground.

A group of young guys arrived from nowhere at the front of the crowd. They wore the same kind of head-gear as the boss, and black-and-white *shemaghs*. Their eyes burnt with zeal. They shovelled sand into the holes to hold the bodies firm. The two women cracked. Both burst into tears. The men rocked back and forth in prayer. The youths shovelled faster to pack them in.

The four AS big dogs headed back inside the building.

My chest heaved. I couldn't help it. My breath quickened. I tried to control it. My skin broke into a sweat. My whole body felt like it was going to burst.

Anna filled my head. I was going to lose the only two women I cared for in the space of the same night.

Where the fuck was Awaale?

The Pakistani led Tracy out. She carried Stefan in her arms. His head was on her shoulder, his legs wrapped around her, her arms wrapped around him. She was struggling to carry him. Both of them shielded their eyes from the bright lights, as they started the long walk.

It took all three of the other al-Shabab to bring BB out.

Skull-cap shrieked, pointing at these evil people coming towards us like they were Satan come to Merca.

BB's eyes darted around. He was trying to suss out

what was going on. It dawned on me. They didn't know what the fuck was happening. Otherwise he would have tried something by now. The three of them were dead men walking. What had they got to lose?

They reached the gates. The old school mullah walked up to Tracy and grabbed Stefan. The boy was his now. But Tracy had other ideas.

She pulled back her child and uttered a long, heart-wrenching cry that silenced the crowd. The women around me moaned quietly. Hands went up to mouths as Stefan hollered out for his mother. His arms clung tightly around her neck as Tracy tried to break the old mullah's grip.

Skull-cap brandished his blood-covered machete at her and yelled to the crowd.

BB didn't move a muscle to help her. He did exactly what he should have done. He looked around, taking everything in, wondering what the fuck he was going to do with the information.

BB then saw the four getting buried, and the two empty holes, and knew precisely what was about to happen.

I moved forward from the crowd, pushing up the *burqa* so I could get the weapon into my shoulder.

5

The Pakistani swung to face the crowd. He would have seen straight away why they were screaming and who they were running from.

As I got the weapon into the shoulder I pushed the selector all the way down to single shot. The Pakistani fixed his eyes on me. I had both eyes open, focused on the foresight. The Pakistani pushed BB out of the way to get his own weapon up but he was too slow. My weapon kicked and he went down. I'd got him with one round into the chest.

The noise around me faded the further the crowd dispersed. Then I heard gunfire. I couldn't tell where it was coming from or where it was going. Tracy was just metres away now. Stefan had disappeared.

One of the other AS big dogs was bringing his AK up but BB had grabbed the Pakistani's weapon and gave him a three-round burst. He helped himself to a chest harness full of mags.

'Tracy! Tracy! Here – with me! It's Nick! It's Nick!'

BB was still firing. He took on the other AS to my right.

'*It's Nick!*'

Tracy couldn't compute.

'*It's Nick!*'

BB looked round. He got it.

I grabbed hold of Tracy and pulled off my *burqa* at the same time. I wanted to get her into the shelter of the wall. Rounds rained in from the right of the compound.

She was rooted to the spot; confused; scared.

'Nick . . . ?'

'*Come on.*'

I grabbed hold of her and began dragging her into cover. BB was changing mags. I got eye-to-eye with him and he started closing in. I pulled her down on her knees, so that her head was below the parapet. The crowd was still scattering in all directions. They didn't know which way to run. The fire was coming from the court-house. They could get a lead on us pretty much anywhere they liked if we tried to make a break for it across the open ground.

BB took up position alongside us and knelt with the AK.

Tracy tried to pull away from me. 'Stefan! I must get Stefan!'

She pointed frantically at the *madrasah*. 'Stefan!' She tried to crawl past me.

Everything was total confusion but her screams were louder than the crowd's.

I looked over the wall. Skull-cap was on the veranda of the main building with the others, weapon up. They were shouting, more in anger than in fright. They'd been done out of a good day's stoning.

To our right, the Somali women scrabbled to get out of the dirt. The lads accused of shagging them were well and truly gone.

The skull-caps on the veranda popped in and out of the doors like Swiss cuckoos, firing indiscriminately at anything that moved. A *burqa*'d figure took a hit at the edge of the square and tumbled into the dust.

A burst stitched along the wall the other side of us. 7.62 is a big-calibre round. The sound of at least a dozen of them thumping into the block-work nine inches from our heads was deafening. I felt the tremors.

I pushed Tracy down flat and crouched over her as BB got his AK over the wall and gave it bursts towards the court-house.

I jumped up, my legs astride Tracy's back, and put some rounds down towards the veranda.

Still no sign of Awaale.

I yelled across at BB, 'They're going to be all over us. Take her down to the beach, turn left, get out of the town. We'll RV somehow. I've got a skiff there waiting. Just get out of the town. You'll see me moving along the beach. I'm going to go and get Stefan.'

More rounds slammed into the far side of the wall. Tracy sobbed into the dust. 'My baby . . . my baby . . .'

We jumped back down.

'Fuck, Nick – did you come on your own? Whatever. Thank fuck . . .' He slapped a hand on my shoulder.

I shook my head. 'I thought I'd brought backup, mate. But the fuckers seem to have left us to it.'

I grabbed another look over the wall. A cloud of grey smoke erupted from a corner of the compound and the back blast kicked up a storm of sand. The sustainer motor kicked in and the round screamed towards us.

'RPG!'

We ducked. But it wasn't coming for us. Chunks of breezeblock and rendering blasted in all directions from the court-house. Debris rained down on us like hailstones.

Screams, shouts and the rattle of automatic fire came from the far side of the *madrasah*.

6

'BB, listen in! That's my backup. We're RVing with them down at the harbour. They've got boats. Make sure they take you down the road, right of the court-house. You've got to stay on the road.'

Rounds zinged in all directions as chaotic and drugged-up shouts and screams echoed around the square. Tracer bounced off the ground and whizzed into the sky. A machine-gun opened up somewhere the other side of the obelisk. More shouts and screams; then a couple of lines of a rap song and taunts from the crew aimed at the court-house. Above it all I heard, 'Mr Nick! Mr Nick!'

Awaale and his crew charged up the alley between the court-house and the compound like the Seventh Cavalry. Muzzle flashes flickered at the windows of another building maybe 150 metres away. BB loosed off a couple of short bursts in return.

'Over here, mate! On me! On me! Awaale!'

The rounds were hurtling in from everywhere and everyone. Tracer zapped into and out of the court-house and from the buildings surrounding the square. We lay in the dust. I kept Tracy covered. Partly to protect her, partly because she kept trying to get up and run.

Awaale arrived alongside us with half a dozen of his crew. Their teeth glistened with *khat* juice. They were totally off their tits. They squatted and bounced, fired a couple of bursts, squatted and bounced, fired a couple more, not really caring who they hit.

Awaale gobbed off into his radio, probably creating even more chaos.

I put my mouth to Tracy's ear. 'It's OK. I'll get him.' I kept my voice level. 'You go with BB. These lads will look after you, OK? I'll get him, I promise.'

She twisted her head. I could see the fear in her red, tear-filled eyes.

BB cut in: 'Yep, no problem. I'll take care of her. I'll keep her with me.'

She didn't want to leave her son. 'Nick – no!'

'Stefan will be OK. I'm going to go and get him. Awaale!'

The fucker was only about three metres away but he still wasn't answering me. He was too busy shouting at everyone else on his radio.

'*Awaale!*'

Screams and howls came from the crews both sides of the court-house as they revved up. An RPG kicked off to our right and flew straight down the middle of the square. It shaved the obelisk and slammed into a building fifty metres further on. There was a bright orange flash and lumps of concrete flew into the air.

'*Awaale!*'

'Yes, Mr Nick!'

'Let's take them down to the harbour. Remember, only on the road, dead centre. Let's go!'

I grabbed BB. 'Take her now, with these lads. I'll get Stefan and we'll RV at the boats. Awaale!'

The fucker had evaporated again.

Two technicals came screaming towards us from the direction we'd taken this morning. The guns' heavy reports reverberated above the rest of the shit around us. Tracer zoomed over our heads. Some hit the obelisk.

'*Awaale!*'

'Yes, OK, I am here, Mr Nick!'

He stepped out of the gloom. He was soaked with sweat. His hands glinted with jewellery. Any passing Black Hawk wouldn't have stood a chance while he was in this mood.

'Get some fire down on those fucking technicals!'

'It's no problem, Mr Nick. It's my crew. They landed in the wrong place so they took the AS technicals. This is very good, Mr Nick. This is a great victory.'

'No, it fucking ain't great! You've got to control them, mate.'

On cue, their tracer kicked into the compound building. Some of it scudded into the shallow graves the girls had finally pulled themselves out of. If they hadn't, they would have been history.

'You got fucking rounds going all over the place. Control them! Get the fucking technicals here, get this lot on board, and let's get them down to the boats. I'm going to go and get the boy. He's in the *madrasah*.'

Awaale waffled into his radio. His crew ran about laughing manically, firing, shouting.

I got up. 'BB, take Tracy. Now. Get her on the technicals as soon as they come over.'

Tracy struggled to her knees. 'No, Nick – no . . .'

'Tracy, it's OK. Stefan will be just fine.' I pointed to Awaale. 'You're going to get the other two white lads out of there as well, remember. Erasto wants to kill them.'

'No problems, Mr Nick. We'll take care of them.'

The technicals came bouncing across the square, all guns blazing. If they'd heard Awaale tell them to stop firing, they weren't taking any notice. As they bounced, tracer arced over the court-house. It was probably landing in the sea or zapping our own boats. Some of it scudded off the dirt and ricocheted into random buildings.

I pushed Tracy down once more. 'Awaale!'

He was busy shouting orders. An RPG kicked off from fuck knew where.

We couldn't move.

7

As the wagons came closer I caught sight of the gunner's star-shaped, white-framed sun-gigs. The sun had gone down hours ago, but that didn't bother him. And the driver, for fuck's sake, was on his mobile. He looked like he was larging it with a blow-by-blow account for the benefit of the girls back home.

BB was out of ammunition. I threw him my day sack with the spare mags. I turned and shouted to one of the crew. I wanted the pistol he had tucked into the back of his jeans. He lay in the dust by the gate, firing at the completely strike-marked court-house. He gave me a big, *khat*-stained grin. 'Fifty dollar!'

'Fuck off! Give me the weapon!'

He shrugged and shouted to his mate the other side of the gate. They both laughed. Another RPG kicked off, this time from AS. It was way off. It almost went into orbit.

The kid with the pistol finally relented. He didn't even check safety before he threw it. As it sailed through the air I could see it was a Makarov, and so old there was no parkerization anywhere near it. I caught it and pulled back the top slide. A brass case was already in the chamber. I pressed the mag-release catch. It dropped into my hand. The mag was full.

BB was now crouched over Tracy to protect her. He held her head down, trying to calm her.

Awaale and four of his crew peeled off and ran towards the compound building. They were going for Ant and Dec. Awaale was in the middle of the gang, still shouting into his radio as if he was controlling this shit. The technicals banged out 12.7 at every muzzle flash within reach. It didn't seem to matter who was on the receiving end.

I got up and started running for the *madrasah*, head down, fast as I could. I reached the massive wooden doors. They were open. I stopped, looked and listened. Nothing. I walked into the hallway. Yellow low-current strip-lights hung from the ceilings. The plaster was pitted. What had probably once been colonial Italy's pride and joy was now close to a ruin. Dark wooden doors led off it, left and right.

The sound of firing was muffled. The whoops of excitement and fear were mumbles. I ventured into the high-ceilinged building. If this place was a school, there was nothing to suggest it. There were no children's drawings pinned to the walls; nothing to show children used the place at all.

The door of the first room I came to was open. Looking down the corridor, I could see a lot of the others were closed. This one was full of low desks. They were just inches from the floor, their tops at a reading angle. Each desk had a little cushion.

I crossed the corridor to the room opposite. The hinges were on the right. I put my ear to the wood but couldn't hear anybody on the other side. I eased it open. The weak light from the strips was enough to show me the room was empty. I went down to the next. My sand-crusted socks rasped on the wooden floor.

This door had a spy-hole bored through it. There was a long bolt at the top. It looked like the schoolrooms doubled as cells; or maybe the kids weren't allowed out until they'd learnt today's chunk of the Good Book. I put my ear to the wood again and went in.

Nothing.

I moved along the corridor, now just checking the spy-holes left and right.

I could hear a voice. An old man's voice, like tyres on gravel. It was coming from the room beyond the next one. The door was ajar.

I moved very slowly, my shoulder skimming the wall. As I got closer, the voice became stronger. I lowered myself to my knees, then flat on my stomach. I inched my head towards the gap between door and frame.

The mullah had a small knife against Stefan's right eye. It looked like it came from a kitchen. He held it with his left arm around his throat so the flat of the blade rested on the little boy's cheek. His right hand covered the kid's mouth.

The old guy sat in a chair behind a desk. He had the boy in front of him as cover.

Stefan was a mini Frank, except that I'd never seen

Frank with that expression on his face. The small boy was petrified. His brown eyes were wide with terror.

I got up and moved forward, the weapon down by my side.

'Do you speak English? Come on, let the little one go. Let Stefan go, yeah?'

I spoke more with my eyes than my mouth. He barked something in dialect, and then he started shouting. He didn't want me to get any closer.

I stopped, keeping eye-to-eye. That was always the most important thing.

I looked at him, almost begging. 'Mate, you're not going to get out of here. Help yourself. Give me the boy.'

I held out my left hand. 'Let me have him. Please.'

I even gave him a bit of a smile.

Stefan's shoulders heaved as he sobbed into the mullah's palm. The old man leant forward, his beard draped over the boy's face. He shouted at me big-time.

My eyes bored into his.

'Mr Nick! Mr Nick!'

It sounded like Awaale was at the main entrance.

I moved my weapon to one side. 'Look, mate, it's OK.' I didn't want to get this lad sparked up. I took a step towards him.

The mullah's eyes darted from me to the door I'd come through. He was unsure. He was getting worried.

'Mr Nick! We've got to leave!'

I could hear flip-flops and the sound of running feet.

Awaale was at the door. I could hear him behind me.

'Mr Nick!'

The old guy's eyes went back to mine. They were no longer tense; no longer unsure. He knew he was fucked. I kept mine focused on his head, brought the weapon up, jamming it into my left hand as he raised his knife, ready to ram it into Stefan's chest.

Stefan screamed. The old guy gripped his hair and pulled back his head.

I took first pressure on the trigger of the Makarov, my eyes glued to a point just above the muzzle. I caught a glimpse of cheekbone and moved the pistol until I had the clear and focused foresight dead centre of the face. The rear sight was out of focus, just as it should be. The first pad of my forefinger squeezed the trigger a couple of millimetres until I felt first pressure.

Stefan struggled. The knife quivered in the air.

I shut Awaale and every ounce of background noise out of my head.

The old guy yelled at me. I could see the veins in his temple swell, and spit fly from his lips.

Then he raised the knife a fraction more to get full force behind it.

His head and beard were fuzzy. My foresight was clear. I brought it up, just above his left eye, and took second pressure. The knife began to plunge. The pistol kicked in my hands and the old guy's face imploded.

He dropped like liquid. The knife clattered on the wooden floor. The boy followed it under the table, screaming, out of control, curling up like a small, threatened animal.

I ran towards him. 'It's OK, Stefan. It's OK . . .'

I had to yank him out from under the table. I

scooped him up and made him face me, encouraged him to wrap his legs around my waist.

'My name is Nick.'

Awaale was gobbing off behind me.

'Shut the fuck up!'

'We've got to go, Mr Nick.'

I got eye-to-eye with Stefan. 'My name is Nick and I'm going to take you to your mum, OK?'

He wasn't listening. He was totally freaked out. I was just one more monster in his nightmare. He was going to need a lot of help. But if his brain was wired the same way as his dad's, he'd probably survive.

'Come on, shall we go and see your mum?'

I turned to Awaale. Four of his crew had piled into the room. I started walking towards the door.

'Mr Nick, you're a lucky man! That was one lucky shot!'

I couldn't be arsed to explain. 'Yeah, yeah. Let's get out. Where are Tracy and BB?'

A stream of gobbing off poured out of his radio. He put his hands up. 'They're OK. Come. We must join them.'

I held Stefan into me as tightly as I could.

'Mummy . . . Mummy . . . I want Mummy . . .'

I did my best to soothe him as we headed towards the gang-fuck outside.

8

The technicals had gone from the compound. So had Tracy and BB. And there was definitely shit on down by the harbour. Tracer swirled into the sky above it from behind the court-house.

Awaale had already reached the obelisk and was standing there as if he had fifty layers of Kevlar, back and front.

'Mr Nick, come on – we are waiting.'

I passed two of his crew kneeling in the open. They were giggling and arguing between themselves at the same time as they tried to load an RPG. Automatic fire still came from the fringes of the square.

Stefan clung to me, his legs trying to cut off the circulation in my waist. I gripped him tight with my left arm. Just as we passed the stoning holes the RPG cracked off behind us. The crew had fucked up. A split second later it smashed into the obelisk. The pressure wave hurled me to the ground. My ears were still ringing as I staggered to my feet in a cloud of sand and mortar dust.

'It's OK, Stefan. We're all right. We're nearly there. Nearly with your mummy.'

Maybe the lads hadn't fucked up. Maybe they'd been aiming at the obelisk. Who knew? There were peals of laughter as they legged it towards us. I wondered if Awaale had enjoyed the joke. I gripped my hands under Stefan's thighs so I could get my feet pounding across the open ground.

Bodies lay all over the place. AS, crew or crowd, it was hard to make out one from the other. Skull-cap's body was draped over the railing of the veranda. Most of the arc lamps had been shot away. The dark liquid pooling beneath him glistened in the light of those that remained.

I pushed Stefan's head into my shoulder. He didn't have to see that shit. He'd had enough drama to be going on with.

I followed Awaale. My throat was so dry it felt like I'd been swallowing sand. It was a long time since I'd had fluids. I was dehydrating.

We turned left between the court-house and the compound and then went right. At its far end, the alleyway intersected with the harbour road. I'd just turned into it when I saw a rocket trail at the bottom of the hill. It was heading our way.

'RPG! RPG!'

I ducked back into the alleyway as the grenade screamed past us, less than a metre above the ground. It hit somewhere the other side of the court-house and exploded.

'Not far now. It won't be long.'

Stefan didn't say a word. He gripped me harder. He

buried his head deeper into my shoulder to get away from this nightmare.

I stuck my head round the corner and yelled, 'Awaale! Where are you? Get them to stop! Not down the road! Not down the road!'

The RPG team who'd demolished the obelisk loaded up again, giggling with excitement, then ran out into the road to return fire towards the harbour.

'No! No! No! That's your crew! Awaale!'

I could hear his radio in a doorway further down.

'It's OK, Mr Nick, come on.'

He sauntered into the middle of the road, waving me on, as if I was holding up proceedings. 'Come on, Mr Nick.'

'Tell these lads to can it. No one's to fire down or up the road.'

'It's OK.'

We'd gone no more than ten paces down the hill when the RPG kicked off behind us, heading back towards the square. I was buffeted by the shockwave, then the hot back blast washed over me. My nose filled with the acrid smell of cordite and spent propellant. My eardrums zinged.

Ahead of us, muzzle flashes flickered the length of the harbour wall. Miraculously, the tracer headed left and right and over us.

9

As we neared the beach I could see the two technicals. They were now weapon free. Awaale stood on the wall. His radio was going ape-shit. All I could hear was whoops and shouts and jibber-jabber.

'Come, Mr Nick, come.'

There were no more rounds heading our way from the town. The lads here were having a good cabbie.

'Two skiffs left, just for us.'

He jumped on board the first with the two lads who had stayed with it.

'Where's Tracy? Where's the boy's mother?'

The rest of Awaale's crew clambered into the one behind. They were still on cloud nine. Mobiles went off. Lighters were struck and cigarettes lit. I heard the hiss of bottles being opened.

'Awaale. Look at me.'

He wasn't on receive. He was stuck on transmit, gobbing off to anyone within earshot.

'*Awaale!*' I finally got his attention. 'Where is the boy's mother?'

'They've gone in the other skiff. No problem.'

'You sure she's safely aboard?'

'Yes, of course. We need them safe. She's with the man.'

'What about the other two white guys? Are they on board as well?'

'They're on another boat. Erasto wants them most of all.'

I passed Stefan to him. Awaale's face creased into a huge grin. 'Hello, big man.'

I didn't know if it was what he said or the scary *Twilight* smile that made Stefan scream, but his little arms swung back towards me. 'Mummy! I want my mummy!'

Awaale patted his head and handed him back. 'Not long now. We'll see her soon.'

The engines revved and we headed into the darkness as the RPG team behind us kicked off one last round. Judging by the laughter, it was just for the fun of it. It made contact with one of the low-level buildings lining the beach.

I took the middle bench. Stefan sat on my knee, legs over one side but face buried in my chest.

I turned back towards Awaale. He wasn't too thrilled to be back at sea. He sat to the right of the outboard, arse on the floor, knees up.

'Awaale, good one, mate.' The lad at the tiller revved the engine to fight the surf, so I had to shout. 'Really good one. Now, can we hook this boy up with his mum? I want to get them together before the airport.'

Awaale curled up into a ball. 'They're out there somewhere. It's no problem.'

421

'We're not there yet, mate. Make sure your guys know to keep the lights to the left. We need to go north. Let's keep everyone together. Control them, mate.'

Awaale heaved himself up and gobbed off into the radio. Six different voices tried to answer at once. I left him to it and pulled out my iPhone. I had one voice-mail message.

'Good evening, Mr Stone, Henry here. Just calling again about that apartment of yours. Could you please give me a ring when convenient? Thank you.'

I felt a bit sorry for Henry. Commission on £150K was never going to make his day, but four per cent of fuck-all was a bit of a choker. I called Frank.

Two rings.

'Yes?'

'Good news. I have Stefan with me. Tracy's in another boat. We're—'

'Is he hurt?'

'No. He's traumatized, but physically he's OK.'

'Can I speak to him?'

I put the iPhone to Stefan's ear. 'It's Daddy.'

He looked up. He didn't believe me but he took the phone with both hands. 'Papa! Papa!'

There was a chorus of oohs and aahs around the boat before he started gobbing off in Russian. He almost fell over his words as he raced to get them out.

They spoke for a couple of minutes while Awaale bollocked somebody for something over his radio. The two crew members in the bow were on their mobiles, sucking teeth, flicking fingers.

We'd left the lights of Merca behind us. There was

no sign of land. No sign even of the other skiffs as we bounced out of the last of the surf and started to ride the heavier swell.

10

Seven or eight tracer streamed up into the sky. We heard the liberated 12.7's heavy report a second later.

'There she is, Mr Nick. The little one's mother.'

Our boat turned in the direction of a second burst. The propeller left the water for a second as the skiff wallowed in the swell and the outboard went into overdrive.

Stefan held the iPhone to my face. 'Papa wants to talk to you.'

'Everything is ready at the airport. How long until you get there?'

'We've been linking up again. I'm not sure where we are. But I'm guessing a couple of hours, maybe three.'

'Very good, Nick. There will be transport waiting at Malindi airport. The pilot has the details.'

'I'll call you before we take off.'

There was a momentary silence.

'Nick, thank you. Thank you very, very much.'

'Don't thank me yet. We're still bobbing up and down in the middle of nowhere.'

There was another tracer burst. Stefan hugged me. I looked down at him. 'It's OK, mate. It's just telling us where your mummy is.'

Frank barked, 'What's happening?'

'Everything's fine. They're just showing us where Tracy is. She's on another skiff. Would you like to talk with her when we meet up?'

That was a no-brainer. 'She and I will talk later. Nick, I know you're not safe yet – I understand that – but I do thank you.'

'No drama. We'll talk soon, OK?'

I slid the iPhone back into my pocket. We were closing on the other skiff. They treated us to another fireworks display even though we were only about ten metres away. The 12.7's muzzle flash strobed the passengers. BB was down by the engine. Pissed-off was written all over his face. 'Stop that fucking racket, you cunts! They're on fucking top of us!'

Stefan gripped me even harder.

I hadn't noticed it before in the frenzy, but he stank. He absolutely reeked. I supposed we all did.

'Your mummy's right there. You're going to see her soon, yeah?'

He nodded into my chest. 'Mummy?'

'Yes. Not long now. Look.' I pointed at the dark shape bobbing in the swell about five metres away.

The two lads in the bow got off their mobiles and grabbed the side of the other boat. We levelled off. Tracy was already leaning towards us, her arms out-stretched. 'Stefan!'

He almost wriggled out of my arms. 'Let me help you, mate. It's a bit late for a swim.' The last thing

I wanted was him falling between the two boats.

The 12.7 from the technical was hanging off the bow of Tracy's boat. It was clearly Star-gigs's turn at the trigger. He couldn't have been happier if it was a giant marlin. There were empty shell cases all over the deck.

I hoisted the boy over the side. Tracy grabbed him and almost fell backwards into her boat. Star-gigs steadied her and eased them both back onto the centre bench.

They were soon stuck together like glue, crying into each other's hair. She pulled back and stroked his cheek. 'It's OK, darling.' Then, as Star-gigs fired up his lighter and lit something that smelt stronger than a cigarette, I saw her face in the darkness.

'Nick . . .'

She tried to say more but her sobs were suddenly the noisiest thing in this part of the ocean.

BB had had enough of this shit. 'Listen, those other two cunts are out there somewhere. How are we supposed to find them?'

I turned back to Awaale. He was on his mobile. 'Mr Nick, is everything OK at the airport? The money?'

'All ready to go. But where are the other two?'

He didn't answer. He got busy with his mobile instead. And he wasn't a happy bunny.

'Awaale, you have got the other two, haven't you?'

BB scuttled across the deck towards me. 'What's up?'

'The other two lads. I think they're Georgians. They speak English? You get anything out of them?'

He shook his head. 'We weren't allowed to talk. But so what?'

He stank as bad as Stefan did.

'We're going to find out for Frank who they are, then hand them over to these lads. We think they killed the clan boss's brother.'

I left out the bit about Jan. Now wasn't the time for Tracy to learn about that. She had enough shit to deal with.

11

Awaale finished his call. 'OK. We split up now.' He gobbed off to the crew and they pushed us apart.

Erasto was smart. It was probably why he was about to become even richer. These three weren't coming ashore until Awaale had confirmed the money was at Mog airport and the deal was in the bag.

I could still hear mother and child sobbing to each other as their skiff was swallowed by the darkness.

'Tracy! It's OK. We're all going to the airport. A plane is waiting. We'll be back together soon. Just a couple more hours. I've got to go ahead and make sure everything's good when we get there. BB will look after you.'

BB grunted. 'My fucking name is Justin.'

We headed out to sea as Star-gigs continued his love affair with the 12.7.

Awaale sparked up his radio and a dozen different voices jibber-jabbered back.

Another line of tracer peppered the sky behind us.

'You see, Mr Nick? Everybody will be together soon.

But we have to make sure the money is there first. Me, I trust you with my life. But Erasto – he doesn't know you like I do.'

I didn't bother turning back. 'Mate, the money will be there. But I'd feel a lot happier if we knew where Nadif's killers were. Have you made contact?'

He had to shout as we picked up speed. 'Do not worry, Mr Nick. I'm not worried. I'm not worried about a thing. We know the sea. I'm happy. I'm a great commander. Everybody is talking about me. Everybody knows about the attack. Even Lucky Justice will hear about it very soon.' He nodded. 'Yes sirree.'

One of the crew was hunched below the bow, out of the wind. He talked excitedly into his mobile.

I moved closer to Awaale. 'That is fantastic news, mate, but remember – success breeds enemies. Just be careful now you're big-time. Some people don't like to be upstaged. You know what I mean?'

We bounced about on the waves. I didn't have a clue if we were pointed in the right direction.

He thought about what I'd said and eventually nodded. 'You're right. But I'm Somalian. We know these things. Erasto will not be pleased. Once he has the money, he'll try to have me killed. But I'll be quicker than him. My father will give me advice. Everybody loves me for the great fighter I am, just like my father before me. Thank you, Nick.'

I smiled politely. I was getting a lot of thank-yous tonight. That always meant a drama was just around the corner.

12

These guys started life as fishermen. I shouldn't have doubted their prowess at sea. Two hours later I began to see the lights of the city over the bow. We were coming in from the east. I didn't have a clue how far out to sea we'd had to divert during the RV with Tracy, but that didn't matter now. All that did was that her skiff made it back too. Ant and Dec's? I still had no idea.

Awaale perked up now he could see land. He had spent most of the time curled up on the deck holding his stomach. 'I told you so. You don't have to worry about anything, Mr Nick. Everybody is now safe.'

We started to approach the airport. The runway was lit up like a UFO landing pad. We headed for the bit sticking out into the ocean. As we got closer, I spotted two technicals. The crews looked excited to see us. Their new conquering hero was home. There was change in the air.

Awaale got on his radio. Then he hauled his mobile out. 'You see, Mr Nick? Everybody loves me.'

We pulled the skiffs into the beach. The sting of salt water reminded me that, after a day in my socks, my feet had taken some serious cuts.

The technical driver shouted down at us through the glare of his own main beams. He thought he was help-ing, but he was just killing our night vision. Blinded, we felt our way up the rock and clambered onto the runway.

We scrambled into the back of the technical, dodg-ing the 12.7's dangling ammo belt, and set off between the twin lines of landing lights that seemed to con-verge as they headed for the terminal.

The driver stuck his head out of the window and shouted to Awaale, who was sitting directly behind the cab on the flatbed. Awaale leant forward and treated him to a blow-by-blow account – complete with 'boom, boom, boom' sound effects. Then he leant even further so he could deliver a high-five. The accelerator pedal never left the floor. It was like the guy was trying to take off. All around me, the boys were back on their mobiles, spinning more shit.

Down-lighters in the roof space made the newly painted terminal building look like it was suspended in its own star system. A Cessna Cargomaster stood in front of it, a weapons-mounted technical alongside. Further down the apron were a couple of closed-down Yemeni airliners.

Another technical had parked up a hundred metres beyond them. The Toyota's headlamps were aimed at a nearby Skyvan. Winner of the Ugliest Plane in the World Award for the last thirty years running, it was basically a train carriage with a tail ramp to freefall out of, a wing and an engine slapped on each side. The twin props had chugged about all over the world since the 1980s, and this must have been one of the originals; the H tail rudders were held together with gaffer tape.

Awaale pointed at the wagon by the Cargomaster. 'Erasto. He's here for the money. I do not want to disappoint him, Mr Nick.'

'Nor do I, mate. Nor do I. But what about Erasto? Will he disappoint *me*?'

He looked at me from the other side of the flatbed. The 12.7's barrel cut a line between us. Finally he put his hands up and shrugged. 'I'm not in his head.'

I pushed the cold steel barrel skywards to clear the obstruction between us and leant across the back of the cab. I wanted Awaale to hear every word of what I was about to say. 'The other two white guys, the boy and the woman, they're important. They're important to someone who can come up with that sort of cash straight away. If this all goes wrong, he's told me that he will declare war on you, on you all. Now that's going to fuck up your future, big-time. And you've got enough on your plate already. Lucky Justice is not a big fan, and now you've got AS on your arse as well. We've got to make this run very smoothly, mate. For both our sakes.'

Fuck it. Things had moved on too far to hide the fact there was a lot of cash flying about, and managing Erasto's expectations had gone completely out of the window. But solving one problem will always present you with another.

'Mr Nick – there'll be no problems from me. Trust me.'

'You've got family in the US, right? You've got to be careful, mate, because my man can get to them. But all he wants is his family back. He gets what he wants, and you get what you want, and everybody's happy. Yeah?'

Awaale nodded. 'I understand, Mr Nick. But you don't need to tell me these things. You're my friend.'

'You're my friend as well, mate. But let's not fuck up now that we're so close to the finish, OK?'

Awaale smiled and leant back. The wind ruffled his hair. I still only trusted him as far as I could throw him. It wasn't as if we were old schoolmates. We slowed. We were almost at the terminal.

Awaale leant back towards me, hand up at the side of his mouth like we were co-conspirators. 'Mr Nick, my money . . . I will need it to pay for loyalty from my crew when I take over the clan.'

'One thing at a time, mate. Let's get in the air before you go and conquer Mogadishu.'

He smiled, and thought for a bit. 'I'll give it some time. I'll let Erasto kill those two guys, of course. I'll give him that satisfaction.'

13

Wednesday, 23 March
04.55 hrs

The second technical faced the Cargomaster head on, its 12.7 aimed at the airframe. We pulled up alongside it. The third one drove across from the Skyvan. Bob Marley sang louder and louder the closer it rolled. Its headlights cast shadows around the Cargomaster; with no windows in the hold area, all I could see was Joe sitting in the left seat. I tried to signal that everything was OK. His head turned behind the Perspex. I couldn't be sure he'd noticed.

The Bob Marley fan jumped out of the driver's seat with a wad of US dollars. He passed it through the cigarette smoke billowing from the rear window of the other double cab.

'Come, Mr Nick, come. We'll go and talk with Erasto.'

We followed the same route as the dollars. Erasto

was settled in the centre of the bench seat, his arms up along the rear.

Awaale waffled away and Erasto nodded slowly. But he wasn't happy. He pointed his cigarette at the Cessna and gobbed off.

Awaale turned back to me. 'Erasto says that the men in the plane, they will not let him count the money. They say they will burn it if we attack or try to come aboard. The money was in— Wait a minute, please, Mr Nick.' He asked the boss to clarify something before turning back to me. 'They told him the money was in "De-Arab" bags?'

'Deniable bags, mate. They'll torch everything in them. It's to stop cash and valuable documents being stolen.'

Awaale looked offended. 'Erasto wants you to talk to them. Tell them that the money must be counted before he'll let anyone else come ashore. As soon as he has the money, Mr Nick, no problems – in they come.'

For all I knew, Erasto might have set out with other ideas. As he drove to the airport, he might have been thinking of ways to have his cake and eat it.

I nodded, turned, and headed for the Cessna as Bob sang about being a buffalo soldier. The guy draped around the 12.7 in the back of Erasto's wagon joined in with the chorus.

Joe leant over and opened the cockpit door. He had his AK on his lap.

I climbed up. In the dim lights, I saw Mr Lover Man – on his mobile – and Genghis in the hold. They were dressed for war in green fatigues and Kevlar body armour. Mr Lover Man had a black set, Genghis a green one. They'd inserted both front and back plates. They clutched M4 assault rifles with telescopic butts, firing handles on the stocks, and the shorter eleven-inch barrel for close-quarter work. No eastern shit for Frank's lads, only state-of-the-art USA. Most telling of all, the magazine pouches on their armour sets were well worn. They'd done this shit before. They looked like they'd been born into it.

At their feet were two black nylon holdalls. Thick steel wires protruded from them, with ring-pulls at the end. Mr Lover Man and his mate had also come pre-pared. There were six-packs of two-litre water bottles; a Bergen-sized medical kit; big plastic zip bags holding spare saline drips and field dressings. Other bags held mountains of *chapattis* and bananas. There was milk in plastic one-litre containers.

Joe was his normal politically correct self. 'Fucking flip-flops, man. I told you, don't fucking trust them. They would have had the money – and us – if it wasn't for these two in the back. They were going to take the fuckers on. All you people are mad, man. You're fucking mad.'

It looked as if Erasto had had other plans, and these two lads had fucked them up.

Mr Lover Man came forward to study the technicals through the Perspex. He waffled in Russian on his mobile.

Joe eyed me. 'You look shite, man. Where are your shoes? Did the flip-flops fucking steal them as well? Where's the other three? We were told you'd got them. Where are they? I want to get out of here, man. It's a fucking nightmare.'

'They're on their way, mate.' I got eye-to-eye with Mr Lover Man in the dimmed cockpit lights. 'Tell Frank they want to count the cash before they let Tracy, Stefan and Justin come ashore. Tell him it's under control. Once you've done that, get off the mobile – we've got work to do.'

I glanced back into the hold. 'You speak English?' Genghis shook his head and slowly stretched out his legs. This lad was so laid back he literally was almost horizontal.

Mr Lover Man closed down and gave me a nod. 'We're ready. I don't trust that old man.'

'Nor do I, mate. I'm going to bring one of them over. We get him to count the cash, then we hold tight until everyone is delivered. They hold us tight, we hold the money tight. Those bags in the back, they really have deniable devices installed?'

Mr Lover Man waffled to Genghis. He unzipped the bags to reveal the shrink-wrapped bundles of hundred-dollar bills. Two black plastic containers, about twenty centimetres square, sat on top of them. Thick steel wire protruded from the corner of each. There were two in each bag, in case one didn't kick off.

Frank probably used them all the time to make sure no fucker got hold of any information he didn't want to share. After all, knowledge is power. If the ring-pull was triggered, the incendiary devices were detonated. The agent was magnesium. It burnt with unbelievable intensity. The problem, especially with two of them in each bag, was that they'd keep on burning – and take out the plane as well.

Mr Lover Man was certainly in no mood for

compromise. Even if he was, his deep growl wouldn't make it sound that way. He was as cold and clear as his boss.

'If they try to fuck with us, we will burn the cash.'

14

Joe wasn't impressed. 'Fuck, man – I just want to get my aircraft out of here, with everybody on board.'

Mr Lover Man had gone back to join Genghis. Joe turned and pointed to the two of them. 'Man, we've got things in our fucking toolbox, man, apart from you fucking hammers. We all need to keep our heads together, man.'

Joe didn't realize that these two had got their heads together. If they had to fight, they didn't give a fuck how it turned out.

Joe turned back into the cockpit. 'For fuck's sake, man. Get that flip-flop on board and get him counting, let's get on with it.'

'Yep, in a minute, mate. Everybody listen in – here's the plan. The guy comes on board and he counts the cash. Make sure that he sees the deniable packs. He goes back to the old guy and gives him the OK. If it then goes wrong, and they go for the cash, we come out fighting. We go for his wagon and take it to the end of the runway. There's a boat there. We head out and we look for the other skiffs. We crack on until daylight, and we keep on looking. That's all we can do.'

I waited while Mr Lover Man translated for Genghis, then I opened the door. 'You got that, Joe?' I stuck a leg out. 'Bet you're glad I didn't take your AK now, eh?'

'Yeah, but what about my fucking aircraft, man?'

'It's going to burn to the ground if those bags kick off. So you'd better hope there are no fuck-ups.'

He nodded, but wasn't too convinced.

I now had both feet on the concrete. 'Awaale!' I beckoned him over. 'Come here, mate. Get counting.'

He nodded. Anybody would be willing to get their hands on that amount of money, even if it was only to count it.

'Go on, mate, get inside.'

I opened the door and followed him in. He headed left into the hold. I got back into the right-hand seat and closed the door.

The bags were opened and Awaale started counting. I motioned to Genghis for some water and food.

It's surprising how small a million dollars looks in hundred-dollar bills. It normally comes in shrink-wrapped bundles, about twenty centimetres high. Six of them are a million, and weigh about ten kilos.

The first two litres of liquid didn't even touch the sides. I crammed bread and bananas into my mouth as fast as I could, then started hiccuping so badly I had to wash it all down with another bottle.

Awaale thought he was going to get some too, but Mr Lover Man just gave him a big growl. 'No eating. Just counting.'

Awaale had done this before. He picked up the bundles and made sure they were the same height. He sliced through the shrink-wrap with his thumbnail to expose the notes along each wad, making sure no one had substituted ones for hundred-dollar bills.

Mr Lover Man and Genghis looked on with contempt.

I mumbled, through a mouthful of bread, 'The extra, have you got it?'

Mr Lover Man gobbed off to Genghis. He fished a bundle out of his map pocket and made to throw it to me.

'No, no. Not me.' I pointed at Awaale. 'It's for him.'

The cash was lobbed over with the same contempt. It hit Awaale hard on the shoulder. He didn't care. It went into his waistband. He sucked in his skinny stomach so it wouldn't show, and pulled his minging shirt over the top of the package. He swivelled to face me. 'Thank you, Mr Nick.'

Another thank-you. I wished they'd stop.

It wasn't long before he was satisfied on both counts: Erasto's money, and his and his dad's. He was still on his knees. 'Everything's good.'

'OK, go and tell Erasto. Tell him the deniable packs really exist. Then what happens?'

'It's easy. Erasto will tell me to call the boats in. You will be reunited.' He turned to the other two and gave them a smile. They looked as unimpressed as Joe.

'You sure you can trust this fucking flip-flop? Listen, man, there's a lot of cash there. These two action men in the back kick off, we're all in deep shit.'

441

I kept my eyes on Awaale. He'd turned back to me, still on his knees.

'Awaale, as soon as we have everybody here inside the aircraft and we are taxiing to the runway, these two will hand over the cash. It gets thrown out the door to you, OK?'

He nodded. 'No problem, Mr Nick.'

'But remember, if anything goes wrong, these two lads will be gunning for you and Erasto. They won't give a fuck, mate, and I won't be able to stop them. Remember what I said, about a war? There'll be many more than these two coming if there's a fuck-up.'

Awaale got onto his feet. He had to stoop so his head didn't bang on the aircraft ceiling. 'Mr Nick, no problem. But remember, Erasto wants the other two white guys.'

'Yeah, but only after I've finished with them.'

Mr Lover Man waffled to Genghis, and that was one part of the deal they both liked.

Genghis opened the cargo hold's shutter door and Awaale was almost thrown out onto the pan. He checked his shirt to make sure his money was safely in place.

I stayed where I was. Mr Lover Man and Genghis kept themselves to the sides of the airframe so they remained in cover. They mumbled away in Russian, weapons in the shoulder, standing by to see what Erasto was going to do now there really was three million just metres away; three million that would go up in smoke if he tried to take it. I hoped he was thinking the best thing to do was just make the deal.

I heard M4 safety catches coming off. It was

followed by one click of Joe's safety lever, to auto.

Mobiles rang outside. Bob Marley gave it large about guiltiness. The two in the back mumbled quietly again.

'Remember, lads – you get the fire down. I'll go for the vehicle.'

Awaale walked to the double cab of Erasto's technical as I got back into the right seat.

The music changed suddenly from reggae to Arabic wailing. I could see Awaale leaning through the window, waffling away. Eventually he nodded and came back towards me. He wasn't looking happy. He had his hands up in an exaggerated shrug.

'Wait . . . wait. Not until they kick off first.'

I opened the cockpit door until there was just enough of a gap for him to talk through.

'Mr Nick, we have a problem. Erasto says it isn't enough.'

I leant down. 'What? What the fuck are you on about? That was the deal, Awaale. You know that was the deal.'

The two lads in the back bristled as Mr Lover Man translated.

The growl was almost a roar. 'We go now, we go *now*!'

Awaale shook his head wildly. 'Wait, wait!' He knew what was coming. 'Everything is good, it's the tax – it's the airport tax. Erasto says you must pay the tax.'

Joe almost blew the windows out with his reply. 'For fuck's sake, man, you want another three hundred fucking dollars?'

Awaale looked at him as if it was the most

reasonable request in the world. 'Yes. You must pay your taxes.'

As Mr Lover Man translated, I couldn't do anything but laugh. Awaale joined in, and then they all did.

15

The laughter stopped as Joe passed the envelope and Awaale stood there and counted its contents.

'Are you going to call the skiffs in now, mate, or what?'

Awaale turned back and waved the envelope towards the technicals. The headlights on Erasto's flashed. Awaale got on his mobile. The exchange was short and sharp. 'It's OK, of course, Mr Nick. The boats are coming now. You see, everything is good.' He flicked his fingers.

I started to get out of the aircraft.

'Yep, mate, it's all good. I want to come with you, and these lads are going to stay here with the money, all right?'

He was already on his way to the technicals. I leant back into the aircraft once I had both feet on the tarmac. 'Listen in, lads. The deal is, I have ten minutes with the two Georgians, or whoever the fuck they are. But I don't want to be on the ground any longer than we need to. What do you reckon?'

I looked at the ones who understood English. They nodded.

'We fuck off the moment everybody's on board. I'm not sure what these fuckers are going to do. They might still try to take us, and go for another round of cash. It would certainly cross my mind.

'But I've got places to go as soon as this shit is over. I need to get away as fast as I can. So I'm now going down to the technicals. I'll collect the two white guys and grip 'em. At the same time, the others should be coming back to you. Then we just get the fuck out of here – agreed?'

Joe didn't take long to cast his vote. 'Fucking A, man.'

Mr Lover Man translated. He and Genghis both gave it the nod. 'What if they don't speak English? What are you going to do then?'

'I'll cross that bridge when I come to it.'

Awaale had climbed back onto the flatbed. He was standing beside the 12.7. 'Mr Nick, come, come!' He had to shout to make himself heard above the music.

I ran over and climbed on board. I stood the other side of the cannon and held on to it for support.

Erasto's technical stayed where it was. Smoke still billowed out of the rear windows.

We headed off down the runway, music blaring, lights on full beam. The blast of air was just what I needed. I was fucked. Awaale was grinning like a psychopath as he checked the cash was still secure under his shirt. 'We're nearly there, Mr Nick. One day you will come to Minneapolis and visit my father. I'll come too. I'll call you, yes?'

'Yep, that would be great, mate.'

He was a good lad, but I didn't plan to get mixed up with the guy who'd shot down the Black Hawk any time soon. That was, if the legend was true, of course. Every man and his Somali dog would want to claim that hit.

'Awaale, mate. Bring the two white guys up first.' I had to shout into the wind. 'They are there, aren't they?'

His eyes rolled as if I'd asked yet another stupid question.

'Good. I want to get them in this wagon for the drive back. The rest can follow. Just make sure you get those two white guys in here first.'

'No problem, Mr Nick. I want them in the back with us, too. I'll be the one to hand them over to Erasto. It will be a great moment for me. What do you think? Do you think it will be great for me?'

'I think it'll be absolutely fucking brilliant. After all, everybody loves you now, don't they?'

'Yes, they do, Mr Nick – *they do!*'

He sank down behind the cab to make the call. Tracy and me, we'd have the gratitude-fest on the plane to Malindi. For now, I still had work to do.

16

We stopped at the end of the runway and I jumped off the wagon. Music blasted. Awaale shouted into his mobile and gave noisy high-fives to anyone within reach. The wagon's crew were still yelling at each other excitedly about the attack.

I hobbled away from them until all I could hear was the pounding surf. I got out the iPhone and dialled. I just got the mad Arab woman again. I tried Jules. Voicemail. But he'd left me a message.

'She's OK. The Brits are sending a warship, the *Cumberland*, to Benghazi to evac UK nationals. No idea when it will get there but I'm trying to get her on board and out of the city soon as. Stand by.'

'Mr Nick, they're here, they're here! Mr Nick, they're here!'

I turned back. Awaale jumped off the wagon. Ant and Dec were being frogmarched along the edge of the tarmac. Awaale yelled, and they were steered towards the back of our technical.

I joined them as fast as I could. Fuck, my feet were

sore. 'Mate, let's get them on board and take them down to the sea, yeah?' If these lads understood English, I wanted them to think the worst. 'Off the runway, down by the rocks.'

Ant and Dec sat against the back of the cab, their arses on the flatbed. There was no fear in their eyes. They accepted they were about to die. Once that happens, it's like a massive weight being lifted. Every minute you're still alive becomes a bonus.

The wagon lurched along the strip. My arm hooked round the 12.7 stand for stability, I squatted in front of them. Their heads lolled with the motion of the vehicle. The runway lights became like strobes as we sped past them.

'You two,' I shouted above the engine noise. 'You speak English?' I jabbed their chests hard. I wanted to be sure they knew the score.

They looked back at me through bloodshot eyes. Both had growth on their chins, and hair on end after hours at sea. I probably looked exactly the same.

I made eye-to-eye with each of them in turn. I wanted to make sure they recognized me. I wanted to see if there was any reaction.

'OK – if you understand me or not, I don't give a shit. But these lads here, they want you bad. The guy you killed in Bristol? Their boss's brother. And you killed a woman. The woman you were with in the AS compound? That was her sister. Both of you have fucked up big-time.'

There was a glimmer of understanding in their eyes. These fuckers knew exactly what I was talking about.

We bounced off the tarmac. Their heads bounced left

and right as the wagon negotiated the rubble-strewn terrain.

'So, lads – you've got to tell me where you come from, who you work for. I'll see what I can do for you. Otherwise, you're fucked. They'll make sure it ain't quick, believe me.'

I kept eye-to-eye, switching between them, making sure they took every word on board.

We juddered to a standstill.

The surf pounded against the rocks below us.

All I got from them was the same look Mr Lover Man and Genghis had given Awaale in the back of Joe's Cessna.

The other technical passed us on the runway, packed with bodies. Tracy was wrapped around Stefan. BB stood behind the cab, one hand gripping the 12.7.

I had to get this bit done quickly.

I stood up.

'OK, then, fuck you.'

I jumped over the side.

'Awaale, let's get them on the ground and stripped. Get their kit off.'

He issued a string of orders. I heard 'Erasto' a couple of times. The crew's reaction was to kick and slap the two Georgians off the back of the wagon.

They fell into the dust. Even the driver jumped out to help deliver the message. The Somali boys pulled off the Georgians' jeans and shirts and tugged at their boots.

'I want them stripped totally. Everything off.'

Awaale and his mates laid into them like a pack of

wild dogs attacking two antelope. Ant and Dec tried to curl up in the cloud of dust that billowed up around them.

17

I let them get on with it for a couple of minutes.

'All right, let's have a look at them.'

Awaale didn't answer. He was somewhere in the mêlée.

I moved forward. They carried on slapping, punching, raining down rifle butts.

'Awaale, where the fuck are you?'

No reply.

'*Awaale!*'

He emerged out of the darkness. A layer of dust clung to his sweat-covered face.

'Enough, mate. You're handing them over to Erasto, remember?'

His eyes were glazed, as if he was drunk or high.

'Awaale, come on, mate, switch on.'

Behind him, the crew kept pounding into Ant and Dec. These lads really did have a different mindset.

I grabbed Awaale's arms. 'Get them to stop. I want these fuckers alive. You're the main man, remember? You've got to step back from this shit and see the bigger picture. Awaale? You listening to me?'

He showed signs of rejoining Planet Earth. His eyes started to focus. 'Yes, yes, of course, Mr Nick. Of course.'

He turned and re-entered the dust cloud, gobbing off as he went. He pushed and pulled the crew off the wounded animals. He had to slap a couple of the boys to make them get out of the way, bollocking them as if he'd had nothing to do with it.

Ant and Dec's grazed and soon-to-be badly bruised bodies were curled up into balls. They looked as though someone had set about them with a cheese-grater.

They coughed and spluttered into the dust. Their tattoos glistened with blood and sweat. They were the normal snakes-wrapped-around-daggers stuff. Plus a couple of tribal tats, all that shit. It was the ones that had writing round them that I was interested in. Ant's was a mermaid with tits. Dec's was a fox. The writing beneath them looked like a row of twisted paperclips, like some sort of elaborate Far Eastern script. But having done some stuff in the Tbilisi neighbourhood, I knew exactly what it was. It was Mkhedruli, the Georgian alphabet.

I still had no boots on. My Timberlands had stayed behind in the AS compound, along with my day sack. But I kicked into them anyway. I wanted to get their attention.

'Who sent you?'

Nothing.

'If you don't help me, these lads will keep on going until you do.'

453

Ant spat a mixture of saliva and blood into the dust, and maybe a couple of teeth as well. 'Fuck you. Fuck all you *bitches*.'

Dec had a mouthful of the same, but he aimed it at me. It sprayed across the calf of my jeans. I turned back to the vehicle. Awaale was looking down the runway. I slapped him on the shoulder.

'You OK, mate?'

He turned. 'Yes, Mr Nick. I must control myself. I'm a leader now, the main man, yes?'

'That's right, mate. You must be able to turn that shit off – keep a clear head when it's decision time.'

He nodded. 'Yes, Mr Nick. Thank you. Yes, I will. I will.'

'All right. Let's get these fuckers back on the wagon. I'm done.'

I'd learnt enough. Now the other technical was at the aircraft, we needed to move.

I watched Awaale get the crew sorted. They dragged Ant and Dec to the flatbed and threw them onboard. We jumped up behind them. The driver ground the gears and we lurched off towards a quick exit out of there.

18

Back at the terminal, Mr Lover Man and Genghis weren't giving Erasto time to think about what he might do next. They were both out of the Cessna with a bag over one shoulder, weapons up.

Mr Lover Man was shouting. Whatever it was about, it meant nothing to the crews around the two technicals. They looked jumpy and brandished their weapons left, right and centre. One lad even brought his RPG into the aim. Another swung the 12.7 on its mount.

Tracy and Stefan were waiting forward of Erasto's wagon, just off to the right, twenty metres or so from the aircraft.

This was the bit I fucking hated on these jobs. In all the excitement, just one trigger-finger exerting a tad too much pressure was all it took to fuck the whole thing up.

BB shouted back at Mr Lover Man, like they were in some kind of *High Noon* stand-off.

We came to a halt behind Erasto's technical. BB was

still bawling out Mr Lover Man. Now I could hear him. 'They don't fucking speak English, you twat! Just give them the cash – give them the fucking cash *now*.'

Mr Lover Man and Genghis stood their ground, M4s still in the shoulder. These guys were chilled. Their expressions hadn't changed the whole time I'd known them.

Now we were closer, I could see the wires snaking out of the bags. Each of Frank's boys had the bottom three fingers of his pistol hand through the ring-pulls, with his trigger-finger free. They were ready to drop the bag and pull, then take casualties before they became one.

Joe was still in the left-hand seat. The electrics started to wind up, blanketing the area with their high-pitched whine.

Mr Lover Man's eyes never left the crews. They bounced from man to man, checking where their hands and weapons were. He shouted loudly over the engine noise: 'Put down your weapons!' The crews screamed back and did nothing, still off their tits.

Genghis and Mr Lover Man stood their ground, one each side of the cargo-hold doors. Mr Lover Man spotted me. 'Get the money-counter to tell them to stand down. We'll all get onto the plane. We'll throw the cash out as we taxi. No hostages, no deal. Tell him.'

BB's head swung between us as he took all this in. It was only as he turned back to me that I noticed he now had Stefan. 'We take the Georgians with us. We can't leave them with these fucking animals.'

I stared back at him. I'd had enough of this fucker already. 'Shut the fuck up or I'll get one of these animals to stick a fucking rifle butt in your face. Shut it. Everyone fucking – calm – down . . .'

Awaale was at Erasto's window. I walked over to him. The boss man was sitting precisely where I'd last seen him, not showing the slightest concern as he sparked up his two-hundredth Marlboro of the day.

'Awaale, tell Erasto we have the two white guys for him. Tell him that we'll now do the one-for-one swap. The money comes to him as the hostages come to us, OK? And then he can have the two lads in the back, and do with them what he feels like. Tell him that.'

'No problem, Mr Nick. We've done this many, many times. You know, you must tell your guys to cool it.'

'Mate, they're not my guys, so that ain't going to happen, is it? Tell Erasto that as soon as he gets the money he leaves with his crew. Tell him he's to take two technicals with him, which just leaves your wagon, the two white guys, and your lads looking after them. All right? So that means everything's calm, everything's good, we can all relax, and you can make sure we get away. But right now, let's all keep fingers off triggers, yeah?'

Awaale turned away from the window. 'OK, Mr Nick.' He gave it the full John Wayne. '*Let's do it.*'

As I followed him towards the Cessna, Awaale started chatting like we were off to the pub for a pint. 'So, I'll give you my father's number. We'll all meet up in Minneapolis.' He leant towards me and went back into conspiratorial mode. 'Once I have taken over the clan I will then visit my father and tell him to come home. But, first, you'll join us in Minneapolis, won't you?'

'Yep, no drama, mate. But we have to get out of here now, OK?'

I looked ahead at Joe and drew my index finger across my throat to signal that he should kill the engine.

We needed calm. No loud noises; no props turning; no fingers on triggers. We'd get the exchange done nicely and quietly and then we'd fuck off. If it did go noisy, at least we'd be doing it from a steadier platform.

Joe got the message. The electrics started winding down.

Awaale carried on talking. 'Mr Nick, please, all is good.' He swivelled and began walking backwards, talking coolly to his crews and motioning for them to lower their weapons.

'That's good, mate. It's high time your lads took their chill pills.'

I could hear another aircraft's electrics winding down in the distance. I peered into the gloom at the bricklike silhouette of the Skyvan.

'Awaale – who the fuck are they?'

'Just guys waiting to pick someone up, I suppose. Like you are doing, Mr Nick. It happens all the time.'

We now stood equidistant between the Cessna and the technicals. 'OK, everyone, listen in!' I felt like I was trying to marshal a school trip. 'Everyone's getting a bit too sparked up so we're going to have a change of plan. This is what's going to happen. I'm going to get the bags and bring them back here, to where we are standing right now. Have we got that so far?'

Awaale translated for his crews and Mr Lover Man

mumbled away at Genghis. Frank's lads still kept their weapons in the shoulder, no matter what the other fuckers were doing. The crews now had theirs down, held by the magazines or slung over their shoulders. A couple lit up. Another two even got on their mobiles again.

'OK, once I start walking back with the bags, BB, Stefan and Tracy come over and meet me here. Has everybody got that? Awaale, make sure these people understand what's going on. Shout at them, mate. I don't want to leave any room for doubt.'

I spun round to Mr Lover Man. 'Your friend getting this?'

He muttered something to Genghis and nodded.

Awaale went into Alexander the Great mode, rallying his troops while another cloud of cigarette smoke drifted from the back of Erasto's technical.

BB couldn't help himself. 'Nick, you've got to fucking grip these boys. We—'

'BB! *Shut – the – fuck – up!*'

The crews fidgeted. The shouting was making them uneasy. Awaale kept giving them commands, but it was turning back into an argument.

I raised my hands again and slowly brought them down, as if that was going to steady the situation the way Awaale had. *'Everybody stay calm. Keep your weapons down.'*

I turned and pointed at Mr Lover Man and Genghis. 'That's you as well. Fingers off triggers, lads.'

One fucking slip and this all went to rat-shit.

19

I gave it about fifteen seconds after Awaale had stopped, everybody had calmed a little and AKs were lowered. 'OK, I'm going to start walking . . . now.'

I moved towards the money and lifted each bag in turn, one over the right shoulder, one over the left, making a point of hooking a finger through each of the ring-pulls. I looked at Awaale, and then at everybody else, to make sure we were all on the same page. 'OK, let's get walking.'

I took the first few paces towards Awaale, making sure I could see the other three coming towards me.

We all converged beside Awaale. I bent at the knees and placed the bags on the tarmac. I kept my fingers threaded through the ring-pulls.

Awaale unzipped each bag in turn and checked their contents.

'Nothing's changed, mate. Check the wrappers – look at where you sliced them with your thumbnail.'

'It's all there, Mr Nick. We trust you. It's all there.'

I let go of the ring-pulls and tucked them inside the bags.

'OK, mate, now you start heading to Erasto, nice and slow, nice and controlled, and then you get your crews out of here.'

'No problem, Mr Nick, no problem.' He lifted the bags and we both turned to go our separate ways.

'Tracy, BB – nice and slow towards the aircraft, when I say. Tracy, don't cross in front of the lads. Keep well to the right of them.'

If it went to rat-shit I didn't want her in the way of their arcs of fire.

I pointed at Lover Man and Genghis. 'We're coming towards you.'

Five or six paces from the Cessna I turned to see the back door of Erasto's technical open and Awaale passing over the bags. The first technical started to roll the moment the door closed again. Bob Marley filled the air once more.

Erasto's wagon followed, but stopped level with Awaale's. Erasto wanted to have a good look at the two Georgians. They were still on their arses on the flatbed, bollock naked, backs against the cab. The two crew guarding them laughed and pointed. Erasto's vehicle moved off.

Mr Lover Man screamed at Joe, 'The engine, let's go, let's go!' He leant through the cargo-hold door, laid his M4 on the floor and turned to help Tracy.

Tracy ignored him and ran straight for me.

'Nick, thank you, thank you, thank you.' As the electrics wound up once more, she threw her arms around my neck and planted kisses all over my face. Her own was one big scabby grin.

'Nick, thank you, thank you . . .' The prop began to turn. Her words were now almost drowned by the engine.

She hugged me tighter, pulling me down so her chin rested on my right shoulder.

Awaale was waiting to exchange contact details and say goodbye but he stood back to let Tracy show her love and appreciation. Maybe he thought it was going to be his turn next. Everybody did love him so.

Her tone changed the instant her lips were at my ear. 'BB is working with the two Georgians. That plane is theirs, Nick. They want Stefan, but he says he will kill him if I tell you. They want my baby. Please help us . . . *Please* . . .'

The navigation lights strobed under the fuselage. Everything unfolded around me like a series of rapid-sequence still photographs.

The Skyvan's props were turning.

Stefan's little legs were a blur as he struggled to get back to his mother.

BB's eyes were fixed on the Skyvan.

'*Nick, please do something* . . .'

Genghis was looking into the hold of the Cargomaster.

Now BB was moving.

Gripping Stefan tightly in front of him, he ran hard into Genghis's back, using the boy as a battering ram. Genghis stumbled and fell.

BB grabbed Mr Lover Man's M4 from the doorway and jammed the short barrel into the back of Stefan's head. His shouts were almost lost in the prop-wash but their message was clear. 'Stand still, everybody. *No fucker move!'*

The boy's clothing was flattened against BB by the force of the propeller. BB moved out of its way.

The M4 barrel was firmly jammed into the base of Stefan's skull.

20

Genghis quickly recovered, weapon back up, but BB kept moving away from the aircraft, making any shot Genghis might take a whole lot harder.

Tracy screamed and lunged towards her son. '*My baby! My baby!*'

I gripped her. I shouted to Genghis above the blast of the turboprop. 'No fire! *Don't fire!*'

He might be able to hit him, but he couldn't guarantee that BB didn't have enough pressure on his trigger to take the boy out with him. I had no doubt that he would. BB might be an arsehole, but he knew exactly what he was doing. If he was in a corner and going to die anyway, he wouldn't give a fuck.

If I screwed this up and the boy got killed, Frank's lads weren't going to give a fuck about us – or anyone else they opened up on as they made their exit.

Mr Lover Man jumped out and I pushed Tracy towards him. 'Take her. *And tell your mate not to fire!*'

I could see no other way of sorting out this shit. It was going to create more drama, but at least the boy would stay alive. Drama I could get to grips with. Dead kids – all I could do was bag them up and take them back to where they'd come from.

I made a move towards BB. Now I was closer I could make sense of his yells. *'Get these fucking animals off the technical now. Get them off. I want them off – now!'*

I turned to comply. Awaale was manning the 12.7.

It pointed our way.

I threw up my hands. *'No, Awaale. No!'*

His hand moved to the cocking handle.

'No! Don't fucking fire!'

The Skyvan rolled towards the runway with its ramp down. Its red interior lights glowed on the tarmac behind it. Its twin props whirled. I kept waving my arms like a madman at anyone with a weapon. *'No firing! No firing!'*

Everywhere I looked, there were too many fingers on triggers.

BB kept edging towards the technicals. 'Get 'em out. *Get 'em out!'*

I shouted and motioned to Awaale to leave the wagon, but he wasn't going anywhere. He had the biggest gun and he was going to use it if he wanted to. I took a pace forward and put myself between them, pointing at BB and bellowing, *'Wait there, fucking wait there – I'll sort it out.'*

BB was almost foaming at the mouth. *'Fucking do it. Get that technical. I'll fucking drop this boy. You know I'll do it.'*

He'd be fucked if he did, but I had no doubt that he would. I held both hands out as if I was trying to stop two lots of traffic. I broke into a run towards the technical. The two covering the Georgians had their AKs pointing here, there and everywhere, screaming at Awaale, desperate to know what he wanted them to do.

Still manning the 12.7, Awaale couldn't make sense of any of this. He could no longer feel the love. I reached the side of the wagon. He stared down at me.

'Forget it. Let him take them.'

'But this will look very bad, Mr Nick. My men . . . I am going to be their leader . . .'

'That's right, mate. But I'm going to beg, make it look good for you. You tell them later that you decided to let them go, for the boy's sake. All good leaders must show wisdom and kindness, mate. The boy . . .'

I got down on my knees, hands together.

'Please, Awaale, please.'

He liked the reaction from the two crew beside him.

'But why does he want that child?'

'Because everything is about the boy, Awaale. The man with the money, the powerful man – that is his son. Just leave the wagon, Awaale. We must keep the boy safe. We don't need any more drama from the father, believe me. I told you, he can reach anywhere he wants . . .'

BB was still going ape-shit, but staying static. He knew this was his best option for now.

The two Georgians, still naked and against the back of the cab, began to taste freedom. They gave me a smirk. Dec gobbed at me as I got to my feet. It hit me on my right shoulder. I wanted to reach over and throttle the fucker, but that would have to wait. 'Awaale, let it go. Fuck 'em.'

The Skyvan had reached the end of the runway.

'And fuck Erasto. You'll just have to take over tonight, won't you?'

He was still struggling to compute. I had to scream like a drill sergeant to get through to him. '*Give – them – the – wagon!*'

His face crumpled. He almost looked hurt. I took a deep breath, forced myself to be calm. 'Please, Awaale . . . *Please* . . .'

He thought about it.

Finally, achingly slowly, he waved an arm at the two crew to debus. The lads jumped off, and he followed.

Ant and Dec got to their feet. The driver was out. Ant vaulted over the side and took the wheel. BB reversed towards the wagon, muzzle still glued to the back of Stefan's head.

The rest of us shuffled backwards towards the Cargomaster. Mr Lover Man shouted, 'Tracy, no! *No!*'

Like a banshee, she zoomed past me.

Her body convulsed with sobs as she ran. 'Take me, take *me*! Not my baby, *please!*'

I bellowed, '*Tracy, stand still. Stand still!*'

But she didn't. Of course she didn't.

BB threw the boy onto the flatbed with Dec and swung round to face the threat. Tracy hurled herself at him. He used her own momentum to fling her to the ground. As he climbed on board, she came back at him. He tried to kick her off but she clung on. The wagon started to move. She slipped and for a second it looked as if she was going to fall, but with a desperate lunge she managed to grab the sill of the flatbed. Her feet dragged along the tarmac.

She gripped the sill and tried to swing her legs onto the back of the wagon.

Dec handed the boy back to BB and took the M4. He moved to the edge and stamped on Tracy's fingers.

Ant swung the wheel from side to side.

Tracy managed to hook a knee over the edge of the flatbed and held on grimly, but her grip was loosening. The force of the seesawing technical was becoming too much for her. Dec took aim with the M4 and gave her a round. Her limbs flailed as she cartwheeled into the ground.

The technical roared towards the Skyvan. BB held onto Stefan like a vice, the boy's face into his shoulder. Dec banged on the cab roof to get Ant to drive faster, then swivelled and gave a burst with the M4 in our general direction. Everybody ducked. I kept eye-to-eye with Genghis. 'No. We don't want anything to hit the boy.'

He got it. He understood. At last.

Tracy lay very still. The wound in her gut glistened. She panted for breath. Supporting her neck, I lifted her gently and leant back to take the weight. Her leg dangled over my right forearm.

'Nick ... My baby ... My baby ...' Every word hurt.

'It's OK,' I murmured. 'It's all going to be OK ...'

Tracy kept trying to talk.

'Stop ... It's all right. We'll get him back, I promise. We'll get him back ...'

Her head fell across my arm. 'I've been so stupid, Nick ... I've been so ... stupid ... My baby ...'

Mr Lover Man helped me lift her carefully into the

Cargomaster's hold. He and Genghis ripped open the medical kit to grip her.

Awaale was at the door, hand outstretched. I grabbed it.

'Listen, mate, good luck to your clan. We've got to go. But you know what? We are friends. We really are friends.'

His face creased into a huge grin. 'Yes, of course, Mr Nick,' he shouted in my ear as the prop revved bigtime. 'Of course, I know it. America, we meet at my father's house.'

'Give me your cell. I'll get your number off it.'

He threw it up to me, then pointed down the runway. 'Mr Nick, they're escaping.'

The Skyvan left the tarmac and lifted over the sea.

'No, they're not, mate. *No, they're fucking not.*'

21

I shouted to Joe as I closed the shutter, 'Get airborne! Get up there – follow that fucking thing!'

The Cessna rumbled towards the runway. I climbed over the two front seats to retrieve my headset. I stared out into the darkness. 'You faster?'

He was at full stretch, pressing buttons, doing pilot shit as he checked left and right of the aircraft. 'Easy. That Skyvan is a fucking shed, man. But they've cut the lights. They know we're coming. Where would they go?'

'It's got to be south. Kenya. Or maybe further. Anything north would be a nightmare. There's the Arab Spring, civil war, and Yemen hates everyone. Why head into that shit? Don't worry about it, Joe. Just get up there, start heading south, and I'll try and find out.'

I checked his watch. We had about half an hour till first light. I looked at him. 'We'll find the fuckers, don't worry.'

We hit the beginning of the strip and the prop

screamed up through the revs. I pulled the loadie's extension lead out of the door pocket and plugged it in.

Headset on, I moved back into the hold. Frank's lads were working furiously to get drips into her. That meant they'd already plugged any leaks.

Genghis pulled the plasma expander from the trauma kit, a clear plastic half-litre container shaped like a washing-up-liquid bottle. He tore it out of its plastic wrapper and threw that on the ground. He bit off the little cap that kept the neck of the bottle sterile. Fuck hygiene – infections could be sorted out in hospital. He knew what he was doing. Let's keep her alive so she can get to one.

Mr Lover Man also had his IV set out of its protective plastic coating. He chewed off the cap to the spearhead connector and jabbed it into the self-sealing neck of the bottle. He took out the plug, undid the screw clamp, and watched as the fluid ran through the line. He wasn't concerned about air bubbles in the line; a small amount didn't matter – certainly not in these circumstances. I willed him on. *Let's just get the fluid in.*

He hung the loop in his mouth to keep the bottle high so its lifesaving contents could run freely.

Mr Lover Man shrugged off his body armour. Genghis rolled the soft Kevlar into a pillow and tucked it under her head. I looked down. He'd plastered field dressings to her stomach, beneath her bloodstained T-shirt.

I leant down towards her as Stefan's two godfathers carried on working on her. I made sure she'd be able to

471

see me before I tried to get her to open her eyes. Her face was screwed up in pain. I stroked her forehead, moving the hair out of the way with one hand and pushing one of the cans off my ear with my other. I had to raise my voice above the prop and engine noise.

'Tracy? Tracy?'

Nothing. I leant in closer, my mouth to her ear. 'Tracy?'

Her eyes opened as the aircraft lunged forward and started to thunder down the tarmac. She studied my face. A smile flickered at the corners of her mouth and turned almost immediately into a grimace.

'Nick, I'm so sorry . . . I've made so many . . . mistakes . . . Stefan, my baby . . .' Her bottom lip trembled. Tears welled in her eyes and trickled down her cheeks. Her sobs gave her even more pain.

Genghis applied more pressure on her stomach to keep the fluids inside her. She strained against the agony.

'Tracy, it's OK. I'm going to get Stefan back. But I need your help . . .'

She was trying to listen through the tears and the pain and the din and the vibration of the aircraft as we gathered speed along the runway.

She gave a small nod. Her eyes closed. She tried to breathe through her snot-filled nose.

'Do you know where they're going? Do you know what country they're going to?'

Her head turned to one side. She coughed, trying to clear her throat. Her nose was blocked. Her face contorted.

The Cessna lifted off the runway. The engine pitch

472

changed. Mr Lover Man held Tracy steady as the medical gear slid down towards the rear of the aircraft. He grabbed a bottle of water as it rolled past and opened it with his teeth. He tried to see if she could take some through her cracked and blistered lips.

'Tracy, do you know where they're taking Stefan?'

She fought to unblock her nose. She tried a drink. It wasn't working. It made her cough even more.

'Kenya . . . They're going to Kenya . . . They're going to . . . take him to Georgia . . . Nick . . . My baby . . . A hostage again . . . Nick, what have I done? My baby . . .'

I stroked her brow some more as Mr Lover Man held her head straight on the body armour. She couldn't control it herself any more. My fingers found the mike, to make sure Joe got the message. 'It's Kenya, mate.'

He came straight back into my headphones. 'I fucking knew it, man.'

I stroked her forehead again. As the aircraft levelled off, a hand came up and grabbed my wrist.

Her grip was pathetically weak. Her lips trembled. Tears fell. She tried to focus on me. 'I'm so sorry, Nick . . . I always mess . . . everything up . . . Why do I always make such a mess of everything?'

She fought the agony. Body fluid leaked out faster than the IV set could get it in.

'No, you don't. You and Mong – you didn't mess that up, did you? You made him so happy, Tracy. He always talked about you. He told everyone how much he loved you.'

473

She gave a weak smile and tried to clear her throat again, but the pain was too much.

Mr Lover Man checked the drips and dressings. He and Genghis mumbled between themselves.

'I always get it wrong . . . The only good things . . . I have . . . are Mong . . . and Stefan . . .' She started to break down at the thought of what might be happening to him.

'It's OK.' I unclasped her hand from my wrist and held it in mine. I rocked with the motion of the aircraft. 'We're going to get him back. He's not that far away. We'll be able to see the plane as soon as it's light. I won't let you down, Tracy. I promised Mong I'd always look after you. And Stefan's part of you. So he's part of that promise, isn't he?'

She gave a couple of half-nods before coughing and snotting up. Her hand squeezed mine hard.

'Nick . . . I want you to understand. I felt so . . . *alone* in Frank's world. He's a good man . . . but his work, his family . . . We could never be together . . . Not truly . . . together . . . Me and Stefan . . . would always . . . be kept in a box . . . I had . . . to get away . . .'

She chugged up a mouthful of blood. I shushed her as she fought for air. 'I don't need to know. Just rest. Let the guys sort you out. Let's get Stefan back.'

'No, Nick . . . please . . . I want you to know . . . BB knew what I was feeling . . .'

'The kidnap plan was his, wasn't it?'

She just about managed a nod. 'I knew there was no . . . happily ever after . . . for us . . . But once he'd set it up . . . he had me . . . exactly where he wanted me . . . I got cold feet . . .'

'But he threatened to betray you to Frank.'

'Frank . . . would have taken Stefan . . . would have kicked me out.'

'BB arranged the hijack?'

'He wanted money . . . He knew the clan . . . from the old days . . . He said . . . Frank would hand over the money . . . then be told we were all dead . . .'

I didn't tell her that BB had always known Frank's cash, if there was any, would be a bonus. The serious money was coming from Georgia.

She worked hard on a smile.

'Me and Stefan . . . We didn't want Frank's . . . money . . . We were going . . . to India . . .'

Her face muscles suddenly relaxed, and I no longer felt the tension in her hand. From the faraway look in her eyes, part of her was already there.

'On the beach . . . Maybe . . . a small restaurant . . . Just be happy . . .'

A coughing fit took her away from her dream. I caught Genghis's eye. For a moment I thought he was going to crack as well. Then the mask of inscrutability was back in place.

'Frank . . . he has . . . so many . . . enemies . . .'

BB had taken full advantage of that. His plan must have seemed pretty close to perfect. But he'd fucked up. He hadn't written al-Shabab into the equation. He hadn't reckoned with people who didn't give a shit about the money and the shagging and the shiny red sports cars.

I gripped her hand and stroked her cheek. I tried to wipe away the tears, but they were falling too fast.

'Tracy, it's OK. You're safe now. Just let these lads sort you out.'

I moved the mike out of the way and bent to kiss her gently on the forehead. 'I've got to go now. I've got to get Stefan back. It'll all be OK. He'll be with you before you know it.'

She struggled to bring my hand to her lips. 'I know he will . . . I trust you . . . Nick . . . I . . . always have . . .'

I smiled at her.

'You . . . and Mong . . . the only men . . . I ever . . . trusted . . .'

She tried to give a smile back.

I let go of her hand and placed it in Genghis's palm. He gave it the gentlest of squeezes.

22

First light was peeking over the horizon to our left as India's bright blue sky and sun prepared to visit Africa again.

Joe was far out to sea. I could just about see the coastline on our right as I moved my head level with his.

He locked eyes. 'How is she?'

'Not good, mate.'

He nodded slowly, letting whatever that meant to him sink in. He pulled on his sun-gigs. 'It's best looking for these fuckers with the sun behind us. Like a fucking dogfight, man.'

'That's exactly what it's going to be.'

I was sure I could see a slight twinkle in his eye behind the shades.

He kept on scanning the area. I joined in, looking for a little dot in hundreds of miles of empty sky.

'Just one thing, Nick. What happens if my aircraft gets damaged? What the fuck would you do about that, man?'

I turned to face him. There was a big smile on his leathery face. 'You going to pay me, man? These fucking things cost over a million dollars. Can you believe that shit? I got a fucking big loan on it, man.'

I smiled right back. 'You won't have any worries on that score.'

He got back to the business of flying and monitoring the sky ahead of us.

'Where are the fuel tanks on those Skyvans?'

Both hands came off the controls again as he started to explain with his hands as well as his mouth. It was like I'd opened the encyclopedia at 'S'.

'On that fucking thing? Two Garrett turboprop engines, each driving a three-blade, variable-pitch propeller. Fuel in four tanks, in pairs on top of the fuselage between the wing roots. Each pair consisting of one 182-litre tank and one 484-litre mother. Total fuel capacity, 1,332 litres. That's a lot of fucking fuel, man.'

'What's its range?'

'With maximum payload, about eleven hundred klicks. But there's no maximum in *that* shed, man.'

'Their tanks won't be full unless they refuelled at Mog . . .'

'No, man, but we didn't either, and they might have extra tanks . . .' He brought his hands down to make sure I was following all this closely, '. . . in the spaces between the fuselage frames on each side, beneath the main tanks. There's provision for another four hundred litres. But fuck it, man . . .' He put his arms up as if he was firing a rifle. 'You drill that area and you're going to hit tanks. That's all you need to know, man.'

478

I picked up the AK and tapped the mag. 'You got tracer in this?'

'No, but you'd better check.'

I grabbed the magazine with my right hand. I pushed the release catch forward with my thumb and released it from its housing. The selector lever, a long spring-loaded arm, was in the upper safe position. I pushed it down to the fully automatic position before pulling back on the cocking handle to check no rounds were in the chamber. I released the handle, fired off the action by pressing the trigger, and replaced the selector lever back to safe.

Tracer are built with a hollow base filled with a pyrotechnic flare material, often phosphorus. In US and NATO standard ammunition, this is usually a mixture of strontium compounds and magnesium that yields a bright red light. Russian and Chinese tracer generates red or green light, using barium salts. Whatever the colour, the point was that it burnt intensely.

I pushed the first round out and used it to start flicking the rest out by the base as the spring forced them forward. I aimed them at the right-hand seat.

I couldn't remember the flash point or the initiation temperature of Jet A1 fuel but I wasn't taking any chances and neither was Joe. He kept looking at the rounds as they fell onto the right-hand seat. I didn't want a big fuck-off firework display. I wanted holes. And the AK 7.62 short would make much bigger ones than Genghis's M4 5.56.

I got to the last round. They'd all been bog-standard plain ball.

Joe sparked up. He was suddenly in full-fight mode.

Very calm. Very precise. No profanity. 'Got him. Half right of the nose. Maybe a klick ahead. Two hundred metres below us. He's following the coastline.'

I hit Joe on the shoulder. 'Well, let's go get the boy, then.'

'Fucking right, man.' There was no smile this time.

I started to move to the rear. Joe came back on my cans. 'You sure this Mr Big Shot will pay for my aircraft if it gets broken? Tell him, if he doesn't, I'll reload that fucking mag and come looking for him.'

My cans filled with his laughter as the prop pitch changed, the aircraft banked to the right and we started to descend.

23

I kicked all the shit further back to clear a space and opened the shutter. A gale rushed in. It was like standing at a station with an express train thundering past. I tried sticking my head out. My face got buffeted like I was in freefall. I couldn't see through my streaming eyes.

I pulled my head back in. All the wrappers from the field dressings and all other bits of crap were caught in a whirlwind around me.

Mr Lover Man had taken my place between the cockpit seats. He shouted at Joe: he wanted to know what was happening. He followed Joe's pointing finger to the Skyvan on our right. Then he looked back at Genghis working on Tracy.

I cleared more shit out of the way. I wanted a good stable platform for the weapon.

Mr Lover Man tilted his head so he didn't bang it on the top of the fuselage and stormed towards me. Joe gave me the heads-up in my cans. 'He doesn't like you, man. He's fucking mad. Those hands are massive. Be careful.'

I came forward to meet him. I wanted metal fuse-lage between me and the sky in case he got weird and tried to chuck me out.

I pulled one of the cans off my ear. 'Listen, this is the only way to stop them. We don't know how much fuel they've got. We don't know if we can outrun them. They might have extra tanks. We don't know what they're up to. We don't know what they're going to do when we get there. So we've got to stop them while we can.'

A big finger jabbed into my chest. 'You kill Stefan . . .' It pressed even harder and his face came closer. 'I kill *you*.'

I let him get on with it. Now wasn't the time. Let him make the threat. If I fucked up, we'd see. I nodded and turned back towards the open door. He was good at jabbing and doing the threats but he wasn't exactly pushing me out of the way to take the shots himself.

I put the can back on as I reached the howling gap. 'All sorted. Where the fuck are they?'

I was looking out as best I could, craning my neck beyond the cargo door. All I could see was clear blue sky, and ocean below.

'They're still half-right. They're about half a klick forward and higher.'

'OK.'

I hauled myself back inside. I braced my back against the fuselage opposite the opening, my knees up and my elbows just inside the creases of the knees so I didn't have bone on bone. I wanted good firm support for the weapon. Legs pressed together, I got the butt of the AK in my shoulder. As the aircraft bumped and buffeted, I pushed the safety to first click.

I was going to have to be good. The AK was designed to deliver massive firepower by hundreds of thousands of Russians advancing over the plains of Western Europe, brassing up whatever was in their way. The AK is at its best firing short bursts on automatic at ranges below about fifty metres. Beyond that, they go wild.

The calibre of the round was in my favour. The 7.62 was designed to take an enemy down first time and keep him down. If Joe could get me in range, whatever I sent across should punch holes in the Skyvan the size of my fist.

I cocked the weapon and pulled the selector down again, onto single shot. I got back on the mike. 'Joe, mate, you've got to get close and level.'

'No problem, man. They got any weapons apart from that M4?'

'We'll find out soon enough. Make it look like we're trying to push them towards the land or some shit. I need to find out exactly where the boy is on that thing.'

The revs picked up a notch and I could feel the airframe increase speed. Moments later I saw the Skyvan out of the door. It was forward of us, to the right, and higher in the clear blue sky. We were about a hundred metres away.

'Get up more, Joe. We need to be at the same level. We need to see through those cockpit windows.'

'They've seen us, Nick.' Joe's voice had gone up a notch too. 'The ramp is coming down.'

24

'Got it.'

I spotted heads on the ramp as it lowered. I lined up my eye behind the iron sights to check I could clear the left-hand side of the door.

The ramp had gone down halfway. I could see Ant and Dec's shoulders. They were standing, and they had longs into the shoulder.

I yelled into the mike. 'Joe! Dive! *Dive!*'

The engine screamed as we tipped instantly right. I struggled against the Gs as the horizon disappeared. Then I was sliding towards the door. The ocean filled the hole. The sea was rushing up to meet me.

I spread my legs, trying to get my socked feet across the airframe as some kind of brake. Both heels hit the door threshold at the same moment. I started tipping up vertically from the floor.

Joe levelled it out. I dropped back. The air stank of burnt oil. He must have taken the engine near its limits. We surged beneath the Skyvan and out of Ant and Dec's weapon arcs.

I checked further down the fuselage. Mr Lover Man and Genghis were holding on to Tracy. Genghis lay over her feet. Mr Lover Man was at his shoulder. They must have had their work cut out keeping her in one piece while Joe did his Red Arrows bit.

I checked back through the cargo door. We were low enough to see the sea. The sun beat down on it and bounced back up into the sky. It was almost blinding.

Mr Lover Man shouted. He was glaring at me.

I gave the calm-down sign I'd been using a lot lately. 'It's OK, mate.'

Joe wasn't impressed. 'They got more than that fucking M4, man. This is what I'm going to do. I'm going to get above him, come right on top of the fucker, crossing the ramp so we can get a good look inside the cockpit. If that ramp keeps open we can still see inside. You got that?'

'Sounds good to me.'

'They're going to be looking for us now. I'm not going to fucking hang about, man. No way. So keep sharp.'

'I'm ready.'

'I'll be able to check the cockpit as I come in on top of them. That heap of shit couldn't outrun a fucking wheelbarrow.'

The Cargomaster tipped right, and then we were suddenly climbing at forty-five degrees, gaining height as the engine screamed. Joe hurled the aircraft round in a tight turn. With blue sky and blue sea and no cloud, I had no point of reference with what was happening, apart from my stomach. I had to grab the struts on the side of the fuselage. I moved to the door, grabbed the rear of the frame with my left hand, keeping the weapon down on the floor with my right.

I saw the horizon. Then I caught a glint of silver. Joe completed his manoeuvre and the Skyvan was two hundred feet directly below us. We surged down. I felt the force of several times gravity. The engine was going ape-shit. All the loose crap inside the cargo hold flew around like slow-motion shrapnel. Some got caught in the drag of the door and was sucked out.

I felt the side of my cheek balloon as I tried to look out.

The Skyvan leapt towards us. My eyes felt like they were about to pop out of their sockets. It was like we were doing a kamikaze dive on it until we were fifty feet away, then Joe pulled the airframe left, towards the rear of the target.

He screamed into my cans, 'The cockpit! *He's in the cockpit!'*

We roared past the open ramp. Ant and Dec, still bollock naked, were kneeling on the threshold of the cargo hold. The ramp was the only protection forward of them.

A thin stream of tracer arced its way towards us. The rounds found their mark. Hot metal ripped through the Cargomaster's floor.

Joe dived still lower.

Suddenly I was looking up at them. They were trying to move forward on the ramp, trying to get some rounds down.

Their tracer really did make it look as if we were in some Second World War dogfight, until we levelled out again, way out of range.

Joe sparked up: 'The boy is definitely in the cockpit. He's with that fucker who took him. They're in the right-hand seat. You see them, Nick?'

'No.'

'He's definitely there. But that's fucking close to the fuel tanks, man. It's going to take some fucking good shooting. You up for that shit?'

'I fucking have to be.'

He laughed far louder than he needed to. 'You told me you didn't know how to use the fucking thing. But I had you drilled down as soon as I saw you, man.'

'Joe, can you come in higher and just slightly to the left, over his left wing? I need a line straight down into the tanks and out the bottom without hitting the boy. Can you do that?'

'As you say, man – I fucking have to.'

The aircraft started to climb. He held the Cargomaster in a tight bank. I tried to look out of the door. I had no idea where the Skyvan was. The engine screamed. More crap got thrown about. We all held on to whatever we could.

Sunlight leapt at me before the blue sky surrounded me, and then all of a sudden I saw it. The Skyvan was four hundred metres away and much lower.

Joe was on the cans: 'As soon as they see us they're going to try and manoeuvre, but fuck 'em. You just get the rounds down, man. Right?'

'I'll tell you when.'

I moved the mike out of the way and screamed to Mr Lover Man. 'Come here! I need you!'

He scrambled towards me. The Skyvan was still below us.

'I need you as a platform. On the door.'

Mr Lover Man knelt down, arms out, gripping the sides of the frame.

25

I knelt down beside his left arm, using it to support the weapon as I leant against the frame.

I pushed the mike back on. 'Joe, I'm ready.'

'Here we go.'

He crabbed neatly across the sky until he was right on top of the Skyvan. I leant forward into Mr Lover Man's arm, bringing the weapon down, fighting the wind.

The Skyvan was two hundred metres the other side of the sights.

The wind was buffeting our faces big-time, but Mr Lover Man's expression hadn't changed. Its message was simple: *You kill him, I kill you.*

The Skyvan was maybe a hundred metres below us now. The strain showed on Mr Lover Man's face as he put everything into keeping his body as rigid as he possibly could. He knew how important this platform was.

Joe's voice came back through the cans: 'I'm going to drop down and move a little over his left wing. They'll see us soon enough. You get drilling as soon as you can.'

'I'm ready.'

We came so close I could identify faces in the cockpit. Stefan was on the right-hand seat, gripped between BB's legs. BB was shifting continuously, twisting and turning, checking the airspace around them. He looked up. The M4 dug into the boy's stomach and his mouth opened in a silent shout.

I felt Mr Lover Man's eyes boring into me, but I knew it wasn't going to happen. Not yet, anyway. Stefan was too valuable to BB now, and the only leverage he had. The only way the kid was going to get shot at the moment was through bad skills and a wayward 7.62.

The airframe tilted left. I had a clear shot straight down into the tank at about forty degrees.

I fired.

I fired again.

Joe came at me on the cans: 'Your old friends are right on the ramp.'

I glanced back. Ant and Dec were manoeuvring themselves into a position from which they could fire without hitting their own wing. The weapons in their shoulders wavered as they fought the wind rush.

A tumbling 5.56 round ripped a hole many times its size in the aluminium floor, missing Mr Lover Man's feet by inches before exiting through the roof.

Mr Lover Man didn't move a millimetre.

I fired again.

I steadied myself for the next shot. Something had changed down there. The fuselage between the

Skyvan's wing roots was staining as fuel escaped across it.

I fired more rounds into the shed, until I got a big clunk as the working parts moved forward, and then nothing. The mag was empty. Ant and Dec just kept on going.

Joe screamed. 'Moving! *Moving!*'

He pulled round in a wide turn.

The Cargomaster threw a sharp left and tilted up. All I could see was sky. Then I caught another glimpse of the cockpit. BB had joined in. He was firing through the side window.

Mr Lover Man and I tumbled back onto the fuselage as the Cargomaster screamed down out of range.

There'd been no sign of Stefan.

Joe was back on the cans: 'Fuck it, we can't afford to take rounds, man. We can't go down before that fucker.'

I looked at the daylight spilling through the holes around me. I was glad he hadn't seen them yet.

Mr Lover Man looked at me, waiting for an answer.

I shrugged.

Joe bellowed with excitement, 'They're heading for the coast, man. You fucking well did it!'

I gave Mr Lover Man the thumbs-up.

He nodded slowly. I moved aside so he could make his way back into the hold.

Genghis screamed up the fuselage at us before he could move a muscle.

26

She looked almost at peace. I thought she even had a smile on her face. I hoped that as she fought to take her last breath she'd known I was going to save her little boy.

I fell back, trying to take it all in. No Mong. No Tracy. Stefan looking down the barrel of a gun. And Anna too. I used to be able to cut away from this shit, but not any more.

Oblivious to what had happened, Joe was almost jumping for joy. 'Definitely, man! That fucking shed is heading for land, man. You shot that fucker to shit.'

The Cargomaster tilted right, heading low towards the coast. 'Let's go see what's left of them when they dump, eh?'

Mr Lover Man was checking for a signal on his mobile as Genghis went and closed the shutter door. I climbed into the right-hand seat. There was fuck-all else I could do for the moment. There was fuck-all anybody could do.

Tracy was dead. That was it. But we still had a job

to do. We had to keep focused on that. I did, anyway.

I didn't have time to mourn her yet. There was nothing we could have done on the aircraft, and there was nothing that could have saved her in Mog. Stefan was the one I was feeling for right now. He had no mother, and if the cards fell badly, a fucked-up, traumatized life ahead. Or no life at all.

Joe shook his head slowly as he took on board what had happened. 'Fucking shame, man. But we'll get the fuckers. Yes, sir.' He jiggled the controls and the Cargomaster's wings responded, waggling like they meant business.

The Skyvan was just a smudge in the distance, heading west. It crossed the surf line, then followed its shadow across the scrub and red sand that seemed to go on for ever.

Joe sparked up: 'He's looking for a place to put down.'

We were soon over the wasteland ourselves. Joe tapped his sat-nav monitor. 'Jilib is a fuck of a shit-hole town, about eighty klicks west. They must be trying to dump there. If they can get to Jilib, they can get a vehicle.' He slapped me on the arm with the back of his hand. 'You fuckers better be quick when we land, man.'

I looked behind me. Mr Lover Man was gobbing off on his mobile. He saw me turn, waffled some more, then got up.

It looked like he was about to give me the phone. I moved the mike out of the way. 'Tell him no, not now. Now's not the time. Cut it. We've got work to do.'

Mr Lover Man's face clouded. He didn't like the fact his boss was being blanked.

I shifted the mike back into position and pointed to the blob ahead of us. 'Can you get us down at the same time without those fuckers taking us apart?'

He nodded. 'When that shed hits the ground it's going to kick up so much shit they won't even see their hands in front of their faces. But we'll have to come in hard. I might lose my landing gear.'

I nodded. 'Then we'll just have to hope we don't have too far to walk.'

Joe's happy face disappeared. 'That fucking boss man of yours better fork out for a new airframe, man. I got other jobs after this shit.'

27

My eyes were glued to the Skyvan through the cockpit window as we rode the thermals across the miles of desert.

Joe had asked for a damage report. He muttered even more darkly to himself when he got the news. 'Fucking shit, man. He *really* better pay up.'

I looked in vain for another AK mag, then unfastened the emergency box between the seats. Inside, among all the other stuff, were two yellow rectangular plastic containers of Pains Wessex mini flares. Each held nine cartridges and a pen ejector – penjector – fitted with a stainless-steel spring and striker pin. These ones would be red. They were rescue kit. The military used different-coloured ones all the time as signal flares. They normally rocketed to a minimum height of about forty-five metres, depending on the spec, and burnt for six seconds. The small magnesium payload blazed so intensely it could be seen for nine K in daylight and sixteen at night.

I grabbed both packs and shoved them in the waistband of my jeans. I checked that the iPhone hadn't gone AWOL.

The flares were easy to fire. They had to be, in case your hands were wet and cold and shaking. You got the penjector and twisted it into the thread projected from the flare cylinder as it sat in its case. You pulled back. There was a sucking sound as the cylinder came out of its holder. Then you pulled back the cocking piece, which would compress the spring. When you let go, the firing pin shot into the back of the flare, and off it went with a loud bang. It started burning immediately.

A massive hand appeared between us and pulled the escape axe out of the emergency box. Mr Lover Man also needed a weapon.

Mr Lover Man gave me his thousand-yard stare. It told me that if this ended up as a gang-fuck, the axe was for me. I moved the mike aside. 'Get your mate up here.'

When Genghis appeared, I moved behind the seats so I was up close to both of them. I pointed to the Skyvan. Its tailgate was still down but we were too far away to see what was happening inside. The point was, we were both much closer to the ground now.

'Listen in. As soon as they land, so will Joe – right on top of them, while the dust is up. We've got to be really quick. Get in there fast and take those fuckers on. Hopefully the ramp's still going to be down. I don't know if you can land with it like that, and I really don't care. We'll find out when we get there.'

Mr Lover Man translated. Then he turned to me. 'We will kill them all. Mr Timis wants them all dead. All of them.'

I got it. If I'd zapped Stefan, that included me.

'I will take care of Stefan. That's still my job, to get to the boy. OK?'

Both of them understood what I was saying that time.

'Justin – he's not going to kill Stefan unless he knows he's lost. At that point, he won't give a fuck. So we must let him think he's got a chance. We let him escape out of the aircraft. If we get in there and corner him, Stefan is dead. Let him run. I know him. I know how he thinks. I'll get the fucker.'

Mr Lover Man wasn't happy at all, but fuck him. 'You want the responsibility of fucking up and getting the boy killed? Do you?' I poked his chest. 'I'll take that fucking responsibility. Just like I did hitting the fuel tanks. Let Justin get out of that fucking aircraft, think that he's running. I'll sort him out. Don't corner him.'

Joe rejoined the party. 'This is it, man. The fucker's dumping down. He can't make it to the town. We're about twenty klicks short. The moment I get you on the ground, I'm going to fuck off while there's rounds flying about. That's if you want an airframe to get you home, man.' He played about with his instruments, his eyes constantly flicking up to lock onto the Skyvan and the terrain below. 'Assuming I've still got fucking landing gear in five minutes' time.'

I ripped off the cans and went and started pulling up the shutter. The Cessna descended. Mr Lover Man put his body armour back on and Genghis checked his M4.

He saw me looking at it and the scowl I got in return told me it was staying where it was.

28

The wind rushed in but not with such force now. We were lower and slower. The scrub was no more than two hundred feet below us.

I stuck my head out into the slipstream. The Skyvan was touching down ahead.

The Cargomaster's engine revved higher as Joe corrected. Mr Lover Man and Genghis watched the action from behind the seats.

Power back. The plane slowed. We hit the final fifty feet.

Frank's lads moved back with me and took up position in the doorway. A huge dust-cloud erupted and swallowed the Skyvan. Grains of sand pitted my face.

I could see the Skyvan's wheel-prints in the hard red crust directly beneath us. Joe was making sure he landed on proven ground.

Our wheels touched. Joe braked as the Cargomaster bounced towards the dust-storm.

Mr Lover Man jumped, curling his body, ready to

take the hit on his Kevlar. Genghis followed. The Cargomaster was bouncing along at about thirty miles an hour. We'd only been down for two seconds.

Fuck it. Why not? I pulled out the mini-flares, gripped one in each hand, and went for it.

The thump as I hit the ground drove the wind out of me. I rolled into a bush, dropping one of the flare packs. Inch-long needles pierced my skin, but I kept on rolling.

I finally got up, spitting out sand and grit.

Genghis sprinted past me. He disappeared into the dust-storm, weapon at the ready. Mr Lover Man was no more than a metre behind him with the axe.

I retrieved the flare pack and started to leg it after them.

29

Joe revved hard, taking off to the left of the Skyvan. The shed was static, but its engines were still running, still stirring up a maelstrom of red dust. There were shouts from inside. I could hear the signature of 5.56 being fired.

I ran to the right of the cloud, to get ahead of it, and dropped into a dip, panting, trying to get oxygen into me. My feet told me there were needles in them too.

There were more shots inside the Skyvan. The props began to wind down. One of them coughed to a halt.

BB stumbled out of the front of the storm, M4 in hand. No Stefan. Fuck.

I willed my body deeper into the sand.

BB turned and ran back, then reappeared almost immediately, dragging the boy. He threw him over his left shoulder. Weapon in the right hand, he headed west, his back to the sun, kicking up grit as he went. He knew where he was going. Even in this heat and with the weight of the boy, BB could cover the twenty K to Jilib in short order.

He didn't look back. He knew there was no need to. He just had to make distance.

A couple more rounds went off as the second prop coughed and died and the cloud began to settle.

I set off behind them, keeping to the right, using the cover of the bush as best I could. The Skyvan soon disappeared behind me.

I pulled off the top of one of the mini-flare sets to expose the penjector. I took it out, screwed it onto a flare, and pulled it out with a gentle pop. I kept on running. It was vital that BB didn't see me. His M4 was accurate to about three hundred metres. The flares weren't accurate at all.

BB disappeared into a stretch of scrub and heat haze and didn't come out again. My feet slipped in the sand as I tried to make ground, still using the cover.

BB might be fronting it. Going to ground, staying concealed. We look for him, we lose him, and at last light he moves off.

It was what his training would be telling him to do. And he would have the bottle for it. He might even know I was behind him, and be waiting for me to move into his weapon sights. What's the point of running if there are people behind you that you can't shake off? Stop, take me on, kill me, and then keep going.

This wasn't a frightened animal I was chasing. It was a highly trained ex-SAS trooper with a score to settle and a big cash prize ahead of him.

I moved right of the point where he had become unsighted.

Slowing down now. Throat burning. Head burning. Relentless heat.

I kept low but fast, not daring to lose ground. Within a few seconds, I came to a dried-up watercourse. It was three metres deep and a couple wide after centuries of angry flash floods. I lay down at the wadi's edge and scanned its bed, left and right. There was no sign. No sign at all. No one had been along here in any direction. He must still be somewhere down on my left.

Feet first, penjector in hand, I slipped slowly down the bank. When I hit the bottom, my left hand supported my right, as if I was holding my Glock. My body became a firing platform. My legs were shoulder-width apart, left foot forward so I turned forty-five degrees to the direction I was heading. I was balanced forward and back, left and right, as I started to move along the wadi.

Only my trigger thumb was free. It was the only thing I allowed to move as I kept the flare ahead of me, in my field of view.

30

Slowly, in bounds, as if I was patrolling, I kept moving, using the wadi as cover. I came to a bend. I stopped and listened before inching round it, weapon up, into the dead ground.

The watercourse twisted and turned, casting shadows, as it headed east towards the sea. The sun was now facing me. It burnt into my face, making it hard to see. I stopped short of another bend, listened again, then carried on, keeping low, hands up in the aim.

I negotiated a left-hander and heard a whisper ahead. I stopped. Leaning towards the sound, left ear pointing towards it, I held my breath so I could hear what the fuck was going on three – maybe even six or seven – metres away.

The whisper became muffled. I could only just hear it.

I dried my right hand in the dust on the side of the wadi then replaced my thumb on the cocking piece. I brought the flare back up into the firing position. Sweat dripped off my forehead and stung my eyes. I shook my head. The sun glared down even more fiercely into my face.

I started to edge round the corner. I could just see BB, sitting beneath an overhang in a stretch of shade, knees up, facing back the way he had come. He had the butt of the M4 in the shoulder, right hand around the pistol grip as he squeezed the forward firing handle between his knees to keep the barrel pointing up to the lip of the wadi. His free hand was around Stefan. He gripped the little boy's mouth, bringing his head tight against him, to keep him quiet.

I took another pace forwards. I needed to get as close as I could before this went noisy. I thumbed back the cocking piece. Stefan was between us, in the path of a clean shot. He was going to see me first. But that was just fine. I *wanted* him to see me. I *wanted* him to start the commotion that would get BB to move, to bring the weapon down and turn it towards me. But not just yet.

I kept the weapon up towards the target, my support hand still wrapped around the dominant one, my shoulder forward so my nose was closer to the target than my toes. My right arm pushed the weapon towards BB as my left exerted rearward pressure, so the platform was rigid.

I kept moving forward, closing in.

Stefan saw me, saw my weapon. He screamed into BB's hand and struggled to free himself as I approached. Not surprisingly, after the events of the last twelve hours, he didn't seem to know whether I was friend or foe.

I kept both eyes fixed on the target, dead centre of

mass of the two bodies. The flare on the end of the tube came into my vision and became my primary focus. The target and the cocking piece were now just blurs. I focused on the flare with both eyes.

BB's head swung round as he tried to tighten his grip on the boy. His eyes locked onto me. No surprise; no anger. Just confidence. Knowing what he needed to do. His unmoving stare didn't leave my centre mass. The rest of his body came round, with the weapon, to align itself with his head. The M4 came up.

He let go of the boy. He needed his left hand to grip the firing handle on the forward stock. As Stefan stumbled and fell, BB's sights came into his focus.

I kept static, keeping a stable platform for the flare.

I let go of the cocking piece and the flare kicked off with a loud bang. A split second later, a blindingly bright ball of flame was burning into his thigh like molten lava. He stumbled backwards, loosing off a short burst into the side of the gully.

The rounds thumped into the dried mud metres away from me.

31

BB's screams echoed up and down the narrow channel. The magnesium would consume the flesh until all the oxygen in it was used up. He lay in the dust, his body jerking as he took the pain and the shock of being hit. Flesh sizzled and dense white smoke poured out of the open crater in his leg.

Stefan stood transfixed.

I grabbed him with both hands, pushed him, trembling, up the side of the wadi. 'Go! Go to your godfathers. *Go!*'

The sounds coming out of him were pure animal fear. 'Where? *Where?*'

'By the plane. Get up there and you'll see 'em. Go! They're waiting for you!'

He got to the lip of the wadi but stayed rooted to the spot, looking down at me. I lobbed a stone at him. 'Fuck off! Go!'

He turned, screaming Russian. I swung back to BB. The M4's working parts were to the rear. The mag was empty. He'd pinned his hopes on hitting me with those last few rounds before moving on.

The flare had stopped burning. His agony was clear to see. But he still attempted a smile. 'It was all about the money, mate. That's all.'

I unscrewed the empty cylinder from the penjector and screwed down onto a new one. There was another little pop as it slid out of the container.

BB heard it too. His head fell back into the sand. His face contorted with pain. The sun beat down on us. He panted as he tried to keep control of his breathing. He'd want to have the last word. He always had.

My shadow fell across him. He looked up, making sure we had eye-to-eye. 'You know I never gave a fuck about Tracy. I never gave a fuck about her slapper sister. Or Frank. Any of them. Even the boy. Fuck 'em all.'

I leant down and held the flare inches from his forehead. But he still wasn't going to beg or try to cut a deal. I knew that.

Through his pain, he did finally manage a smile. 'Know what? I didn't even give a fuck about Mong. I let him die. Risk getting myself killed for a bunch of slopes? Fuck that. He wanted to fight, so I let him. Fuck it. Fuck him.'

He looked up at me. 'Fuck you, too.'

His breath quickened. Sand coated his face.

I got down on my knees. I wanted to get as close to him as possible. I didn't want him to miss anything that I was about to say and do.

'Mong wanted to fight to give me time to do the job we were there to do. He was protecting me. That's what mates do when they've spent time being wet, cold and hungry together. Real mates put their lives on the line for each other. We're members of the same tribe. That's something you never, ever got.'

I pressed the flare against his temple. He didn't even flinch.

'You're not going to hear me begging. It's not going to happen.'

I nodded slowly. 'Yeah, I know.'

He laughed. 'Better to burn out than fade away, eh?'

'You're about to find out.'

I pulled back the cocking piece and let go.

The penjector jumped a little in my hand and I rolled back to see his head already frying. His body jerked about as if he was in an electric chair for the whole six seconds.

I sat in the wadi, not even bothering to move into the shade. I looked at the charred remains of BB's head. Smoke curled from the entry wound as the last of the magnesium ate down to the bone. It poured out of his closed eyes. The wound in his thigh glistened in the brilliant sunlight.

I kicked off flare after flare into the sky. It was only minutes before Frank's boys appeared on the bank above me. Stefan was firmly wrapped around Mr Lover Man. He kissed the boy gently, murmured to him; smoothed his hair, shielded him from the sight below.

Genghis was lugging a blue tarpaulin, the sort you find in pound shops. I realized what he had inside it as he slid down to the wadi bed with the bloodstained axe in his hand. It took him three swings to take off

BB's head. It joined Ant's and Dec's, and another I supposed must have belonged to the pilot. He spun it closed and slung it back over his shoulder.

He motioned for me to fire more flares. I kicked off another one and followed him up the wadi.

I could hear the Cargomaster up there somewhere but the sun was getting higher so I couldn't see it. I sat in the sand, loosing off the last two as Mr Lover Man continued to comfort Stefan. Genghis threw the axe into the sand. We all just waited, not wanting to talk, not wanting to celebrate, not wanting to do anything. I was totally fucking drained. Mentally and physically.

The Cargomaster screamed overhead and banked and turned as I started pulling the thorns from my feet.

32

The engine noise was a constant drone in the cargo hold. We were following the coastline, flying low. The lush greenery to the right was Kenya. I was perched between two bundles. Tracy was swathed in a tarpaulin like an Egyptian mummy. The heads were in another. They'd been stowed right at the rear, out of Stefan's sight.

Genghis was between me and the cockpit. He was either asleep or just lying there, I wasn't sure. His head lolled on his discarded body armour. The boy was next to Joe, sitting on Mr Lover Man's lap, being cuddled, cajoled and comforted.

Stefan held a nearly empty bottle of water. Mr Lover Man was fooling about, trying to get him to finish it. He needed to get some liquids down him. There still wasn't much reaction from the boy at all.

I sat staring at the bundles. Mong dead. Tracy dead. Now even BB. It was as if a part of my life had ended too. Maybe it was meant to be. Anna was the important one now. This situation I knew about; hers I didn't. I just hoped we'd be able to pick up where we'd left off.

I pulled the iPhone from my pocket. There wasn't much power left but there were three bars of signal. To try to find some shelter from the noise, I lay down next to Tracy. It wasn't much help. Finally, with a finger in my other ear, I called her. No mad Arab women this time, just a long, uninterrupted tone. Maybe the French and Brits had bombed the infrastructure to shit.

I cut off. Then I called Jules and went straight to voicemail. 'Mate, I'm in Kenya, heading to Anna today. I'll call when I get some more power on this thing.'

Mr Lover Man turned and shouted at Genghis. The cockpit suddenly became a hive of activity. They both peered out of the pockmarked windscreen and Joe gobbed off to air traffic control.

I got up and moved forward. Mr Lover Man was pointing Stefan's gaze in the direction of his dad. The G6 couldn't be missed, even at this distance. The airport was not much more than two tarmac runways, big black scars in the ground that joined each other at a right angle. There were a couple of small buildings and hangars, and light aircraft dotted about. Sunlight flashed on the top left corner of the screen as we began our final approach.

The boy peeped at me over Mr Lover Man's shoulder. He looked more like Frank by the second. I gave him a smile and a wink but got no reaction. The boy turned, the water bottle still in his hand, and nestled into his godfather's chest. His hair was plastered with sand.

I looked down at him and realized he was going to be OK. His father loved him; his godfathers loved him. Kids have survived war, famine, even the Holocaust, and still become good, stable people. And, besides, Stefan had something other kids didn't have. The Frank gene. No doubt even this experience would be turned into an advantage later in life.

I felt a little jealous of him. Both his parents had loved him so much, and Mr Lover Man had given Stefan more cuddles and kisses on the cheek during this trip than I'd ever got in my whole childhood.

The wheels touched down, smooth as silk, and Joe taxied towards the G6 by the junction of the runways.

The boy craned his neck towards the jet. Mr Lover Man took the chance to turn and glance at me. His expression hadn't changed. Fair one. What the fuck did they care about me? The job was the job. The boy was safe. That was all that mattered.

It wasn't much of a movie ending, but Frank and the lads had what they wanted more than anything. It was all about the boy.

We stopped behind the G6 and the prop spluttered to a halt. It was a bit of an anti-climax. No bands; no welcoming committee. No mayor to give us the freedom of Malindi.

Joe flung open the cockpit door and climbed straight out to start his inspection. 'Fucking hell, man. Look at this.' The Perspex was crazed. The fuselage had a lot of new air-conditioning.

Mr Lover Man left the plane carrying Stefan. I followed Genghis out of the shuttered door. I left them to it and joined Joe. It was very clear that my part in the Frank road show had ended. I just let them get on with it.

Joe pushed a fist into a gash in the aluminium and peeled it back a little more. He peered inside his airframe. 'What happens now, man? What the fuck's going on?'

'I don't know, mate. All I know is that I've got to get to Benghazi.'

His hand shot down to his side as if he'd been given an electric shock. 'What? You really are fucking crazy, man. Haven't you had enough of this shit already?' He nodded towards the hold. 'Who are they?'

'Georgians – and a guy who used to be a mate. They wanted the boy. His dad wasn't on their Christmas-card list, if you know what I mean.'

His hands came up to cover his ears. 'Don't want to know any more of that shit, man. Just make sure the dad makes good on my airframe. I'm going to be down the beach very soon, getting some beer and doing fuck-all. While that's happening, my new machine can be on order. That's me sorted. What you crazy fuckers do is up to you.'

I heard footsteps behind me. I turned to see Mr Lover Man with Stefan still attached to his hip, and Genghis.

Mr Lover Man kissed the boy on the cheek and murmured to him in Russian. Stefan nodded slowly. Mr Lover Man looked at me. His expression hadn't changed. He still looked like he wanted that axe in the top of my head.

'You have given us Stefan back. Now you must hand Mr Timis his son.'

He passed him over to me, and I finally got a smile. 'Thank you, Nick.' He nodded and stood aside as Genghis held out a hand. Even he came out with a thickly accented 'Tank you.'

I finished the handshake and headed for the G6. Stefan rested his chin on my shoulder, looking down at the pan.

As I reached the bottom of the steps, Frank appeared in the doorway. He was still dressed in immaculately creased jeans and a crisply ironed, short-sleeved white shirt, with a pen in the breast pocket. But his face wasn't in such pristine condition. He was crying.

33

As I started up the steps I whispered into the little boy's ear, 'Daddy's here, Stefan! Look!'

His head lifted and turned. At last there was a smile on the boy's face too. He struggled to release himself. 'Papa! Papa!'

We reached the door.

Frank held out his arms and took him from me. They hugged each other hard. Tears streamed down Frank's cheeks as he kissed his son's face. 'Oh, my Stefan . . .'

Frank carried him into the interior, a feast of white leather La-Z-Boy type seats and sofas and thick-pile carpets. I stayed where I was, just inside the door. Frank walked further into the aircraft. He sat down on a curved settee with his son. They embraced and kissed.

Stefan sparked up in Russian. I didn't know what he was saying but he was tripping over himself as he raced to explain everything that had happened. I heard, 'Mama, Mama,' a couple of times.

Frank wiped the boy's tears from his cheeks. His own were drenched. He couldn't control himself.

Soon Frank was talking to him gently in Russian and stroking his face. He made some sort of funny, as you do with kids. It didn't work.

An older woman emerged from the door nearest the cockpit, set into a wall of varnished walnut veneer. She said a gentle but cheerful hello to the boy and stroked his hair.

Stefan knew her. She led him away by the hand, but not before he got one more kiss on the forehead from his father.

Frank watched him all the way to the bedroom, where his son turned and waved.

His Zenith rattled as he beckoned me into the cabin. 'Nick, please. Come. Sit.'

My attention stayed for a moment on the bedroom door, and then I joined them.

'Stefan's wounds need to be cleaned, Nick. And then she will give him something to help him rest until we get back to Moscow.'

I dropped my arse into the curved sofa opposite him. He wiped his eyes and leant forward. His hand came up and shook mine. 'Nick, thank you. Thank you.'

He offered me a real glass bottle of water. The cap gave a hiss as I untwisted it. I glanced out of the window as I took a couple of big thirsty gulps. Mr Lover Man and Genghis were transferring the tarpaulin bundles into the hold.

'What happens to the heads?'

'They'll be sent to certain people in Tbilisi. As a gift.'

'Some gift.'

'I will make the regime in Tbilisi crumble and my country will be free. Georgia is an enemy of Russia, Nick. An enemy of South Ossetia. There will be violence on the streets of Tbilisi very soon. The people I support and finance will make sure of that. Those heads – they are a gift to those who would try to use my son as a weapon against me.

'I am treating them to a vision of their future – because soon I will have their heads as well. My mother and my father, they were in their seventies when the Georgians came into my country. They were old, gentle people, no threat to anyone.'

When Georgia launched its military offensive in 2008 to retake the breakaway South Ossetia, about fourteen hundred locals were killed. Frank's parents must have been among them.

We both went quiet as Tracy's body was loaded.

There had been anger in his voice when he spoke about his parents, but now sadness replaced the more familiar Terminator look.

'We'll bury her in Moscow. Stefan needs to be close to her always.'

Frank suddenly couldn't meet my eye.

'What are you going to tell him?'

He shrugged.

'If it helps, Frank, when I first saw Tracy in Merca, she was stroking his head and singing a nursery rhyme. What about telling him that his mum has gone to heaven to teach the angels to sing "Three Blind Mice"?'

The tears welled up again in Frank's eyes. I didn't

518

think they were just for Stefan. A hand came up, trying to push them back into his head rather than wipe them away.

'Yes, that will be a very good idea. Thank you, Nick.'

My job was done, but I suddenly felt this might be a new beginning, not the end of days. Maybe what I'd told Tracy was true. Stefan was a part of her. And she was a part of Mong. And Mong? Well, Mong was a part of me, always.

I gave Frank a couple of seconds to sort his face out. 'And what's going to happen with Stefan now? Is he going to be kept away from your family?' I nodded over at the bedroom. 'Kept in a box with a nanny for the rest of his childhood? It wouldn't be right, would it, Frank?'

The tears had gone and the old Frank, maybe not the real Frank, was coming back. 'You really have been working very hard to find out about me.'

I nodded. 'Part of my job, mate.'

He leant in towards me, the eyes now able to fix on mine. 'Stefan will be part of my family. My wife's name is Lyubova. It means "love". She has much of it. She has had to, Nick. I have not always been a good husband. Some of the women, Lyubova has known about – but she has always loved me.'

He pointed a finger at me. 'She knows nothing of Stefan. But she will, very soon. I will tell her everything. I believe she will embrace my son as her own. I hope she will forgive me. I hope that I may become the husband she has always deserved. So maybe something good has already come out of this.' He sat back. 'But enough, Nick. What about you – what do you want? What do you need?'

I sat back too, taking the last of the water down my throat. 'I think Joe the pilot needs a new aircraft. He's got more holes in it than my socks.'

Frank looked down and saw the state of my feet. He laughed.

He put his hands up. 'Of course, that will all be taken care of. But you, Nick – what do you want more than anything in the world?'

That was an easy question to answer.

'Frank, I want a lift to Benghazi.'

His eyes widened. He laughed again, a deep, warm, sonorous laugh. This was the real Frank, and I liked him.

PART EIGHT

PART EIGHT

1

Friday, 25 March
01.17 hrs

The Muslim Without Borders convoy of six white
Mercedes Sprinter vans passed through yet another
Free Benghazi checkpoint on the outskirts of the war-
scarred city. With all the 12.7-mounted technicals and
AKs and RPGs, it could almost have been Mogadishu
– except that these Africans were Arabs.

After he'd laughed himself out, Frank had ordered
the G6 to fly to Sallun, the Egyptian border-crossing.
Near the Mediterranean, it was about ninety miles
from Tobruk. The small airport that greeted me there
looked exactly like Camp Hope in Aceh Province six
years ago. The only difference was that transport
planes could land a lot closer.

Aircraft disgorged humanitarian supplies 24/7. Lots
of people ran around looking very busy in khaki
waistcoats and cargoes with a huge number of pockets

full of very important stuff. The white Toyota 4×4s had already turned up with their big antennas and NGO and MONGO stickers.

The G6 looked totally out of place as it taxied to a standstill. Even the happy-clappy crowd who'd just arrived to convert the Libyans and Egyptians to Christianity stopped and stared, as if Obama had turned up to take a personal look. The locals just watched suspiciously. They needed to make sure it hadn't come to help Gaddafi's family do a runner.

When I emerged in a pair of Frank's centre-creased jeans and a green and yellow checked shirt they all looked very let down. Frank knew how to make a billion or ten. He also knew how to dress like a knob.

Getting into Libya was a piece of piss, mainly because nobody wanted to. There were no officials on the Libyan side of the crossing. It was getting out that would be the problem: the Egyptian side was heavily policed. Sub-Saharan migrant workers waited for days in makeshift camps to do so, drinking bottled water and eating bread doled out by the agencies. Every one of them carried at least one large market bag with that tight tartan weave, tied up with string. Some even had TVs wrapped in cardboard. These lads had worked hard to buy that shit, so it was coming with them.

And even when they finally got across, it was only to step into yet another camp. Where would you go? There was fuck-all for miles in any direction apart from some Roman wells and a Second World War Commonwealth cemetery.

At least those who'd made it this far were getting fed until somebody, somewhere, somehow, got them home. It wasn't like the Egyptians didn't have problems of their own. They'd just had their own Arab Spring and were still trying to sort their shit out.

The Bangladeshis faced the worst hardships. There were thousands of them, and they were thousands of miles from home.

Militias controlled the main drag along the coast, and the eastern part of the country – or so rumour had it. Whatever, they looked ecstatic to see our convoy coming through. They knew we were on our way to help their brothers.

Wahid Kandawalla, the young Pakistani guy in command of the line of vehicles, was negotiating the war zone for the fifth time in ten days, bringing supplies to the hospital. His fresh face full of goodwill, he sat in the right-hand seat, still trying to grow his beard like a good Muslim.

He glanced into the rear of the van from time to time to check I was OK. I was. I'd made myself reasonably comfortable, lying on the boxes of dressings and surgical sterilization kits. I was also completely fucked. The rocking of the vehicle, the darkness and the heat had me asleep in no time at all.

And now I was just lying there relaxing. I had no control over what was happening. I couldn't do anything about it. So: whenever there's a lull in the battle, get your head down. You never know the next time you're going to get the chance to sleep.

I'd thrown Awaale's mobile away at Sallun. I wasn't fucking him off: it was just that these 'meet up again' things never really work. Events had brought us together for a moment, but that was all it had been.

525

Besides, Awaale wasn't going back to Minneapolis for a while. He'd be too busy taking over the clan, brassing up Lucky Justice, and standing his ground against AS fighters coming from the south. That was if he stayed alive long enough. Piracy was a dangerous business on both sides of the deal.

Everything Kandy had in the way of information about what was happening on the ground was a product of the rumour mill. Rumour had it that defecting Gaddafi troops had ransacked Benghazi's main police barracks, looting tons of weapons and ammunition. That meant the local militia had been rearmed and resupplied and could take on anything Gaddafi threw at them from the west.

There were rumours, too, that Turkey would soon be sending its navy to defend the route between Benghazi port and Crete, and their troops to take over the airport to secure humanitarian sea and air corridors.

Kandy did have one fact. Turkey already had five warships and one submarine off the coast. They were stopping Gaddafi's navy laying mines to deny the port.

Kandy received a fresh batch of rumours at every checkpoint. The militias had just been told that the French and British fast jets had mounted raids on the oil town of Ajdabiya. Gaddafi's forces had been hammered. The town had been retaken. Further west, however, the fighting went on.

Another low-flying rumour was that Gaddafi had offered $100,000 to anyone willing to fight for him, payable on victory. That rumour was met with the militia head-shed telling all the rebels that if they defected they would be classed as traitors and shot as soon as hostilities were over. That was the problem with this type of war. It was fast-moving, and communications were poor. There was still no signal on my iPhone, and no one really knew what the fuck was going on.

2

The dark streets of Free Benghazi were littered with the hulks of tanks that had been totalled by French and British fast jets. They were already covered with graffiti. A lot of it was in English, for external consumption. One message read: *Thank You Obama, Thank You Cameron.* If Sarkozy saw that on breakfast TV, there was going to be one very pissed-off Frenchman.

A poster on a shell-blasted wall showed Gaddafi looking defiant but without a hat, and blood all over his head. Words like 'Murderer', 'Terrorist' and 'Dictator' were scrawled all over it. Another wall mural had the president's face repainted with a big yellow smiley. I'd seen hundreds of those giving Saddam the same treatment just hours after the US tanks rolled into Baghdad.

As we moved through the blacked-out city, there were plenty of signs that Gaddafi *had* lost control. If it wasn't covered in graffiti, every physical sign of the dictator had been taken down and shot or torched. The solid green flag was no longer flying above ramshackle and ransacked government buildings that Gaddafi's troops had wrecked when they withdrew; the old royal standard – red, black and green with the crescent and star at its centre – hung in its place.

A storm was raging out there in the Mediterranean. I spotted several passenger ferries offshore, all lit up as they rode it out. They'd been waiting for days to come in and evacuate foreign nationals.

Another rumour was that because the Turks, NATO's second biggest army, had provided a large naval contingent, the Brits had been forced at last to up their game. They were sending a frigate. It would park up in the port in the next couple of days and take off Brits and anyone else it had room for. Kandy laughed at that one. The Turks, Italians and Russians had already been and gone. Even the French were back home drinking coffee and watching the war on the news. But the *Cumberland*'s late arrival was good news for Anna. Jules had booked her a place on board.

The vehicle slowed. Kandy turned in his seat. 'Nick, here we are.' A big friendly smile wreathed his face. 'Nick?'

I was dozing.

'The hospital – we're here.'

I stretched in my Timberland-effect fleece that I'd bought at the border crossing. Even in war and desperation, there will always be a Del Trotter setting up his stall.

'That's brilliant, Kandy.' I passed him the bundle of a thousand US dollars. 'Thanks, mate.' Two dollars a kilometre, as promised. He waved the cash before putting it into his pocket, uncounted. 'This will buy us fuel to go back and make another run here the day after tomorrow. Thank you.'

I had no doubt that it would.

We got out of the wagon as the lads hooked up with the waiting militia. We all shook. 'Good luck, Nick. I hope that you find her.'

I nodded. 'And good luck to you, mate. Hope you get back in one piece, eh?'

From the outside, the main hospital, Al-Jalaa, looked like most of the rest of the city: concrete, rectangular, plain. The courtyard and car park were a blur of news crews, ambulances, 12.7-mounted technicals, and casualties from the fighting in the west.

A pair of fast jets screamed through the darkness somewhere overhead. Nobody looked up. They could only be French or British. Although someone had said that the Italians were about to join in too.

For the news agencies, war was business. They set up shop outside hospitals to be close to the action, but also for protection. Gaddafi wouldn't hit a hospital, would he? Hmm. We'd see.

I hobbled up to the nearest crew. 'You know where the foreigners are being looked after? I'm looking for a Russian reporter, Anna Ludmilova.' I nodded at the three lads sitting on blue nylon folding chairs. 'You know her at all, lads?'

Even in the middle of a war zone, the Germans were always immaculate. Even the military contractors protecting them were perfectly turned out, right down to their national flag on the front flap of their body armour. Me, I still hadn't washed or shaved since landing in Mog. Frank's clothes and trainers would probably start to dissolve quite soon.

One of the coffee drinkers pointed me towards the main doors. 'They'll know inside. There's a couple of media who can't be moved yet.' He threw a bottle of water at me. 'Good luck.'

3

The interior of the hospital was cleaner and brighter than a lot of the NHS ones I'd been in. It was also a whole bunch busier.

Medical teams in green aprons and masks rushed past with trolleys laden with militia, kids, old people blasted by Gaddafi's artillery and mortar fire. I walked across the freshly polished floor. I almost felt embarrassed to wait in line for the receptionist behind a group of militia who'd run in with a badly injured comrade. She pointed in the direction of what I guessed was the emergency room, and then asked them something in Arabic. I guessed it was to unload their weapons, because they did.

The girl manning the desk was still in her teens. The phone rang. She answered it efficiently before nodding at me. This was the future of the Arab Spring. A head covered by a purple scarf, but face powdered, eyes made up, lips glossed. I didn't think the jihadists were going to get much of a hold in this country.

'Do you speak English?'

She smiled. 'Of course. What do you need?' She was surprisingly calm and pleasant. It made me feel even worse. 'I'm looking for a Russian reporter, Anna Ludmilova. She was shot in Misrata a couple of days ago.'

'OK. All the foreigners are on the second floor, Ward Seventeen. If you're armed, please unload your weapon.'

'I'm not armed.'

'Can I see?'

I unzipped my fleece, lifted it up, and turned round so she could admire the crease in my jeans.

'Thank you. I hope you find her.'

Two more militia came in. They'd linked arms to improvise a seat for a guy who couldn't have been any older than the receptionist. His right leg had been blown away below the knee. His blood trailed all the way back to the main entrance.

4

The second-floor corridor was grey lino, clean and polished. I came to the main hub. Phones rang. Staff shouted for help. The wounded moaned. But at least they were in beds and the dressings were clean. The place functioned. There was an air of total efficiency.

I wasn't sure what I was going to say or do when I saw her. When people I knew got shot, they were normally mates and I just took the piss. But this was different. She was more than a mate. She was the most important person in my life.

Yes, I was punching above my weight. Yes, she might well tire of me one day. But I knew I'd have the best time of my life while it lasted. I was even looking forward to taking care of her until she was fit enough to go back and play reporter and leave me watching her on TV at Gunslingers.

Ward 17 went on for ever, a classic Nightingale ward with fifteen or twenty beds each side. Some had screens. Some had solid partitions. I walked down the centre of it, checking the beds I could see. Most were occupied by militia. A couple of white guys lay with wound dressings. Maybe they were oil or military contractors, or media. I didn't give a fuck. I just wanted to find Anna.

I kept walking. The last two beds at the end were partitioned off like little cubicles. Maybe that was where the women were.

The one to the right was open. An old woman lay with her family gathered round. She'd been hit in the stomach. Blood seeped through her dressing, and onto her sheets. Her face was pockmarked with red scabs. A mortar round had probably zapped her.

I went to the left-hand door and knocked gently. I didn't wait for an answer.

She was sitting up, half asleep, supported by pillows. She was wearing a green surgical gown.

'Nicholas?'

5

Her blonde hair was a mess. Her face was washed out and knackered. But she still looked great to me.

'I called. I tried but . . .' I leant over and kissed her on the cheek. 'You OK?'

She looked me up and down. 'Are you, more to the point?'

'Fine. I'll tell you later.'

I sat down on the steel chair beside her and took her hand in mine.

Things were strained. Or maybe it was just me.

'Where did you get hit?'

'Left-hand side. Lower gut. It came from nowhere. There were bursts in the distance. There was an air raid, but nothing too close. Then down I went. The crew were fantastic. They got me here and I had surgery. No organs hit. But it hurts and I can't be moved just yet.'

The family opposite started to wail and cry. Medical staff came rushing down the ward.

'What's wrong, Anna? Why can't you be moved? It hit nerves on your spine or something? Your legs? Can you move them?'

She was welling up. She bit her lower lip to try and control it.

'They said it's the wound track, Nicholas. The round passed through but . . . very close to my womb.'

I looked at her, waiting for more.

Her hands were now gripping mine.

'They need to make sure the baby isn't damaged.' Tears ran down her cheeks. 'I'm three months pregnant, Nicholas . . .'

It was like I'd pulled ten Gs in a fast jet. My arse pushed down into the seat. My whole body felt like I was getting rammed through the floor.

'Everything's OK, Nicholas. I just have to rest, and get checked out again in a few days. It's just that until I get the all-clear I can't move.'

The family the other side of the partition were led away down the hall. I heard a trolley rattle into the room.

'That's good. That's good . . .'

She kissed my cheek. Her breath was rancid. I was sure she'd thought the same when I kissed her. Her hands brought my head onto her chest. 'I was so worried about you.' She stroked my hair.

Eventually I summoned up the courage to put a hand on her stomach, so gently it was hardly touching. I moved it carefully, like I was expecting something to be there apart from the wound dressing. What the fuck did I know?

'Nicholas, I've been really worried about how you'd

take the news. I wasn't sure how you'd react. We haven't been together for long and—'

'Why did you stay out here in this condition?'

'My grandmother gave birth to all her children while working in the wheat fields.' She tried to laugh. 'Stupid, I know. But I guess it was because I knew this had to be my last foreign job.' She managed a lopsided smile. 'I've got responsibilities now . . .'

I grinned back. 'Sounds like I have too.'

I thought of Mong, of Tracy and of Stefan. Maybe it was the end of an era after all. A new one had just begun.

She held my face in her hands and I kept on staring at her and smiling.

Then she looked at me more seriously. 'Have you finished *Crime and Punishment*?'

I pulled a guilty face. 'I've got to tell you – these classics are doing my head in. I keep telling everybody who asks me that I'm reading it, but you know what? I'm even having trouble with the cheat notes.'

She kissed my head and then gave it a big slap.

I stood and held her close, until long after the old woman was wheeled away and another casualty was brought in to replace her.

RED NOTICE

ANDY McNAB

A NEW THRILLER AND A NEW HERO

Deep beneath the English Channel, a small army of Russian terrorists has seized control of the Eurostar to Paris, taken 400 hostages at gunpoint – and declared war on a government that has more than its own fair share of secrets to keep.

One man stands in their way. An off-duty SAS soldier is hiding somewhere inside the train. Alone and injured, he's the only chance the passengers and crew have of getting out alive. Meet Andy McNab's explosive new creation, Sergeant Tom Buckingham, as he unleashes a whirlwind of intrigue and retribution in his attempt to stop the terrorists and save everyone on board – including Delphine, the beautiful woman he loves.

Hurtling us at breakneck speed between the Regiment's crack assault teams, Whitehall's corridors of power and the heart of the Eurotunnel action, *Red Notice* is McNab at his devastatingly authentic, pulse pounding best.

Red Notice: You have been warned...

COMING THIS AUTUMN!

BRAVO TWO ZERO

ANDY McNAB

HIS MIND-BLOWING NON-FICTION BESTSELLER

In January 1991, eight members of
the SAS regiment embarked upon a
top secret mission that was to
infiltrate them deep behind enemy
lines. Under the command of Sergeant
Andy McNab, they were to sever the
underground communication link
between Baghdad and north-west
Iraq, and to seek and destroy mobile
Scud launchers. Their call sign:
BRAVO TWO ZERO.

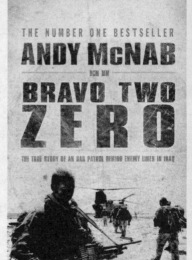

THE NUMBER ONE BESTSELLER

ANDY McNAB

BGM MM

**BRAVO TWO
ZERO**

THE TRUE STORY OF AN SAS PATROL BEHIND ENEMY LINES IN IRAQ

Each man laden with 15 stone of
equipment, they patrolled 20km
across flat desert to reach their
objective. Within days, their location
was compromised. After a fierce
firefight, they were forced to escape
and evade on foot to the Syrian border. In the desperate days that
followed, though stricken by hypothermia and other injuries, the
patrol 'went ballistic'. Four men were captured. Three died. Only
one escaped. For the survivors, however, the worst ordeals were to
come. Delivered to Baghdad, they were tortured with a savagery for
which not even their intensive SAS training had prepared them.

Bravo Two Zero is a breathtaking account of Special Forces
soldiering: a chronicle of superhuman courage, endurance and dark
humour in the face of overwhelming odds. Believed to be the most
highly decorated patrol since the Boer War, BRAVO TWO ZERO is
already part of SAS legend.

WAR TORN

ANDY McNAB
& KYM JORDAN

With two tours of Iraq
under his belt, Sergeant
Dave Henley knows what
modern war looks like. But
nothing can prepare him
for the posting to Forward
Operating Base Senzhiri,
Helmand Province,
Afghanistan. This is a
battlezone like he's never
seen before.

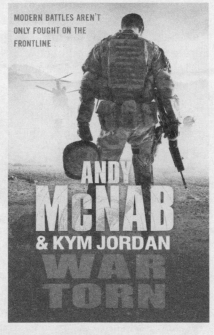

MODERN BATTLES AREN'T
ONLY FOUGHT ON THE
FRONTLINE

ANDY
McNAB
& KYM JORDAN
WAR
TORN

He's in charge of 1 Platoon,
a ragbag collection of
rookies who he must make
into a fighting force – and
fast. But this is a brutal,
unforgiving conflict which
takes no prisoners. Their
convoy is ambushed on the way to the FOB, leaving two men
grievously wounded – before they've fired a shot.

Back at home, Dave's wife, Jenny, seven months pregnant,
must try to hold together the fragile lives of the families left
behind, who all wait for the knock on the door and the arrival
of bad news . . .

SPOKEN FROM THE FRONT

REAL VOICES FROM THE BATTLEFIELDS OF AFGHANISTAN

EDITED BY
ANDY McNAB

Spoken from the Front is the story of the Afghan Campaign, told for the first time in the words of the servicemen and women who have been fighting there. With unprecedented access to soldiers of all ranks, as well as pilots, reservists, engineers, medics, Royal Military police, mechanics, cooks and other military personnel, Andy McNab has assembled a portrait of modern conflict like never before.

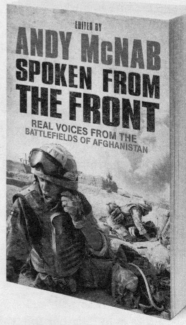

This is the full experience of our troops on the ground and in the air. The horrors, cruelties, drudgery, excitement and banter of these soldiers' lives combine to form a chronological narrative of all the major events in Helmand during the British Army's time there.

From their action-packed, dramatic, moving and often humorous testimonies in interviews, diaries, letters and emails written to family, friends and loved ones, emerges a 360-degree picture of guerrilla warfare up close and extremely personal. It is as close to the real thing as you can get.

ZERO HOUR

THE SCORCHING
NEW NICK STONE THRILLER

ANDY McNAB

ONE MAN

When the beautiful
twenty-year-old daughter of
a Moldovan businessman
goes missing from her
university, British
Intelligence are unusually
interested in her safe
return. They will do
anything in their power to
track her down.

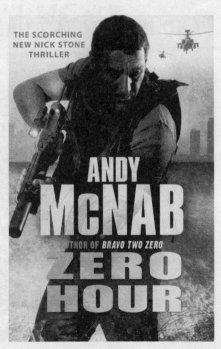

ONE MISSION

Only one man is skilled and
ruthless enough for the job
– but for the first time in his
life, Nick Stone doesn't
want to play ball . . .

ONE HELL OF A READ